MW00770817

Jolie's Story

Moon Child

Moon Trilogy – Book 2

GUITTA KARUBIAN

Copyright 2015, by Guitta Karubian

All rights reserved.

The characters and events in this book are fictitious and the product of the author's imagination. Any similarity to real persons is coincidental and not intended.

The scanning, unauthorized uploading, or distribution without the author's written permission is theft of intellectual property.

The exception is for a published review in which case the reviewer may quote passages for the review.

To request permission, kindly contact the author. info@guittakarubian.com

Thank you.

ISBN: 978-1-7330151-8-9

DEDICATION
Women, Life, Freedom

I dedicate this book to Life, which is, in the end, all we have.

The strong women of Iran are fighting for a better life; for the ability to pursue happiness and live life to the fullest. That requires having choices in all facets of our lives, and the more choices we have, the more empowered we are.

We all have the right and the responsibility to live a life that defines who we are, regardless of where we happen to live.

The men and women who have chosen to give their precious lives for the cause will never be forgotten. Their memory is honored as the cause continues…

Let us toast to Life!

ACKNOWLEDGMENTS

I thank the many people who have supported me in writing this book, both by encouraging me in the pursuit and by helping along the way. And thanks to you, the reader about to begin *Moon Child*, Jolie's story.

CONTENTS

"Whatever you can do or dream you can do, begin it… Boldness has genius, magic and power in it. Begin it now."

Johann Wolfgang von Goethe

PROLOGUE

Gardena, California — 1980

The music was loud and funky. The drinks were affordable. The men were of all ages, all colors, and all backgrounds. There were blacks and whites, Russians and Asians, Latinos and Arabs.

The girls were there to entertain them all. College boys paid for their night out with student loans; old men paid with their Social Security checks. Businessmen, stopping by before riding the freeways home, paid with their dreams and guilt. If they liked a girl, they'd shower her with money, and money was why these girls were there.

Ruby was a veteran stripper. She couldn't do office work or sell worth a damn, but she could wriggle her tight body like a snake and she made the money every night to prove it.

Her routine, like that of the other girls, was made up of three dances.

She used the first to get into her groove, strutting, wiggling, and shimmying in the skimpy, flashy outfit that was all about gold and

1

ruby-red sequins, all the while licking her lips seductively and suggestively gliding her hands along her ample curves.

Early in the second number, she teased the men, removing her flashy top and glittering short skirt, leaving her in a gold bra and red thong. She slithered up and down the pole with the suppleness of a serpent, then turned her back to the men and unsnapped her bra. The men whistled. She'd tease them, moving it back and forth, left and right. They knew she would do that; she always did.

When at last she let the sparkling bra drop and turned to face them displaying the bounty that lay beneath, the gold glistening on her dark nipples, she was met with a welcomed uproar. The men hooted and pounded on the tables.

She promenaded up and down the catwalk, then stood center stage, her long, chemically straightened hair brushing against the floor, and suddenly her legs were in the air, one following the other as she executed a perfect cartwheel and came up onto her red stiletto heels. The men went wild and shouted for more.

"Way to go!"

"Do that again, Sugar!"

The energy in the room heightened. Ruby smiled ingratiatingly but didn't do it again. Instead, she strutted back and forth on the catwalk. The men understood and reached into their wallets and brought out more cash. They hurried up to the catwalk to shower her with fives and tens, tempting her as she had tempted them. Ruby took their money and only then gave them what they wanted. They were ready for her third and final dance.

Untying the thong, she eased the breath of red silk off. She was completely naked now and in total command of the room. The whistles, roars, and rakish comments flowed as freely as the money that flew onto the stage.

"Show me that sweetness!"

She repeated two cartwheels in succession, and, with every parting of her legs, Ruby collected more cash amid shouts of appreciation ranging from demands for more of the same to proposals of marriage.

When the final curtain fell, Ruby hurried to jam the bills into the nylon bag she'd left at stage side. She frowned. The bag wasn't completely filled.If she was going to pay for Tyrone's braces next month, she'd need to take home a lot more than this. She would ask Tony to give her more sets.

Coming off the stage, Ruby saw a girl standing at stage side. She'd never seen the girl before and correctly assumed she was new to the club. She was young and exceptionally pretty, with an elegance that made her look out of place in this milieu. She wore street clothes, a simple pair of black shorts and a flowered halter-top. But she was a looker, even in that simple outfit.

The girl seemed nervous."You were great!" she gushed to Ruby. "I'll never be able to do anything like that."

"You'll be just fine, girl!" Ruby said, giving her a pat on her shoulder. "You just go on out there. They'll love you. You'll see." *She was so pretty! Of course,* Ruby thought, *they'll love her.*

Ruby watched as the girl inched her way onto the stage like a frightened preschooler. As she moved to the center stage, the announcer introduced her. "Now, let's all welcome Sally, our newest girl, here for her first time on any stage. We know you'll agree she's a peach."

The music started and the men welcomed the pretty young newcomer with catcalls and long whistles.

The girl stood frozen.

"Hey, girlie, don't be shy," they called.

"Come on, gorgeous, wiggle that pretty ass."

The girl heard the comments and blushed. And then a big burly man, a regular, sitting at a front table stood up, wobbly on his feet. He pointed a wavering index finder at the girl and when he spoke, his words slurred.

"Look at you," he said. "Damn! How in the hell are you gonna show us your pretty little titties and that pretty thing you got between your legs if you're too scared to move with all your clothes on? Hell, you're so shy you're pink!"

And the name stuck.

PART ONE: THE ADOPTION

1

JANE ALBRIGHT

Dallas, Texas — 1961

he Albright Ranch lay quiet in the stillness of the early Texan morning but for the sound of Sugar, Jane Albright's galloping horse. Jane rode, her long red hair glowing in the morning sun as she headed out to the gently sloping hills at the western end of her ranch.

Summer had peeled back to expose autumn, Jane's favorite time of year. Jane loved taking Sugar out for these early morning rides across her land. The sound of hooves hitting the dirt, falling into the silence around her, was comforting. She needed this time of solitude to relax and recharge. She dealt with people all day long and people sapped her energy. A horse was so much easier to deal with.

She brought Sugar to a stop at the western boundary of her ranch and looked out at her two hundred acres, the fruit of her labor and the growing seed of her future. She'd bought the parcel with the rundown house five years ago with money from her marriage settlement and was pleased with what she'd made of it.

In fact, Jane Albright was pleased with herself in general. At forty-two, she never admitted to being a day older than her new thirty-five year old husband. She was a shrewd businesswoman who had done well for herself and predicted that in a few years she'd be a millionaire. Then she'd return to Los Angeles to show her ex-husband what she had made of herself and dangle his handsome replacement in front of his eyes.

She turned Sugar around so she could look at the southern vista where her ranch met the Shelton ranch. Yesterday, she'd overheard that this adjacent parcel was coming onto the market. From her vantage point, Jane could readily see that if she acquired Shelton's property, all the land south of the creek would be hers, almost doubling the size of her ranch. Dallas was stretching, and her land was within a thirty-minute drive of the growing city. Jane didn't doubt that prices would continue to climb as the city continued to grow. Dallas was already a major center for the manufacture of electronics and electrical equipment and was on the way to becoming the center for the manufacture of aircraft and missile parts as well. She reasoned that the presence of these large companies in the city would only ensure its continued growth and expansion.

Buck Shelton was apparently anxious to reap the sizable profits from the early rise in value of his land. But unlike her neighbor, Jane could wait. She would hold on to her real estate for a few more years. She decided she would make a strong offer to Shelton and buy his land before it officially hit the market; she would far rather deal with the man directly than with any realtor he'd retain who would, no doubt, be a nuisance.

Having made up her mind, Jane turned Sugar around and headed back home. If she hoped to stop by the Shelton ranch on the way to Abigail's and make her neighbor's ranch her own, she would have to hurry.

At the gate to her house, she handed the horse over to Cesar then hurried up the porch and into the farmhouse she'd renovated. Once in her upstairs bedroom, Jane moved quietly. Dean needed more sleep than she did, and she didn't want to wake him up or he'd be crabby all day. Looking at his long, lean body in bed, she smiled. After their lovemaking last night, he deserved his rest. He'd outdone even himself. There really was not enough to be said for younger men. Dean was everything Jane needed in a man – a fantastic lover who never got in her way outside the bedroom.

She hurried to shower, then dried herself off and transformed herself from a morning cowgirl in jeans, chaps and boots with long hair flying, into a professional woman in an understated dress, her hair pinned primly back into a bun. Her jewelry consisted of simple pearl earrings, her gold wedding band and a watch.

She went to the bedroom window and pulled up the shade to look at the land she planned to buy. She was leaning on the windowsill, smiling at what she saw, when Dean awoke, rubbing the sleep from his eyes.

"Good morning," Jane said, her voice as warm as the sun outside.

Dean raised his head and shoulders, propped himself up on his elbows, and squinted. "I've asked you to keep the shades drawn in the morning. Damned sunlight blinds me every goddamned day."

Jane went to the cushy bed and kissed his cheek. "Sorry." Her husband tried to pull her close to him in an embrace, but she laughed and moved away. "Save your energy for tonight. Hopefully, we'll be celebrating."

Suddenly wide awake, Dean sat up. "Celebrating?"

"Take a good look out the window when you get up," she said. She walked back to her dressing table and picked up her lipstick. "By tonight, everything you see will belong to me." She looked at Dean's face in the table mirror, expecting to see something other than what she saw. Dean had covered his head with the blanket.

She stopped applying her lipstick. "What's wrong?" she asked.

Dean didn't answer until he'd sat up and adjusted the pillows and leaned against the headboard. He was pouting. "Oh, nothing much. Just thought you might be pregnant. But I'm starting to think I'm the only one here who wants a fucking kid." He crossed his arms. "Christ, Jane, I thought I finally knocked you up! Jesus knows I try hard enough."

Jane flinched. Kids be damned! And *she'd* be damned if she was going to get fat and ugly and lose Dean all because of some kid he

9

thought he wanted – until it was there, crying and screaming. Didn't she have enough of babies all day? Enough of pregnancies? She'd seen what childbirth did to a woman's body, even a young body, and there was no way in hell she would ever let that happen to her. And she wasn't about to share Dean with some snotty-nosed kid who'd want to play ball or whatever with him. She liked having him all to herself, thank you. And then, if you're dumb enough to have a kid, after all is said and done and they've aged you and used you, they toss you aside. There wasn't a chance in hell she'd ever be stupid enough to have a kid.

She went to her husband and stroked his hair. The burnished gold curls were beautiful, even tousled like this. "I know you want a child, darling. Don't you think I do, too? Don't you know how badly I want your baby growing inside me?"

Dean took her hand. "But we've been together two years, Baby, and it doesn't seem like you really care."

"I enjoy trying," she said lightly. Seeing that Dean remained long faced, she changed her tone to match his sullenness. "I try not to show how much I care," she said. She pulled her hand away from his, turned away, and covered her eyes. She sniffled.

The effect on Dean was brilliant. He jumped out of bed, the muscles of his hard body moving like a panther. "I'm sorry, sweetheart." He put his arms around her, and she felt the warmth of his nakedness through her dress. "I'm so sorry! I'm just an insensitive, fucking oaf!"

She buried her head in his chest. After a moment, she lifted it and smiled feebly. "No, Dean, *I'm* sorry I haven't been able to give you the child you want so badly."

Dean held her chin up and smiled into her face. "It'll happen, honey, I know it will. We'll just try harder."

He walked her to the open window and looked out at the view, his hand shielding his eyes from the sun. "So, how are you going to make all this yours in one day?"

"I've decided to buy the Shelton ranch," she said.

"I didn't see any 'For Sale' signs on it." He returned to bed.

Jane returned to her mirror and applied her lipstick. "I plan to buy it before there's a sign up." She collected her keys and checkbook and put them in her purse. "I've got to get moving, Hon, I have a big day." She spoke with no residue of sadness. "Tell Rosa to have dinner ready about 6:30, okay?"

"Come over here and give your husband a goodbye kiss."

Jane did as she was told. "Last night was wonderful," she said, stroking Dean's face.

"I'll make sure to get some champagne to celebrate tonight," Dean said. Then he slapped her rear. "Now go get it."

With that Jane walked out of the room, bounced down the stairs, grabbed an apple from the ceramic fruit bowl on the dining room table and left the house. She got into her light-blue Buick Invicta and drove off to make a deal with Buck Shelton.

On the way to the Shelton ranch, Jane wondered how long she could keep Dean from taking this kid thing to the next level, how long before he'd start talking about seeing specialists. She didn't want to lose him. She was certain she loved her husband as much as she was capable of loving anyone. She'd buy him a gift and give it to him tonight.

But first she had to go to Shelton's, then straight to Abigail's where she had an early afternoon appointment to interview a job applicant. Charlene, the most senior and most trusted member of Jane's staff, believed the Home needed another hand to help with the laundry and cleaning and had already interviewed several applicants. She had identified the woman Jane would hire; all that was needed was Jane's stamp of approval.

Following that meeting, Jane had an appointment with a couple coming to Dallas from the east coast to adopt. Hopefully she'd do well with them. She needed all the money she could get to pay for Shelton's ranch. After that she'd be free to find Dean the perfect gift and prepare herself for her evening with him.

2

ABIGAIL'S

*I*t had been an excellent morning. Jane had closed a deal with Shelton that was as sweet as any she could have hoped for and had returned to her office in time to meet Matilda.

Jane Albright was the sole proprietor of The Abigail Home for Unwed Mothers and, except for Dean, no one – not the parents of the unwed girls who boarded there, not the pregnant girls themselves, not the couples that came to Abigail's eager to adopt the little bastards at birth, and not a single person on staff at Abigail's, including the trusted Charlene who kept the place running so well – no one knew that Jane was Abigail. Now, as she entered the Home right on time for her meeting, Charlene greeted her.

"Good morning, Abigail."

"Good morning, Charlene," Jane answered.

The Home had the air of a mansion with sixteen bedrooms, some private, others larger, with two beds. It was built in a park-like setting on acreage Jane owned some twenty minutes away from her ranch and housed young women who were pregnant out of wedlock.

"She's waiting for you. Her name is Matilda."

"Thank you, Charlene."

With abortion illegal in the United States and the birth control pill not yet readily available to the public, Abigail's was a product of the moral climate in America through the early 1960s.

The State of Texas had no laws addressing statutory rape; thus, it was not a crime per se to have intercourse with an under-aged girl. Furthermore, most often, consent was deemed granted as the violated girl rarely reported the incident. She feared marring her reputation and knew that if word got out that she'd had that carnal experience, her name would immediately become synonymous with *slut* – even if she had been a helpless victim.

The young girl who wanted to file a report envisioned a future fighting off armies of boys without any support from other girls, all of whom would abandon her overnight – as if a reputation for sexual promiscuity was contagious. It was no wonder then that she had not gone to the authorities; she'd hoped no one would know. Only too late, she might discover she was pregnant.

Then there were those young, romantic, fertile girls who fell in love and got pregnant. And, of course, those who simply liked boys and got unlucky.

The job applicant was in her office waiting room. "Good morning, Matilda. I'm Abigail."

Girls from poorer homes who found themselves "in a family way" would most likely find themselves on a bus headed for a facility run by a religious organization. They'd spend their pregnancy living a drab existence dressed in generic, colorless smocks or whatever else had been charitably donated, while being subjected to daily lectures admonishing them for their sins and encouraging them to repent.

Not so at Abigail's. Abigail's was a very different sort of place. It sheltered the young, pregnant, unmarried daughters born to only the wealthiest and was almost always running at full occupancy.

At times, families would engage in what amounted to a bidding war for an available bed, buying their daughters first place on the waiting list of prospective residents, hoping to send them on a prolonged "vacation to Europe" or "to visit family on the coast" before their young bellies enlarged so much that their embarrassing condition became obvious to all.

"You are to understand that under no condition are you to mingle with the guests," Jane said to the applicant.

Parents who could afford Abigail's high-priced accommodations for their daughters were assured their child would enjoy six, perhaps seven months of a pristine room and healthy food. There was also the company and emotional support of other young women of similar backgrounds caught in the same unfortunate situation. Friendships would develop that helped pass their time at Abigail's congenially, playing games, discussing the latest fashions, chatting over tea, and taking walks in the gardens, all lasting only as long as their stay.

Abigail's provided professional services as well, boasting two gynecologist-obstetricians available around the clock.

Birth certificates of children born to Abigail's guests were creatively completed and often lost in the shuffle of papers they received from the House upon leaving.

Jane soon learned that the most appealing thought to the unborn child's grandparents – parents of the pregnant girls, and the people who paid her significant fees – was the promise that their grandchild would be placed in a fine home that ensured a secure life, and preferably, to a home of someone important. Jane presumed this helped absolve them of any guilt they felt as a result of abandoning the infant.

As a result, when these people found themselves enjoying tea and lemon cake in Abigail's office while they registered their pregnant daughters and paid the upfront fees, Jane often made confidential mention of a mayor, governor, well-known business tycoon or Hollywood icon whom she'd heard "was looking to adopt." This elicited yet additional sums of money to Abigail from these newest patrons of the Home, anxious to ensure that their bastard would be duly remembered at the time that adoption was ripe.

"You are not to pry into their private belongings, Matilda. You are to remain invisible to the boarders, not broadcast their names, do your job well, and keep to yourself."

The endless stream of young mothers would deliver their babies and part ways without laying eyes on the infant or even knowing its sex; the attending obstetrician mae sure of that. They'd leave their newborns behind with Abigail, never to be seen or heard from again.

15

They would simply return to their parents, schools and lives with their reputations intact and a second chance to live their upper-class all-American lives.

Jane found a new home for every Baby Girl and Baby Boy born at Abigail's. Though she sympathized with the girls who'd been knocked up and could understand why they would leave their babies behind, it was the adopting parents who confounded her, for they were clearly paying for other people's throwaways — and pay they did.

Jane never exactly charged the new, adoptive parents for their newly-adopted baby; no, Jane couldn't possibly bring herself to do that! But invariably, there were fees and charges that had been "over-looked by the distraught parents of the poor young girl" who, "in their distress had, unfortunately, failed to make full payment of their bill." Abigail would shake her head then and sigh, as if life were just too unfair.

"But of course, that's not your problem," she would say, "I felt such compassion for them. They'd been through so much!" and then, "And, of course, there's this perfectly lovely innocent baby that you're taking home – which is why I opened my Home in the first place."

Not surprisingly, the adopting parents were always ready to pay any and all balance due on their baby rather than to feel they had scrimped on the purchase of their child.

Matilda, duly warned and adequately submissive, was hired and would report to work the next day.

Charlene's choice had been perfect.

3

GOLDEN CHILD

*J*ane sat at her desk facing Phil and Stella Gold.

Her morning had been perfect. She'd closed the deal with Shelton and hired Matilda.

Then these two New Yorkers came in looking dismal and completely devoid of the bright-eyed excitement she'd come to recognize in parents-to-be. Jane stifled her curiosity about them. This meeting wasn't about chitchat; there was business to be done.

Mr. Gold was a short, stocky man with a nose too big for his face and a circle of curls resting on his otherwise hairless head like a doughnut with a very large chunk bitten off in front. He had a way of blinking his large round brown eyes that unnerved Jane for it made him look like he was staring at her and was continually surprised at what he saw. He spoke with the thickest of New York accents, as if his jawbones had softened to mush, and as a consequence his vowels were all dreadfully flattened making him sound as uneducated as, in fact, he was. He spoke in spurts, breaking sentences off into pieces with a gruff voice that didn't match his sorrowful bearing.

Mr. Gold told Jane he and his wife were heading west, moving to California. "My cousin's got a movie business out there. Theaters. I'll be working with him." He blurted it out as though confessing to a cop, holding the brim of his New York City hat between his open legs, turning it round and round with his stubby fingers as he spoke.

The woman was also a sight, sad and ugly. She hadn't responded to Jane's greeting. Her mouse-brown hair fell just past her ears. Her jowls drooped, and her complexion was uneven, the thick skin of her face, ruddy in places. Oddly, her lips were cemented into a definite downward arc, a natural frown. But her most outstanding feature was the blanket of pain that covered her face and the glaze of sorrow that hooded her eyes.

Mrs. Gold seemed oblivious to her husband and Jane as they spoke. She sat gazing at some spot on the green carpet, gripping the black strap of her handbag on her lap with both hands. It didn't escape Jane that the handbag – like the coat she wore, her shoes, and the Gold's new Cadillac parked outside – was expensive. That was good, Jane thought. These babies were her inventory and worth good money.

Jane noted that the Golds wore wedding bands. She checked for that whenever she first extended her arm to greet potential candidates for adoption. In those days, adoption procedures, lax in all states, was particularly so in Texas, where all that was needed of an adopting couple was a valid marriage; Jane deemed the presence of wedding rings was adequate proof of that.

It was as though the Texas state legislature was too embarrassed to admit that there were unwed mothers who spawned illegitimate babies; how could it possibly begin to regulate the adoption of the illegitimate infants? Any legal requirements that were to be met by those wanting to adopt in Texas were *never* checked. Paper trails were *not* kept. *Nothing* was recorded. In fact, record keeping was discouraged.

Jane smiled. "So. You want to adopt one of our beautiful babies."

Phil stopped playing with his hat. His thin purple mouth closed tightly, and his full jowls became fuller before he answered. "Right," he said. "But the kid's gotta be Jewish." He pointed his hat at Jane. "That means the mother's gotta be Jewish. You got any of those?"

Jane was caught off guard by his request, but she answered smoothly. "Of course, Mr. Gold. Why that's no problem at all."

The man dropped his hat on his thigh, passed his palm across his brow, and shook his head. "It's terrible that a Jewish girl would be in a place like this."

"Yes. But unfortunately, it does happen."

Suddenly, Mrs. Gold, still clutching the black strap of her bag, began to wail. Tears streamed down her face. "Oh, my Jeffrey!" Jane had no idea who Jeffrey was or why Mrs. Gold was sobbing. But she saw Mr. Gold's chest collapse as he got up to go to his wife's side.

He gave her a handkerchief from out of his pocket. "Stella, please." He mumbled with closed eyes.

Mrs. Gold looked up at Jane, pushed her husband away, waved the handkerchief and cried out, "He just had his bar mitzvah! I want my son back!"

Jane didn't know what a "bar something" was, but she gathered that the woman was mourning the loss of Jeffrey, most likely, her son. As understanding took hold of Jane's mind, she felt waves of pity for this woman wash over her.

She leaned towards her. "There, there. I am so sorry for your loss, Mrs. Gold." She didn't know what else to say. She wanted to add she was so glad she would never have a child. "And for you, Mr. Gold."

Mr. Gold wiped his brow with his palm again and shook his head. "Stella," he said to his wife, "remember our promise on the Torah."

Jane had no idea what he was talking about but was glad to see that, though her tears didn't stop, Mrs. Gold was now silent. She also realized that she had to refocus the Golds on the reason for their visit soon or this maudlin show could go on forever.

She rose from her seat and approached Mrs. Gold, speaking to her in a tone she hoped sounded earnest. "Come, come. I know this must be very hard for you, Mrs. Gold. I know it's impossible for you to believe me, but I've seen other mothers in this situation. Trust me, you will come to love your new child every bit as much as you loved your own son."

When the miserable woman, still crying, looked up at her, Jane had never seen eyes filled with so much pain. She had to look away and when she did, she caught sight of the clock on the wall. Time was marching on. She had to seal this deal quickly and be done with the

Golds. What if they became so distraught that they changed their minds about adopting?

She placed her hand firmly on Mr. Gold's arm. "Well now, Mr. Gold," she said, "I'm sure you're anxious to choose a baby. Let's all go see what we have, shall we?"

With that she headed briskly toward the door. When she saw Mr. Gold reach to give Mrs. Gold his hand and saw the woman rise from her chair, she thanked her lucky Texas stars. The woman moved as slowly as one twice her age and sniffled all the way, but she did follow along.

Jane called to the couple trailing her as they made their way downstairs. "You're in luck. We have five babies here today, and two of them are lovely Hebrew babies."

Downstairs, they entered a large room painted soft yellow with windows that were graced with short, yellow gingham curtains looking out onto a garden where four girls, all about sixteen years old and all obviously pregnant, sat chatting in a covered patio.

Jane introduced the Golds to Charlene, sitting in a rocking chair against a wall, a baby cradled in her arms, nursing from a bottle.

There were eight cribs in the room and several bassinets. Phil looked around the room and muttered, "This baby had better be Jewish."

Mrs. Gold had her eye on the girls outside the window. "What happens to these girls?" She wiped away her newest tears. "I mean after they leave their babies. Do they ever see them again?"

"No, Mrs. Gold. They simply return to the lives they had with a second chance at happiness," Jane said.

Then, as the three of them stood between two cribs, she fanned her arms out at her sides as if displaying new cars in a showroom. "Boy or girl?"

Simultaneously, Mr. Gold said, "Boy," and Mrs. Gold answered, "Girl." They turned to one another, Mrs. Gold's mouth hanging open, her husband's round eyes opened wide. It became apparent to Jane that the couple hadn't previously discussed the sex of their baby-to-be!

Mrs. Gold turned back to Jane with her down-turned lips set, her eyes steely. Clutching her black handbag in front of her, she spoke assertively. "We want a girl, Abigail."

Jane quickly picked up the baby in the crib tagged "Baby Girl (560)" and placed her in Stella's arms. Jane was anxious to unload this baby. There were too many strikes against the infant. Though petite, this was by far the oldest baby in the House, more than three months old. This was also the newest baby in residence and the only one not born at Abigail's. She had been hand-delivered to Jane only two days before by Jane's old girl friend Maggie, who had driven in with the infant from Los Angeles.

Recalling that Maggie had a daughter of college age, Jane had initially assumed that the baby was Maggie's grandchild. But over a salad and martinis, with the infant lodged at Maggie's side, Jane's friend related the story of a young Persian girl who had come to UCLA from her home in Iran.

"She was a lovely girl, beautiful and probably quite intelligent. While she was here, she fell in love with a young doctor. He asked her to marry him, but she refused. You see, she was a Muslim, and he was Jewish, and she knew her parents would be dead set against it. He wanted her to marry him and go with him. She loved him enough to sleep with him – you know, that's totally against her religion and her upbringing – a Persian girl is supposed to stay a virgin until her wedding night – still, she refused to marry him. She felt obliged to do as her parents had expected; you know, return to Iran when she finished UCLA and marry a Persian man. So, the poor doctor left for Israel without her to live on a kibbutz there – a sort of Israeli commune.

"After he was gone, Layla – that was her name – Layla realized she was pregnant. Well, poor thing, she wanted to die. She couldn't believe abortions aren't legal here. Apparently, they're legal in her country. Can you believe that?

"Anyway, she had to keep her pregnancy a secret from her parents. Poor thing! Can you imagine? Alone in a strange land, pregnant, and having to keep it a secret from your family? She couldn't let them find out. She was so scared, so miserable. Anyway, she didn't tell anyone. Not even the baby's father knew. She kept it from everyone – except my two children who were friends of hers from school.

"She'd been to our house countless times, truly a lovely girl. When my kids discovered that she was pregnant, they insisted – bless them – that she move in with them. She had no one else. Poor girl! They completely cared for her during her entire pregnancy. It was a very hard time for her." Maggie had paused then to sigh and take a long sip of her drink.

"Anyway, to make a long story short, she delivered the baby around the middle of May and named her Jasmine ... like the flower. Then it was June and she had to return to Iran — you know, her parent's house — for a month. She couldn't not go. She was supposed go back every summer. She was so lucky that the baby had already been delivered!" Maggie gestured to Jasmine wrapped in quilts and a blanket alongside her.

"Well, obviously, she couldn't take Jasmine with her – God only knows what they'd have done to her if the'd known. So, she left this beautiful baby with my two kids while she was gone."

Jane had almost choked then.

"I know, I know. She was only supposed to be gone for a few weeks and they had no school and they felt so sorry for the poor girl; like I said, the she had, absolutely, no one else. What could they do? They cared about her.

"The baby was only a couple of weeks old, and Layla was going to put her up for adoption when she returned, obviously — she had to. She didn't give Jasmine up at birth because she didn't want to leave the choice of new parents to an agency; she was determined to be involved in finding the best home possible for her baby. So, she decided she'd wait till she returned from Iran.

"My two kids actually took care of this baby, Jane! Well, the couple of weeks turned into six weeks, then *two months* and she *still* didn't return! Then she called them and said she was getting married to some Persian man and that she would be coming to L.A. for her honeymoon. She told them that her husband knew nothing about Jasmine! He probably believed he'd married a virgin! Anyway, she swore she'd be back by early September."

"She never came back?" Jane had been unprepared for such a dramatic story, so different from that of the girls who came to the House, all white upper-class Americans, spoiled by wealthy parents who cared for their errant daughters, and arranged their stay at Abigail's. And she was in awe of the two college kids who had watched over someone else's newborn while the mother was gallivanting halfway around the world getting married.

Maggie shook her head. "Jane, my poor kids spent their summer taking care of a newborn infant! Imagine! Two college kids! They couldn't go to the beach, or a movie, date ... they couldn't do *anything*! Poor things! My heart broke for them!

"Whenever they'd come to home to visit, they'd bring Jasmine and her diapers, formula ..." Maggie put her fingers at her temples and rolled her eyes.

"Anyway, she's still not back. I don't know if her wedding plans fell through or what the problem was. My kids think, now that she's married, she just doesn't want to bother with a baby that no one knows about. They think it's easier for her to simply forget about Jasmine. And honestly? I get it."

Then Maggie had gazed over at Jasmine somewhat lovingly before picking her up and nestling her in her arms. "Look at her. She's a beauty, isn't she?"

Jane had agreed. The infant was pretty, much prettier than most babies she'd seen. Yet to Jane, bottom line was, a baby was a baby was a baby, and you can have them all – so long as you pay for them.

Maggie had sighed then continued. "Anyway, classes have started and there's no way that they can continue to care for Jasmine. And they don't live together anymore, either. I don't blame them and I'm sure you don't. Jane, imagine you and me when we were in college. Can you see us taking care of an infant?" Maggie had chuckled then, and Jane rolled her eyes. "And to tell you the truth, I wouldn't let them if they wanted to. I'm completely amazed that they'd done it for what turned out to be three months! Poor babies!

"In any event, Layla wanted to put her up for adoption anyway.

She would already have been adopted by now if Layla had been here."
Maggie downed the remainder of her martini.

"I know this isn't your usual, Jane. But if you could do me this
huge favor, I'd appreciate it. I've grown fond of the little girl, poor
baby," Maggie had hugged the baby closer to her then, "and I know
she'll be in good hands with you."

Jane had made an exception as a favor to an old friend and so, little
Jasmine became Baby Girl (560), the newest addition to Jane's
inventory.

The Golds would be the perfect buyers, *if* she could pass the infant
born to a Muslim mother off as Jewish.

Meanwhile, with the baby in her arms, Mrs. Gold had stopped crying.
That was a good sign. The little thing shuddered, as babies do in their
sleep, and Mrs. Gold's face relaxed as if her heart had melted. In fact,
Stella's nurturing instincts, along with her earliest memories of mothering, had come to life. The plain woman looked at the baby's beautiful
little face, her lush lashes, tawny skin and dusky rose-colored lips that
had a definite upturn as though the infant girl was smiling even in her
sleep. She was beautiful.

"Stella!" Mr. Gold's face flushed as he watched his wife cradle the
she-child. "We want a boy!" But his wife paid no attention.

Mesmerized by the child in her arms she was already imagining
her life as the mother of this pretty girl. She saw this baby growing up
surrounded by friends and boyfriend, and the kind of social life that
she had never experienced; entry into the world of good-looking
people, sought after by others ... and there was Stella at her side,
advising her daughter and sharing all that attention, acceptance, and
love.

She thought of her Jeffrey. She would forever compare a boy to her
lost son but wouldn't be able to do that with this girl. She hugged the
baby in her arms.

Phil pursed his lips and addressed his wife again. His eyes were
imploring, his voice, softer this time. "Stella ... Honey ..." He wiped off

the perspiration on his brow and put the hat he'd been holding back on his head. "What are you doing? It's a son we want, isn't it? A son – to take his place."

Stella spoke to the floor near Phil's feet, her voice dismissive and bitter. "We had a son. No baby boy will take his place."

Then, with a voice devoid of all acridity, she asked Jane, "Is she Jewish?"

Having stood by serenely, fingers intertwined, anxiously watching and listening to the duel between the Golds, Jane now answered, smiling sweetly. "Oh yes, Mrs. Gold, she's as Jewish as can be."

"Stella. Call me Stella."

Jane smiled. "Stella."

Stella was sure. If they were going to adopt, she wanted this pretty girl who slept so peacefully in her arms. She looked at the baby once more and turned to Jane.

"We'll take her, Abigail," she said.

"Now hold on, you two!" Mr. Gold said. He again wiped his brow and looked at the baby, then at his wife. Jane thought the eyes of the short purple man might explode. But Stella just returned his look with an expression of challenge, a mix of pure misery, hatred, and ultimately, defiance.

"Hold her, Phil." Stella never took her eyes off the infant she passed to her husband, but it was only at the last millisecond, when Jane was certain the baby was about to drop, that Mr. Gold took hold of the baby. "Look at her," Stella instructed him. "Isn't she beautiful?"

"Yeah, yeah," he said, barely looking down, "but she's no boy."

Stella spoke over his head to Jane. "It feels so strange to hold a baby again."

It was time to close the deal. "If you're sure, I suggest we go back to my office and finish this up. Shall we?"

Jane shepherded the couple toward the stairs. "Charlene, please have some tea and lemon cake sent to my office for Mr. and Mrs. Gold, then see to the baby's requirements and ready a bag."

As they made their way back upstairs to Jane's office, Stella followed Jane and Mr. Gold trailed them, holding the beautiful girl like a time bomb and shaking his head in dissatisfaction the whole way.

As soon they'd returned to Jane's well-appointed office and Stella Gold had sat down, she put her arms out for the infant and her husband gladly obliged. Jane took her seat at her desk across from the Golds. Stella removed the baby's pink blanket and examined every part of the little girl, as if examining a dress for possible imperfections before buying it.

Jane recalled seeing a red beauty mark in the shape of a crescent on the little girl's calf. "Look at this, Phil." Stella had found the mark. "It looks like a crescent moon."

"Let me look," he said. "Maybe she's got a problem there. Don't tell me you went and got us a kid with a problem!" He turned to the baby in his wife's lap, eager to find a defect so they could trade the girl in for a boy.

"Don't be stupid!" Stella said, slapping his encroaching hand away. "Look at it. It's just a pretty little birthmark, a lot prettier than yours!" He sighed.

Jane was already shuffling through various sets of papers on her desk, held together with clips. "Let's see. There is some paperwork we have to deal with." She smiled at the folks across her desk sitting in the elegant chairs. "I hope you like lemon cake?" The tea and lemon cake sat before them. As if on cue, they both took a bite of the cake, nodded appreciatively, then took a sip of the tea.

"All right," Jane began. "As you may know, it is our policy not to charge for our babies. It's enough for me to know that each one of God's little miracles finds a good home. However, there is an outstanding bill for medical services. Apparently the doctor who delivered your baby is, unfortunately, still unpaid."

She had yet to see a set of new parents unwilling to dish over money due the obstetrician. None had so far been willing to look at their new baby and think there was an unpaid balance owed on their new child.

"How much?"

"Let's see. Five hundred twenty dollars." Jane said, moving the sheet of paper this way and that.

Mr. Gold looked over at his wife. She was stroking the baby's hair. "Okay."

"Very good. He'll be pleased." Jane flipped through more papers. "Hmm, there's a birth certificate to think about."

"How much?"

"Well, if you'd like some discretion, there are costs involved in maintaining that–"

"How much?" Mr. Gold asked taking another forkful of his cake.

"Nine hundred dollars."

Phil whistled. "That much?" He looked over at his wife again. She was stroking the baby's cheek. "Okay, fine!" he said grudgingly. He opened his wallet, counted out fourteen one hundred-dollar bills and put them on Jane's desk with one twenty. Then he put down an additional eighteen dollars.

"What's that for?" Jane asked.

"For luck. Eighteen is the number of chai. Luck."

Jane nodded. She had no doubt that this new family would need all the luck they could get. 'The birth certificate will be mailed to you. What's your address?"

"I don't have one yet. I'll let you know where to mail it when I have one." Phil would ultimately forget to forward their new address to Jane and so they would never receive what he'd just paid for.

"Well, then, we're done. Congratulations!" Jane put the papers away and looked at her watch. With less than an hour before the bank closed for the day, she was ready to send the Golds on their way. "I'm sure you'll make excellent parents. And your daughter's family will be thrilled to know she's with Hebrew folks. That's what they wanted."

Stella's head shot up. "Will they know we have the child? Abigail, I'd rather they didn't. What if one day they change their mind and come looking for her? They'll take her away! I don't want that. Do they have to know where she is?"

Thanks to the great state of Texas, it was easy to reassure Stella. "That won't happen. Rest assured that once you take this baby out of Abigail's, no one will ever know where to find her. It's against the law for your baby's whereabouts to be divulged to her natural mother.

"You should know that not once have any of these girls returned to ask me about their child; not a single one. But if they do, the law prevents me from giving them any information. Nor can the birth mother's identity be disclosed to you, to the child, or anyone else. It's the law. The law of Texas is very clear on that." With that, Jane stood up, the meeting, officially ended, the transaction done.

At the front door of Abigail's, Charlene handed Mr. Gold the bag she prepared for all new parents, containing several diapers, two T-shirts, a small yellow blanket covered with tiny white sheep and three cans of formula. After that, the Golds would be on their own.

Mr. Gold took the bag and looked at Stella. He tried one last time. "Are you sure about this, Stella? I mean … a girl." Stella's answer was to walk to the light blue Cadillac holding the baby tightly in her arms.

Jane Albright watched from her upstairs window and smiled as the newly expanded Gold family settled into their Cadillac and drove off. She'd had a stellar day. She got paid on both ends of the baby trade, getting more money per pound for her babies than any Texas cattleman ever got for his meat.

On her way to the bank, Jane was humming. Business was booming.

4

ALL THAT GLITTERS

– Phil –

*O*n the twelfth day following Jeffrey's funeral, at 3:24 in the morning, Phil Gold got up off the couch, sealed all the windows of the small apartment, went into the kitchen and turned on the gas. Then he went back to lie down on the flowered couch in the living room and wait.

At approximately a 7:45 morning, Phil and Stella Gold's next-door neighbor was in the hallway waiting for the elevator when she smelled the gas. She knocked on their door. When she got no answer, she called the police. They broke into the apartment and sent for an ambulance. Phil and Stella were rushed to Bayside Hospital. At that point, the police notified Stella's sister, Sophie.

Phil's attempted suicide-murder was botched. Both he and Stella survived. But the debacle changed the course of their lives.

While they were in the hospital, their two families had met and decided that something had to be done and when Stella and Phil were discharged, they were presented with their future: they would leave the east coast forever and move as far away as possible. They would go west, all the way to California where Phil would work with his cousin in Maury's thriving movie theater business.

Their belongings were packed, and they were given an itinerary for the trip across the country making note of a stop in Dallas where they would adopt a child before continuing on to California as a new family.

Before departing on their road trip, they were escorted to a synagogue where they vowed on the Torah that they would speak of Jeffrey no more.

They would erase their past and make a fresh start.

Phil had left Route 66 somewhere in Oklahoma to head south toward Dallas and Abigail's. Now he returned to a northwestern route.

The couple resumed their silence.

As they drove the desolate prairie roads, clouds of dust continued to dirty their light blue Cadillac. Neither paid attention to the landscape around them. Instead of seeing the rolling hills belted now and then with more rugged ones, Stella only had eyes for the sleeping baby on her lap. Phil's eyes were glued to the asphalt ahead.

He ached to talk to his wife about Jeffrey. He longed to tell her how much he missed their son, how he wished Jeffrey was in the car with them now, sitting in the back seat singing, so Stella could comfort him. But he knew that was impossible. She was incapable of comforting him, and anyway, he didn't believe he deserved any solace, certainly not from Stella. He didn't dare speak of his lost boy to her, and so, he said nothing.

He turned the radio on. Tony Bennett was lamenting the heart he'd left in San Francisco. Phil's vision blurred with thoughts of the heart he'd left with his son in a New York cemetery.

He jabbed at the radio buttons and stopped at the news. John F. Kennedy, the country's new president, was in meetings with his brother, Robert, the newly-appointed U.S. Attorney General. Plans were being finalized for Kennedy's first trip abroad as President of the

United States. The President's wife would be traveling with him, and there was enormous speculation as to what the First Lady would wear on the trip. Jacqueline Kennedy had wowed the nation with her sense of fashion and style. Everything she did was news and everything she wore took headlines.

Phil shook his head. *Women! That's all they think about, schmutzahs and decorating. Just wait! This Kennedy woman will redecorate the White House. God, how Stella loved decorating that Florida house. Oy, veyz meir, Florida!*

Phil's tears resumed and he heaved a heavy sigh, wiping his eyes with his stubby hand. He repositioned himself on the seat and gripped the steering wheel tighter. Stealing a look at his wife to see if she'd noticed his tears, his eyes followed hers down to the still sleeping infant she held in her arms. It was strange to see his wife holding a baby again after such a long time.

Stella had aged in the weeks since Jeffrey's death. *She's been through Hell!*

And now? They were on their way to a new home in California, a place neither he nor Stella had ever been to. They had a new child, a baby girl. He had thought he would never have to work again but he'd be starting a new job, nothing at all like the construction business he was used to, and he wasn't as young as he used to be. He and Stella would need to stay close, support one another. Instead, Stella had acted outrageously, insisting on adopting this girl and not changing her mind no matter what he'd said.

Ah! What difference did it make? He snapped off the radio. After all, he'd tried to kill them both.

But they had decided they'd make a new start, hadn't they? Phil squirmed in his seat. *Still, we were supposed to adopt a boy! A daughter? Oy, what a disaster! What am I, here, chopped liver? If I had known Stella was thinking of a girl, I'd have changed her mind before we got to that damned baby house. Why even bother with a girl? It's a son we lost! A son we're replacing here. What the hell is Stella thinking?*

He glanced at his wife sitting beside him. She'd set her cigarette down in the ashtray and was stroking the baby's face with her finger. The pain caught in his throat and he opened his window for fresh air.

"Close the window," Stella said almost immediately, reaching for her Salems. "It's too much for the baby,"

"For Pete's sake!" He rolled it back up. "I should close the window, but you should smoke? There's no goddamned air in here."

Stella didn't bother to answer him as smoke curled out and up from her lips.

Phil eyed the infant, trying to kill the kernel of resentment he felt toward the baby he would be living with from now on.

Once she had you in her arms, her mind was made up. How could I say no when that was the first time she'd smiled since Jeffrey died? Such a tired smile … she's a mess.

I suppose she thinks you can make her happy. God knows she deserves that chance. Well, you had better make her happy or I'll wring your neck, you little bastard.

He sighed. *I guess I don't really know if a boy would've made us happy … someone else's kid … not Jeffrey … Ahh, who am I kidding? Stella had every right to adopt a goddamned monkey if she wanted to.*

Still, she should have taken a boy.

They passed a sign that read, "Welcome to New Mexico, the Land of Enchantment," and the infant began to gurgle in her sleep. They were in a town called Tucumcari.

The baby stirred. She opened her eyes. Stella smiled down at her and put her cigarette out in the ashtray. "Stop, Phil. I want to change the baby's diaper."

"*Aw*! Again? For Pete's sake! You just changed her. We're never gonna get to California." He looked for a place to pull over. "You haven't stopped with the kid. Formula, diapers, feeding her, changing her, taking her out for fresh air." He was sneering as he pulled up in front of the Blue Swallow Motel, a perfect prototype of an American roadside motel popping up all across the country, a concrete box lined with windows separated by red doors bearing numbers and cars alongside the rooms parked in the black asphalt lot.

Stella got out of the car and laid the baby down on the front seat where she'd been sitting. "Come help me," she said.

Phil arose reluctantly, stretched his back, then shuffled his way around the Cadillac and stood ready to help his wife. A slight after-noon breeze blew dust at their feet.

Stella unpinned the baby's diaper. "I've been thinking of a name for her. She's just so pretty. She should have a pretty name. Don't you think?"

"Name her whatever you want. Look at that, will you? Her diaper's still dry, for Pete's sake!"

Stella changed it anyway. "Okay, already! It won't hurt her to air out." The breeze brought the scent of Johnson & Johnson's baby powder to Phil's nose. "I think she should have a foreign name," Stella said.

"Why? She's a foreigner?" Phil's eyes opened wide.

"Look at her skin, it's kind of rosy-olive."

Phil's eyes widened but he didn't look at the baby. He ran his palm across his forehead. "Don't tell me you went and got us a foreign baby!"

"Don't be an idiot. She's American. And anyway, you heard Abigail. She's Jewish."

Phil sighed and they got back into the car. As Stella replaced the baby, now fully awake, on her lap he thought, *at least she's a quiet little thing*.

A few miles later, Phil braced himself when he heard Stella's first *goochi-goos*, then relaxed and decided to let Stella enjoy herself. Her cigarette was down again, and she held the baby's hands. Then she stroked her ample black hair and put her finger on the baby's nose. He had to agree; the baby girl was unusually pretty. Jeffrey certainly hadn't been good-looking; God rest his soul …

How was he supposed to forget?

Phil aimed the Evinrude back toward the dock behind their new house on the lake. The hottest part of the humid Florida summer day was over, and the water was taking on deeper shades of blue as the glare of the dazzling sun was finally ebbing. There were fewer boats out on the lake now than when he and Jeffrey had started out a couple of hours earlier, but the whir of running motors could still be heard. Phil slowed his boat then killed the engine. The boat began to drift.

"Do we have to go home now, Dad?"

Phil nodded. "I need to get cleaned up and get going. We can't be late for the Starlight." As he spoke, they neared the dock. "I'll bet your mother bought herself some new *schmutza* for tonight, cost me a goddamned fortune."

"Do you have to tie her down? Can't I please stay out? Just a little bit longer?"

Phil wasn't surprised by his son's request. Though he never allowed the boy to stay out on the boat alone, he continued to ask. Jeffrey's greatest pleasure was spending time on the boat, and Phil suspected it was not only for the time spent with his dad. It was also his refuge.

When they'd first moved to this Florida town, Phil had assured his son that soon the boy would have lots of friends. Yet school had started months ago, and the boy was still a loner. At least back in New York Jeff had sometimes played board games with that little fellow who lived in their building. In this town, he had no one at all. He was one of a kind here, not just the awkward new kid in town, the awkward and apparently unwanted, new *Jew* kid in town.

Phil's heavy eyebrows converged above his thick nose as he answered, flapping his short and stubby arms, "*Aw*, come on, Jeff, don't you start that with me."

"Dad, I don't get it. I just had a bar mitzvah. Doesn't that mean I'm a man now? Isn't that what a bar mitzvah means? That you don't treat me like I'm a kid anymore?"

Jeffrey was looking somewhere behind his father. Phil turned to follow his son's gaze to the group of boys stationed on the shore close by their dock, lazily tossing a football. They were around his son's age.

"I … I … I don't want to go ashore right now, Dad. I promise I won't go beyond the lakefront. I'll just drift around right here for a few minutes and then come in. I can tie her down. You know I can."

Phil looked at his son's thin, lanky arms, his frail hands set on his lap, the large nose set between Stella's small brown eyes now fixed on the grassy area where the boys played, the smiling boys with fair complexions, obviously passing amiable comments back and forth as they tossed the ball. If they left now, Jeffrey would have to pass into their midst.

"Please can I stay?"

Phil was a simple, uneducated, working man and a self-made millionaire who was as surprised as everyone else when he had struck it rich in the post-war housing boom of the late Fourties. As a contractor, his business flourished before he'd sold it a year ago and moved to this Florida town he had read about with his wife and son. The article in Life magazine had predicted that the town, located on the intracoastal waterway on Palm Beach Island in southern Florida, would be one of the most sought-after places to live in the U.S. within the decade.

He'd built the house they now lived in. It was the last home he would build and the best he had ever built. The house was designed in the style of new wealth, stocked with every new appliance made. Still, they hadn't yet entertained a single guest. The townspeople had been downright cold to the family and Phil was starting to wonder if he'd made the right move.

This would be a pivotal night for his family. His banker had invited him and Stella to a dinner party at the Starlight Country Club. Located by the bridge to the island, the Starlight was the only country club within a radius of a hundred miles.

Phil had put off applying to the club until people got to know the Golds better and realized they were friendly, they had money and class, and — in case his ever-increasingly perception of the town's anti-Semitism was accurate – they weren't all that religious. To that end, they had been fortunate that Jeffrey's bar mitzvah had been held in New York where all their guests resided.

Tonight, Phil hoped to impress on the members of the Starlight that he was one of them. He couldn't stay on the boat with Jeffrey any longer or he'd be late. It was time for him to go home, shower, and dress for the evening that could change their lives.

He sighed and ran his hand up the boy's forehead and into his hair, his gesture of affection. "Okay, Jeffrey, you can stay," Phil said. He held the key out to the boy.

"Thanks, Dad!" Jeffrey clapped his hands like Phil did when things went his way and took the key from his father.

"But," Phil wagged a stubby finger in Jeffrey's face and eyed him sternly, "don't turn the boat's engine back on until you're ready to dock her. Just sit for a few minutes. Only for a few minutes. You hear?" Phil instinctively gestured to the boys. "Then come home." Jeffrey nodded. "Me and your mother have to get going. Got that?"

"I promise. I'll be in soon." The boy smiled, looked up at his father and clapped again.

"Okay, then. I'll see you inside the house." Phil turned his back to Jeffrey, caught hold of a plank, and got onto the pier. The wooden boards creaked as he stepped onto them. His short legs moved gracelessly toward his new home. Propelled by the excitement of his first dinner at the Starlight Country Club, Phil clapped his hands. He was also pleased that he'd made Jeffrey so happy.

He never again saw his son alive.

5

THE ROAD PAVED WITH GOLD

– Stella –

*T*he land that had been as flat as a tortilla gave way to hills and mountains as the blue Cadillac moved west.

"Oh look! She's smiling!" Stella's exuberant voice brought Phil back to the moment.

"How could a mother leave a child with a *punim* like yours? Your mother must have been one of those pretty girls with no brains." The ashtray was full, so Stella cracked her window open and tossed out the remains of her lit cigarette. "I'm going to make sure you use your brains, you pretty girl."

She turned to Phil. "Let's give her a French name. Something pretty like, Georgette, or Cheri." Phil nodded. This was as animated as he'd seen his wife in a long time. "Cheri means 'dear' in French." Stella had taken a year and a half of French in high school and used her limited French vocabulary as often as she could. Early on, her dream had been to go to France and speak French to the natives. Phil wondered if she still had a dream.

"You're just so pretty," she said to the little girl. *"Vouz et tres jolie!* Jolie means 'pretty' and you, *mademoiselle,* are very, very pretty. Yes, you are." Stella kissed the infant's cheek and left another Revlon Million Dollar Red imprint on the baby's soft face. She continued fondling the baby, repeating. *"Vouz et tres jolie! Tres, tres jolie!"*

She sprang up in her seat. "That's it! I'll name you Jolie! It's perfect. That's who you are. Mama's pretty little girl!" She hugged the infant to her chest. "Hi, Jolie! Hello, my pretty baby! Mama went out and got herself a pretty little Jolie. Yes, she did and that's who you are! Jolie Gold!" She looked at her husband. "Phil, that's her name! Jolie Gold."

"*Shayna. Shayna* means pretty in Hebrew," Phil mumbled.

"Phil, say hello to Jolie. You're my pretty little Jolie Gold and you're adopted, Jolie, but we love you just as much as if you were our own."

The new Gold family passed their first night together in New Mexico, near the Arizona border. The next morning, they started out on what would be the most difficult part of the trip, the drive through the deserts of Arizona and Nevada. The air became increasingly dry. The temperature continued to rise.

Phil and Stella felt like they were in a sauna. The ice they had packed quickly melted and the water soon became too hot to drink. Phil pared down to his thin white undershirt and Stella, who wore a light summer skirt and sleeveless blouse, had already taken her stocking off and now she opened the buttons of her blouse. Jolie, asleep in Stella's arms, wore only a loosely pinned diaper.

The hot drone of the desert overtook everything but the dull whoosh of cars that occasionally passed by.

Stella closed her eyes.

She was in her newly completed bedroom in Florida talking on the telephone, a Salem between her lips. She was proud of her new house and of the magnificent job she had done decorating it. She loved the master bedroom, the walls and carpets in a trending soft green. The bedspread was a light beige and the curtains, beige with lots of green in a floral design. Everywhere she looked, her impeccable taste reflected back to her.

Phil came into the bedroom. Later, he said that he'd started to tell Stella right then that he'd allowed Jeffrey to stay on the boat for just a few minutes, but she had gestured for him to be silent because she was talking to Ida, telling her about the Starlight and her new dress, and by the time she'd put the receiver down, he had emptied his pockets, taken off his short-sleeved shirt, stepped out of his sneakers – and forgotten to tell her.

"For Pete's sake, Stella, you talk to that woman more than you talk to me."

Stella took another drag from her cigarette then put it out in the green ashtray that sat on her nightstand. The smoke poured out of her mouth along with her words. "Well, thank God for Ida! If it wasn't for her, I'd have *no one* to talk to! It's not like I have any friends here yet."

"Well, maybe it's cause you're on the phone with Ida all the goddamned time! And why do I have to be quiet? Doesn't she know I live with you?"

"Oh, hush up! Hurry with the shower. You stink! I can smell the sweat from here. Throw your clothes *in* the hamper, your socks, too, and shave again."

"Christ, Stella!" Phil flicked his fingers off his chin. "I shaved this morning."

"Well, it won't hurt to shave again. You want to make a good impression, don't you? Shave. People notice."

Phil bent down and picked up his clothes, dumped them into the bin in the corner of the large bathroom, then went into the shower and turned on the water.

Stella, with her hands on her hair, yelled, "And don't make steam. My hair will go bad."

She was excited. So far, this new town hadn't treated her well, but tonight she would turn the tide. She had expected the people here to accept her family immediately. After all, Phil had bought one of the most expensive lots in the area and built a grand house, which she had capably transformed into a showcase. But no one had yet seen the inside of it! They drove a new Cadillac and had bought the newest in motorboats. She shopped at all the right places and they all wore the right clothes. But all her efforts had been completely unacknowledged. *It was so frustrating!*

Just that morning she'd again said hello to her next-door neighbor, the thin, pasty-skinned, strawberry-blond woman. The name on her mailbox said *Cunningham*. Stella wondered what her first name was. She had looked forward to befriending her neighbor. Maybe she played pan or mahjong. But the woman just didn't seem to warm up at all and hadn't even returned Stella's greeting this morning.

What was with these people? Her family was being completely ignored! She was being snubbed! Well, she'd had enough of that!

Maybe Phil wasn't as handsome or as educated as most of the men in town, but he had as much money as any of them. She wanted to make friends of their wives and she wanted Jeffrey to make friends of their sons and daughters. He was miserable here without even one friend. True, he had been an insecure, shy boy in New York, but here he was totally alone. He was growing up and needed a social life.

Stella believed that as a result of tonight's dinner, the family would join the country club. Certainly, membership at the Starlight would be the undeniable stamp of approval that would put an end to their problems. Their attendance tonight would ensure membership. Just wait until they got a load of her in her new dress! She'd get their attention tonight, and no one in this town would ever snub her again. She could just see them dying for her company, begging for her advice on decorating and clothes, and their children eager to invite Jeffrey into their homes.

She was already wearing the new girdle and low-cut brassiere that went with the dress she'd bought. The wires and elastic bands that circled her body, constricting it, were uncomfortably tight. But she didn't care. She sat at her vanity table and heard Phil singing his favorite song in the shower, *Because of you, there's a song in my heart.* She lit another cigarette and shook her head, trying to tune out Phil's gruff voice as she turned her attention to the face in the three-way mirror and looked at herself.

Nothing had changed since the last time she'd looked. There was the uneven skin tone that showed through all but the heaviest of foundations. There were her small eyes that all but got lost in her fleshy face. And there, impossible to ignore, was the largest and most unusual feature of her face, the lips that pointed sharply down where they were supposed to point up and stayed down even when she smiled.

Her mother's friend had matched her with Phil. The night they met, she'd worn a red sweater with tiny black beads at her bust line. Not expecting this "wonderful catch" to be quite as short as he was, she'd also worn high heels. As a result, Phil – unknown to her, a breast man – had passed a most enchanting first date bumping into Stella every chance he got.

It was easy for her to get him to propose after that. All she had to do was emphasize her breasts, jiggle them a bit and, like any good, decent Jewish girl, allow him no more than a feel before marriage. The promise of their unveiling was too much for Phil to resist. Three months after their first date, they married. Stella was twenty-nine and Phil had been her first boyfriend. Aware that she wasn't an attractive woman, Stella was more than grateful for her life with Phil, and she adored their son.

All the girls Stella knew – including her younger sister Sophie, who was undeniably prettier – were already married to men far more appealing than Phil. Then came the end of World War II and a huge boom in the housing market.

Phil's construction business became excessively lucrative. Stella enjoyed flaunting their new wealth. She wore expensive clothes and new, flashy jewelry. She demanded that Phil pick up the tab on evenings out with her girlfriends and their husbands.

In the early days, if her husband dared to contest her will, Stella would punish him when they got home by wearing her brassiere under a long flannel gown and taking to the far side of their bed. Phil soon learned to do her bidding. Years afterward, when he'd learned that she was almost always mad at him for something and almost always off limits, he still did her bidding.

Stella applied a second coat of thick foundation, then powder, artfully evening out her skin tone. She applied brown Maybelline eyebrow pencil, extending her thin brows, doubling their length and filling in their shape. Then she spit onto a small, thick, black brush and pushed it deep into the cake of black mascara, which she applied onto her lashes until she was satisfied that she could not possibly make them any blacker. She carefully applied Revlon's Million Dollar Red lipstick and blotted her lips, smudged on red rouge and again primped her brown hair. The sound of the shower had stopped and a moment later Phil was standing in the bedroom, wrapped in towels with a small piece of toilet paper stuck onto a nick under his chin.

"Phil! You should have been more careful. Ah, never mind." She was about to pick up her Salem but realized it had burned out. She got up and went to the far side of the bedroom, opened the closet door and reached for her gown while Phil hurriedly dressed.

"I'll be ready soon," he said. "Are you almost done?" By the time Stella had squeezed into her dress, Phil had donned his white dress shirt, socks, and black tuxedo pants, and was clipping on a black and gray silk bow tie.

"Zip me," she said. "There's two hooks, one at the waist one at the top."

When he'd finished hooking her up, Stella put on her high heels then went to her jewelry chest and returned to Phil who was donning his tuxedo jacket. She again turned her back to him so he could fasten the clasp of the diamond necklace. That done, she was ready. "Well, what do you think?" she asked, turning for him.

Phil looked at his wife and whistled. Her new gown was bright-red silk. The bodice was tight with a low neckline that showed off her cleavage before falling in soft folds to her hips and ending down just below her knees. She wore the drop-dead diamond necklace Phil had given her on their last anniversary in New York, when he was coaxing her to leave her family and girlfriends behind and move to Florida.

"You look like a goddamned fortune, Stella."

"I should. It cost a fortune."

"How much?"

"Don't ask. A year's rent in our first Brooklyn apartment. Brush your hair. Then we'll say goodnight to Jeffrey."

Stella walked out of their room calling, "Jeffrey?" She went into the hallway, went into Jeffrey's beige, brown and blue room. She came back to their bedroom door. "Phil, where's Jeffrey?"

Having adjusted his gold cufflinks, Phil was about to brush his hair. "I don't know. Isn't he in his room?"

"No. Jeffrey?" She was heading for the guest bedroom. Of course, Jeffrey wasn't there either. "Where is he?"

"Probably downstairs," Phil said. He hurried down the stairs calling their son's name. "Son? Jeffrey?"

Stella was right behind him, holding up her skirt. "Where is he, Phil? Where could he be?"

Phil's palm swiped his forehead. "I left him on the boat. But he promised he'd come in soon."

The panic began. "You what?" she yelled at Phil.

After searching downstairs and checking the garage, mother and father ran outside. It was growing darker. With a scan, they realized that the boat was not in its dock. It was nowhere in sight.

Stella froze. They both knew that Jeffrey could not maneuver the boat well. "You left my son on the boat?" Stella screamed. She ran at Phil and beat his chest with both her fists. "What did you do with Jeffrey?"

Phil waved her aside and stumbled back toward the house and the telephone. "Get out of my way. Let me get the patrol."

Stella and Phil waiting silently until the patrol arrived and watched as they flashed their floodlights onto the water. Time passed. Phil looked like a madman, shoeless in his black tux and tie, his fringe of hair, unbrushed.

Stella's tears had taken her black mascara down over her red cheeks and onto her open bosom. Her lacquered hair had become a mangled nest. Two manicured nails had been bitten off. Her new dress was soiled with dirt and mud. She had kicked off her high heels long ago, and her nylons had multiple runs.

"How could you leave Jeffrey alone on the boat? How could you? How could you? He's your son. I swear I'll kill you if anything happened to my boy. I'll kill you."

Phil, face to the sky, began reciting prayers in Hebrew.

The two stayed outside by the water throughout the night, thoughts of the Starlight, long forgotten. They didn't try to comfort one another. Stella was at the bottom of an abyss of fear and knew she would always blame Phil if anything had happened to their son.

Around three a.m., they saw the patrol boats head in. They rushed to the dock. When Stella realized that the grim-faced patrolman walking toward them was slowly shaking his head, she fell to the ground.

"We found your boat. It hasn't been damaged." The patrolman spoke to Phil, shuffling nervously on his feet. "But there was no one on it. We … we did find your son … in the water."

Stella looked up at him with a last burst of hope.

"I'm sorry folks, but he's gone. Looks like he drowned. We're awfully sorry."

Stella unleashed mournful wails, pounding the dirt. Phil crumbled down to meet her.

The authorities believed that Jeffrey had accidentally fallen overboard, but Stella and Phil were never sure that the boy hadn't been intentionally drowned. He was an obedient son and had promised not to drift far, yet the boat was found a good distance away from the dock. Jeffrey was not a strong swimmer. If he had been thrown overboard, he would not have been able to swim his way to safety.

They disagreed with the official findings and suspected foul play but decided against an autopsy. The Golds would bury their son whole, according to Jewish law. If Jeffrey's death had been maliciously caused, the perpetrator would remain undiscovered.

The funeral was no more than a blur in Stella's memory. They'd returned to New York with the body. Somehow, she had gotten through that day. She recalled very little, only the image of her son's casket being lowered–

What was moving on her lap?

⁓

Stella opened her eyes to Jolie. It took her a moment to arrive back to the present. When she did, she was determined to free her mind of the memory of the funeral, bury the sad thoughts, and focus on the beautiful infant that was her daughter.

"Are you restless, Jolie? Oh, look there, out the window." Stella held the infant up, hugged her tightly and pointed to a sign on the road. "Let's read what that says. *His cheek was rough/ His chick vamoosed/ And now she won't come home to roost/ Burma-Shave.*

"Isn't that a silly Burma-Shave ad? You know what Burma-Shave is, my pretty girl? Burma-Shave is something men use to take the hair off their face. "It's a silly-willy ad."

Jolie made a noise. "Stop the car, Phil. She's hungry."

Phil pulled off the highway and found a market where he bought fresh formula and a new bag of ice for the cooler.

When he returned to the car, Stella was angry. "Why did you kill the engine? It's like a furnace in here. We almost melted without the air conditioner."

With the bottle in her mouth, the baby looked so peaceful. Her eyes were large with lashes already long and curling up. Her little lips looked like two parts of a rosebud coming together, and Stella confirmed again that the corners of her lovely mouth turned up – definitely up. She was perfection.

God forgive her, as excruciating as it was, Stella had to admit that this little girl was a far cry from her Jeffrey. The name *Jolie* would fit her well. And she was sure she'd done the right thing not to adopt a boy. A boy would want to be close to his father as he grew up. Not so with a girl. Stella resolved to keep the vow she'd made on the Torah. She would never to breath Jeffrey's name to this new child. As much as she loved him, she would not allow her beautiful daughter to grow up in the shadow of a dead son.

They spent the last night of their road trip in Las Vegas, still only a small town in the desert with a smattering of casinos and hotels amid an ocean of dust.

Garish neon lights and slot machines met them at the gas station and at the market where they stopped to shop for more diapers and formula, at the restaurant where they ate dinner and inside their hotel lobby, where Phil and Stella, hot, weary travelers, luxuriated in a cool, air-conditioned room.

Phil spent the evening in the casino of the Stardust Hotel sitting in front of the slot machines with a gin and tonic in his hand while Stella stayed in the room with Jolie, enjoying a cold shower and watching television. She repacked for Los Angeles, setting out what she would wear to meet Phil's cousin, Maury and his wife, Marie.

They set out for their last day on the road, refreshed with another several hundred miles of desert to get through. Though neither of the Golds had paid much attention to the scenery for most of the trip, it eventually did register with them that they were leaving behind the colors of the desert and the vast vistas of empty sand dotted with cacti, sagebrush and thistle-like foliage.

As they entered California, brown telephone poles, stilted as a child's rendering of soldiers, stood at repetitive intervals connected by black rope along the highways. New freeway systems of gray cement wrapped around their Cadillac in incomprehensible circles.

When they finally entered the city of Los Angeles, it was late afternoon. Stella raised her head and looked around at the vast stretches of flat emptiness, devoid of any substantial skyline. She saw bare streets littered with refuse. There were no parking meters, no traffic and no pedestrians.

Her first impression of the famous city was anticlimactic. They'd entered a vast urban desert of concrete and asphalt, a sea of emptiness., "This is Los Angeles?"

6

THE HOUSE OF GOLD

*I*n the early 1960s, Paradise was named California. Los Angeles was like a budding starlet, full of hope and not yet jaded.

As the curtain fell on World War II, California was swamped with ex-servicemen who had been based there during the war and swore to return after serving their country. They settled and raised families there, primarily in Los Angeles.

Easterners, many of whom had earlier aspired to move to Florida, began migrating west to California where the weather was consistently good and the air was drier.

California – and Los Angeles, in particular – came to symbolize the American dream of wealth, fortune and social and economic mobility, available to anyone. By 1961, Los Angeles was welcoming nearly a quarter of a million new residents annually. Added to that number were the hordes of immigrants who moved north into California from Mexico illegally in search of jobs.

Though the population of Los Angeles continued to swell, the people of the city lived in areas set apart from one another; communities developed like short hyphens separated by vast stretches of roads and freeways continually expanding to reach them all.

People from around the world brought their frustrated dreams and their hopes for a better future to what was then the country's western-most state, often rebelling against all they'd known. They also brought their anxieties, delusions, broken hearts and neuroses.

Los Angeles watered the imagination. Excess became its mainstay and a unique culture of extremes developed. The city was marked by exhilaration and occupied by mavericks who made movies, created art and architecture, and started up industries, the likes of which the world had never before seen.

Alongside all this, was the movie industry that attracted every rest-less beautiful girl and every wannabe actor making Los Angeles the city with the most attractive waiters and salespeople in the nation.

When Phil and Stella entered the city with their new baby girl, they were looking for refuge from their memories and a fresh chance for happiness.

Though he'd left much of his wealth behind him, Phil had enough money in the bank to settle comfortably in California. If his venture with Maury proved successful, Phil had no reason to be concerned about his finances – and he prayed his venture with Maury would be successful.

They began looking for a home and headed straight to Beverly Hills, which lay just six miles east of the Pacific Ocean and eight miles east from the heart of downtown Los Angeles. The city, barely six square miles, had long been considered the prime place to live, popu-lated by celebrities and movie stars. It was initially a planned city, reaching as far north as Sunset Boulevard. Beyond that, the verdant hills with horse trails and hunted game defied planning.

The hillsides between canyons were motorcycle wonderlands that served as an open-air backdrop for a multitude of lovers' trysts. But that was to change when hoards of newcomers demanded homes in these hills yielding both privacy and panoramic views.

Soon enough, trees were cut down and roads were built, tar slith-ering up the slopes to newly built hillside residences. Choice lots offered views that extended west to the Pacific Ocean and Catalina Island and east to downtown Los Angeles and beyond, virtually sunrise to sunset.

Maury urged his cousin to buy in Trousdale Estates, the place to live in the 1960s for the Westside nouveau riche desirous of a leisurely lifestyle and high-style entertaining.

"I should live on a hill why?" Phil asked Maury.

"It's *the* place to live." Maury said. "The developer's name is Paul Trousdale. He had big dreams.

Edward Doheny, the most successful oil producer, owned four hundred twenty-five acre of land. In 1925, he gifted some of his land to his son. That became Greystone, the largest private estate in the city's history. It's at the bottom of what's now Trousdale Estates. In 1954, Trousdale bought the lion's portion of the land from Doheny, the easternmost hillsides of Beverly Hills, and he's been building homes there since."

"What's so special about the houses?"

Maury shrugged. "You've got swimming pools, lots of glass, plenty of room, and amazing views. And they're all Jews living there." Stella said she wanted to see them.

When Phil and Stella went to view several sites, Trousdale was still busy grading the area, cutting down what needed to be cleared and building his expensive, modern, family homes where snakes, possum, raccoons, owls and other wild animals roamed.

Stella favored a three-bedroom home high in the hills with an additional maid's bedroom off the kitchen, a family room, a pool, and a view that boasted the much sought-after southern view of the city.

They stood outside the model house. "It's so big! This is a perfect house for parties!" Stella envisioned hosting many gatherings for Jolie's friends and their parents who would become her own new friends.

"So, we'll buy it, huh, Stella?"

As Stella moved her eyes away from the baby in her arms to agree with Phil, she saw a sudden movement in the dirt nearby. She let out a scream and ran to their car, huddling Jolie deep in her bosom. She had seen a rattle snake.

There was no way in hell Stella Gold was living in those hills.

The following week, they viewed a house that had gone on the market that same day. It was in the flats of Beverly Hills on North Beverly Drive, an expansive street with expensive homes, just south of Sunset across from the famous Beverly Hills Hotel. The asking price for the newly built home was just under ninety thousand dollars.

Stella loved everything about the house. Phil swore he would install a childproof fence around the pool before they moved in and the deal was done.

The couple was surprised at how soon they felt comfortable in their new home. Their neighbors on both sides owned new Cadillacs. Realizing that with Jolie to care for Stella would need her own car, Phil bought her a new white convertible Cadillac and Stella learned to drive.

7

THE GOLDEN LIFE

*S*tella loved her new life. She was delighted when her doorbell began ringing as neighbors came to welcome the Golds to the neighborhood. She happily decorated the new house.

She'd put the baby in an open stroller and walk her to stores on Rodeo, Beverly and Canon Drives, enjoying the many comments she got on Jolie's beauty. She often took the baby to the park so Jolie could be seen and she could meet other mothers.

For his part, Phil was surprised at how happy he was to leave Stella at home with her baby and join the work force again. Work left him with less time to think about his home life.

As it happened, Maury was doing well as the owner of four movie theaters around the city. One was in Sherman Oaks, the other side of the hill from Beverly Hills; another was in the heart of Hollywood; one was on the Miracle Mile on Wilshire Boulevard; and the newest was in Westwood.

Maury set Phil up as manager of the one in Hollywood, the oldest of the four, and watched as Phil threw himself into the job, soon proving he had the needed acumen for success.

"Maury, you got trouble at the theatre."

"What trouble?"

"Don't worry. I fixed it."

"What trouble?"

Phil wiped his forehead with his palm and shook his head. "The numbers weren't right. The cashier was in cahoots with the two guys working the door."

Maury frowned. "What do you mean?"

"So, a guy pays for a ticket, but he don't get a ticket. Guy at the door lets him in without it – like the he's a VIP or something. They split the price of the ticket."

Phil's knowledge of the construction business proved to be advantageous as well. He first suggested that Maury put in additional seating, then suggested that he remodel the lobby to make the concession stand – the biggest money maker for Maury – far more prominent. Maury agreed to both suggestions and each led to handsome profits. Next, the theater's facade was redone to look more like the Las Vegas casinos Phil had recently seen, more neon lights and glitz added, outdoing the lights on the other, nearby theaters. Ticket sales increased substantially.

Maury was close to convinced that Phil could do no wrong. He gave the go-ahead when Phil suggested that they offer their patrons not only cold drinks and individually wrapped ice cream but tea as well, both iced and hot. Again, overall profits rose considerably as patrons welcomed the additions. As a grand show of gratitude, Maury extended a full partnership to Phil in the ownership of the Hollywood theater.

The first few years of living in Beverly Hills went by. History repeated itself when Phil successfully renovated and brought new ideas to the other three theaters as well. Phil and Maury became partners in all four theaters.

Phil had also had luck in the stock market. He ventured into the market following the advice of Barry Stern, a fellow New Yorker also replanted in Los Angeles. Chewing an unlit cigar after dinner at Maury and Marie's home, Barry had commented that, "anyone who doesn't run out and buy shares of Haloid Xerox is a goddamned fool!"

The company was newly listed on the New York Stock Exchange and was already doing remarkably well with its Xerox copier, the first machine of its kind. Phil and Maury had purchased one, and both were impressed with its capabilities.

Giddy with his enormous profits from the rise in the value of the stock, and confident now of his ability to manage theaters, Phil dared to strike out on his own.

He purchased a rundown, bankrupt movie house located in the West Hollywood area, remodeled it, then reprogrammed the movie fare from mainstream movies to graphic films that appealed to the large and ever-growing homosexual community in the area. He changed the theater's name from Central to Tommy Boy.

The 1973 ruling by the Supreme Court defining 'obscene' as only "that which is patently offensive" had helped to legitimize porn theaters. "Obscenity" was to be measured by *local* standards, and that meant theaters like Phil's had tremendous leeway in what they could show.

Tommy Boy proved to be so successful that Phil bought a second theater, this one a movie house that had long been abandoned in the heart of downtown Los Angeles. Boots, as he renamed the theater, also pushed the limits of obscenity.

"So, now that I've taught you all you need to know and you've bought another theater, you should make me a partner in both of yours."

"No. I want these for myself."

"But Phil, I made you a partner in all my theaters. I brought you in when you knew nothing and gave you a job."

"I earned the job and the partnership. I've more than doubled your profits. That helped the value of your investment."

Maury folded his arms, somewhat surprised at Phil's business sophistication. "You really won't make me a partner?"

"I really won't." Maury proved to be unforgiving.

When it became obvious that Phil's ventures were resoundingly successful, Maury became insulting, calling his successful cousin "shamefully immoral" for catering to – and exploiting – those who are "sexually maladjusted." He wanted nothing more to do with Phil. Their partnerships were dissolved.

Phil turned his attention to his new solo ventures with a vigor that surprised even him. Just as he'd highlighted the concession stand and introduced new drinks and snacks at Maury's theaters, he now highlighted the concession stand at his own theaters. He introduced the sale of sexually explicit photos, sexual fare, and eventually, videos.

Yet the same sharp eyes that had caught scheming employees at Maury's theater were now closed to the sexual acts that sometimes took place in his theater's bathrooms and in dark corners and blind to the fact that the theaters had become a favorite place for fast and casual, informal sexual liaisons and contractual sex.

Unable to resist the high profit margins he realized in catering to the sexual needs of his clientele, Phil eventually stretched his movie fare to include material that clearly fell outside the legal definition of "obscene."

After all, Phil was a businessman.

It was obvious to Phil that Stella had also come alive. As he saw how radically his wife's outlook on life had changed since Jolie was in her life, he came to feel grateful to the little girl who gave Stella a reason to get out of bed every day.

He deeply craved his wife's forgiveness for his part in Jeffrey's death and mistakenly took his wife's new interest in life as a sign that she had forgiven him.

In fact, Stella never stopped blaming Phil for the loss of her beloved son and she never forgave him. Any love she had for Phil died with Jeffrey that horrible night.

In another time, Stella would most probably have divorced Phil. In a later decade, she might have taken Jolie and left him after they established themselves in Beverly Hills. But in 1961, the thought of divorce was not a viable alternative for a woman like Stella. Few women divorced then and those who did were either financially independent or young, attractive and soon remarried.

Stella had no marketable skills and knew that her chances of snagging another man were slim. So, she continued living with Phil and set about creating a life apart from him. Jolie was the centerpiece of that new life and the key to her happiness. She filled her days with Jolie and built her life around the girl's schedule.

She was there to pick up her daughter after school every day.

"Melinda, have you seen Stella?" Judy asked, positioned in the crowd of waiting mothers at the end of the school day. Judy was Bella's mother. "Bella is supposed to play with Jolie today, but I can't find Stella."

"Look for a lacquered blonde with smoke curling up into the air," Melinda said. "She should be easy to find." Their chuckles were too faint to be heard by the other mothers.

"Really!" Judy said. "Can you believe what she walks around in? With those flabby thighs and flaccid arms! I mean, I know it's hot out but my God! Save us from the sight, please!"

"How old do you think she is?" Melinda asked.

"Old enough to know better, that's for sure." Judy replied. "Anyway, Bella has her heart set on playing with Jolie today. She's been talking about it all week. She brought her favorite doll to school to take with her to Jolie's house. That little girl really is a sweetheart."

Melinda smiled. "Darren likes her too."

So long as Jolie was the attraction, Stella was tolerated by other, younger mothers and enjoyed an acceptance she'd never before known. They would have taken a number and stood in line to schedule play dates with Jolie. The girl was lovely to look at and, more importantly, she was very popular with all the children. She had no problem sharing and was kindest to those who were ignored or bullied by others. For that, the mothers not only tolerated Stella, they enfolded her in their arms.

For her part, Stella dressed Jolie in flouncy Shirley Temple dresses and patent shoes and put bows in her long hair. She involved Jolie in as many activities as possible.

Having started her in mommy and me classes, she moved on to dance classes, art classes and gymnastics, then added piano lessons and ice-skating lessons and every other class and group she could find. Everywhere, everyone loved the girl, and as her mother, Stella was acknowledged. She was indeed a happy woman.

What Stella hadn't realized was that one day, Jolie would grow up.

As Jolie grew up, Stella place in Jolie's life gradually lessened.

She no longer had a part in Jolie's social life and returned to her former loneliness. She felt hurt that Jolie had cast her aside, rejecting her, and she resented the girl for these increased feelings of frustration and depression. She complained to Phil, whom she had long blamed for her underlying desolation and gloom, and Phil, in turn, stormed at Jolie.

Though Phil had come to care immensely for Jolie, as he watched Jolie grow up and away from Stella and saw his wife's unhappiness increase as the distance between mother and daughter grew, he became angry with Jolie for disappointing his wife and blamed his adopted daughter for hurting Stella. He convinced himself that since Jolie had been the cause for Stella's happiness, so she must be the reason for the loss of that happiness. He felt that his wife deserved nothing but total compliance from the daughter she worshipped.

He never forgot that he had wanted to adopt a boy and had been forced to accept Jolie. If Stella had adopted a boy, he reasoned, she would never have been hurt as Jolie had hurt her.

In any event, he was not willing to have his wife's misery bounce back onto him. When dealing with Stella, Phil felt meek and impotent, filled with guilt and shame. He was mollified when she complained to him about Jolie for it justified striking out at the girl. certain he had a lot to be angry about; he was his wife's protector. It was just too easy.

Hitting the defenseless girl made him feel powerful, no longer weak and impotent.

And Stella, feeling Jolie deserved punishment for rejecting her, and raised in a generation when physical discipline was all too often an accepted form of parental discipline, did nothing to stop him.

PART TWO: THE ADOPTED

8

NOT SWEET SIXTEEN

Beverly Hills, 1976

I remember looking at other girls in HS that were thinner than me. There were these 2 girls, Heidi and Carol and I would walk behind then and look at their legs from behind as they walked. I could see their thin Achilles' heels. Where the flesh went in so a very thin point at the rear of their ankles.

Teachers hated me because I was ugly. I never wanted to go to school I hated it.

Three stages:

Aged 2-5, Parents get mad at you for the first time and you sense something is wrong. You've disappointed your parents for the first time. I'm bad. They keep the lights turned off at night in your room, etc.

Aged 11-13, I'm different. Adolescence, not like others, different house, clothes, looks,

Aged 15-18, I'm on my own. Financially independent I'm stranded

I used to wish that my parents would divorce. They were very happy together and there was absolutely no tension between them.. But I was so uncomfortable with my parents that I wanted to break up the parental unit. I used to think that if they were separated, I could deal with them one at a time and they wouldn't be so formidably strong.

I pound my fist on the soft yellow comforter covering Nora's queen-sized bed.

"But I don't *want* her to throw me a Sweet Sixteen party!"

I'm miserable. Again … still.

"It's all about her! She doesn't want to invite my friends. She wants to invite the kids with mothers she likes so they'll invite her to lunch or something."

Nora, lying alongside me, is leaning her head on her hand, elbow bent, facing me. "What will you do?"

"I don't know. What can I do? It's just so dumb!" I pound my fist again. "She does this every year!"

Nora shrugs. "I don't know, Jo. I mean, I get it. But you're her daughter."

"I'm *not* her daughter!" I say, pulling at my hair as I roll away on the bed. "All I ever hear from her is, "You're adopted, but we love you like you were our own." She's told me that ever since I can remember, and I'm sick of hearing it! I think it was first thing I ever heard!" I sigh. "I so wish they'd never adopted me."

Of course, Nora is thinking of something to say to make me feel better. "My god, Jo, don't say that. I get it. Your mom's weird. But, there are so many kids out there who are never adopted; they'd love to be in your place. You have a home and people who care about you – even if they're weird."

"But I don't want to live with them! When they get mad at me, you know what they say?" Without waiting for an answer, I continue. "They say my real parents are *lucky* they never knew me! How do you think that makes me feel?"

"Shitty."

I turn my gaze to the chandelier above us. I love that chandelier with the colored flowers, but today, I hardly see it. "I really, really, want to know who my real parents are! I so want to get out away from them!"

"You've already your parents asked about them. I know. But you need to keep asking, so they know you're serious."

"They won't tell me! And I can't do much about it until I'm older. I'm not an adult yet." I shake my head, feeling defeat. "The day I turn eighteen, I'll hire a detective."

Nora strokes my arm. "Poor Jolie."

I haven't even told my best friend that Dad hits me. I think Mom's hormones are out of whack. She gets incredibly bitchy and complains to my father about me for the craziest things and he goes total whacko, hits me, then grounds me.

I'm so unhappy! I'm miserable living with them! Mom is always saying that they love me as much as if I was their own, but the thing is? I don't believe her. I think they love me much less.

9

FOOL'S GOLD

Spring, 1976

*I*t's 7:15 in the morning on the Monday after my stupid Not Sweet Sixteen party. I'm leaving the house. My mother hears me and hurries out of the kitchen. She's smoking.

"Jolie! You come back here and change. And brush your hair!"

"Bye, Mom." I'm sixteen, a junior in high school, and my mom's telling me to brush my hair! I fly out the front door. "Don't forget," I call out, "I'll be home late. I'll be with Nora after school."

Nora's been my best friend since forever. We were together in first grade at El Rodeo. The four primary schools in the city all pour into Beverly High for ninth grade so there were a lot of new kids around last year, but Nora and I have stayed best friends.

My mom races to the door, her pink fuzzy slippers flopping. "Jolie! You're not wearing that to school!" I've got on a knit top with jeans and a denim jacket. Mom nags me like this regularly, still expecting me to wear Shirley Temple dresses or pleated skirts to school. She either doesn't realize the world has changed or she doesn't care.

"I won't be home for dinner," I call back to her. "I'll call you."

She's coming down the path after me, waving her cigarette in the air. "I said, you come back here and change!"

"Can't. I'll be late for school."

I escape, turning up the sidewalk. I'm too young to drive, so I walk to Nora's house two blocks away and she drives us to school. I love Nora. She's the best. I tease her cause her car is nowhere near as fancy as most of those in the school parking lot – Jags, Vets, and other expensive cars, not to mention the limousines that line up in front of the school every day.

I'm not really going to Nora's after school today; I just use her as an excuse. I have a date with Steven. I met Steven at Tower Records on Saturday. I was looking for the soundtrack from Saturday Night Fever, and he was looking for the newest Sex Pistols album.

I lie a lot to Mom and Dad. Nora is usually my cover. It's not like I love lying, but I learned a long ago that it's the expedient thing to do.

The thing is, if I told them the truth, they'd want to meet Steve and ask him a zillion questions. First, they'd want to know if he's Jewish – even I can tell he's not; so, they'd forbid me to see him. If they did like him, Mom would probably want to go to lunch with his mother. So, I lie.

And why is it their business if I want to see a boy a few times? It's not like I'm not going to marry him! But they wouldn't understand. I see who I want. Lying is easier for them and for me.

I mean, really? I deserve some fun.

꧁꧂

We're having our usual Tuesday night dinner: broiled chicken, mashed potatoes and green beans.

As usual, we eat at the same table in the den where my mom plays cards. She wears a cotton duster like she always wears when she's home. This one is white with small blue flowers on it. And, as always, a pack of Salems is lodged in one of the two large front pockets; her lighter is in the other.

It's always weird to see her in these frumpy dusters with her hair all done up like she's going to a ball. She used to change the shade of her blonde hair every week or so, but it's been this same golden shade for a few months now. She hasn't changed her hairstyle in forever, a perfect French roll, teased high in the front and full on the sides, sprayed and lacquered and as hard as wood, so every hair stays perfectly in place between her Saturday morning hair appointments. I wonder how long she'll keep this same French twist and this same shade of blonde.

Dad's wearing his favorite brown pants with a short-sleeved shirt, checkered in brown and white. The top two buttons are undone, so his scraggly light brown chest hairs peek through the thin wife beater.

The television is turned on to "All in the Family" and while the rest of the country is either laughing hysterically at Archie Bunker's view of the world or amazed by his bigoted, over-the-top remarks, my father is feeling sorry for him! A brother!

As usual, no one says a word at the table except when my dad says, "Gimme the potatoes," and his mutterings, almost in perfect synch with Archie's. I space out — let my mind wander — a skill I've perfected. I can pretty much totally space out without letting on.

When my mother gets up and begins clearing off the table it brings me back to the present, and I get up to help while Dad moves to his favorite chair in the den to watch the next show. I clear the table and start the dishwasher, then head for my room. I have a ton of homework.

"She took money out of my wallet," Mom says, lighting first after-dinner smoke. The statement comes out of nowhere.

Dad tears his eyes away from television. "Who?"

"Who do you think?" Mom points her chin at me. "Little Miss Innocent." I look at her and plop down on a chair in amazement. "I didn't steal anything!" I should have run.

"Are you, kidding?" Dad asks her. Even he finds this hard to believe. "Why would she do that?"

"You're asking me?" Mom stands in front of his chair and exhales a line of smoke. "Ask your precious daughter! All I know is what I had. I had sixty-eight dollars in my wallet last night, today there's sixty-five and I haven't been out all day. Did you take it?"

"No, *I didn't take it*," Dad says, his tone reeking of sarcasm. He's already on his feet heading toward me, his hand wiping his brow, while Mom finds an ashtray and carries it over to the couch where she sits down, puts her slippered feet up on the coffee table, inhales and waits.

"Did you take money out of your mother's wallet?" Dad asks me, his hand already poised to strike.

"I didn't steal it. I needed three dollars for lunch."

"So, you stole money from your mother's wallet?"

"I didn't *steal* it! You'd already left, and mom was sleeping. I tried to wake her up, but she'd probably taken a sleeping pill."

As I speak, I start up from my chair, preparing to dodge the strike I know is coming. He hits me, and, because I moved, the impact falls on my ear. My hand goes to the hot sting and tears fill my eyes. "*Ow!*"

"Don't you talk about your mother like that!" Dad is turning purple.

"What did I say?"

"Don't you get fresh with me, girlie! You little thief! We give you everything you need … and you steal? That's *khotspah*! Your real parents are lucky they don't know you! How dare you steal from your poor mother?"

He raises his hand to smack me again, but I dodge out of his reach this time and crouch down against the wall. I know there is nothing I can say to make him believe that I hadn't meant to *steal* the money.

"Okay, Dad. I heard you. I'm sorry. It won't happen again. Really. You don't have to hit me again. I learned my lesson. I'm sorry. Really. I promise."

Dad glares at me. "Don't you do that again, Missy! You hear?"

He goes back and sits down in his chair. Mom is watching the sitcom. She takes a drag off her Salem and smiles. I go to my bedroom, shut my door and cry.

10

GOLDEN MINUTES

Beverly Hills High School, Spring, 1977

*I*t's Thursday morning and I wake up tired.

I was up late last night doing homework due in four classes and studying for a quiz in my Government class. I'm no mood to play nice.

On top of that, we're going to Maury's and Marie's tomorrow night for their stupid housewarming. They just bought a new house in Trousdale, and for some stupid reason, I have to waste a perfectly good Saturday night staring at their daughter Marissa. Except for me and her, everyone there will be old.

I can't stand Marissa. I've hated her since we were little kids. Besides, Dad and Maury used to be partners and real friendly, but things between them soured. So why do we even need to go to their stupid party? Why did they even invite us? And why do I have to go? *Whatever!*

Anyway, I have problem with a teacher today. Again. Another one. This one in English.

We have a substitute in my first period, English class, Mrs. Gerber, a picture of an old school marm from some movie, with ear-length, frizzy, gray hair, a low-budget shapeless dress and black orthopedic shoes.

Mrs. Gerber and I disagree about whether or not I was late to class. It's a long story. I'll just say I was right, but she wanted to argue. When she decides I should stay after class, I tell her I can't because we have a quiz in my next class (Government).

I thought it was all over. But I'm wrong. I barely turn in my quiz when I'm called into the office of the girls' vice-principal.

"Jo-*lee*?" Mrs. Rutherson says.

I hate the way Mrs. Rutherson pronounces my name, like it's two separate words, and I can't stand how every sentence out of her mouth sounds like a question.

"Jo-*lee*? We both know that this is not by any means the first time ya'll have been sent to me for displaying a bad attitude? Now, ya'll's a top student? But? As I've said before? Attitude is *as* important as intelligence?" *How does anyone stand listening to her?*

"I didn't display a bad attitude, Mrs. Rutherson. All I did was tell the teacher the right time."

Mrs. Rutherson doesn't want to hear it. "Jo-*lee*? Ya'll seem to consistently have trouble minding authority? Ya'll are a junior this year? And next year ya'll will be hoping to graduate? This is a good time to mind that attitude? Now, since this is not the first time ya'll have had this problem? There will be two hours of detention served today?"

But I have a date after school with Andre! "Oh, Mrs. Rutherson, I have a doctor's appointment today. Can I please do it Monday? I need to see the doctor – it's a … female thing. Please?"

She sighs in exasperation. "All right then? Monday?" She writes something down. I'm ready to get up and leave her office. But she sits back and just looks at me and I can feel that she's waiting for me to say something. The silence becomes awkward.

"I'm sorry," I say. "I'll try to do better."

The principal looks me in the eyes. "Well, I fully expect ya'll to do just that?"

"Can I leave now? I don't want to be late to my next class."

11

HAMMERED GOLD

Beverly Hills High School, Winter, 1977

Okay, Major Important Fact: I'm different than other kids.

Yes, I know, we're all different. That's great. But look, I'm different in a different way. I'm not just another shade of the same color, I'm a different color altogether.

Sometimes I wonder why other people can't see that. It's painfully obvious to me. It's not that I behave strangely. I mean I don't do anything weird. I don't constantly pick my nose in public or wear cocktail dresses to school and I'm not like Chrissy who explains everything in terms of where she's at in her cycle and stands people up because her ovaries hurt.

You can't always tell right away that someone's strange. You might think they're fine, normal, and then you find out they're not. Like this sixteen-year-old girl I read about. She joined a billion cults. She'd hear about one and join it right away. The article said she belonged to something like 18 cults at the same time and none of them knew about the others. She said she did it because it kept her busy and she met a lot of interesting people.

Strange, right? So, there's strange and then there's *strange*.

I'm like a flower in a garden that looks like all the other flowers around me, but I'm without roots in the dirt. They do. They *fit*. They fit in class, they fit in a family.

Maybe they don't get along with their mom or dad, but they *connect* with them – if not with both, then with one or the other. I don't have a connection with either of my adopted parents.

I wake up every morning waiting to go home. I don't belong in that house. It's hard to explain. It's a spacey, detached feeling.

Nora is the only real connection I've got.

I don't know what I'd do without Nora. I really love her. She's the best friend anyone could have. It's strange that we get along so well, cause we're way different.

For starters, I can't imagine anyone whose home life is more radically different than mine. Nora's parents are great, her life is calm and stable. If you want to find instability in Nora's life, you'll find it in her closet. I kid you not. That's the only place that's constantly changing. She just about buys a completely new wardrobe with every new fashion and she always looks hot.

I'm the better student, no doubt about that, but Nora does well, too, and she's way prettier. Mom says Nora reminds her of the blonde girl in magazine shampoo ads from the 40s and 50s, with flaxen hair and baby-blue eyes set in a creamy complexion. Her body's all curves, too, and she got it all from Carol, her mom, who was an ex-beauty pageant queen — a fact Mom doesn't like to talk about.

This year, Nora's been voted Junior Class Princess. Next year, she'll most likely be voted Prom Queen. Me? I don't go out of my way to look good for school.

My usual – as Mom will tell you – is pretty much jeans and a top. If my long hair happens to fall into a wave that day, so be it. If it's straight, cool. I suppose I'm sort of shapely; Nora says she wants my long legs. Modesty aside, I think, it's mostly my coloring that people like. It unusual. I have hazel eyes and chestnut-colored hair and my skin color is kind of dark, but in a slightly suntanned kind of way. People say I look exotic. I don't know. Maybe I am.

"Bottom line," as Maury would say, is that our differences mean nothing. Our friendship and our mutual love is genuine. And though our family lives are the antithesis of one another, we're sisters to the core.

⁓

Earlier, Nora and I went to the shopping mall at Century City. She bought a really neat crushed blue velvet skirt and a matching blue velvet jumpsuit with hot pants. You're supposed to wear them together then take the skirt off and show off the hot pants. She's also bought two pairs of long pants, three tops, and two pairs of shoes.

From Century City, went to Nora's house. I told my parents I'd be spending the night there. I didn't tell them I have a date with Jay tonight. I'm excited. This is going to be the first time we're going to a party as girlfriend and boyfriend. Nora's got a date too. They four of us are going to a party.

Jay's smart. He goes to UCLA. He's nineteen, gorgeous and a great kisser. He has a black Jag but I love riding behind him on his bike, hugging his back, my face up against him, smelling his leather jacket and feeling the bike's vibrations moving through me, wind rushing up against me.

I meet him a distance away from my house where my parents won't see him and we ride up through Topanga, up and down Pacific Coast Highway or spend time in the canyons of Beverly Hills. They're building houses everywhere, chopping down the trees and making asphalt roads where there was grass, wild vegetation, even a creek. But we rides to an area where they haven't yet built and to a spot where we can't be seen. We smoke a doobie Jay's brought with him and then, well, then we do our thing and I like being out there in the semi-wild.

Jay doesn't talk a lot about the usual things — you know, like movies and music ... his love is math. His family's got money, but he's at UCLA on some sort of math scholarship, working on an equation. He tries to explain it to me but it goes way over my head. There are lots of terms special to math like *binomials*. There are words like *neighborhoods*, *monotone* and *convergence* that I understand in plain English but not mathwise.

I like that Jay is smart. He seems to have his life together, kind of a male Nora. I wouldn't mind having the kind of home he's got. His parents are happily married. I haven't met them, but they sound cool. He talks about them like they're teenagers, always going away together or going out somewhere cool, like they're dating. I'll bet they don't fight all day, and I'm guessing his father doesn't beat him. He's got an older sister who's married and lives in Sacramento.

I've been hanging out with Jay as much as possible. I've been seeing him for about three months. That's way longer than I've ever been with a guy. I think he cares about me as much as I care about him. I've come to think of us as a couple. I feel like I've gotten lucky; maybe we'll really connect. It's exciting.

And so, for the first time in my life I say the words, "I love you."

The party tonight is at Marcia's house. Marcia FuckAll Masoni. Her parents are out of town, so she's put the word out for all of us to go over. Nora's going with her date; I'm going with Jay. This will be the first party that Jay and I are going to as a couple and I'm looking forward to it. It should be fun.

Geezo! We're not even inside the door before Marcia FuckAll is all over Jay. He's cool; he's definitely not into sluts.

Oh, my god! Her tits are hanging out of her top.

"Do you guys want a beer?" FuckAll's supposedly asking all four of us but she's looking right at Jay and she's so in his face that he moves his head back. I swear she just rubbed her tits against him – like *whoops! Sorry! Accident! Excuse me, I'm a little tipsy.* She's so totally ridiculous. Does she really think she's turning him on? *Hysterical!*

Jay and I walk around. I introduce him to some of the kids. We talk to a bunch of people and just kind of move to the music a little while Jay guzzles down another beer, until at some point, he needs the bathroom.

While he's gone, I'm left talking to some other kids. I talk and talk until I realize I miss Jay. He's been gone a while and I decide to find him. I go stroll around the house looking for him. I knock on the bathroom door and look in all the rooms. I really want to be with him. No one seems to have seen him. I open the front door but there's no one on the front lawn. I go through the kitchen to the back end of the house and into the backyard; he's not there either and he's not in the driveway. I've looked everywhere.

Where's Jay?

There's a detached garage at the end of the driveway. I'm definitely not going to find him in the garage, but since it's the only place I haven't looked I check it out. It's some kind of converted garage, a guesthouse or something with French doors. I try the doors. They're locked. I cup my eyes and press against the glass so I can see inside the room.

No! There's Marcia with her top off, bent over a daybed or something. Her breasts are hanging down and ... *oh, my God!* There's Jay standing behind her! And ... and ... *oh, my God!* Jay - Jay... *Jay! Oh God!* He's facing me, but his eyes are closed and ... *God! the look on his face!*

I run, crying. Nora finds me in the backyard. I'm in so much pain. Her date drives the three of us back to her house. I feel like my heart's been slashed. Nora wipes my tears and tries to comfort me. But to I know I'll never forget what I saw. I'll. Never forget the look on Jay's face.

My eyes burn badly; they're on fire. The image of Jay in the guesthouse is burned into my eyes and all my tears can't put the fire out. I cringe with repulsion!

Jay fucked Marcia and my head and my heart all at once. I'm sick, so sick with pain, *How could I have trusted him?* He didn't give a damn about me! He couldn't have been more careless with my feelings and my heart or show less respect for me .

I trusted Jay! He was the first boy I ever said those three words to. He didn't just hurt my feelings or break my heart; he destroyed my faith in love. After that night I vowed never again to say those words to anyone.

How can I ever again believe that love is wonderful and unselfish all roses and warm hugs?

I'll never find someone to connect with, someone who will care about me and make me feel I'm okay. Someone I can trust. I thought I'd found that person in Jay, but I was very wrong. I'll always be alone.

Stranded. Alone in a world of others.
Abandoned.

Alone.

If you ask me, love sucks.

12

JAMSHEED

1978: Senior Year, Beverly Hills High School

I'm sleeping over at Nora's again tonight. She's got a date with Fred. He goes to Hamilton High. I agree to tag along with Fred's cousin, Jamsheed.

When Fred rings Nora's doorbell, Nora and I are dressed in jeans. She's wearing a white buttoned-down blouse, and I've got a soft blue work shirt on.

Jamsheed is waiting for us in the backseat of Fred's car. As soon as he sees me, he smiles the brightest smile I've ever seen, nods, and extends his hand.

"Hi, hello. I am Jam*sheed*," he says, his name with a very definite emphasis on the second syllable. "You are Jol*ly*." I smile, not bothering to correct him, but Fred does. "Oh," Jamsheed says, hand to mouth and nodding his head again, "Okay! Excuse. You are Jolie." He pronounces my name perfectly.

"Yes. But you can call me Jolly." He smiles again.

Jam*sheed* calls Fred by his Persian name, Far*sheed*.

While we're driving towards Santa Monica and the beach, Fred tells me and Nora that Jamsheed's father is a rarity in Iran, a Jewish man who holds a high position within the Shah's offices. He openly associates closely with the royal family. When he says the name of the Iranian *Shah* or King of Iran, he goes on and on - the man has a really long title. In English, it translates as "His Imperial Majesty, the King of Kings, Mohammed Reza Shah Pahlavi." And I think, this shah must be quite the dude.

Jamsheed recently arrived in California. He came with his grand-parents. The two boys tell us why Jamsheed is in America.

This past January, there were demonstrations against the Shah in the Iranian city of Qom, They tell us that Qom – they pronounce the name of the city with a hard *'gh'* as though they're gargling – is a religious city in the predominantly Muslim country of Iran where lots of Muslim religious leaders live. According to them, there has been a long- standing feud between the Muslim clerics and the king. The demonstrators wanted more religious freedoms. When the king - or 'shah' - sent the army to disperse the crowds there, students were killed.

Though this sounds bad, I can't understand what this has to do with Jamsheed and his family who are Jewish and live in Tehran, the capital city.

They continue. In February – a month later – students in cities throughout the country marched against the Shah in memory of the students who had fallen in Qom. Buildings were burned and more people were killed. Over one hundred people were killed in a city called Tabriz.

That's when Jamsheed's father suspected that dissent against the government would snowball. He immediately sent his aging parents and Jamsheed, his only child, here to safety.

So far, his father was right. The country has become politically instability. If the shah stays in power when the dust settles, they'll go home. If not, it'll be super dangerous for Jamsheed's parents to stay in Iran. I get it. First, his father is really close to the shah's family, and second, they are Jewish. If the shah loses his throne, Jamsheed's parents will immediately join his their son and his grandparents in America.

I've watched what's going on in Iran on the nightly news where they've shown clips of movie houses, hotels, banks, and other buildings in Iran going up in flames.

My father watches and curses "those damned A-rabs," believing that Iranians are Arabs – which they're not. I've tried to tell him, but he doesn't listen. He's hopeless.

Farsheed explains. "The demonstrators believe the buildings they burn are symbols of the monarchy." He looks over at Jamsheed and says, softy, "And every day brings less hope that Iran will return to stability under the shah."

"I want see my parents esoon," Jamsheed says. He is afraid they will be killed in the violence, or arrested and hung.

I'm full of compassion for Jamsheed. He's the same age as me and I relate to his feeling of rootlessness, though his is newer and hopefully, temporary.

Still, he's been torn from all he's ever known, his parents, his friends, and his home and thrown into an unfamiliar country where people speak a different language, live life differently. He has no idea what street he's on right now, or where we're going, or what tomorrow will bring.

He must be so worried about his parents' future and filled with fear as he scans our daily newspapers and watches the news! Most of the extended family are already in the U.S. and they're all worried about Jamsheed's parents.

I try to imagine how Jamsheed feels, afraid that he might never again see his mother and father. Yet he smiles.

When we arrive at Johnnie's Rotunda, I sit facing Jamsheed and take a better look at my date. His short-sleeved white Polo shirt, too large for him, was probably borrowed from Fred. The white sets off his dark skin, a bit browner than mine. His thick, jet-black hair is cut unstylishly short, as though ease of maintenance was the priority. His full eyebrows seem to reach longingly toward one another above perfectly shaped brown almond eyes surrounded by thick, long black eyelashes. Looking into those eyes, I see the bits of cautiousness and anxiety they hold behind the endless bright smile and cheery disposition he presents.

Scanning my menu, I look up to see Jamsheed gazing at his. Realizing there are items on the menu he can't possibly recognize, like artichoke hearts and the array of Mexican foods they offer, I ask if he knows what he wants. I try to describe the dishes, but it isn't easy, and I depend on Fred a lot, often interrupting him in his conversation with Nora to ask for Persian translations.

Choices made, Jamsheed thanks me with that wonderful smile. He's trying hard to speak English well.

I ask him to tell me about his life in Iran and he says he often "esleeps" of home. His mistakes are sweet. I explain the difference between "dreaming" and "sleeping," still depending a lot on pantomime. He tells me that in his language the word is the same for both — you see one and do the other.

I smile at this and he says I'm pretty. "Thank you."

"In Farsi, we say "you the moon.""

After dinner Nora suggests we go to the pier at Santa Monica Beach to ride the Ferris wheel. But when we get there, I see that Jamsheed's sights are set on the ocean, so I suggest that he and I take a walk on the beach and meet up with Nora and Fred later.

"Do you go to the beach in Iran?" I ask him.

"No. It is not near from my house," Jamsheed says, his gaze still on the waters. He gestures to the vast ocean. "I like esee this. It is so much!"

"Yes. Did you learn English in school in Iran?" I ask.

"No, in my eschool very little." His answer leaves me with the impression that more English is taught in other Iranian schools. As I'm deciding whether or not to ask if that's the case, knowing what that would take from us both, he kicks up some sand and chuckles.

He gives me the feeling that despite his anxieties, he's the happiest person I know.

"I will tell you esomething. You like. Okay?"

I sit down in the sand and nod, "Okay."

He sits as well and points to the vast ocean. I marvel at the expressiveness of Jamsheed's face and the utter delight he seems to have in sharing. And then he recites what I take to be Persian poetry:

Ketobeh fazleh toroh obbeh bahr coffee neest

Keh tarr conee sarr angooshtoh safheh beshmoree

When it ends, I ask, "What does it mean?"

Jamsheed licks his lips and shakes his head. "Very good." He repositions himself in the sand. "My English not good, but, okay, I try splane." He licks his lips again.

"*Ketab* meanbook; *Fazl* mean esmart or ... how you esay? Very, very esmart." He gestures, opening his arms wide, taking in the entire ocean. "Water here not enough to ... wet ... " He points to his index finger.

"Finger?" I ask.

He shakes his head and grazes his index finger against his tongue then points to the wet portion and looks at me questioningly.

"Fingertip," I say.

He nods and starts over, making as if he's turning the pages of a book. "*Water of ocean not gonna be enough for wet ... fingertip? ...* I nod and he goes on, *"one, two, three ... for book of your esmart."* He points to his head to indicate, I think, brains.

I think I understand. "Wow! That's quite an exaggeration," I say.

"What means that?"

"Exaggeration? An exaggeration is, um, you know, to say something is much, much more than it is. Like what you just said."

"Yes, yes! Persians we love this ... exaggerations," Jamsheed replies, squeezing out the word he's just learned with his bright smile.

We head back to the boardwalk to meet Nora and Fred and I realize that I am thoroughly enjoying myself for the first time since that night Jay hurt me so. I'm completely relaxed and comfortable with Jamsheed and I am surprised – and disappointed – when he says his grandparents expect him home by 10:30 tonight.

We arrive at his address first, an apartment in Westwood. "Good night, Jamsheed," I say. "I enjoyed tonight. Too bad we don't go to the same school! I'd like to see you again."

"I enjoy meet you, Jol*ly*. I gonna ask Fred, he gonna take me esee you," Jamsheed says. His hand is extended, and the bright smile is back.

"Great!"

But then I meet Rocky and everyone else is forgotten

13

ALIEN

"Well, Jo-*lee*? I am truly sorry to see ya'll here again? Now, I know ya'll have your side of the story? always do, so please, tell me your side before we go further?"

"I don't know why I should. You won't believe me."

Mrs. Rutherford slams her hand down on her desk, uncrosses her legs as she leans towards me across her desk, drops the pen she's holding onto the desktop and shakes her head.

"Well, if that not just – Jo-*lee*? That is *exactly* your problem? Ya'll have one *huge* attitude problem. I truly doubt that Mr. Cobent was to blame? And I for one, I'm am quite tired of your games? How many times have ya'll been it my office 'cause of your bad attitude? I say, it is disgraceful? Ya'll is a top student? But good grades or not? I can bar ya'll from graduation exercises?"

I sit up and scoff in disbelief. "Are you serious?"

"Yes, I *am* Jo-*lee*? Now ya'll are just too smart a girl to jeopardize attending your graduation? And I might just take away your Senior Class Princess title?"

I shrug. "I don't care about that."

"Now, I know ya'll don't mean that? Why, any girl would *die* to be

Senior Class Princess? And what with your girlfriend being Prom Queen?" She pauses.

She sits back and re-crosses her legs. An unpolished fingernail plays at her lips and says, "I just don't know what option ya'll leave me?"

I utter a curt, "Huh?" wondering if she will actually have the guts to bar me from graduation exercises, and if this is the most difficult decision she'll make as the girls' vice-principal of Beverly High. Mrs. Rutherson makes look shocked, like I've just let one loose and shakes her head.

"Ya'll *must* be punished? Your parents will be notified? But, apparently? They have absolutely *no* effect on ya'll whatsoever? So ..." She picks up a stack of files from her desk and drops them with a thud an inch or two away from where they were. "... I am barring ya'll from attending the Senior Mother and Daughter Tea?"

She leans her elbows onto the desk, leaning forward at me. "I *am* sorry? But perhaps it will send a message to you *and your parents?* Ya'll will *not* be able to attend the Tea with your mother next Wednesday? I am *also* barring ya'll from Senior Beach Day? Jo-*lee?* I'm afraid ya'll just left me no choice? I do hope this is the last of our meetings about your attitude?"

"Me, too."

Meeting over.

Thank God I'll be done with this place in less than two months. On the way to Drama class, I think how glad I'll be when I leave this place.

I'm scheduled to perform a scene today in Drama class. It's from "Cat on a Hot Tin Roof" and I've been assigned to do the scene with Paul Moss. I became friends with Paul at the start of this school year.

I didn't like him before that. I thought he was really stuck up. Granted, I didn't really know him well. He didn't seem to have any friends; whenever I saw him, he was alone. But then I saw him at a club one night, both of us obviously having gotten in with false ids and more than tipsy. He was with another guy and the body language was clear enough; I got it. After that, I set out to make him a friend and didn't give up. I had to let him know I wasn't interested in him as a guy. He finally caved in. We became friends, then followed Nora and then Jonah and now we're a sort of foursome.

We decide to practice our lines at his house after school. At his front door, a servant answers. He's wearing a tuxedo! In the afternoon! He tells Paul his parents left for out of town that afternoon.

From there, Paul leads me through the huge house to a rear door. We cut across a major yard with a pool and cabana on one side and a tennis court on the other and Paul opens the door to the fifteen hundred square foot guesthouse with private jaccuzi that is his home.

"Pretty private here, Paul." I say. "Parents can't bug you; it must be heaven."

He scoffs and drops his head down. "I don't need to live here for privacy. Mr. and Mrs. Harold Moss, my esteemed parents are rarely in the country, let alone at home."

"Oh."

"Yeah. I see more of them in magazines than in person. And they know very little about me besides the fact that I go to Beverly Hills High and have two weekly appointments with Dr. Louise Fletch."

"Why? Are you sick?"

He shakes his head. "Dr. Fletch is a psychiatrist they know, with offices on North Bedford Drive. If an appointment is missed, they're to be notified. I suppose it's their way of knowing I've still alive; I keep the appointments."

Among the things that his parents don't know about Paul is he's attracted to boys. I don't think the kids at school know either. He's chosen not to come out and that's his choice.

The two of us share the irony of our assigned scene when Paul's character is meant to lust after my character; it's our Drama teacher Mr. Westan that Paul actually lusts after.

I suffer from major stage fright – always have. I imagined Drama class might help. Today, I'm coming to class straight from my meeting with Rutherford, still leading with an 'I just don't care a friggin' bit" attitude.

On stage, I just throw it all out there, and somehow, we pull it off.

In fact, when we're done, the class applauds and we both get an A on the assignment! Paul and I are hysterical as we congratulate one another. I suggest we celebrate.

"How?" He asks.

"Let's see a movie then hang out back at your place afterwards," I say. "A mellow Friday night."

"Right. It'll be fun; I'll make sure." Paul's place is *always* fun.

"Cool." I say. "Nora and Jonah are going to see 'Alien.' Wanna join them?" I ask. He's in.

When Jonah Hansen transferred to Beverly Hills High this fall, it took about five minutes before he was acknowledged as one of the most popular boys at Beverly and waltzing right into Nora's arms. I'm good with that. I like him.He's a good guy. He's totally gaga for Nora; he'd never ever hurt her, and Nora is crazy about him. And really? They are *The Perfect Couple*.

I had everything to do with bringing Jonah and Nora together.

On his first day at Beverly, I noticed Jonah standing his locker. He's not my type, but you can't miss him. He's not exactly handsome, but he's nice-looking. Anyway, you definitely know he's there. He's tall, big — imposing, impressive. Turns out, he's a jock. He became the star player on Beverly's football team.

Anyway, I'd never seen him before, and I was curious, so I went over and asked if he was new. He said he was.

"Hi, I'm Jolie."

We started talking, and by the time he'd closed his locker, I knew more about him than he knew about himself. Turns out he's from Missouri. His father had been wanting to move to California for years. Then last year, the family discovered that Jonah's older brother had a pretty major drug problem and was hanging with "the wrong sort" as Jonah puts it. Jonah was totally open about that. His parents figured a change of environment would be the best thing for his brother, so the family moved. Fortunately, big brother's doing a lot better.

"Alien" frightens the pants off of all of us with those yucky things popping out of everyone.

Afterwards, we stop to eat at Ships, then move to Paul's place. As soon as we get there, a doobie appears and Paul lights it and we pass it around. He turns on his super crazy stereo and blasts "I Love the Nightlife" by Alicia Bridges. Nora and I start dancing a little disco, singing, *I love the night life, I love to boogie ...*

Paul's phone rings. He answers it with a "Yo!" He listens and says, "just chillin'" then smiles and says "cool" before he hangs up. He joins us then, moving his lean body with the smoothness of a natural dancer, his dark blonde hair flying around his face.

Jonah's just watching the three of us until Nora takes him by the hand and pulls him up. Reluctantly, he starts to move his feet. This is the first time I've seen Jonah on a dance floor.

"Jonah," I tease, "I've never seen you not dance before." I say. "Is that how they don't dance in Missouri?"

"I wish I could dance like Paul and you guys," he says, and I'm immediately sorry I've teased him. He shrugs. "They really don't dance like this in Missouri."

We show him some basic steps then, and after a while he's doing okay. I guess football keeps him agile on his feet.

"Once you've got the basic rhythm going, all you need is attitude," I say.

When the music ends, Paul applauds. "Good work, Jonah," he says, thumbs up."

I'm feeling a slight buzz off the weed. "Hey, Paul," I say, "this isn't the same insane weed you had last time."

"That's long gone," Paul says.

The music ends and Nora comes to sit alongside me on the couch. "So, what exactly did the witch say today?"

I take a hit of weed and pass her the joint. I recount my meeting with the girls' vice-principal that afternoon to Blondie's, "Heart of Glass."

My three friends laugh at my imitation of Rutherson's accent, but when I finish, Nora gets huffy. "That really sucks," she says.

"Who cares? I don't care about the beach or some stupid tea party,"

I say. The joint is again in my hands and I exhaled a stream of smoke. It's true; I really don't care.

"She's still a witch!" Nora takes the joint from me, takes a hit and hands it to Jonah then heads for the kitchen.

"It's not a big deal! I can go to the beach on my own. And I don't want to go to the Mother and Daughter Tea. With my mom? Please! It's a joke."

Nora turns around to face me. "Well, I'll bet your mom wants to go." She says it like it it's a sure bet.

Nora knows my mom pretty damn well, and I start to consider what my mom's reaction will be when she finds out she'll be missing the Senior Tea. Nora returns from the kitchen with three beers and a Coke. The Coke is for me; I can't stand the bitter taste of beer. She passes the drinks around and makes herself comfortable on the carpet against the wall, alongside Jonah.

"Yeah, my mom's really looking forward to it," I say. "I guess she wants to punish my parents too."

"Hey, Paul," Nora says, "this weed is okay, but that shit you had last time was amazing."

"Yeah, that was dynamite!" Jonah says. I nod.

Paul nods. "I know, I know. I'm scoring more of that tonight."

"You're going out?" Nora asks.

Paul's at the stereo, thumbing through his tapes, deciding what to play next. "Nah, he's coming here. He called to say he's on his way. Should be here soon."

Nora sits up, alarmed. "What?"

"He's bringing over some of that same weed; gunja." He's still deciding between two tapes in his hands.

"You didn't say anyone was coming here," Nora says. She sounds offended.

"Rico." Paul said.

"Wow." Nora starts to get to her feet. "I can't believe that. We're getting out of here. Come on, Jonah."

"What's wrong?" Paul asks.

Nora stares at him like he's crazy, her mouth hanging open. "I can't believe you don't know! You actually gave this guy, Rico or whatever, your address?"

"Yeah. Why shouldn't I?" Paul asks.

"Don't you know you just don't do that? You should have met him somewhere. He shouldn't know where you live."

"Why not?"

"Paul, he's a *drug dealer*! Don't you know about Charles Manson? Helter Skelter?"

"Hold 0n, Nora," I say. "Paul, how do you know this guy, Rico?"

"Through some people I met at a rock concert," he answers. He seems baffled at Nora's reaction.

Nora's found her handbag and she's heading for the door. "Great!" She says, sarcastic as hell. "That's just great! We're out of here." Then, to Jonah, she says, "Can we please go now?"

Jonah's still where Nora left him, taking another hit. Paul walks over to her. "Look, Nora, he's not a drug dealer." he says, "Rico and his brother are cool musicians; good people. Rico's brother, Rocky, was playing with his band and afterward a bunch of us went backstage with Rico and we all got high. We've become kind of friends since then. I've been to their house. They were supposed to come over last night, but couldn't. Why shouldn't they come here?"

I look at Nora. "Nora," I say, "Maybe you're getting a paranoid. I'm sure this guy is no Charles Manson. Paul's a good judge of character."

Nora isn't listening. "Right. I just don't want to be here. We'll see you guys later."

Jonah stands. "Okay," he says. "Just a sec. Let me take a quick leak." He's off to the john.

Paul is exasperated, but forces a smile. "Nora, he's not a drug dealer," he says. "He's a musician with some really amazing weed gunja that he's willing to part with for money. He gets it from Jamaica...or Cuba...some island somewhere."

Nora's at the door. "Fine. Great." She looks at me. "So, are you coming?" I shake my head. "I think you should come with me and Jonah. We can drop you home." I shake my head again. "Okay, you go ahead and stay. We're out of here."

14

ROCKY

*J*onah returns to the living room just as the doorbell rings. Paul opens the door and Nora, taking Jonah's hand, tries to escape as the Calvo brothers walk in.

Rico enters first, his head, full of tight brown curls reaching out. He's rather small, what my dad would call a "featherweight," with skin that's the color of vanilla caramel. He's wearing a black leather jacket over a black T-shirt and black jeans. A tiny gold hoop is set in one ear.

Rocky is behind Rico, taller than his brother by a head. He's swarthy, with thick, straight, chin-length, black hair, naturally falling into a center part and lustrous in the light over Paul's front door. Like his brother, he's wearing one tiny gold hoop earring. He's also wearing a black leather jacket over a black Rolling Stones T-shirt with blue jeans. His Roman nose is just large enough to complement the full lips beneath. The gold, wire-frame glasses he wears seem to magnify his chocolate-brown, shining eyes, warm and soulful. As I look into them, I find them looking back at me. I feel shock waves of recognition ripple within me, a dizzying sensation.

Paul introduces everyone.

"Hi," Rocky says. His voice is soft, his full lips, exquisitely shaped. The two brothers give Paul a high-five. "Hey, man."

I am riveted by Rocky's looks and disarmed by his soft voice. I hardly hear Nora speak. "Excuse us, we were just leaving. Are you coming, Jolie?"

"No, I'll stay."

Nora's neck moves forward, and her eyes are open wide as she looks at me as though she'd just realized I'm crazy. She moves directly into my face and speaks slowly, her voice strained, as if speaking in code. "Are you sure?"

"Yeah."

She hesitates a second then said, "Okay. Come on, Jonah. Bye all." They hastily leave.

"I bring you peace and good things," Rico says as he reaches inside his jacket. He brings out a small brown bag that looks overly used. "Here's a lid," he says.

Paul gets his wallet out, counts out some cash and gives it to Rico in exchange for the bag. "This is that same shit you gave me last time, right?"

Rico nods and quickly counts the cash. "The very same gunja," he says. He stuffs the green bills into his pocket "Okay, so that's it then."

Paul smiles. "This is really great shit, man."

Business is over, but I want these guys to stay; I want *Rocky* to stay. "So, Paul tells me you two are musicians," I say. "What do you play?"

Rico raises his hand like he's in class. "Bass," he says.

"Keyboard," Rocky says. His sensual lips are shaped into a small smile, and, as he looks at me and speaks in that soft voice, I feel my heart being pulled to him.

I try to keep my own voice steady. "I'd love to hear you play sometime."

"Oh, these guys are really good – I mean, they're bad-ass musicians," Paul says.

"You want to jam, man?" Rocky asks him.

"Are you kidding?" Paul is about to wet himself.

"Okay, man," Rico nods. "We'll get our tools."

"Tools?" Paul repeats.

"Yeah," Rico says. "My bass and his keys. They're with Homer."

"Homer?" Paul asks, looking through the window.

"That's what we call the van," Rocky explains softly.

"Right," says Paul.

I watch the brothers bring in Rico's bass and Rocky's keyboard with their amplifiers and plug them in. Rocky moves as unhurriedly as he speaks, like he has all the time in the world. While the brothers are setting up, Paul is taking out seeds and stems, then quickly rolls a couple of joints.

"Those your wheels outside?" Rico asks me.

"The Porsche? No. That's Paul's. Nice, huh?"

He shrugs. "For some. Me? I don't go for that bourgeois shit," Rico says. Then to Paul, "Let's light up and grab your guitar."

Paul plugs in his amp and connects his electric guitar, then they take time tuning up. The room takes on the scent of fresh strong marijuana and I'm impressed once again by the potency of this weed. They're about ready to start playing.

"Where is this from?" I ask as I take a second hit.

"Jamaica," Rocky answers.

"They call it gunja," Rico adds.

"Is that where you're from?" Curious me.

"No." Rocky sounds as if he just doesn't have it in him to speak louder. I look into his eyes. They're amazing! Big and shiny … and I know I can't just keep staring into them, but I really want to. I want to stare for as long as it takes to decide if what I'm seeing in those eyes is kindness, sadness, or inner peace. Maybe it's all three. Or maybe it's something else entirely. Whatever it is, there's a lot of it. The guy has already hooked my attention. Now it's just a matter of reeling in the rest of me.

"It from a loyal; a groupie," Rico offers.

Paul is impressed. "You guys have groupies that give you this shit?"

Rico shrugs in comic apathy. "Some of us have Porsches; we have groupies."

They start playing. There is no doubt about it: the brothers make good music. I'm stretched out on Paul's green couch relaxing, enjoying the combined effect of the grass and their music. They're playing their own compositions, a mix of jazz and soft rock. Paul is playing the guitar surprisingly well.

"You write nice music," I say when they are done.

"Thanks. You play any instruments?" Rocky asks.

"No. My mom made me take piano lessons when I was a kid – along with ballet lessons, skating and gymnastics – but I put a stop to all that as soon as I could."

"I bet like you and your mom get along pretty well," Rocky says with a gentle smile.

I smirk. I may not like my mom, but I'm not about to tell a stranger about it. "She's not too bad."

Rocky grins. "Sure."

"Jolie writes poems," Paul volunteers. "She's really good."

"Don't say that, Paul. I'm not."

"She's kind of modest," Paul says. "But I bet if someone put her lyrics to music they'd be really good."

Rocky just nods. "Hmm."

I shake my head modestly, fervently hoping Rocky believes him.

15

ROCKY ROAD

*J*t's early Saturday morning.

Nora's calling. "Jo! Thank God you're still alive."

"You missed a good time last night," I say. She asks how I got home, and I tell her Paul drove me. She apologizes for leaving me. "I just couldn't stay. I was scared. I wanted to drag you out of there with us. I've been worried about you since."

I tell her the brothers are nice guys. I want to tell her Rocky's a *real* nice guy, but instead I say, "They brought some great pot and played nice music."

There's a smile in Nora's voice. "Jonah and I played some nice music, too."

We laugh and make plans to meet for lunch. As I'm leaving the house, my phone rings again. It's Paul. "So, Rocky called. Asked if you were hooked up with anyone. He thinks you're cool, wants to ask you out. Interested?"

My blood pressure jumps. "I don't know." Is he kidding me? *Of course, I'm interested!* "What do you think?" I ask super-coolly.

"I think he's hot." We laugh, and I know Paul wouldn't admit that to many people. "But he's not going to ask *me* out. He's a great guy, great musician, he's good people. You two would be good together."

My heart is racing, and I can barely find my voice. "Yeah?" I hope I sound unsure.

"Yeah. So okay?"

"I'll think about it."

"Good deal. He'll call. May the force be with you."

In fact, I think about little else. I'm anticipating Rocky's call with more excitement than any call ever. Each time my telephone rings, I'm surprised at how nervous I get before knowing it's not him. Yet, on Sunday, when I finally hear his velvety soft voice, I'm totally comfortable. I feel like I've known him forever.

We make plans to meet after school on Friday at The Pink Turtle. I can't wait. The rest of the week is impossible to endure. I'm distracted, obsessed with thoughts of Rocky, recalling his voice, his face, his smile and his eyes.

TGIF!

As the bell signals the end of the school day, I race to the used Benz I got on my birthday.

I take the short cut, driving the alleys and make it from the high school parking lot to the Beverly Wilshire Hotel in record time. I scoot out of the car and turn it over to the hotel valet, more than willing to pay them if I can save a few minutes looking for a place to park. I dash to the Pink Turtle and almost enter the corner coffee shop, but then I see Rocky sitting at a table inside and hesitate. Rather than rush in, I stand outside and watch him.

He looks terrific just sitting there at a table doing nothing. He stands out. Maybe it's because he's a musician. There's something special about him and it's palpable. He looks around, and my heart goes wild at the thought that he's looking around for me, anticipating my arrival. I'm eager to sit next to him, to be with him and have his attention.

I open the glass door and walk over to him as coolly as I can. The moment he sees me, he's up from the booth hugging me, and I take in the mingled scents of his freshly laundered blue T-shirt, his clean hair and his own warm body musk; it's arousing. On the fringes of my awareness, I register that he's not as tall as I'd thought, just an inch or two taller than me.

"I was looking forward to this," he says. His voice wraps around me in sensuous velvet.

"Me too," I say.

Even when he speaks to the waitress, his voice is free of urgency. It's as if he knows he doesn't need to exert himself because people will do what they must to hear him. We order coffee and a slice of apple pie to share, but I won't remember if I actually eat any. Rocky has one hundred percent of my attention. He draws all of me to him just by being there.

"Tell me about your music," I say. I sense that's what he's all about.

"Well, I've been writing songs forever. As far back as I can remember. I'm twenty-three, and there was never a question in my mind that I'd be a musician. I played in bands all through school, and as soon as I graduated high school, man, that's all there was for me."

He looks me in the eyes, and I'm lost in his. "I've been lucky. I get calls to play keyboard and synthesizer as back up at recording sessions and people like my music. I've already sold one song. In fact, I sold it on my last birthday ... in March." I wonder if he's trying to impress me and hope he is. I'm impressed.

He continues. "I've always been with women who dig my music, but they've never been a part of it, you know? I like the idea that you write lyrics."

I'm overwhelmed by his implication and almost gasp. "I don't write lyrics. I just play around with some poems."

"Well, I'd really like to hear some." His hand touches mine, but no, it doesn't rest there. He just sort of grazes it. "I'd like to try putting some music around your poems ... you know, just play around." He smiles and I realize 's playing with me, teasing me.

I tease him back. "Sure. That would be great," I say. "If that's how you like to play around."

Rocky's eyes dance when he laughs, looking here and there as if too delighted to stay still. He moves his glasses back up on his nose. I will learn he does that whenever he laughs. "You're a funny lady. You're pretty but you're smart too. I can see that. Not too many like you in my space. Let's see how it goes, okay?"

"Okay." With a rush I realize we're not kidding anymore.

He goes on, "Why don't we try next week? One night when I'm not playing a gig and you're free, we'll have some dinner, and spend some time in my studio. Bring your lyrics – poems," he salutes in deference to my term, "– and we'll kick."

"Okay." I don't want to wait. "What about tonight? I'm free. Are you?"

He nods. Give me your address. I'll pick you up."

"No, I'll meet you."

"Don't your parents insist on meeting the guys you go out with?" he asks.

"Only the ones they know I'm going out with."

"And I'm a secret?"

"Let's see how it goes, okay?"

He nods again, rapping the tabletop with his knuckles. "Okay, boss lady."

I go home, shower and dress. Then I drive over Benedict Canyon into the Valley. I will meet Rocky at a small no-name Italian place off Ventura Boulevard in Van Nuys.

When I arrive, he's already seated at a booth. We order and can't stop talking. I had assumed Rocky's background was Mexican, but I discover that his mother was Puerto Rican, his father, Cuban.

"Our last name is Calvo Borinquen. Calvo was my mother's maiden name, but we use it cause it's easier."

"Rocky Calvo Borinquen," I hear myself say the name. "Sounds nice."

"Borinquen means 'the land of the noble lords.' Our father's family had *mucho* bread once upon a time." Rocky smiles slyly. "But it's all gone." I discover he was born in Puerto Rico.

"Where are your parents now?" I ask.

"Gone. They both died."

"I'm sorry."

"Yeah. They died together … in a train wreck." He raps the edge of the table with his fingers, as though he's trying to lessen the sting of his comment, but it makes me shiver.

"I'm so sorry! When?"

"About twelve years ago. Rico was really freaked out. He was eight."

"So, who raised you?"

"We came to L.A. and lived with our *tia*, my mom's sister." He's drumming again. "What about you?"

I don't usually disclose that I'm adopted when I first meet someone, but I immediately open up to Rocky.

"My quote, parents, end quote, are all from Russia. But I'm adopted, so I don't know where I was actually born or where my real parents are from."

He's right there with me. "When did you find out you were adopted?"

I chuckle. "Oh, I've always been told I'm adopted. I was adopted as an infant and I think the first thing I ever remember hearing was my mother telling me I was adopted." I shake my head and continue.

"But I never really understood what it meant until Marissa – she's my father's cousin's daughter – told me at my fourth or fifth birthday party that I didn't come out of my mother's stomach. She called me a *freak*, so I pushed her into our pool. She started crying and ran to tell our mothers what I did. When they asked me why and I told them, they said it was true. My mom said, "Honey, I've told you so many times that you were adopted." I couldn't believe it!

"Ever since that day, I've felt like the freak Marissa said I was." I lean back against the leather. Anyway, I've really never known *where* I came from. I kind of feel that I came from nowhere." I pause and feel a little foolish then. "It's hard to explain."

Rocky listens intently. I see what I take to be understanding in his eyes. He reaches for my hand across the dinner table and says, "Go on."

His hand feels warm and protective and wonderful. I'm almost certain he's held my hand before – though I know he hasn't – and I know he'll hold it many times again. It just feels so right.

"That's it. I've hated my cousin ever since. I know it's not her fault, but I don't like her anyway. My adoptive parents probably do love me – I suppose – in their way, but I don't feel connected to them."

Rocky doesn't try to convince me that I'm not a freak, he just listens. I like that.

"Do you ever wonder about your real parents?" he asks.

I slam the table. "Are you kidding? All the time!" I sit up straighter. "Okay, that's everything. Back to you. How did you get the name Rocky? Is that your real name?"

Rocky leans back in his seat. "Our dad loved boxing. He named both his sons after boxers. There was a Puerto Rican boxer, a middleweight champ who spent some time in the U.S. in the late 50s. He was great and going places, never lost a fight. His name was Rafael Acosta. They called him 'Rocky.'"

"Why?"

"He was a little hard to handle. Couldn't stop himself. Unpredictable. He finally died in a bar brawl. Anyway, that's it about me." He drums the tabletop with his index fingers to signal the end of his story.

"No! I want to hear more about your life." I say.

"There's not much to it. Music is my life. Rico and I play in separate bands.

"Rico plays mostly rock. He plays clubs in all the beach communities up and down the coast," he waves his hand, "from Laguna to Santa Barbara and even farther north.

"I write some music, and I'm part of a band. I play keyboard and manage the band – NightFlight. We play gigs here and there, some of my stuff and some jazz, blues, rock," he laughs, "and even disco."

"I envy you. You've got a brother you're close to; you've got your music … you have a life you love."

"Yeah, it's cool. We're different, though. Rico's angrier. He's been like that since mom and pop died. I've got to watch him. But we're tight." He reaches over and moves a strand of my hair off my face. His touch is a feather.

He asks, "So, what will you do with your life?"

"You mean if I ever graduate from Beverly? I don't know. I'm pretty excited about it, though. I can't believe I'm almost out of there.

"I'm going to go to college. I've been accepted at Arizona State, so I get to go away to college and that's sweet, getting away from my parents. After that I'll do something to make sure I'm independent. And, of course, I want to find my real parents."

"Have you thought about writing lyrics?"

"I'm really not that good," I say.

"Well, let's make tracks to my studio and we'll see what we can do with what you have. My house is around the corner. Ready?"

We leave my car parked in the lot and walk there.

16

FOR A SONG

*T*he brother Calvos' rented house is in obvious need of a new coat of paint and a gardener, but inside, the house is clean and organized.

"Be warned: There's no bathroom in the studio, so use it now. It's down the hallway." Rocky motions ahead, past the dining room to a long corridor.

I use the bathroom, then Rocky leads me out of the house to the studio, a converted two-car garage. The door has a serious set of locks on it. The brothers have put an indoor-outdoor carpet on the cement floor and cork-board on the walls. There's a coffee table that may have been abandoned in an alley and two large square pillows in one corner of the room. There are also three amplifiers and three guitars, two electric, one acoustic, an electric base, a synthesizer and a black standup piano with a tambourine on top. The room has the smell of stale incense, blended with marijuana.

"Welcome to our studio." As Rocky takes my hand and guides me to the piano, I'm again aware of the warmth in his touch.

He leaves me standing at the side of the piano and sits on the bench, quickly running his fingers up and down over the keys. He looks at me and smiles before serenading me with a song he's written about looking for someone to love. I wonder if he's chosen this particular song to send me a message.

When he finishes, I ask him to play more of his compositions. He indulges me.

His voice is soft and raspy, interesting and nice enough, though certainly not the best voice I've ever heard. But I like his style of music. It has a fresh, upbeat sound. And he is definitely on very familiar terms with his piano. His fingers are flying all over the place.

"That's beautiful!" I mean it.

"Thanks. Now let's hear your lyrics."

I'd prefer that he take me into his arms right now and kiss me. I so want to kiss those incredible lips.

I haven't really liked a guy since Jay, and that was over a year ago. But this feeling I have for Rocky comes from a different place, deeper within me than what I felt for Jay.

And Rocky is way different than Jay. After the pain Jay put me through, I should probably be running the other way. But instead, I yearn for whatever Rocky will offer me. In fact, I can't wait; I want to rush to it.

"They're really just poems," I say. I don't want him to expect much. I'll be crushed if he's disappointed.

"That's cool. Recite one. Maybe I'll come up with a melody for it."

"Okay. It's called 'High on Love.' I'm a little nervous." I clear my throat and begin to recite the words to a poem I wrote when I was with Jay and still blind to who he really was. I'm praying Rocky will like what he hears.

If he does, maybe he'll love me.

Yes, I'm feeling all the changes that your love has brought to me.
All this magic. It's fantastic! It's what love's supposed to be.

I am gliding, yes I'm flying, soaring free and high above
Unsuspecting, I'm just dangling, flying high on all this love.

Look at me up in the sky. I'm high ... on you.
Let me take you with me so you can feel high, too.

Yes, I'm blindly moving clearly toward the love light in your eyes.
It's my love for your sweet loving that has gotten me this high.

Now I've found you, and together we can fly up to the stars
Come with me and let me love you. Let the world of love be ours.

I finish with the pressure of anticipation in my chest. Then I hear Rocky's applause. I exhale. I'm thrilled!

"You really like it?"

Rocky nods. "Very cool. I'll have no problem putting a melody to that. It's a natural, much more a song than a poem." He plays some chords on the piano.

Maybe he'll make love to me soon.

"Okay, *High on You*," he says. "Did you write it for one of your boyfriends?" He doesn't sound jealous, just curious.

I'm not taking any chances. And besides, there's no way Jay deserves even one line of that poem.

"No. It was really kind of weird. I just woke up in the middle of the night and there was this first line with a melody in my head, so I started to write more words to it."

"Then you have the melody," he says. It's not a question.

I shake my head. "No."

"Well, let me hear what you heard that night."

"Okay." I'll do anything he asks. I step closer and face him. I want him to look at me. I begin to hum.

"That's good, Baby." He's smiling "You can carry a tune, too." He taps the piano bench. "Now come sit here beside me and sing your words to that melody."

He called me *Baby!*

I sit beside him on his bench. I'm so close to him that I can count the hairs on his neck, smell him, hear his breath. There is a terrific magnetism about him and the closer I am to him, the stronger I'm pulled to him.

I don't tell him about my phobia. I run my tongue over my lips and begin to sing, trying to stay focused on the song and not on Rocky; trying to be brave. As I sing — I'm really barely whispering at first — I'm watching his fingers glide over the black and white keys. When he strikes chords, his reach is wide. His fingers are long and beautiful, well proportioned and strong and as I continue singing, I picture his fingers pleasuring me. My pulse quickens, my voice falters. But Rocky doesn't seem to notice. His eyes are closed and he's totally into enhancing the melody he hears.

I'm in awe of how easily he can take the tune I gave him and create beautiful music around it. I'm so distracted by Rocky that it's only later that I realize how soon I'm comfortable singing in front of him; my fear of performing disappeared.

"This is good, real good," he says and I'm floored that a talented musician like Rocky seems to like my poem and even my melody. "It needs some work," he says. "We'll shorten it. And it needs a musical break. Sing it one more time, Baby."

Ecstatic me! This time, I actually have the confidence to murmur the words with my lips close to his ear. Rocky stops playing and turns to face me. I continue singing softly. Our lips are no more than a hair away from brushing against each other. He pulls his head back and watches me as I continue to sing, gazing at my lips.

Let me take you with me so you can feel high, too.

"Baby?" So soft.

"Hmm?" My heart is hammering.

"Can I kiss your lower lip?"

I am thrown by the question. "My lower lip?"

"Yeah. I've been watching it. When you speak, it bunches up in the middle. I really want to kiss it. Can I?"

I take a breath. "Yes."

I have never before felt lips as warm, as full and as soft as these and never before have been kissed like this. True to his word, he's kissing only my lower lip, nipping at it softly with his lips and tongue, exploring it from one corner to the other. I'm torn between wanting to respond and wanting to do nothing but simply be still and receive his kiss. I do nothing. Our first kiss ends.

106

"I've been wanting to do that since the night I met you." He stands and leads me back into the house.

I'm about to experience heaven.

Inside, the house is filled with the fresh smell of gunja. Rico sits on the living room couch behind a line of smoke, smoking a blunt and watching television.

"Hey, Rock Man, how's it hangin'? You were right on again, man. The gig busted early."

Rocky nods, then points his head toward the studio. "We were making music. Jolie here has written a dynamite song."

Rico puts a hand up like he's giving me a high five. "Good to see you again, Jolie." I'm not close enough to him to reciprocate.

"Hi, Rico. Your brother is incredible. He wrote some amazing music to my poem."

"No," Rocky says modestly. "I just pumped up the music she already had. You'll hear it. I think I'd like the band to play it … if she'll let us."

I look at Rocky in disbelief.

Rico nods and holds out the doobie. "Hey, you guys want a smoke?"

I want to hear Rocky say we can't because we're on our way to heaven, but instead I hear him say, "I'll take a hit. It'll mellow me out. You want some, Baby?" He sits down, accepting his brother's offer and takes a hit. My heart sinks. The rest of the night can easily be lost.

"No thanks," I say. "The last time I smoked your weed I was high forever. I'll just go home." I pick my handbag up from the sofa.

"Okay, just a second, Baby, I'll walk you to your car."

I am beyond disappointed. Rocky doesn't even try to dissuade me from leaving. He takes another serious hit, coughs, and gets up.

I say goodnight to Rico, and we head back to the restaurant's parking lot.

Outside, a heavy fog has fallen, characteristic of LA's early summer nights.

It's nighttime but the gray-white sky obscures the moon and fills the air around us. We walk towards my car, talking about working on the song. As soon as it's ready, Rocky wants to introduce it into Night-Flight's repertoire.

"Maybe you'll sing it with us," he says as he takes hold of my hand.

The fog is so thick that, as I shake my head, I feel cool light moisture on my face. "Rocky, I can't sing in front of people. I have major stage fright. I don't even know how I was able to sing in front of you."

Rocky tightens his grip on my hand. "You'll do just fine, Baby."

The silver mist is almost the same color as my Mercedes.

"I should have known you'd drive a Benz," he says.

I'm embarrassed. "It's old! They got it for me because it's heavy. They thought it would be safe."

Rocky nods and opens the car door for me. "I had a good time," he says.

"Yeah," I say, "me too." It's time for me to sit in the car. But I don't want the night to end.

He moves inside the open car door that was between us, holds my face between his hands and gazes down at me. "You're a beautiful woman, Jolie."

No guy has ever called me a woman. I feel a shiver move through my body. Looking up, I wait for his lips. He kisses me gently, so gently that his lips feel like a warm flutter. Like his earlier kiss, this kiss has nothing rushed about it. It seems the softer his kiss, the greater my yearning for him. This time I return the kiss.

When we come apart, Rocky asks if I have to go home. I nod and he says, "Okay, then go. Drive carefully in the fog."

I feel sensual, aware of the mist that has moistened my eyelids, the subtle change of temperature inside the car and the touch of the smooth leather seat all at once. And Rocky. I'm reluctant to leave his warmth.

"Come sit inside a minute," I hear myself say.

Rocky is beside me in a heartbeat. Wordlessly, we kiss again. I'm kissing Rocky in the same slow way he kisses me.

Without realizing I've moved, I'm lying down on the front seat, my head by the steering wheel, watching him pull my jeans down and seeing him gaze at my thighs. He is toying with my panties. I am out of my mind.

"Can I kiss you here? I've been wanting to do that since I saw you walk into that coffee shop today."

Rocky is unquestionably stranger than any guy I've ever known. I've never heard anyone who's asked permission like he does. It makes him seem gentle and maybe harmless, but at the same time the anticipation gives me a mini orgasm before he even touches me. I nod and discover that my consent, like his question, gives way to another.

Rocky is positioned with his mouth on me, and my body is flying away. Holding my pelvis in his warm hands, he lifts me up while exploring my most sensitive parts with his mouth in the same slow, sensuous way he'd kissed my lower lip. I'm lying there having orgasm after orgasm and he's not stopping, not changing his pace. When, finally, he lifts his head, I have no idea how much time has gone by, maybe five minutes, maybe five hours. It's black outside. Inside, the car the windows are white, covered with the thick fog of our breaths.

"You liked that," he says. I can only breath. "You taste good, Baby." He takes hold of his car handle. "Can I call you tomorrow?"

"Yes. Call."

He kisses my forehead, then smiles and gets out of the car. "Go slow and drive carefully, Baby."

I drive home slowly. I'm in no rush. I hold on to the feeling of Rocky's lips on me all the way back to Beverly Hills. I visualize the light in his eyes when he said I was a beautiful woman. I'm singing my song … *our song*.

Forevermore, my lyrics set to Rocky's music will link us together.

1 7

BANG! BANG!

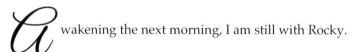wakening the next morning, I am still with Rocky.

> *I sleep in peace dreaming of you.*
> *The first breeze of morning*
> *glides through my window,*
> *Passes over my body*
> *like baby's first kiss.*
> *I awaken to thoughts of you.*

He calls me. NightFlight has a gig at an airport hotel tonight. I'm dying to go but cannot get away. My parents have planned my Saturday night, absolutely insisting that I join them at a Moroccan barbecue at our neighbor's house down the block. He calls the next day and I plan to meet him at the hotel that night, but then Dad grounds me because he says I got fresh.

And then it's Monday and the grind is on. It's like our teachers know they're going to lose their grip on us soon and they want to make us as miserable as they can between now and graduation.

High school is *finally, actually, really* coming to an end! Nora reigns over her court at the Senior Prom as Prom Queen. I'm Senior Princess, which had surprised me when I first found out.

There are so many other girls – cheerleaders and girls who come to school wearing great clothes with their hair all done up. They're absolute artists at putting themselves together, and, if you ask me, they're lots prettier than me.

When I found out that the witch hadn't taken away my title, I was happy, proud to tell Rocky that I'm Senior Princess; my class thinks I'm really pretty.

Rocky's response is, "Baby, I'm not surprised."

I want so much to go to the Prom with him. I know he'll stand out. It would be like taking a rock star and not only because he'd be the oldest guy there.

I ask him. He declines. I say, "I'm not surprised."

I assume he's past high school proms. Then he explains that he would like to go but NightFlight is booked to play at another prom that night. I go to the Prom with Paul.

I hang out with Nora on Ditch Day and stay home on Senior Beach Day, talking to Rocky on the telly for hours.

The Senior Mother and Daughter Tea is today. Just as I feared, Mom's been sulking since I told her that we're not going. I knew she'd take it badly, like Nora had guessed, so I only told her yesterday when I came home from school. I'm sure I'll be punished, but Dad's in Las Vegas at a convention of theatre owners until Sunday, so I have that to look forward to when he gets back.

At some point after breakfast I wander back into the kitchen for a glass of orange juice and regret it as soon as I walk in. Mom's still sitting at the breakfast table, running her hand across the wavy glass top while looking at the clock. She's sulking. The steam is rising from her cup of coffee and I'm sure it's not her first because there are already two cigarette stubs in the ashtray at her hand. Her doctor's given her diet pills and she says caffeine adds an extra kick.

"Are you okay, Mom?" I ask. She looks glassy-eyed and tired.

"I'm so upset, I couldn't sleep a wink last night, Jolie. I was looking forward to today. But you don't care one bit!You just don't think of anyone but yourself. You never do! "

"I told you, Mom. It wasn't my fault."

"Yeah, you always have the same answer," she says, taking a cigarette from the pack on the table. It's the last one. "It's never your fault. But if you thought about your mother for a change, you'd have kept your big mouth shut." She shakes her head and then says, "Its your mouth's fault."

She looks – I guess the word is *forlorn.*

"I can't believe it!" she goes on, almost wailing. "The Senior Tea! I've been looking forward to it since you started high school!"

She plays with the empty pack of Salems, and I see her hands shake as she takes a drag off her freshly lit cigarette and tips it into the ashtray. "Everyone will be there except me."

Watching the her exhale the stream of smoke, I wonder how many times I've seen it and how many more times I will.

She continues complaining. "I paid good money for that dress – and the hat! I would have looked so good."

She's pushed her chair away from the breakfast table. She gets up and shuffles over to the garbage can. She tosses in the crumpled pack of Salems then joins me at the refrigerator where I'm replacing the bottle of orange juice. She reaches in and brings out a cellophane-wrapped carton of twelve fresh packs of green and white Salems.

"I could just die!"

The refrigerator door closes and she turns to me with one hand on her hip. "Now where am I supposed to wear them?" She shakes her head. She puts the carton, now holding eleven packs, back in the refrigerator and closes the door."I'm not going to return them. Oh, no! I'm not letting some little *nebbisheh* saleswoman at Saks know I didn't get to wear them today. All because of my daughter! Everyone will be there but me. Jolie! I'm just dying!" She turns to me with one hand on her hip.

"Didn't *you* want to go to Greystone?" she asks. I just look at her. "The Doheny family lived there. Imagine, Jolie! The man gave that huge mansion and all that land to his son as a gift! I've heard it's fantastic. Oh, I really, really wanted to see it."

"So, you'll see it some other time, Mom. I said I'm sorry."

"Listen to you! *I'll see it some other time?* I've waited years." She opens the pack of cigarettes and drops it into a pocket of her cotton duster (this one, pink with red hearts).

I stand at the counter drinking my juice, watching her shuffle back to her seat like an old woman. Forgetting that she has a lit cigarette in the ashtray, she lights yet another one, then notices the other and puts it out.

"You're smoking more than usual, aren't you Mom?"

"It's the new pills the doctor gave me. They make me want to smoke. I told you. I'll be fine. I've lost seven pounds already!"

Her gaze is fixed on the small chandelier hanging above her. "Ahh, they had their *tzurus*. You better believe it. They weren't living such a happy life either."

"Who?"

She looks at me. "The Dohenys."

What could my mother possibly know about the lives of the Dohenys? "Why do you say that?"

"*Oy*, you should only know. Imagine that poor girl. She marries a boy that's unbelievably rich, with a father as rich as Rockefeller, so rich they name streets after him, the richest family in Los Angeles.

"She lives in this huge mansion with him and has five kids with him. She's got servants and chauffeurs and I don't know what else. She's got everything money can buy. There's a ballroom! A bowling alley! A switchboard in the house for God's sake!" She takes a hit off her cigarette and exhales.

"Then *boom!* One night, six months after they've moved in she hears a shot.

"A gun shot?" I ask

She nods. "11.30 at night. And there's her husband, lying dead on the floor." She's pointing to a spot on our kitchen floor. "He's laying right there on the floor, shot to death."

"He was murdered?"

"Murdered, *schmurdered*." Mom puts out her cigarette. She takes a sip of coffee, makes a face and puts the cup down. There's a fair amount of ashes on the table; smoking is a dirty habit.

"Her husband's secretary is lying there. He's dead, too. They said his secretary shot him and then committed suicide. But no one knows who killed who. They were mixed up in some kind of government scandal – bribery, I think, something with a silly name. I don't remember, something like Teapot or Teacup –"

"The Teapot Dome?" I say and she nods. "We read about it in History. It was when Harding was President. Bribery, I think it was the early Twenties. Is that when all this happened?"

"Yeah," she says, "that must be it." Why does my mom care about a rich guy that died decades ago? "Anyway, " she says, "the two of them had a thing going on."

"What do you mean, 'a thing'? Were they having an affair?" She nods. There's a smirk on her face. "So, who killed who first?" I ask.

"We don't know," Mom says.

"Okay. Who cares? They were having an affair and for some reason, he killed her, or she killed him."

Mom looks at me slyly. "Well, for one thing, *she* wasn't a *she*; she was a *he*." She nods. "His secretary was a *man*." I must look startled. "That's right! The big important Mr. Doheny was a closet queer!"

She knows she has my attention. She takes another drag off her cigarette and goes on. "They met at the gas station the secretary's father owned. And he was married! The guy started off as Doheny's chauffeur. Eventually he divorced his wife and became Doheny's personal secretary."

"Oh, that's so sad." I say. I know Mom thinks I mean it was sad that he was into men, but I'm thinking how torturous it must have been for Doheny to live a lie. "Did his wife know about them? I mean, Doheny's wife."

"She must have. She hated the guy," my mother says, brushing ashes off the kitchen table. She looks at me with such longing. I feel awful. "I really would have liked to have seen the place," she says.

I feel terrible. I'd never have guessed she cared this much about Greystone. "How do you know all this, Mom?"

"I've been reading about it. I'm fascinated. The family, so rich and powerful, and look at their lives!" She shakes her head again.

"The two bodies were moved before the police got there. They weren't even *called for three hours after* the shots were fired." Then I see a strange expression cross her face. "They never found out who did it." She says.

"Three hours? Wow! Then it could have been Doheny's wife. Maybe she was jealous."

Mom shrugs, "Maybe." She gets up and carries the ash-filled ashtray to the garbage can. On the way, she says, "You know, there were no fingerprints on the gun. How can you shoot someone – or shoot yourself — and not leave fingerprints on the gun?

"Anyway, the two ended up buried near one another. How do you like that?" As she empties the ashtray into the garbage, a few ashes land on the kitchen floor. She sighs. "But not in the church cemetery. You can't be buried there if you're a suicide because it's a mortal sin. They're the same as us Jews. I didn't know that. Anyway, you never know about families. They have their *tzurus*."

She sets the kettle on the burner and there's a *whoosh* before flames appear. "If Greystone were built today, it would probably cost over two hundred million dollars. It was designed to look like that French palace. I used to know the name, but I can't think of it now. It starts with a V."

I say nothing. "Anyway, I've always wanted to go to France and see it. Maybe one day I'll go." As she empties her cold coffee into the sink preparing to make a fresh cup, she turns to me and repeats, "I was really looking forward to the Tea."

Now I wish I'd have talked that witch into letting us go today – or at least letting my mother go.

I'm absolutely sure Dad punish me when he comes back.

18

ROCK ME

*G*raduation ceremonies take place on Beverly's multi-tiered front lawn.

Invited guests are seated along the lowest tier. Graduates are sitting on the second highest tier, our white folding chairs turned away from family and friends, facing the top tier where the Phys Ed teacher sits with the Principal and both the Boys' and Girls' Vice Principals. The podium is set up there too.

It's a hot June day. A lot of us girls are wearing shorts and camisoles under these long white robes. It's torture sitting in the sun listening to all these endless speeches. *Geez!* We get it already! We'll all be successful and true to ourselves, take hold of the future and make our high school proud.

At last the final speech ends to applause and each of us is called to the podium where we receive our diploma, curled and tied with a black ribbon. As I'm handed mine, Mrs. Rutherson smiles at me, and I smile back, a smile that comes from my heart and acknowledges that I've finally leaving behind all I've endured. *Goodbye, Mrs. Rutherson? I'll never have to see ya'll again? Or listen to the crazy way ya'll speak?*

The graduating class of 1978 moves our tassels from one side of our square cap to the other. Ceremonies end and white caps go flying. High school is over and is forever in my past.

I'm feeling a mix of emotions. Though I'm ecstatic that high school is over, I know the end of my relationship with Rocky looms ahead of me.

When I was applying to college in Arizona, Mom and Dad tried to persuade me to go to UCLA. I didn't blame them. UCLA is a really good school and only about a fifteen minute drive from our house. But I was adamant about getting away from home, so I didn't even apply there.

That was before I met Rocky. Now, I'd give anything not to leave L.A. I have contacted UCLA and, though my grades are acceptable, they're filled to capacity. So, I'll be leaving for Arizona around September 5. *Shit!* What a bitch life can be.

I'm determined to squeeze as much time as possible with Rocky before I have to go. I spend every possible minute with him.

By mid-August, Rocky still hasn't once been to my house. In fact — *thank God!* — my parents don't know he exists. I tell myself I'm hiding Rocky from them. But the truth? I'm also hiding them from Rocky. I drive to his place in Van Nuys or meet him on some neutral turf almost daily.

Not having met my parents, it's hard for him to understand. "Baby, is it possible you're making this a bigger deal than it is?" He asks.

"No Rocky, I'm not. Believe me. My parents will hate you. A, you're a musician; B, you're not Jewish – no, that's wrong. A, you're not Jewish; B, you're a musician; C, you're 'ethnic' and my dad is such a bigot he makes Archie Bunker look cool; D, you're not in college; E, you drive a used red van; F,-"

"Okay." Rocky smiles. "I get it. You don't need to go through the whole alphabet. I guess I'm never going to meet your parents or see your house. Too bad. I've never been inside a mansion."

"It's not a mansion. Paul's parents have a mansion."

Then, *Oh my God!*

It's mid-August and my parents get news that Dad's father is about to pass away. My parents pack their bags and arrange to fly to New York immediately. I try not to jump for joy when they tell me they'll be gone for two whole weeks!

I telephone Rocky. "How would you like to see the inside of a big Beverly Hills house on North Beverly Drive?"

After delivering a lecture on what I'm supposed to do with the mail, who not to let into the house, what time I'm to be home every night, how and when to water the plants and so forth and so on, my parents give me some money and tack a list of phone numbers I might need onto the kitchen wall and I finally drive them to LAX.

I call Rocky. "Okay," I say, "the coast is clear. Come on over. Bring a toothbrush and your swimming suit." I hang up and realize he doesn't need to bring a swimming suit.

I see Homer parked in our driveway and I've never been so excited. Rocky enters and tours the house. His eyes light up when he sees the baby grand and his fingers are immediately on it, probably testing the sound and stroke. No one has played it for years. He notices all the couches and chairs in the house have zippered plastic covers on them, as Mom says, "to keep the dust and dirt off." He says nothing, just sort of twists his head around and nods knowingly as if to say, "You told me you mother wraps everything in plastic, and now I'm seeing it for myself."

I can see he loves the backyard. It is pretty, with all the trees, flowers and plants.

He sits on the swinging chair for a minute, and I watch him, then he gets up to inspect the recently retiled pool, fingers in to confirm it's warm, and then nods at the adjoining Jacuzzi. He wants to get into the water but I'm anxious to show him my bedroom. I hope he'll like my posters and my collection of music. Then I realize he will actually be sleeping in my bed tonight and my insides shiver.

He's thirsty.

In the kitchen, I bring out a glass from the cabinet to get him a cold drink and he sees plastic covers all the china in the cabinets ."Your mother's got a plastic jones," he says.

Embarrassed, I shrug half-heartedly and laugh. "Some people have heroin jones, my mom's got a plastic jones."

I open the refrigerator door. When he sees Mom's two unopened cartons of Salem's on the top shelf holding a total of twenty-four packs of cigarettes, I add, "and a Salem jones." He looks from the cartons to me. I nod. "She goes through over two packs a day."

He continues to survey the contents of the fridge then closes the door and shakes his head. He claps his hands as if he's just thought of something, and asks me if I'd like to try some Cuban dishes. He says he likes to cook, and would like to cook for me.

"Of course," I say, "I'd love that."

He downs his drink and we get in his van. We're on the way to the Valley to his favorite little market.

At the small market, where he seems of know most of the people there, I watch as he seeks out the plumpest tomatoes and the juiciest guavas and mangoes. He small talks to the butcher while he has him turn over some cuts so he can select the perfect cut of beef, then follows with lamb and then pork. He examines every piece of salmon fillet before making his choice. I wonder how he will use all this food.

The first dish Rocky prepares is guava-glazed pork ribs with a side of rice and black beans. I go crazy for it. The second night he serves the fillet of salmon. I watch him prepare it, lovingly stroking the fist with rum, mango and honey before adding cracked pepper and "pan roasting" it. The combination of flavors is a merry-go-round of tastes. I ask him to make it again when Nora, Jonah, and Paul come over to swim and stay for dinner. They all go as crazy for it as I did. And, when they taste the fried bananas he's made for dessert, they're full of compliments.

Afterwards, we light up some gunja, plentiful since Rocky's arrival, and laugh, remembering how Nora ran out of Paul's place that first night, afraid that Rocky and his brother were dangerous, possibly crazed and murderous. Nora is embarrassed at first, then laughs along with us.

It feels good to be with Rocky around Nora and Jonah.

If I've envied my best friend's relationship with Jonah, I never admitted it to myself. But now that I'm with Rocky, I'd be lying if I said it didn't feel good.

Yet, though Nora is being sweet to Rocky, I sense she's not crazy about the idea of the two of us as a couple. She's neither stuck up nor a snob, but I know that if you asked her, she'd say that because she loves me, she hopes our relationship won't last.

She probably wishes I was with someone more educated, or with someone that has more money, or with a guy that's more established by the age of twenty-three than Rocky is, with a brighter future – someone kind of like Jonah … or Jay.

I get it. If I think about it, it is weird that I can be so strongly attracted to someone who is almost the complete opposite of everything I liked in Jay – that unfaithful asshole! But, though he was an asshole, he was also real smart; a mathematician who was methodical and analytical. Rocky is a musician who just sort of flows, with nothing to answer to but his heart.

What's obvious to Nora would be obvious to anyone: Rocky is a guy with no college education, not a lot of money, a run-down van and a limited wardrobe, who probably has no idea what *pi* is except for the kind filled with fruit. And yet, he emits a kind of warmth that Jay lacked. He makes me feel valuable and I feel as though I do everything better when he's around. I want to shine for him.

He's also a more exciting lover.

As the days go by, Rocky and I are like two kids playing house.

We spend our days naked either in the Jacuzzi or floating in the pool. Rocky enjoys playing the baby grand and I spend time working on our song. Evenings, Rocky usually cooks a delectable dinner, then we clean up together and listen to music or we'll catch a movie and get ice cream. Sometimes Nora and Jonah come over. Paul hangs out too, maybe playing his guitar with Rocky on the piano.

I love living with Rocky like this.

I'm trying hard to suppress my feelings for him, but they're only deepening. I try not to think about how much I'll miss him when I leave for Arizona State. He hasn't once brought up the subject of my departure and sadly, I assume it's because our relationship doesn't mean as much to him as it does to me.

It's true, I've never felt this deeply about anyone before … but I vowed I would never again say those three little words . I'm determined not to get hurt again.

19

ROCKY 'N ROLLIN'

*O*ne afternoon, I accompany Rocky to a NightFlight practice session.

The rambling cedar house, a classic rustic Laurel Canyon, is edged on a winding dead-end.

We climb the outside stairs to a large second-story room. Though the August sunshine is bright, the room, nestled in the shade of the large trees outside, is cool and almost devoid of sunlight.

"Yo! How's it hangin', Rocky?"

Danny, our host, sits perched on his seat at the drums in the center of the room. His arms are muscular. I notice his fingers are unusually thick. When Rocky introduces me, Danny says, "No wonder you're lying low, dude. The lady's a fox." I smile.

Josh is the vocalist who also plays guitar. He's probably the youngest member of the band. He certainly looks younger than the others, squatting there, playing with the dials on an amplifier. Then he rises to strap on a red Kramer guitar. He greets us with a nod as he reaches for an open can of beer sitting on top of the amplifier.

I also meet Raul, the bassist and Ray who plays the flute, saxophone, and clarinet.

Rocky sets up his keyboard.

In the far corner by the windows there's a worn velvet purple loveseat and two straight-backed chairs. A large, round piece of glass sits atop three wooden logs. A couple of joints sit in a large, red ceramic ashtray in the shape of a woman's naked torso.

"We're going to try something new tonight," Rocky says as the band tunes up. "Jolie here's written a song and we've been working it. We'll try it out when we're done."

My heart is beating at hyper speed. Rocky didn't tell me he'd be sharing our song with the band tonight. I should be angry, but I'm not. I'm surprised, shocked – and proud.

"Cool," Jimmy says.

"You play?" Danny asks, craning his neck toward me.

"No."

They're all nodding, knowingly. "That's cool," Danny says.

They start going through their numbers.

They're so good, so in synch with one another, that I don't know why they bother to rehearse. They could be playing to a crowd right now. All the songs are great, and once again I marvel at Rocky's compositions and his talent, as his fingers float over the keys.

When they've gone through their usual songs, true to his word, Rocky introduces our song to the band. He plays it on the keyboard while the various instruments experiment around him. The drummer picks up the beat, the bass comes in, the guitar follows. Danny improvises with the flute then the clarinet and returns to the flute. After a while, the combination of sounds around the melody is lovely. They play the music through several times, varying slightly as it gains sophistication.

Rocky asks me to sit on the bench next to him. "Sing with me, Baby."

I am deathly shy, but with my with eyes fixed only on him, I do as he asks, singing along in a voice so soft, it's almost inaudible.

With Rocky by my side, singing with me, smiling at me, caring for me, I begin to relax and grow a little more confident. My voice gets continually louder until it can be heard along with Rocky's. Then his voice slowly, fades away and I'm singing alone.

When the song ends, I see four thumbs go up.

"Here, here."

"Nice. Very nice."

"The lady's got a voice, too."

I don't know if they really liked my voice or the lyrics or if they're approving out of respect for Rocky but whatever the reason, I love it.

Rocky tells them he's anxious to work on the song, polish it up and play it publicly as soon as possible.

I'm ecstatic.

But when he mentions that I'll be singing it on stage, my stomach flounces.

Rocky has no idea how amazing it was that I could sing in front of *him*! And then in front to *them*. Singing *on stage*? For a roomful of *strangers*? *No way!* Cannot be done! It's absolutely impossible! I need to tell Rocky. I'll explain it to him later, when we're alone. Josh can sing it.

The band ends their session with "Let's Go Get Stoned" – and we do.

On our way home, I snuggle up to Rocky on Homer's long front seat and wrap both my arms around his right one as he drives. "Rocky, it was amazing to hear them play our song! And no one but you could have gotten me to sing like that in front of people. I feel so good when I'm with you."

"It's the music we make, Baby. And our lovemaking"

My smile broadens and I feel my heart expand. He calls it 'our lovemaking' and not just 'sex.' I smile up at him. "The music?" I say, "Yup, absolutely. But our lovemaking? I don't know … " He pushes me off his arm in mock hurt and I set my feet up on the dashboard. "It's the music we make and the way you've been feeding me," I say.

"Funny lady."

One late evening, we're in my backyard cuddling on the swinging chair, enjoying the night. Looking up at the starry sky I feel content. Rocky is feeling philosophical.

I'm overcome by the beauty I see. The moon is silver and set amid thin clouds as though placed there by an artist. For some reason, I flash on my parents in New York. "Isn't it strange to think a gazillion people, people all around the world, are looking up at the same sky?" I bury my head deeper into his wonderful chest.

Rocky nods. "Some are looking up at the sun now," he says. "It's all pretty magical, isn't it?"

"You mean how beautiful it looks?" I ask.

"Yeah. All of it: the moon … the stars … the sun … life. How we're all born, and we all die … and how we all want the same thing."

Curious, I look up at him and ask what he means.

He keeps his arm wrapped tightly around me. "You know what I'm saying, Baby," he says, looking down at me and smiling. I can see the light dancing in his eyes even in the night. "You're a poet. You write about love. You know the only thing we all want in this life, the only thing that's worth anything is love … just to love and to be loved …" His soft voice drifts off. He can't see the look of awe on my face. He's looking back up at the sky.

I put my hand in his and grope for words to tell him that in this moment I'm realizing I can let myself love him because I know he understands me as no one else does. But the moment slips away. I bring his hand to my lips and kiss it tenderly then reach to kiss his lips.

We make love in the moonlight, as gently as the summer night breeze kisses the grass around us.

2 0

CAUGHT!

$\mathcal{I}$'m completely aware that Rocky is taking up most of my heart.

For all the days and nights that Mom and Dad are out of town, Rocky and I make the house our private heaven. I'm enjoying my home for the first time since I was a little girl in flouncy dresses.

Throughout these days of hazy happiness, we make love in every room and every nook of the house. I savor Rocky's cooking. We laugh a lot. At night we wrap ourselves around one another. I relish each minute of being with Rocky.

And the days go by.

On the twelfth day, we go to the market where Rocky adds a box of neon-colored markers to his purchases. I ask him what he wants them for.

"A project," he answers.

We return home, strip and eat lunch in the warmth of the sun in the backyard. Rocky brings out the markers.

His 'project' turns out to be drawing all over my naked body. He writes 'Rocky' inside of a heart in several locations including my buttocks and stomach and draws pink and green hearts around my nipples. The different neon colors shine brightly on my skin in the mid-day sun. He has my legs parted and he's at my groin, intent on covering the rest of me with an intricate design. What I can see looks rather nice. Colorful with an interesting design.

"Damn! I'm out of green."

I can't stop laughing. "No problem! We can get another box from the market and finish tomorrow."

"Jo, be still. I need to finish this part."

"I can't help it. It tickles."

We don't hear him until he's there. Standing on top of us, taking in the entire scene. He scares us out of our bijessis.

"Who the hell are you?" Rocky jumps. So does my heart.

"Who is it Phil? Who's there?" Ah, having heard my father's bellowing voice, my mother comes running up behind him. She stands transfixed, her cigarette hanging at the lowest point of her down-turned lips.

Dad's round eyes are opened wide, staring.

I look up at Rocky in complete panic. He grabs two towels off the grass and throws one down to me, quickly wrapping the other around his waist.

I'm trying to get up while trying to cover my breasts with my arms and keep my legs locked, but I'm having trouble. I'm finally up and I cover myself as best as I can with the towel Rocky gave me. It takes a second for me to gain my balance and in that second, Rocky holds his hand out to my father.

"Hello sir, I'm Rocky."

Dad's eyes slide up and down Rocky then move back to me. Despite my towel, the colored markers are definitely visible. Both he and Mom have seen Rocky's artwork.

With his nostrils flaring and his round his eyes squinted in anger, Dad looks like an animal that smells prey close by. He seems ready to pounce on Rocky but then his nose turns up. "What's that smell?" he asks, wiping his forehead with his hand. "Is there hashish or marijuana in my house?"

Rocky looks at me and I glance down at the ashtray that's holding the joint. My father sees it too. His stubby legs move as quickly as they can over the cloth we've spread on the grass.

He picks up the joint and brings it to his nose. "What's this?"

He looks at me. I say nothing. He looks at Rocky. "It's a marijuana cigarette, isn't it?"

Rocky doesn't answer. "Why you – I'll have you arrested for this," he says. "I'm calling the Beverly Hills police right now, you son of a bitch!" He turns toward the house with the joint in his hand.

"That's not his, Dad."

Dad turns back. He's holding the joint out in front of him like he'd hold a dead rat.

"What?" he screams. "Not his?"

Mom's mouth opens and her lit cigarette drops from her lips onto the grass.

Rocky puts his palm up to me. "Don't Jo –"

"No! It's mine." I say. "You can't arrest Rocky. I'll tell the police it's mine!"

My father explodes. "Yours?"

"Yes. They'll have to arrest me."

Dad passes his free palm across his purple forehead, wiping away beads of sweat while my mother has continued staring at my body since the first second she saw Rocky's creation.

Both my parents are staring at the almost totally naked female in their backyard with the painted body who smokes marijuana with the almost naked boy they've never before seen they call their adopted daughter.

"I'm very sorry, Mr. Gold." Rocky says.

Now Phil is ready to attend fully to Rocky. "You! You're sorry? Who the hell are you, you bastard son of a bitch? What's your name?" Dad is breathing so hard that the rise and fall of his chest is easy to see.

With his left hand at his waist firmly holding the towel, Rocky again extends his right hand out to Phil. "Rocky Calvo Borinquen, sir."

My father totally ignores Rocky's outstretched hand. "Fuck you. What are you doing here?"

I can't believe he's speaking like this to Rocky. "Dad! Rocky's my boyfriend!"

Dad stares at me. "Your *boyfriend!*" He makes a face, his voice mimicking mine, filled with hateful sarcasm.

"Yes. My boyfriend." I repeat emphatically.

Dad looks at my mother. "You hear that Stella? This is your daughter's *boyfriend*." He cocks his head toward Rocky. "Is your boyfriend Jewish?"

Before I can answer, he addresses Rocky. "You're not circumcised." Rocky shakes his head.

Dad looks at Rocky as though he's covered in shit.

I hear him swallow as he turns slowly back to Mom, shaking his head and rubbing his forehead with his palm. "Your daughter has an A-rab for a boyfriend," he says to her.

Then to me he says, "How dare you bring an A-rab into my house?"

Despite all this, Rocky can't hide the shadow of a smile. I'd warned him that my father is a prejudiced racist and he's probably seeing Dad as a character straight out of the comics. He's going to clear up Dad's confusion; it'll be easy. With his voice still soft, Rocky replies, "I'm not an Arab, Mr. Gold."

"Baloney," Dad waves him away with a sneer on his face. "Don't lie to me. I know an A-*rab* when I see one. I knew right away you were an A-rab. All you Middle Eastern scumbags are A-rabs."

Rocky's shaking his head, his smile now stale. He's simply dealing with an ignorant bigot. "No, Mr. Gold, really, I'm not. I'm half Puerto Rican, half Cuban."

Dad nods, turns to my mother and then to me. He has a ghoul's smile on his face. "Great," he says, "your boyfriend's not an A-*rab*. He's half spic, half banana monkey."

Rocky and I speak in unison.

"Hey, man, it's not cool to talk like that," he says. The smile is gone. I'm horrified. "Stop that, Dad!"

"You shut up!" Dad says pointing the joint at me as though it's a dagger.

Then he points it at Rocky. "And as for you, you son of a bitch," my father says, "I'll tell you what's cool. Cool is I go inside right now and call the Beverly Hills police, you prick, and have you arrested. You'll be deported the hell back to wherever shit hole you came from sooner than you can say banana monkey."

Still looking at Rocky but pointing at me, he says, "You know how old she is? Seventeen! You know what statutory rape is, you son of a bitch?" Saliva splatters in the sun.

I go for broke. "Dad! I wasn't a virgin."

My father's round, bald head turns. Very slowly. He looks at me as though seeing me for the first time – and loathes what he's seeing. His eyes bulge out so far, they almost reach me just before his hand slaps me across my face, hard and fast, like a whip. I think my neck cracks.

Rocky starts toward him. "Hey, man, that's-"

I grab his arm. "Stop, Rocky. Don't."

"You're a slut," my father snarls at me. "But you're still underage."

"You expect me to tell the police that Rocky raped me?" I say. I force a laugh under my breath. My face burns where he slapped me. "I won't! I won't even talk to them."

His jaw is shaking. He points to the sliding doors as he speaks to Rocky. "You! Prick! Take that trash parked outside my house and get the hell out of here now! This *minute*! And don't you dare come back. Don't you dare ever touch my daughter again! Don't call her, don't speak to her. You hear me? You come near my daughter or my house again and so help me God you'll be one sorry spic prick!"

"Stop!" I scream. I appeal to my mother. "Tell him to stop calling him names."

Mom doesn't move. She hasn't yet closed her mouth. The cigarette at her feet has almost burned out.

Rocky hangs his head low. "It's okay Baby, I'll leave."

"Don't go!" I say.

"It's okay, Baby." We leave my parents outside, passing my mother who still hasn't budged and stands staring at Rocky.

I follow him inside and into my room where I throw on a robe while he collects his things, then I walk him to the front door.

I am incredibly embarrassed and super angry. They've managed to ruin this, too.

My time with Rocky is ending horribly. Rocky doesn't kiss me before leaving. He barely touches me. "Be cool," he says. He's forcing a smile. "I'll see you."

And he's gone.

～

I return to the living room.

My parents have retreated back into this room, and the three of us form a triangle. My father is stationed in the groove of the baby grand with his hands stirring in his pockets, his face dark. My mother is sitting on the couch, still wearing her suit jacket though it's even hotter inside the house than outside. I notice her jacket has a coffee stain at her breast. Her face is frozen and pale. I stand at the threshold of the room. The middle of the room is taken with their luggage.

They're quiet now and I can't tell if they'd been talking before I entered the room. Either way, I don't care.

When he sees me, my father's hands jerk. His short-sleeved brown shirt has large wet spots under the arms. I don't want to sit. I stay on my feet by the entrance to the room. My anger hasn't subsided, and I feel like a boxer about to begin the next round.

The most important person to me is no longer here.

My father wastes no time. "Well, if it isn't the little slut! Our daughter, the whore." He might be expecting me to say something, but I don't. "As soon as we turn our backs you let the scum of the world into our home. You sleep with trash in our home. A *spic*!"

I'm fuming. The bigoted language I've heard for years still jars me – and it has never jarred me more than it does now, directed at Rocky.

"That's all we needed, was for you to become a marijuana-smoking slut whore!" My father's hands return to his pockets and he shakes his head.

When he speaks again, he's looking at the woman frozen on the couch. His voice is laced with disgust. "No wonder your mother didn't want you. She was probably a slut, too, gave birth to a bastard. You'll probably get knocked up, too – if you haven't already."

Oh, I truly hate him! My anger closes my throat and I stand before this stupid, sick man who is supposed to be my father, listening to him slander both the mother I've never met, as well as me and the person I care most about. Then he takes a step in my direction, and his hand flies out of his pocket as he gestures with his arm up like he's a flamenco dancer.

"If I ever catch you with that no-good piece of shit again, I'll throw you out of this house. You hear, Missy? *Out of this house!*"

Still, I say nothing.

He expects me to be afraid. He *wants* me to be afraid. I see my mother stir. "If you're going to whore yourself," he says, "at least don't whore yourself to spics, banana monkeys, Chinks, apes, and A-rab camel jockeys! And don't you *dare* ever bring drugs into my house."

I speak as softly as Rocky would. "You forgot degos and cholos," I say.

Dad starts to nod, then realizes I'm ridiculing him. "Why you …!" He rushes up to me and moves his arm to smack me, but I step sideways, away from his reach.

"Don't you dare hit me, Dad. Touch me and I'll call the authorities and tell everyone you know. You're insane."

When she hears me say that, my mother starts. I point to her. "Look at her! She's killing herself with cigarettes. There's always one hanging out of her mouth. And you talk about a little weed?"

He's taken aback, surprised at my outburst and looks uncomprehendingly through the glass doors to the backyard.

"Weed! Grass, Dad! Rope, hooch, dope, pot, J, dooby, MaryJ - *whatever!*" I throw my arms up. "Marijuana!"

"Don't you shout at me, Missy!"

But I'm just getting started. I want nothing to do with this man or with the woman sitting on the couch. I stomp past him to Mom. "And you, you're one hell of a mother. You don't even try to stop him when he talks to me like that. He hits me, and you just watch!"

She looks at me as if I've turned into a zombie, but she's the one acting like one. I haven't heard her say a word since she's seen me.

Now she speaks for the first time, her words coming through a fog of bewilderment. "What has he done to your body?" She's not waiting for answers. "How could you let him do that? When did you start sleeping with boys, Jolie? And taking drugs? I hardly know my own daughter."

I can't hold back. "You don't know me at all! And I'm not your daughter! You're not my mother! And you're not my father! I hate you both!"

My eyes suddenly well up with tears. "If you two couldn't make a baby, I'm sorry, that's really too bad. But why did you have to adopt me?"

My mother looks like she'd been hit in the stomach with a cannonball and my father is horrified. "How dare you talk to us like that?" he says.

Maybe he's angry, but I've never been angrier. I'm going all the way.

"You don't care about me at all. If you did, you wouldn't say the things you do about me … or hit me! And you wouldn't talk to my friends like that!"

"Friend?" Dad bellows. "For Pete's sake, that boy is goddamned trash!"

"He's not trash! You don't know Rocky. He's a wonderful person."

"Don't be stupid. He's a goy. He's wonderful until he turns you in."

"Turns me in? For what?" I'm confused. *For the weed I said was mine?*

"For being Jewish." He throws it out instantly.

"What are you talking about? Turns me in for *being Jewish*? Turns me in to who?" When he doesn't answer, I repeat, "To who?"

I scour my mind but the only thing I can come up with is what he's alluded to so many times before. But it's so beyond ridiculous that even he can't be that insane.

"Are you that nuts?" I say. "Are talking about the Nazis?"

"You think the Nazis are gone?" he says. "You don't think there are

Nazis today? You don't think people are anti-Jewish anymore? Ah, come on. Don't be stupid, Missy. They hate us."

"Oh wow!" He is definitely, *totally* off his rocker. "I can't believe you're really saying this! You're insane!"

Fingers are moving like crazy in his pockets. He glances quickly at my mother, then says, "Yeah, I'm insane. No, I'm not insane. You're just stupid. You don't know. Thirty-seven Israelis in a bus were killed just yesterday. You ever heard of the PLO?"

"This is the United States!"

"They're killing us here too."

"Oh, wow! Really? Tell me where."

He glances at my mother again, then drops his head down as he answers, sullenly. "Everywhere. Every day."

His eyes turn back to rest on me, and his tone becomes more emphatic. "And they're passing laws against us Jews every day, too. They're killing us with laws. They say it's this or it's that, but they know where the Jews are and they're killing us – quietly – and no one bothers to look into it."

As bafflement takes root and fills me, he adds, "And your 'friend' is no different."

I stare at him. After a moment, I turn to my mother. "What's he talking about? Why don't you tell him he's wrong?"

She's stone-faced. "Because he's right."

I throw up my arms. "This is great! It's 1978. The blacks have won their civil rights. But, according to you two, Jewish people in the United States are discriminated against by the government *and being killed*? Whatever!"

I turn, ready to leave the room, but I realize I have more to say.

I gather my truth and confront Phil. "And, you're five hundred percent wrong. Rocky would never 'turn me in.' He cares about me. He's great … and for your information, he thinks I'm … " I can't continue this. I stop and hang my head.

It's sad but true: they'll never understand.

My father's voice is like a roar. "I don't want you seeing your Mr. Wonderful ever again. You hear?" He's waving his finger in my face.

"I'm going to see him, Phil."

He freezes and looks from side to side. "What – what's with this 'Phil'? Now I'm 'Phil'?"

"That's your name. You're not my father. I'm not going to call you that. You're Phil," I gesture to the couch, "and she's Stella."

He speaks with finality, emphasizing his words, poking his finger in my face with every word. "You're not to see that bum again. As long as you live under my roof, you go out with Jewish boys or you don't go out."

I turn and walk out. "I'm getting out of here."

Stella is sitting on my bed. I've dressed and started packing.

I figure I'll go to Nora's house and decide what to do from there. Her mom is cool. Carol won't even ask why I'm there.

"What are you doing?" Stella asks.

"I'm leaving."

"Where are you going?"

I'm not about to tell her where I'll be. "I don't know, but I'm not staying here."

"Are you pregnant, Jolie?" I just look at her, then throw up my hands and the nightgown I'm holding goes flying.

"Is it so bad that your parents care about you?" She says

I retrieve the nightgown, then continue bringing things out of my drawers and tossing them in my bag.

"You're not my parents. And if you cared about me at all, you wouldn't have treated my boyfriend like that. And Phil wouldn't hit me."

I hold a T-shirt in my hand for just a second and gaze at her before packing it. "And you wouldn't let him."

I throw some bras into the bag with a pair of jeans and a few more tops, a pair of shoes, and slap the dresser drawer shut.

"Jolie, we love you so much. If you had been our own child, we wouldn't love you any more than we already do." She stands and takes hold of my shoulders. "I won't let you go."

I pull away from her grasp. "Do you know how sick I am of

hearing that? Well, I'm not your child. You won't even tell me who my real parents are. You've – you've kidnapped me."

Stella gasps and covers her face with her palms. "Kidnapped you? My God, Jolie! You think I know who your parents are and won't tell you? You've asked me, so many times! And I've told you the truth. Sweetheart, I swear, it's the truth. I don't *know* who your real parents are!"

I give Stella a stone-faced look – I've heard this too many times before – then shove some toiletries into my bag.

"I swear on everything holy. I have no idea who they are."

I ignore her. I don't believe her; it's just not possible. She sinks onto the bed, her shoulders hunched over.

"Jolie, whatever happened to that little girl who used to kiss me all the time? We'd go to ballet class together, go shopping together. I used to go to all your friends' parties with you and you used to love me so much–"

I interrupt. "She grew up."

I see tears on Stella's face and something inside of me breaks a bit. I stop packing, but I don't go to her.

"I'm sorry. I don't mean to make you cry. And I'm sorry for what I said about you two not being able to make babies."

Of all the things I feel, frustration is in the lead.

"Maybe I'm just going through a phase. Or maybe, if I was the way you expected me to be, it would be easier, but I'm not.

"I was probably lucky that you adopted me, and I should be more grateful. But I feel like a stranger here. And I don't want to be hit anymore. I can't stay."

I zip up my bag. "I just don't see how you could let him do that to me."

I remember my watch. It's on the dresser. I take it but I'm too upset to strap it on, so I throw it in the pocket of the bag.

"Anyway, I think you may have adopted the wrong girl. I'm just not the daughter that you want. Nothing I do is good enough for you. Everything I do is wrong."

"Please, Jolie. Don't leave."

"It's just a matter of time before he'd kick me out anyway."

"Be fair, Jolie! We come home from a funeral and we see you with a strange boy in our backyard coloring your naked body. You're *both* naked and doing drugs. He's slept with you. We're supposed to welcome him with open arms?"

"No, he's supposed to slap me so hard my neck snaps and throw my boyfriend out. Yes! Yes, if he respects me and the guy is my boyfriend! What did he call him? A banana monkey? A spic? That's disgusting. And what did he call me?"

I'm ready to go.

"You don't love this boy." It's a question. She's looking at me waiting for an answer, but I don't give her one. I pick up my jacket.

She shakes her head and sighs deeply. "You're so young, and there's so much you don't know Jolie, so much I hope you never have to learn."

"If it means turning into an abusive bigot, I hope I never do."

With that, I leave Phil and Stella's house forever.

21

VALLEY GIRL

*a*s always, Nora is there for me.

I arrive at her house. Carol hugs me and asks if I'm hungry.

When Nora and I are alone in her bedroom, I tell her – for the first time – that Phil hit me. She comforts me. She's extremely upset and calls him a bully. But, she says, trying to be gentle, though he had no right to lay a hand on me, and though it was detestable for him to call Rocky names, she can understand that he and Stella would be upset by what they saw going on.

Again, I suspect that Nora doesn't really support my relationship with Rocky and it saddens me.

I call Rocky from Nora's house. He's surprised to hear that I've left home and keeps saying it's his fault. Though I tell him that's not true, he keeps apologizing, saying he's really sorry.

NightFlight's playing a gig tonight and it's time for him to get on the road. He will pick me up from Nora's house around noon tomorrow.

I see him and no one else matters.

He drives us to The Saloon on Melrose, a casual place with swinging saloon-style doors and sawdust on the floor. We take a corner table and order.

"Baby, you shouldn't have left home because of me," Rocky says. "You'd warned me about your dad, so I knew he's not cool. And why did you say it was *your* weed?"

I don't answer his question; the answer seems too obvious to me.

Our food comes. "I didn't leave only because of you, Rocky. I just couldn't stand them anymore. I've disowned them. They're not my parents."

"That whole thing wouldn't have happened if it wasn't for me," he says, calmly, before taking another bite of his burger. He chews and swallows. "I feel responsible."

He looks at me over his glasses. "You know, I lost my parents. Don't take them for granted."

"They're not my parents! I never knew my parents." I don't want to make this about feeling sorry for me, so I give him a tired smile.

He asks, "Did you really have to leave?"

I nod. "I was bound to leave, or they'd eventually kick me out."

"Baby, I know they're difficult. And I know they're not your parents. But these people raised you."

"So, now I'm raised. I don't want to be with them anymore.

"And you know something else? I don't think they even really like me. They only like me when I'm the way they want me to be. They loved it when I was a little girl who did whatever they wanted. And when I graduated at the top of my class. And when I was Senior Princess," I say, rolling my eyes. "But not unconditionally."

I put my hamburger down and sit back as the familiar wave of self-pity washes over me again.

"My real parents discarded me, and I'm not good enough for Phil and Stella, either." I'm itching to add that I think no one will ever love me, just so that Rocky will tell me that he does. But, like I said, I don't want to push the 'pity thing' and besides, I doubt that I can make Rocky say that.

From Rocky's questions, I sense that he doesn't really understand why I left home, though I want him to. It's important for him to. "Rocky, as soon as they got the first inkling of who I really am, they hated me. The way they treat me, the way they talk to me ... the way they think ... I just can't be around all that anymore.

"Dad says I should date only *Jewish boys*. Why? Cause *he* says so? I don't think so! I'm going to do what I want and not what he tells me to. I was raised Jewish, but how do I even know that my real parents weren't Catholics? or Muslim? or Buddhists?" I sigh.

"I'm glad I left. Maybe, I'm wrong. Maybe, I'm making a mistake and maybe I'll make a lot more mistakes. But I think I did the right thing. And this is my life, not theirs."

I'm glad to see Rocky's nodding now. "So, what happens next?" he asks. His hand reaches across the table to enclose mine in its warmth. "I mean, where do you go from here, Baby?"

I shrug. I try to sound light-hearted. "Don't know." It's time for me to think about what comes next.

"Change of plans, I guess. I certainly won't be going to Arizona State. I didn't really want to go there anyway. I won't be going to school in September. It looks like college will be on hold."

"What about a college here?"

I shake my head. "I can't afford school – tuition, books and all that. It'll have to wait.

"I'm going to have to get a job and work. I'll need money to pay for an apartment and money to live on. I can't stay with Nora forever. I have a little money saved in my bank account, but ... it's not much."

"Where will you live?" he asks.

I shrug and shake my head. The question overwhelms me. "I have no idea."

"Hmm," Rocky says. He taps his fingers as though giving the matter a lot of thought then looks up at me suddenly. There's a light in his eyes. "I just thought of something." Then he sulks back into his bench. "No."

"What?"

"Nah. You wouldn't want to."

"Tell me."

"Wait. I need a refill. Let me get the waiter's attention." It almost seems to me that he's purposely delaying his answer, putting it off to create suspense; and he's doing a good job.

He calls the waiter over, orders another Coke, and the server takes his empty glass away.

Then, "What was I saying? Oh, yeah, you wouldn't want to."

"Wouldn't want to *what* Rocky?"

"Well, okay, I'll tell you. You'll probably think it's a bad idea, but that's okay. It was just an idea."

"Yes?"

"I just thought, maybe …"

"Rocky, what?"

"Okay. I just thought that maybe, since you have to leave Nora and you have no place else to go and you need to save money …. maybe, if you want to – or if you think it would make it easier for you –" he pauses and smiles "you could live with me for a while – and Rico, of course."

I am absolutely thrilled! My heart is racing. I'm actually trembling. "What?"

"Well, I mean, you're homeless. Right?" I stare at him, my mouth hanging open. I nod. "And, I still feel that it *is* on account of me even though you say it's not. So, the least I can do is offer you a place to crash – at least until you can afford your own place."

"Rocky, you're asking me to move in with you?"

"Yeah, if you want. You're cool people."

"But I won't be in the way? I mean, you've got Rico, and your music, and the band, and –"

"And, I'll have you, too. You won't be in the way."

I jump up move to his side of the table to hug him but Rocky puts his hand up to stop me. "Hold on there. There's one condition."

I freeze. "What?"

"You get fat off my cooking and you're gone."

The waiter spills Rocky's drink as he rushes over to see why I'm screaming. When he gets to us, we're kissing.

I have no desire to run into Phil or Stella, so I return home only when I know Phil is at work and Stella's car is gone.

I quickly pack up what I can of the rest of my belongings, and stick a note on the refrigerator: "I'll call, J."

Homer is around the corner and he drives me to his home. I move in with Rocky and Rico.

I telephone home on the third day I'm at Rocky's to let them know I'm okay. Phil answers. He asks where I am. I tell him I'm with Rocky and he turns incredibly angry. Still, I tell him I'll stay in touch.

"As long as you're with that spic trash, you're not our daughter," he shouts before he hangs up. *I never was your daughter!*

I don't get to speak with Stella. I decide not to call again.

I celebrate my eighteenth birthday with Rocky, about two weeks after I move in. It's the first birthday I've spent away from Phil and Stella.

Rocky takes me to dinner at the little restaurant we ate at that first night and gives me the best gifts ever: a cassette tape of my singing "High on Love" with NightFlight and a small leather-bound notebook with a pen attached.

"Baby, this is for lyrics," he says handing me the book. "I want you to keep it with you always, wherever you go: in the car, sleeping, at work – keep it nearby. Even when you're in the shower. Whenever the words come to you, Pop!" He flicks his finger inside his mouth to create the sound, "you write them down."

Two weeks later, in mid-September, I start a job and three classes at Santa Monica City College. I hostess at Sierra's, a high-end restaurant on Ventura Boulevard. I work full time on days I have no class and work after class on days that I do.

When Rocky first sees me dressed for work in heels and stockings, he whistles. "Looking' hot, Baby J!" I love it.

I begin to drive to school, back and forth over the hill three days a week. I could take the freeway, but I enjoy the drive through the canyon, up Beverly Glen to Mulholland and down Benedict Canyon to Sunset Boulevard then making my way south to Pico Boulevard and west to the campus. It's a scenic drive and I'm familiar with the curving canyon roads so I maneuver them easily.

Tall telephone poles stretch up toward the sky and line the street, joined together by thick black wires running across them. Mulholland, the narrow, winding road at the top of the hill is fenced off from the steep drop of the canyon by a short railing that strangely appears and disappears then appears again at arbitrary spots, like so many twisted strands of metal spaghetti.

There are posted signs warning that the area – like so many others in the city – is prone to brush fire. Other signs warn drivers to be on the lookout for deer and, though I have seen them in the brush, I have yet to see any try to cross the road.

The changing sunlight of early autumn begins to change the foliage from greens to oranges; later it will turn to golds and browns. Overhead, the branches of the weeping willow trees come together to form arches above me. No matter how many times I take the same drive, there's always something new to see.

A variety of flowers appear and lend color with every turn of the winding road. Purple and orange morning glories climb up walls and grow wild everywhere. There's a lot of bougainvillea, most of it a rich cranberry color, with bits of white and shades of pink. Banana trees seem to lift their heads among the plentiful white and pink oleander bushes. Every now and then a single daring stem of a dramatic scarlet flower shoots out of the ground as if to say, "I'm here, too! Don't forget me!"

As I make my way to the Westside in the mornings, I plan my day, perhaps review for an exam, or simply daydream. I'm always more anxious on the afternoon drive back to the Valley, filled with the anticipation of seeing Rocky again.

Rocky. The more time I spend with him, the deeper my feelings for him grow. I've just never felt so ... *safe* with anyone.

As amazing as it is, Rocky seems to accept the real me – me as I truly am. In fact, he actually makes me feel valuable. He's so tender and mellow and loving.

And yet ... and yet, I still haven't told him I love him. I'm just too scared ... afraid it won't last. I'm afraid that he'll leave me; get bored with me; grow tired of my looks; tire of having me around; find out I'm not as smart as he thought; that I won't be able to write any more lyrics he'll like; or, that he'll meet someone else and be unfaithful … a thousand reasons why he'll leave me.

I am so afraid he'll abandon me that though my feelings for him continue to deepen, my ability to express them remains futile.

I want to share everything with him. I share as much as I can, and that includes his love for Rico. I hope his younger brother doesn't resent me for getting in the way of the two of them.

I used to be really embarrassed knowing that Little Brother was in the house when Rocky and I made love, but I got over that. Besides, Rico is hardly ever home. When he is, he sleeps into the late morning or early afternoon, then finds his way into the kitchen where he makes himself a cup of coffee and grabs some bread. Rocky and I – if we're home – join him, and I listen as the brothers talk about their past and future gigs and share news about mutual friends.

I long to share their bond. This is the closest thing I've had to a feeling of family.

When I'm not at school or at the restaurant I'm with Rocky. I go to NightFlight rehearsals with him and take along a textbook so I can read until the band is ready to work on our song. Rocky and I continue to work on it when we're alone, too, perfecting it. I'd never realized how much joy there is in two people creating something together.

As NightFlight is gearing up for rehearsal this evening, Rocky informs us that on their next gig I'll be singing our song on stage. I'm horrified! I've been telling Rocky I can't sing on stage, that I'm as shy as a kitten in public, but he just laughs every time.

"You're a good singer. I'll be with you. You'll be fine, Baby J."

At some point, I realize Rocky won't take no for an answer, so I resolve to do my best and make him proud. He's is coaching me. He's taught me to bring my voice up from my diaphragm, and not my throat or chest. He's encouraging me constantly.

I remind myself of the "A" I got on the scene I did with Paul in Drama class. I repeatedly tell myself that I can do this! I'm determined to break through my stage fright and get through the performance without breaking down.

Then the night arrives and I'm about to go onstage.

The band's played well so far. People like them. All my friends are here, and everyone is cheering me on.

Until this minute I've done my best because I want to make Rocky proud, but I've realized that I owe it to myself to do well, too. I want our song to shine; and it would be so cool to get past my stage fright. It's time for me to sing.

Wonder of wonders, I do fine. I sing the entire song without a hitch and when we're done, it's great to hear the applause. It's a wonderfully exciting night.

I sing two more times that weekend and by Sunday night, I *enjoy* being on stage with Rocky and the band.

22

PASSION BURNS THE
HOUSE DOWN

*C*lasses at Santa Monica are meant to cover basic, general requirements for transfer to a state college or university.

I'm hoping to do that. For the language requirement, I've enrolled in a Spanish class so I can converse with Rocky and Rico in their native tongue.

On my break today before Spanish class, I go to the patio to grab a quick meal. It's a clear October day, and I'm sitting at one of the round white tables, eating a chicken burrito and enjoying the lovely weather, my Spanish book propped open. I'm reviewing today's lesson. A shadow falls over the table.

———

"Hi, mind if I join you?"

I look up. Against the glare of the sun, I see a thin boy standing by the vacant chair to my right, carrying a tray. He wears glasses and his wavy brown hair is combed into a side part. I avert my eyes from the sun's glare, but not before I notice that a couple of tables nearby are empty. I turn my focus back to my Spanish book and shrug.

He sets his tray on the table and puts down his red backpack. The tray is holding a burger, fries and a drink. I sneak another peek at him while he's settling down. His arms are super thin. His red and white checked short-sleeved shirt is perfectly pressed. His lips are long, and his ears are large. He gestures to my book.

"Spanish," he says. "You're in my class. Starts at 1:30."

"I'm studying." I'm hoping he'll be quiet; but that's not happening.

"I've been watching you," he says. I don't like the sound of that. I look up at him. "Yeah, you're gorgeous." It's obvious that the state meant is not intended to be a compliment. It's like he's just stating a dry fact and one he's not happy about. "But I guess you know that."

The offhanded way he says that sounds almost mean. I don't thank him. I don't respond or change my expression. I just turn back to my book.

"You probably hear that from a lot of guys," he continues, taking hold of his hamburger. "You probably get asked out a lot, too."

Is he for real? Finished with my burrito, I get up and toss the wrapper in the nearby garbage can. I return to the table and begin to gather my things. "I have a boyfriend," I say.

He takes a huge bit out of his burger and gazes up at me. "You look so much like her," he says, dreamily. "You're younger. But you could be her daughter."

I don't care who I look like, and I have no intention of asking him.

He takes a sip of his drink and as I'm walking away, he drops the rest of the hamburger on the tray and says, "I sure hope you're not a home-wrecker." Then he takes his glasses off, lifts his hands up to his eyes and wipes them. *He's crying!*

"Are you okay?" I ask. *Shit!* I can't believe this! The clock on patio wall shows it's about twenty minutes before class starts. His arm is covering his eyes and he emits a tiny sob.

"Listen," I say, as if I've made him cry, "I'm not a home wrecker. I told you, I have a boyfriend."

His arm comes away. He's still tearing. "I know," he says. "I'm sorry. I really am. It's just that … " he's sobbing now.

Someone burned this guy badly. "Was it your girlfriend?" I ask.

He laughs. "I wish it were that simple. No." He shoots me a piercing look. Behind his lenses his enlarged eyes are so sad.

Then he makes a ghoulish laugh. "You want to hear a story?" He asks.

I check the clock on the patio wall. I have some time, and we both need to get moving soon. "Sure." I put my books back down on the table and sit down.

Between sobs, he wipes his eyes with a napkin and puts his glasses back on. "You probably won't believe it."

"We'll see," I say.

"Okay. But you won't."

He begins. "Okay. Here's the thing. I used to be super close to my dad. He's an accountant, a successful CPA. He used to be a champion skater. He still loves it. Now he coaches skaters who compete. I also have a brother. He's about six years older. My dad's always been real close to both of us." He chuckles. "He's almost been like another brother." This seems to make him happy and also miserable. "I mean we always do – or we always did – everything together: fishing, camping – and, yeah, he taught us to skate."

It sounds like heaven to me. I can't imagine why he's crying.

I say, "You're lucky to have a relationship like that with your father." I'm thinking, maybe the dude died?

It looks like he's about to start crying again, but he stops himself and continues. "My parents have been married for over twenty-five years. They live Las Vegas; that's where I'm from. And they've always been pretty happy." He swallows, takes a breath, sighs, and then continues.

"Anyway, like I said, Dad became a skating coach. Dad was training a woman in Colorado. She paid him a lot to fly to Aspen and coach her for a state-wide skating competition up there. He'd go there every few weeks, first for a day and then, when the competition drew closer, maybe two or three days."

I can't imagine where this is leading. I don't interrupt. I wait.

"Anyway, she won the competition."

"Great!" I say, wondering where there's room for sadness in all this. Yet, he is miserable.

"Yeah, sure. The night she won, she insisted on taking him out to an expensive dinner to celebrate."

149

My suspicions are aroused. "How old is this woman?"

He eyes me. "Early fifties. Dad's in his fifties, too. But she looks a hell of a lot younger! She's real pretty. Gorgeous – like you."

"So, what happened?" I ask, with a hint now of what might be coming.

He looks so high up that his head falls back. "Ah! What happened." He's turning his head this way and that as though to relax his neck.

He sighs again and continues. "That night at dinner, they drank too much, or at least Dad did – I know he's not a drinker. Afterwards, she invited him to her hotel room and … they had … they … they started an affair." He pauses and throws his jaw forward as if he's determined to accept that fact without tears.

"Afterwards, he went back to Colorado a few times. Sometimes they met in Vegas. She has a second home there. I think it went on for about four or five months."

I want to ask him how he knows all the details about his father's affair. They can't be *that* close.

"They both talked about their children. She has a daughter who used to be a showgirl in Vegas. My Dad told her about me and my brother. My brother Bob's a successful investment advisor who works for a firm in Vegas. She told Dad she wanted to talk to my brother about making some financial decisions and Dad – I don't know what the hell he was thinking, maybe he was drunk out of his mind then, too – he gave her Bob's card."

Did this woman come on to his brother? *Oh, yuk!*

"She actually made an appointment with Bob. She went to see him. She told him that someone had referred her to him but didn't specify who. She showed him a picture of her daughter."

He looks at me and sighs, yet again. "Bobby's always been a fool for pretty girls. He's dated lots of pretty ones. He's always especially loved showgirls, so he said he was open to meeting her."

Okay, I guess they hooked up. *But why is he so miserable? And who's the home wrecker?* "Bob was married?" I ask.

He slowly shakes his head. "Not then."

"Okay, go on."

"My dad's … friend … liked Bob. In fact, she liked him so much that when he agreed to meet her daughter, she invited him to her house in Vegas so they could meet there. Bobby went to her house, met her daughter, and went crazy for her.

"They started dating. When she told my father that their children were dating, he thought nothing of it. He figured it would blow off, you know, end soon. But it didn't."

I sense that he's getting to the bottom line. In the back of my mind, I know we'll need to leave for class soon, but I want to hear the rest of this story.

"Well, next thing, Bobby invites Mom and Dad and me to dinner at Caesar's Palace. When we get there, Bobby's there, with this woman's daughter, Clara. And this woman is there too, with her husband. Bobby and Clara announce they're engagement."

"Oh, no!" I say.

"Oh, yes!"

"But your father-"

"Yeah, my father. It was a surprise to him, too, and he immediately told the woman they had to break it off. He typed up a letter to her and mailed it. No way was he having an affair with his son's mother-in-law. "

"Of course!"

"Meanwhile, the woman's husband started calling my dad."

"He found out?"

"Hell! Turns out he knew all along! The old man's in his late eighties, probably almost ninety years old. He knew from the start!

"He called to tell Dad he absolutely had to continue seeing his wife – and keep having sex with her. He told him he loved his wife very much and he could give her everything she wanted, except sex. He was sure his wife loved him; but she was highly sexual and needed to have sex and she enjoyed my father, so Dad had to continue the affair."

"Oh, my God! How weird!"

"Dad said he wouldn't, that it had been a mistake from the start, the only time in his life he'd been unfaithful to my mom, and they had to stop. But the old guy wouldn't hear of it and he wouldn't leave Dad alone. He kept calling.

"Dad would say he was going out of town, he'd say he was sick, scheduled for surgery … but the guy wouldn't go away. Nothing he said made the guy stop calling. Meanwhile, Bobby and Clara got married. It was a small wedding. That was a year ago. Then Mom found out."

"Oh, my God. What happened?" I ask.

He takes a deep, deep breath and mutters, "Oh God!" and then goes on. He speaks slowly and deliberately as though trying to keep himself from bouncing off the walls or pulling his hair out.

"Clara was six months pregnant when the shit hit the fan. Mom saw a copy of the letter he'd sent. Her husband mailed it to the house. She started divorce proceedings.

"My father apologized. He begged her to stay with him. They'd been married for so long! Dad swore that he'd never been unfaithful before. He begged my mom to forgive him, but she wouldn't.

"So, after all those years together, they divorced. She said she wants absolutely nothing to do with him ever again, and that he's despicable – Dad said she'd used that word.

"But all that time, Mom never said a word to Bob or me about what any of what he'd done. Bob and I knew nothing about their affair. Nothing."

I've never heard anything like this. He's still talking.

"Dad insisted on giving Mom the house, his BMW, and money every month, so she won't have to work.

"Meanwhile, this joker is still calling Dad. Dad refuses to see the woman again no matter what he says. Then her husband tells Dad that, if he doesn't continue sleeping with his wife, he's going to tell me and Bobby about the affair."

"*He* told you?"

"No." He pauses. "Dad did. He said he wanted us to hear it from his own mouth. That way he could stop the affair and her husband couldn't threaten him with anything.

"The day he told Bobby was the day their baby was born." He swallows hard and shakes his head ever so sadly.

"Bobby doesn't talk to him anymore. He won't see him, and he won't take his calls. I don't know that I blame him. Then, two days ago

Dad came here to tell me. He took me to lunch and told me the whole story. That's when I found out why my parents broke up."

"Wow!" I say. "That's a sad story."

"Yeah. Dad's a mess. He's changed a lot.

"You know, he raised us saying we had to have values, that we had to be honest, never do anything we'd be ashamed of if the world found out, and that family is sacred." He's crying again.

"He broke every one of the rules he taught us. And when I asked him *why* he did it, why he had an affair, why he started seeing her and why he continued it after that first night, you know what he said?" I'm already shaking my head. "One word." He puts his index finger up, high up as though demanding justice from the world. "Just one fucking word: *Passion!*" He looks at me with misery in his eyes. *"Passion!"*

People around us are moving now, heading into the various school buildings. It's time to head for Spanish class. As we enter class together, he says, "Thanks for listening." I ask his name. "Steve," he says. I'm about to tell him my name but he stops me. "I know, you're Jolie."

All during Spanish, I barely hear the teacher. My mind is stuck on the amazing story I've just heard. If it weren't for his father's relationship with the skater, his son wouldn't have met and married the girl of his dreams.

Had that really been the only affair Steve's father had ever had? What would have happened if his wife hadn't never seen the letter he'd written?

But she did. And Steve's father lost his wife, his relationship with both his son, his money and –hell! He lost everything he had! Steve and his brother lost their father. The repercussions of the affair were incredibly hurtful to the entire family.

His dad had been playing with fire and he'd gotten burned. Badly burned. They all had.

Passion! Passion burns!

All at once I hear a man screaming it, an electric guitar and drums playing loudly. *Passion burns!* I start to write.

> *Passion burns! Passion burns!*
> *Passion burned my house down.*
> *Passion burns!*
> *Passion burned my house down.*
>
> *Burned down all the rules*
> *Made me act the fool*
> *Then it burned my house down.*
>
> *Lost my wife and kids.*
> *Then I lost myself.*
> *My life went up in flames*
> *Passion burned my house down.*
>
> *Passion burns! Passion burns!*
> *Passion burned my house down.*
> *Passion burns!*
> *Passion burned my house down.*
> *Charred and burned my life down.*

All the way home my head throbs with the song. I hear drums, loud and unrelenting.

Passion burns! /Passion burned my house down!

It is so different than anything I'd ever written and yet it somehow wrote itself.

I can't wait to share it with Rocky. Hopefully, he'll like it. At least sharing it with him might ease the loud screaming, the thunderous drums and steel guitar playing in my head.

When I finally mimic what I hear in my head for him, Rocky adjusts his glasses on his nose and smiles.

"Well?" I ask.

"You're taking us into heavy metal, Baby. Def Leppard, Black Sabbath."

"That's what I hear. Torture."

"It's good. But what made you write it?"

I kiss him and smile. "Let me take a quick shower and I'll tell you the story."

Making music with Rocky is pure excitement. Combining his talent with my words and ideas, having his attention, winning his approval, the sheer satisfaction of knowing I'm his partner in actually writing a song and hearing it evolve, is heaven.

I recall that when we met Rocky said he'd never before had a girlfriend who was able to share his music with him and here I am, actually part of his band!

We're on our way home from our next rehearsal when I'm skating — pardon the pun — on thin ice.

"What would you say if I told you I might be falling in love with you?" I ask him.

Rocky smiles at the road ahead. "Why would you say something like that, Baby J?"

"I don't know. Maybe it just slipped out. Maybe because I feel like I finally belong with someone … or to someone." Rocky's looking at me, his head cocked questioningly.

"Why are you looking at me like that?" I ask. "You know I've never felt connected to anyone before you," I say. What I mean is, *I've never felt loved and accepted for what I really am by anyone before you*. But I don't say that.

"I remember walking into Marissa's new home before they'd actually moved in. I was really young. There was a new stove standing in the living room with all the tags still on it and I asked my mom why Marissa's parents had put it there instead of the kitchen like our house. I've always felt like that stove, like I'm in the wrong place. I don't know. I just don't know.

"I don't know why my parents abandoned me. You make me feel like someone really cares about me … and I love that."

"You've said that before, Baby J. But what about Nora? You two

155

have been friends for years. Don't you feel connected to her? You've told me she's a cool friend. She cares about you, no?"

I nod. "I do feel connected to Nora and yes, she does care about me. She's the best friend in the whole world and I'm really lucky to have her in my life. But I'm not sure how close we'll stay now that Jonah is so much a part of her life."

"I want to add, *and you've become such a big part of mine*, but instead, I say "She's like a sister to me. But even the closest of sisters have limitations."

I don't add that I'm pretty sure Nora doesn't totally accept Rocky, or that he's the love of my life.

I push myself to say, "You make me feel like I'm able to love."

"Well, that's good, cause I love you, too, Baby J."

He's said those words so easily! And he's said them to me! I feel my cheeks flush, my eyes well up with tears.

Rocky loves me! Oh, thank you, God! Everything is wonderful!

Now there's no holding back on my part. I let myself fly and I soar to new heights of ecstasy.

Rocky has touched my very core.

23

OUT OF THE BAG

*R*ocky is tapped by the studio to play keyboard for a new album on the Polar label.

The album's producer, Bob Seidman, has hit a wall in a stellar career, and the pressure is on him to make this album a winner.

The artist, a singer named Smokey Ray, is a newcomer who emerged on the music scene more than a year ago with a smash single, then came out with a lackluster album and is just about forgotten.

They're both hoping this album will revive their star status and make the singer, Smokey Ray, a major force in the industry.

The call that comes to Rocky in late October asking him to play keyboard for the album is most welcomed, not only because of the money, but also because it's a great compliment to his musical ability; there is no margin for error in making this record.

NightFlight has rehearsed only once since he got the job, and Rocky has stopped booking new gigs for his band. There's a rush to finish the album. It's to be completed two weeks before Christmas.

The first week or so, the tempo of work at the studio is unhurried but as October ends, and November begins, the atmosphere there is more hectic and it is becoming increasingly frantic with every passing day.

Rocky is at the studio.

I'm in the kitchen setting out some cheese and crackers and slicing some fruit for lunch when Rico comes in. He's wearing bright red boxer shorts with scattered green clovers and a wife-beater. His uncombed hair looks like a monster bramble bush. He's playing with the silver cross that hangs on a chain around his neck; he does that a lot.

"Hi, Rico. You're up early this afternoon. How're you doing?"

"Tired." He looks tired. He rubs his eyes. "Not much time. Need to make tracks. I've got an appointment with a new band member."

He checks to make sure the kettle has water in it then turns on the stove. He brings out the jar of instant coffee, leans against the counter and looks at me.

"So, how are you and big brother doing?"

I sit at the kitchen table and start to eat. "Good. Really good. Things are *tight.*" He doesn't realize I'm teasing him, mimicking one of his favorite expressions.

"Cool," he says, spooning some coffee some into a mug. "Yeah. So, like, Rock Man and you are tight. That's cool. I like you. You're good people."

I know he's being sincere. "Thanks. I like you too."

"Yeah." He opens the refrigerator door. He has two pieces of white bread in one hand and a bottle of milk in the other. He kicks the refrigerator door closed and it's almost like he's speaking to himself. "It's good to see big brother bounce back and stay," he says nodding.

"Bounce back from what?" Had Rocky just ended a hurtful relationship when I met him?

The kettle whistles and he pours the boiling water into his cup. "The accident." He says it like it doesn't need to be said. I'm initially too surprised to react.

He tops off his mug with some milk.

As he passes me to sit at the small table, I smell last night's weed still clinging to him, mixing with the aroma of coffee. He swings one leg over a chair and joins me at the table, holding the two slices of bread and slapping the mug down in front of him, harder than he needs to.

I watch him fill his mouth with white bread and wash it down with a swig of coffee. "The accident?" He doesn't answer me. Instead, he takes another bite of the white bread and another swig of coffee. "*What* accident, Rico?"

"With his bike." Again, that casual tone, as though we both already know the answer.

"You mean a motorcycle?" I say.

"Yeah."

"He has a motorcycle?"

"It was wiped out in the accident," he says.

I put down my fork. "When was that?" I try to make it sound like it's slipped my mind.

He shrugs. "Two and a half, three years ago."

He's holding the last bit of bread crust, looking at me as if he's beginning to realize that he doesn't know what to make of my questions.

"You don't know?" he asks.

My heart skips a beat. "What happened, Rico?"

"He smashed into a car?" He says this and nods, hoping to jar my memory. He waits for me to remember, for things to click into place.

"Was it his fault?" I ask.

"Yeah." It's dawning on him that I don't know about the accident. "He hasn't told you?"

While he's registering disbelief that Rocky hasn't told me, I'm registering, *What the hell?*

"Was he hurt?" I ask.

"Yeah, he was hurt! He really hasn't told you?"

"Tell me, how bad was he hurt?"

He scoffs. "He was pretty badly fucked up for a while. He had a concussion and a small but nasty cut here," Rico points to the crown of his head. When he sees the fear on my face, he adds, "He got off easy; the other guy was a hell of a lot more fucked up bad."

I'm suddenly scared, chilled to the bone. Rocky hasn't said a word about any of this to me.

"My God! Was Rocky speeding?"

Rico backpedals. "Hey, listen, if The Rock Man hasn't told you, it's not my place. Ask him."

"You said it was his fault."

Rico jumps off his seat like it's electrocuted. He's walking away, even leaving his coffee unfinished. "I gotta go, gotta make tracks."

"*Rico!*" He doesn't respond, doesn't even slow down his pace. I get up and chase after him. "Rico, what happened?" He's entered the hallway, but I block his way.

"Was Rocky speeding? Was he high?"

Rico scratches his head. "Look, Jo. Don't hassle me. Ask the Rock Man."

"You started something, why won't you tell me?"

"Look, you two are tight … " he shifts his feet. He rubs the back of his neck and turns his head this way and that. "I thought you're tight. I figured he'd told you. My mistake."

"Told me what? Rico, talk to me. What do I need to know? Is there something I need to know?"

Rico stretches his neck up and back then starts rubbing it again. "The accident?" He smirks and bites his lip. "It happened cause The Rock Man has a uh…" he drops his hand, sighs and looks down. "A condition. A medical problem."

The world is falling out of orbit. "What … medical problem?"

Rico has gone too far to back off now. He has to tell me what I want to know. I don't care how unhappy he is about it.

He's got his hands at his hips and he's shifting his weight from one foot to the other, and back.

"Shit, man! The Rock Man has this problem … "

"Yes?"

"Leave me alone! Fuck! Ask him!"

"I'm asking you! What problem, Rico?"

He's looking up again. "It's only when he drinks."

"Drinks?"

"Liquor."

"*What's only when he drinks?*" I can't stand his reluctance.

"He … sometimes … he kind of …"

"Yes?"

"He sort of … shit!" He looks at me.

I stand my ground, arms folded, wanting – demanding – more information. And the more Rico stalls, the more frightened I'm becoming, surer with ever word he doesn't want to say, that it's really bad.

Rico scratches his head with both hands and rolls his eyes. "Oh, Jeez. Fuck this!" He sighs. "He really hasn't told you *anything*."

"Tell me!"

"Okay, well, look. Here's the thing. It's really nothing. No biggie."

"Tell-me-Rico! *Now!*"

"Okay! Damn it! He just forgets sometimes. That's all. He kind of goes blank, passes out. He gets fucked up, okay? He blanks out, becomes, like, unconscious for a second, and then doesn't remember anything."

"*Oh, my God! Rico! Rocky!*"

"Okay, so now you know! Shit, Jolie, look, if The Rock Man hasn't told you, then forget it. Okay? Just forget it. Really. I to gotta go."

"Does weed do it?"

He passes me and answers with his back moving away. "No, only liquor. Hard stuff. And he doesn't touch that shit anymore."

He turns around and faces me. "The doctors called it *petite mal epilepsy*," he chortles.

"Fuckin' French name. Fancy fuckin' French name for what The Rock's got. Anyway, Jo, it's the fuckin' booze! You know, whiskey, vodka, shit like that. Weed's cool." He sees the look on my face.

"Look, Jo, no worries. Don't look so blue! It's not a big fucking deal so long as he stays cool and doesn't drink. I've really gotta get moving now."

"Not a big deal? He blacks out! He had an accident! A *major* accident and hurt someone!"

"Well, yeah, it's in the past," Rico says, arms up in the air, resuming his walk down the hall. "And he's still here."

"Why hasn't he told me, Rico?"

"Who knows?"

At the threshold of his room, he turns to me one last time. "Listen, be cool, huh? Don't tell big bro I said anything, okay? I shouldn't have told you. It's not my business what you guys talk about … what he does or doesn't tell you. I don't want him to think I ratted on him – that's definitely not cool."

"Yeah," I nod as he closes his door.

I stand in the hallway, trying to digest what Rico has just told me. Rocky has epilepsy. He's so mellow, so calm and confident, so sure of himself. Strong as a tree!

Petite mal epilepsy – that's what Rico said. It's hard to picture Rocky passing out from just a drink.

Come to think of it, I've only seen Rocky drink alcohol once and that was wine, red wine, a glass he ordered after we'd left Gazzari's, and he'd shared it with me.

"Rico said it is only the hard stuff, like whiskey and vodka; I don't think it includes wine.

Rocky's never mentioned an accident or a medical condition to me and I've never noticed any scars anywhere on his body. But I don't doubt Rico. I'll just have to accept it and deal with it.

But why hasn't Rocky told me?

Here I am all this time assuming that Rocky feels as close to me as I do to him, that he's as trusting of me as I am of him, that – as Rico says – we're tight. But I'm wrong.

It may be true that I haven't told Rocky every little fact about my past, but he certainly knows all about my skeletons, all the important stuff.

Of course, I don't have of epilepsy. If I had, I'm not sure I'd want to talk about it, and knowing he's hurt someone else badly must be really hard, too.

And the diagnosis must be painful for him. I get that. I get that he's not anxious to talk about either.

But I love and trust him so much … if it were me, I'd want to tell him. I'd want him to know.

Maybe he's just waiting for the right time to tell me. That must be it. I'll wait. I'm sure Rocky will tell me in his own time. Besides, I really have no choice. I can't betray Rico.

November unfolds.

Studio sessions become longer and longer, and Rocky gets home later and later.

Cocaine appears at the studio to make it easier for the musicians keep up with the grueling schedule. Rocky is snorting, then he comes home and smokes weed every night just to come down from the coke. He's smoking more and more, and I can only guess at how much coke is going up his nose at the studio. I wait, wishing this stupid recording job would end so that Rocky stops snorting coke.

I see how it's changing him, and I don't like the changes.

"Hey, Rock Man, what's happening?" Rico asks. "Is the thing almost done?"

We three are in the kitchen this Sunday. Since Rocky's recording job began, it's rare for both Rocky and Rico to be home and awake at the same time.

"Nah, the cat can't sing worth shit," Rocky says.

"Yeah, well, bro, you must be doing mountains of snow, cause you're going through my stash of gunja faster than I can get the shit."

So! I'm not the only one watching. Rico's got eyes, too, and he's also registered how much Rocky must be taking up his nose and seeing the bags under his brother's eyes.

"You want me to pay you for it?" Rocky asks.

Rico ignores him. Rico must also notice that his big brother is becoming increasingly irritable and short-tempered.

"Yeah, Rocky, you're overdoing the coke, aren't you?" I ask sweetly.

He shrugs. "I've got to stay on top of it, Baby J. We'll be taking it up a few notches. They want it in the bag by Christmas."

"Of course, 'they want,' man," Rico says. "First they wanted it done two weeks *before* Christmas. You know it's costing them money every day you guys are in there. But can they have what they want?"

"Ask me? No way in hell," Rocky answers, "but it's their party. They're paying for it. I get paid double beyond the fifteenth."

"And a free coke habit," Rico murmurs.

The album is progressing much slower than expected and we're all paying for that fact. Rocky is barely sleeping. He's spending almost all his time at the studio. There's still a long way to go.

"Rocky, I wish you'd stop doing so much coke," I say, days later.

He isn't interested. "No way. Can't cut down right now, Baby J."

And a few days after that, "Rocky, I can't wait until this job is over. I hate it. I wish you'd stop the coke now."

"Don't nag me, Baby."

As usual these days, I'm asleep when he gets home, but tonight he knocks something over when he enters the bedroom, and the noise wakes me up. When he gets into bed, alarms go off in me as I realize he smells of alcohol.

"Have you been drinking?" I ask.

"I had a shot of vodka. One of the guys brought in a bottle."

He casually volunteers the information and falls asleep. I lie in the darkness, a solid wall of fear between us. I'm scared all the time now. Rico's been out of town for four days and will be gone for another two.

I open the freezer to get some ice cream and there's a bottle of Smirnoff vodka sharing the shelf with a quart of Dryer's chocolate ice cream. I shut the freezer door and fall back against it as though I've just seen a monster inside, and in fact, I have. I'm beside myself all day.

When Rocky comes home, well past midnight, I'm sitting at the dining room table in front of an open textbook pretending to study.

Rocky comes up behind me and kisses my head. "Baby J, it's late. You have class tomorrow. How come you're up?"

"I have an exam."

I stand and embrace him, kiss him, God help me, just to know if he's been drinking. His skin is cool and clammy but I'm relieved that he doesn't smell of alcohol. I saddle up against him.

"And," I add, "I want to give you some loving, baby. It's been a while."

We both know our sex life has taken a definite plunge as the recording job has become increasingly stressful.

Most nights, I'm asleep when Rocky gets home, and he never wakes me. On weekends, or the odd night when we do indulge, the effect of the stress, the long hours, the exhaustion, the cocaine, the weed, and now the alcohol, have taken a toll — on his body's physical endurance, his attention span, his patience, and unfortunately, his sexual reaction to me.

Slithering against him, I need to feel his body respond.

"Looks like you're finished studying," he says playfully.

"The A is in the bag." I take his hand and start to lead him into the bedroom. He pulls away.

"Get into bed, I'll be right there," he says, heading to the kitchen.

"I'll come with you," I say. "I'm thirsty."

As I open the refrigerator door and take out the orange juice, Rocky opens the freezer door and takes out the Smirnoff.

"I saw that bottle," I say, my throat tight. "You're drinking vodka now?"

Rocky shrugs. "A shot helps me crash off the coke."

I want to punch him. I want to strangle him. I want to scream. But I can only watch as he opens the bottle and pours some vodka into a glass and then downs it.

The lump in my throat is so big I can't swallow. I turn and pour the juice into the sink.

"Come on, Baby," he says. "Let's go to bed."

Will he black out? If he does, what should I do?

Naked under the covers, my stomach knots in anxiety. I cradle myself into Rocky's arms, craving the protection I've always felt there. I so need to be reassured of our mutual love. I need to know that Rocky will always be there.

Determined to defeat the enemy, I move on top of him and kiss the mouth that tastes of vodka, then move from his lips to his neck. Rocky embraces me, holding me close. The feel of the stubble on his chin, the warmth of his skin and the feel of hairy places I know so well, comfort me. He kisses me, stroking my hair and casually grazing my breasts.

Soon I'm turned on. I want him. I adjust myself and spread my legs, wanting him as much as I ever have. The moment before he enters me is always incredibly arousing as my body prepares to welcome his. I wait … and wait.

"I'm not hard, Baby J."

I feel my blood drain. I fall back on the bed, drained. This is a first for me. Rocky is spread-eagled on his bed, his arm over his brows. I take hold of his dick and gently stroke it. I'm praying it will be hard in seconds; it isn't.

"Sorry, Baby J. It's no good."

Wordlessly, I slide down and put my lips around that part of Rocky I know so well, amazed at how lifeless, cold and small it feels. I stay there, working it with my lips and tongue, trying to bring it to life. I cannot let it die. But nothing I do creates even the shadow of an erection. It is as though his dick will never again be what it once was and wants only to be left alone.

Rocky coaxes me back up to him. "It's not you, Baby, it's me. I'm sorry. Let's just leave it."

Leave it? He's holding me against him. "You're just tired, Rocky," I say.

Leave it? I feel as cold and as useless as Rocky's manhood.

Soon he's asleep, but I lay there, a mess of emotions I'm unable to hide from as long as I'm awake.

Leave it? This is our passion he's talking about! Our lovemaking! Not only have I failed to win Rocky's trust, I can't even excite him! And I have no idea how to get him to stop drinking.

Soon Rocky is snoring. I switch the nightstand light on and slowly draw back the blanket and the sheet. I want to examine Rocky's sleeping body. I'll find the scars I've somehow missed, some sign of the injuries he suffered in the accident, anything that I can point to and ask him about. I find nothing.

I gently probe his scalp as I feel for the scar Rico spoke of. I comb his thick hair with my fingers and find nothing.

Was Rico wrong? Was he lying? I'm certain he was being truthful.

I have no idea what to do.

24
TARNISHED GOLD

I am crazy with fear.

Rocky has started drinking regularly now before heading home.

I've come really close to confronting him about the accident and his medical problem several times. I know Rico's fear that Rocky would be angry with him for having told me is, in the long run, less important than getting to the truth.

Yet every time I'm about to say something to him, I imagine how much better it would be for him to tell me, and so, though my frustration level is high, I silently wait.

I consult my best friend. "How can I get him to stop drinking, Nora? How do I get him to tell me? What would you do?"

"I don't know. Maybe you should speak with a professional, Jo," Nora answers. "Too bad you can't tell some kind of a counselor – you know, like a psychologist – about it."

"That's a great idea!" I say. "Why *can't* I?"

Nora shrugs. "I don't know. If you tell them about the drugs, they might have to report Rocky and he'd be busted."

"I almost want them to bust him. That would be the end of the coke. He only drinks to come down off the coke, so no coke, no vodka.

Besides, I won't have to give them Rocky's name. I'll just ask the counselor to help *me* figure out what to do, so *I'll* be the patient."

I call Paul and ask about his therapist. "You like your shrink, right?"

"Jo, you're the most together person I know! You want to see a psychiatrist?"

"Yes. How expensive is she? Is the first visit free?"

Paul is laughing hysterically. "You kidding? Dr. Fletch? She charges three hundred fifty dollars an hour, and the first visit is three hours long"

I'm mortified. "I can't afford that!"

"Try the Maple Center," Paul says. "Their counselors are psychologists-in-training and cheap. The city of Beverly Hills will pay part of the fee since you're a Beverly Hills resident. You'll only pay what you can afford."

I call Jonah and ask him how his brother's doing, glad to hear he's doing "really great." I ask where he goes for counseling.

"The Maple Center referred him to a drug center that has special addiction counselors," he answers.

I call the Maple Center. I have an appointment there in two days.

I immediately tell Gloria Ramos, a woman probably in her forties with a sweet face, that I am there to seek guidance in handling my boyfriend's drug problem.

"Why don't you start off by telling me about yourself? Then we'll talk about your friend's problem."

"Sure, Mrs. Ramos. But I don't want to spend too much time on me."

"Call me Gloria."

"Okay. I'm eighteen. I was adopted. I don't get along with my adoptive parents and I haven't talked to them for a while.

"I graduated from Beverly Hills High and I'm at Santa Monica College now. I have no idea what to major in.

"I love my boyfriend. I've known him for about six months now. I met him last May. He makes me feel really good and for the first time, I feel like I belong.

"Everything about him is so caring and so strong and everything was great until he started snorting cocaine, lots of it. He's a studio musician and they're doing coke to get the work done fast.

"He's been smoking marijuana to come down off the coke. But now, the really big problem is that he's drinking vodka again to help him come down and he shouldn't drink any alcohol at all.

"He has *petite mal epilepsy*. You know what that is?"

"Why don't you tell me what your understanding of it is?" Gloria says.

"Well, he can get out of control if he drinks liquor. He blacks out.

"He had a bad accident because of it before I met him. He was in the hospital. That's when he was diagnosed with that epilepsy.

"And he's drinking again now, and I'm really scared!"

I can see that Gloria is listening intently. Her face reflects involvement in what she's hearing, which I take as a good sign. She'll be able to tell me how to make everything good again. I continue.

"Anyway, he doesn't know that I know about his condition or about the accident or any of that. His brother told me and made me swear not to tell my boyfriend that he did. I don't know what to do because I'm not supposed to know.

"But because they bring coke to the studio every day, he's started drinking vodka to come down off it and he's drinking more and more … "

I bite my lip to hold back tears. "I'm so afraid he'll hurt himself … or someone else."

"And you want me to help you?"

I nod. "I need to make him stop and I don't know how to do that."

The psychologist crosses her legs and sits looking at me silently. I return her look, wondering why she doesn't say anything.

"Is there anything else you want to tell me about yourself?" she finally asks.

"No. Like I said, only that I love him, and I really want him to stop drinking cause I'm scared and I need your help."

"Jolie, if you want to talk about yourself, we can do that. But unfortunately, I can't help your friend."

I feel like she just threw a bucket of cold water on me."Why not?"

"Well, without him being here, it's impossible. I would have to talk to him.

"It might be a long process. But even if he were to come in, I'm not really equipped to help him. I suggest you take him to a drug counselor, someone who specializes in these things.

"You seem like a bright young lady. You might want to explore why you're involved with a man who has a problem like this. If you're ready to do that, we can start."

I respond icily. "I'm involved with him because I love him. I told you. It's not his fault that he has this – this condition."

"I'm not speaking of his medical condition. I'm wondering why you are involved with a man who knows he shouldn't be drinking, knows how dangerous it is, and yet does so."

I get up and take hold of my purse. "I'm sorry but if you can't help me help him, there's no reason for me to be here, so I'll just leave. Thanks for your time."

The psychologist gets up too. "If you ever decide to explore your own motivations, Jolie, please come back."

I won't be returning to the Maple Center.

It is beyond me how this supposedly well-trained woman could think I have a problem when it's Rocky I'm seeking help for.

It's Saturday.

Rocky and I on our way home from an early movie, the first we've seen in months. Rocky fell asleep at the show. He's heading for the market to pick up some things. He pulls Homer into the lot and looks for a parking space.

"Rocky," I say, "I've decided not to smoke any more weed."

"Oh yeah? Why, Baby J?"

"I'm starting to remind myself of my mother – I mean, of Stella. She always has a cigarette in her mouth. You've seen the full cartons she keeps in the refrigerator.

"When I was a little girl, she was always blowing smoke in my face. I'd come home from school and there she was with the TV on, wearing a cotton duster, and smoking. She'd be sitting on the couch talking on the telephone with one of her friends and finish every conversation by saying, 'Thank God, as long as we have our health ... ' and the cigarette would be hanging out of her mouth.

"The living room — the whole house, and everything in it — smelled of stale smoke and so did she.

"I hated the smell, the ashes all over the place ...

"Anyway, now the constant smell of weed and the ashes that are everywhere remind me of Stella and it bothers me. I don't want to be like her."

All he has to say, is, "Okay, Baby J." *Damn him!* He's accepting, and unmoved, more interested in finding a parking space.

"Besides, drugs suck." I continue in the same voice.

"Whoa!" He brakes so hard that Homer jolts. "Hold on." His two hands are up in front of him.

"Now look, you want to stop smoking weed so you won't be like Stella, that's fine. Great. But don't suddenly get all about anti-drugs. You do your thing, that's cool, Baby, but, hey! Don't get all judgmental, okay? That's not cool. Are we clear here?"

Rocky is accusing me of being judgmental! He has me sounding like Phil!

Somehow, I've fallen into my own trap and I have to find my way out.

It's Tuesday afternoon. Classes are over for the day and I'm not on the schedule for work at the restaurant today so I'm with Nora, shopping at the Century City's mall – rather, I'm accompanying Nora who's shopping like crazy for herself and buying holiday gifts for a long list of people including Jonah – although she's already bought him three gifts.

We're browsing through some dresses at J. Magnin's.

"Look at this," I say, holding out a dress. "It's so soft and sexy."

"You'd look great in that, Jo."

"Maybe. I'll never know. Look at the price tag."

Nora looks and says, "It's not that much."

"Hah! Maybe for you it isn't, my sweet little friend who's supported by her dad, but I can't afford this. I'm a working girl, remember? And I don't live at home anymore, remember that? My dad doesn't support me."

"Try it on," she says. "I'll buy it for you. Your Christmas gift."

"You don't have to do that, Nora. I can't afford a gift for you."

"Don't worry. Just try it on," she says.

"No, Nora, I can't accept it."

"Okay, don't try it on. You can do that later." Nora looks at the tag. "Great. This one happens to be your size."

Despite my protests and much to my delight, Nora buys the dress. The cashier puts it in a plastic bag and Nora hands it to me. "Merry Christmas, Jo."

I hug the best friend any girl could have. "Thanks, Nora."

"You know, it's really no a big deal," Nora says. "You saved me the trouble of guessing what to get you."

As we walk out, Nora gives me a sideways look. "Jo, That was the first smile I've seen on your face in a long time. No offense, but you haven't been looking all that happy lately."

"Sorry."

"Don't be sorry. It's not your fault. I know Rocky's making you crazy." She looks at me. "And, of course you won't leave him."

With that comment, I get that Nora thinks her low estimation of Rocky is proving justified. I have to defend him.

"He's going through a hard time. He's under a lot of stress and I'm just scared because of his epilepsy thing."

"So, what are you going to do about it?" She asks.

"I don't know. But I wish that shithead producer would stop feeding him coke!"

Nora stops in her tracks and takes hold of my arm. "Jo, why don't you just tell him?"

"I just might. I'll go to the studio on my way home and tell the son of a bitch what I think of what he's doing."

"Why there?"

"You think I should call him up?"

"What are you talking about? Tell him when he gets home."

"You want me to tell Rocky?"

"Yes! Tell him you know he's sick and that he's being a major jackass to take the kind of chance that he's taking."

"Oh! I thought you meant I should tell the producer."

"Why would you tell him what a jackass Rocky is?"

"I wouldn't! I'd tell him what a jackass *he* is for feeding Rocky the fucking coke! If it wasn't for the coke, Rocky wouldn't drink!"

Nora rests her hand on my arm. "No, Jo. I'm sorry, but you can't control the world. The hell with the producer! This is Rocky's problem. Rocky needs to learn to take care of himself."

I have no reply. We resume walking, entering the food court before she continues.

"Jo, you go through hell every day all day until he gets home at whatever time of night. I'm amazed you haven't already confronted Rocky a hundred times. This is so unlike you! The Jo I know would be in his face with the truth in a second!"

"Yeah."

"So why haven't you told him?"

I shrug. "I was hoping he'd open up to me." At this point, that sounds lame, even to me.

"Well, he didn't. Get over it."

I present her with my last excuse. "I promised Rico I wouldn't say anything. He'll get mad at Rico and Rico will get mad at me."

Nora stops me again. "Jo, Rocky seriously hurt someone and hurt himself! It can happen again. He could kill someone – or himself – next time," I release my breath.

Nora's absolutely right. In fact, she's a lot clearer than I've been about this. What I have to do is suddenly clear.

She goes on. "You know, Jo, maybe that psychologist you went to had a valid point. I'm sorry, but's it's not like you not to confront Rocky about this."

I bristle at the recollection of what the psychologist had said. "You're right. I won't wait any more. I should confront him. I have to. I will. I'm sure he'll stop drinking."

"Right, okay, good. But let me ask you a question. What if you talk to him and he doesn't stop?"

"He will."

"I hope so. But what if he doesn't? What if he keeps drinking after you confront him?"

I have no answer for her. I can't even think of such a scenario.

She fills in the blank. "If that happens, I'd hope you wouldn't hang around, best friend. I mean, if he doesn't get it, he doesn't get it."

I shrug away the possibility that Rocky wouldn't get it. "I really love him."

"Does that mean you'd stay with him?"

"He'll stop."

I really don't like winter's shortened days.

As I'm making my way home, it's barely 4 o'clock, and the sun's already going down.

I mull over the conversation I had with Nora and again conclude that she's right on about everything she said. I must confront Rocky with what I know. Now I can't wait to talk to him.

What will I do if he won't stop drinking?

That would be horribly sad.

It hurts like a bitch to admit it, but if Rocky still won't get his act together or at least try, deep inside me I know that I shouldn't stay with him. There'd be no point in hanging around.

It kills me because he's so good and I so want to stay with him forever. But, as much as I love him, and as wonderful as he is, if he's just going to go on taking the chance that he'll kill someone – or die – that's exactly what might actually happen. And I'd be pretty stupid to hang around waiting until it does.

I can't let myself be pulled down into that … if he doesn't care

174

enough about himself or me … if he doesn't show some courage and strength …

A news bulletin breaks into the music on the radio and interrupts my thoughts.

This report just in: The bodies of many hundreds, perhaps over a thousand people have been discovered in Guyana, South America. The dead – including hundreds of children – are believed to be members of the People's Temple Christian Church led by Jim Jones.

Apparently, death in all cases was caused by poison. Authorities are calling it mass suicide.

Again, hundreds of people, believed to be members of a Church led by the Reverend Jim Jones, have apparently joined in mass suicide in Guyana, South America.

This station will continue to bring you news of developments as they occur."

The regular program resumes and the music returns, as if we can now continue enjoying the music as we did before we became aware of this travesty against human life.

I switch the radio off.

Mass suicide? People agreeing to kill themselves? And their children? What the hell were they thinking? How could they do that?

It's just crazy! I pull into the driveway and go inside the dark house in a dismal mood.

Though I want to talk to Rocky and get through this, I know I'm facing another evening alone, wondering if and when he'll get home from the studio.

Again, I pray this studio job was over.

Then, suddenly, I realize that the end of this studio gig is not the end of the problem.

Rocky has set himself on a daily pattern of coke, weed and alcohol and, though the coke supply may wind down once the album is done, whenever that may be, I doubt his drinking will cease if he is in denial of his problem. In fact, ironically, every day that he survives only leads him to believe he can go on drinking.

As these thought go through my mind, I hang my new dress in the bedroom closet and sit on our bed. I stare at the wall. My thoughts ping-pong back and forth between the news bulletin I've just heard – *hundreds of people poisoning their children!* – and my thoughts about Rocky — *how can he take such unnecessary, huge, stupid chances with his life?*

In the hope of pulling myself out of my depression, I take my new dress out of the closet, remove the plastic cover and try it on.

The fabric feels soft. It's paper-thin but it looks like rich suede and the color of roasted yams.

Looking at myself in the mirror, I can hardly help from running my hands down my own body; I know I look fabulous in it.

The neckline is low and drapes softly over my bust line. The skirt has slits up the sides and shows off my legs. It will be perfect to wear at Nora and Jonah's Christmas party.

Rocky will flip when he sees me in it. Rocky....

And then, while I'm watching the news reports on the mass suicides on television and getting ready for bed, he arrives, smelling of alcohol yet again, looking and sounding exhausted.

He's not hungry. He says he's already had dinner 'with the guys.' He plops onto the couch, puts his feet up and lights up a doobie. When that's done, he retreats to the kitchen and downs a shot of vodka then strips and gets into bed.

He's hardly said a word to me. I'm beside myself. And the fact that I'll soon confront him doesn't comfort me at all.

In bed, listening to him snore, I cry. I'm so scared I'll lose him, yet he seems like he's lost himself. He's somehow diminished.

I resent him for what he's is doing to himself and to us and I hate myself for not stopping him.

Why have I just stood by watching?

I struggle with that question through the night, and sleep, the sole refuge from my obsessive thoughts, is elusive.

2 5

FADE OUT

I awaken raw and tired.

I'm dressing for school, determined to broach the subject with Rocky before he leaves for the studio. I watch him put on a clean T-shirt.

⟡

"Rocky, you've got to stop all the snorting and drinking."

"Hey now, Baby, be cool."

I'm determined. "No! This isn't about being cool. You've got to stop."

"I will. Meanwhile, *you* stop," he says.

"When?" I ask.

"The album has to be done by Christmas. Seidman's scheduled a trip to Tahiti with his family for Christmas and New Year's. That's less than two weeks away."

"That's too long a time. This has been going on for a while now. You can't snort coke all day, drink before you come home, then smoke and drink again the way you do. It's out of control."

177

"Jo, don't nag. Nothing's out of control." He takes off his glasses, wipes them with his T-shirt and puts them back on.

My fear morphs into anger. "Oh really? You think you can quit any time?"

"I'm out of here."

"Rocky, I mean it! Don't you think all this coke and vodka is going to hurt you?"

"Ciao." Rocky is ready to walk out of the bedroom. I block his path.

"You think you can stop whenever you like?"

"Yes, I can. Now get out of my way." Rocky's voice is as stern and what's more, as loud as I'd ever heard it, yet I go on. I fold my arms defiantly in front of me.

"Okay, then, let me see you stop!"

Rocky peers at me over his glasses. He's calm. He says, "I'll stop when I want to." Then he walks around me, and he's gone.

I leave for school frustrated, angry, hurt and very scared. Rocky has been acting increasingly insensitive toward me and seems immovable. His drugging and drinking are coming between us.

I take the winding canyon roads as fast as my Mercedes will allow, thinking about what I know of drug problems, the schoolmates I've had who seemed to have dug themselves into a hole.

I think of Jonah's brother. He's in therapy because he wants to save his life. He's also had huge support from his parents who moved the whole family to California.

I recall Gloria Ramos' words and remember how incensed I'd been when she suggested I need counseling to understand why I'm in a relationship with someone who has a life-threatening drug problem but doesn't seem to want to do anything about it. Maybe she's right. Maybe there's something wrong with me. Maybe I shouldn't be in this relationship.

At this point, with Rocky apparently out of control and acting so differently towards me, our relationship is pretty much in shreds.

Funny, addiction was the one thing my endless insecurities never thought might be a reason for our relationship to end. As it turns out, it may well be the reason *I* leave *him*.

I just keep thinking that he'll stop if I just know how to make him. I'll have to confront him again, this time, head-on.

I'm in a rare deep sleep when he gets home late that night. In the morning I start up from where I left off the day before.

He looks terrible. Too thin, pale, not like himself at all.

My first words: "Rocky, you need to stop drinking."

He looks around the room for his jeans. "I feel like shit and I can't find my jeans," he says "so don't start that again."

"I mean it, Rocky. You have to stop now. Today."

He seems surprised by my calm yet assertive tone.

Meanwhile, he's found his jeans and turns around to face me. "Yeah?"

I take a deep breath. "Rocky, is there anything you want to tell me about yourself?"

He glides into his jeans. "What do you mean?"

"I mean, is there something about yourself you haven't told me that maybe I should know?"

"Well, let's see … " He zips up his fly then takes on a pensive look. "I've already told you I feel like shit. Let's see … I don't know what T shirt to wear, Baby J – oh, and I lost my shades."

"Rocky, I'm serious! I know."

He speaks ever so softly. "What do you know, Baby J?"

"I know. Rico told me. That's right, he told me. Everything. I know."

I count on fingers extended towards him. "I know you had an accident on your bike, I know that it almost killed you, and I know the other person was really badly hurt. I know that it was your fault and I know that you were in the hospital for a long time. I know…" I slow down and drop my arms.

It's exceedingly difficult to say the next words. "I know you have epilepsy."

Rocky's eyes react like he's been hit with a bullet, but only his eyes.

I hurry to ease the pain. "Not epilepsy. You have *petite mal epilepsy.*"

Rocky seems to crumble before my eyes. "Rico told you that?" It's a whisper.

"Yes. But only because he thought I already knew. He thought you had already told me."

Rocky takes off his glasses and rubs his eyes. He seems to have curled into himself.

"He's your brother. He loves you. It's not like he meant to rat on you, Rocky. He saw what happened to you and he doesn't want it to happen again. You're all the family he has."

The words just tumbled out and I've finally told Rocky that I know. He knows I know, and the truth is there in the room with us.

I move toward him tentatively, not sure how to approach him, how to get around the effect the truth has on him.

"I love you too, Rocky. You're the best thing that's ever happened to me. I want to stay with you more than anything in the world. But you're acting crazy!"

I stand in front of him. "You're acting like there's nothing wrong with you. Rocky, I don't want to watch you kill yourself … or anyone else."

He sinks down onto the bed, his head down. He puts his glasses back on then sets his hands at his brows, covering his eyes as if to shield himself from me.

"There's nothing wrong with me," he mumbles.

I sit down next to him. "It's not the end of the world, baby. It's not a terrible thing. You just can't drink. That's all."

I put my hand on his thigh, but at my touch, he gets up and stomps away. He picks his belt up off the back of the chair and moves as if he's going to weave it through his belt loop, but then, suddenly, he holds it high up then whips it against the wall leaving a long black mark there.

I'm startled. I'm stunned. I'm scared. This is way more violent, more aggressive than anything I've ever seen him do.

"Goddamn it!" He turns back to me, and I see how anger has changed his face. "I can drink! I can snort and I can drink as much as I goddamn want!"

His red-rimmed, black-circled eyes stare at me from his ashen face, and I want nothing more than to take him in my arms and hold him, tell him he's right and I'm wrong, that it was just a mistake on my part, and everything is fine.

"You think I can't drink?"

He tosses the belt onto the bed and jabs at his face, poking with both hands. "Look at me. Is there something wrong with me?" His voice is breaking. "You see something wrong?" He laughs a ghoulish laugh.

"Epilepsy? Right! *Petite mal epilepsy!*" He turns away, picks his wallet up from the dresser. "Fuckin' doctors, don't know piss about anything."

I am absolutely and totally dumbfounded!

Never in a million years would I ever have imagined he'd have *this* reaction. My voice reflects my bafflement. "You think the doctors are wrong? They don't know what they're saying?"

"They're fuckin' idiots!"

Oh, my God! He is actually trying to persuade me that he's fine! That he's been misdiagnosed!

He comes to me with a wide, ingratiating smile and takes both my hands in his.

"Baby J, look at me. Do I look like a cat with a fuckin' brain lesion?"

I look at him, but I stay mute. I'm in some kind of shock.

Why is he denying the truth? I don't understand. Could he be delusional, mentally ill?

He continues. "Look, Jo, Rico's young. The kid was scared. He's a good boy, but he's not as bright as you or me. He knows his music, but, hey …"

I have no idea how to respond to him. *What is Rocky saying? How can we deal with the problem if he denies that he has one?*

"Okay, Rocky, then you tell me what happened when you had the accident." Rocky smiles and throws his hands up as if the answer is all too obvious, but he says nothing. "Come on, tell me. Tell me you didn't black out. Tell me you remember who you hit, what color the car was, where it came from… *tell me!*"

"Hey, what's this shit? The Spanish Inquisition? You don't believe me?" My head moves slowly, barely from side to side, my eyes pinned on his, my heart racing. I'm so scared.

"Look, you're a cool lady and I love having you around. You're cool people. But, hey, if you don't believe what I'm telling you, then …"

I know I'm fighting for Rocky's return. I'm fighting for my future. Our future.

"Rocky, I hope you don't believe what you're saying. I don't think you do. You're the smartest guy I know. You've got to think about this – what you're doing – and stop it. I beg you, please, Rocky. I don't want to lose you. Stop drinking!"

He has to love me enough. He has to see that I don't want to leave him or lose him to another accident.

I go to him and lovingly stroke his cheek. "Rocky, I'd climb mountains for you, I'd do anything you asked me to. I love you that much. But if you won't even admit to yourself, let alone someone who loves you, what's going on with you, if you won't help yourself, then … we don't have much going on here."

Tears begin to cascade down my cheeks.

He takes my hands off his face and looks at his watch. "I gotta make tracks. I'm late." He finds his keys on the dresser top then walks away leaving me standing where he's left me, watching him go.

I remain standing there in silent wonder at the surprise of it all, trying to digest what just happened. I confronted Rocky, exposed my heart to him, betrayed Rico's trust … and the bottom line is that he denied everything – all of it – and left me cold.

I'm left with no choice. I must leave.

I lie on the bed, soon no longer to be mine and cry.

Why? Why can't I stay with Rocky, keep on loving him and being loved by him? Why does our love have to end like this? *Why?* Why is life is so *fucking unfair*? Why does my love have to end so bitterly?

At eighteen, I can give it to you in writing: life sucks!

Abandoned by my mother and father. Not accepted by my adoptive father and mother.

Guys before Rocky just wanted to sleep with me. The first boy I told I loved, fucked a slut in front of my eyes. I swore I'd never love anyone after that.

But how could I not love Rocky? And now I have to leave because he turns out to be so fucked up that though he's had a major terrible accident because of an illness, he totally denies the problem!

He's not strong, not strong enough to save himself. And he can't even see what's right in front of his eyes, so I guess he's not so smart either.

It's so goddamned unfair! Why does he have to have some stupid condition? Why doesn't Jonah? Or Jay?

Life sucks. And love sucks. If loving someone means I have to tie my life up to theirs and take on their addictions, it's too painful. I don't want it in my life.

I miss school that day, call in sick to work and lay on the bed for hours, crying, feeling sorry for myself, thinking about my options and realize I have none. I call Nora and leave a message on her answering machine. It's strange to leave this message on an answering machine.

"Nora, it's me, Jo. I'm leaving Rocky. I … have to. Please … please let me know if you can help me get my stuff out of here today and maybe stay at your house tonight. I … I really need to leave."

I roam around the house, go into the studio and sit at the piano for a long time then wander into the alley where I find two boxes and start packing my things.

Hours later, Nora calls back saying she's sorry it turned out like this, but she's proud of me for finally talking to Rocky and knows I'm doing the right thing to leave.

She'll help me, of course, but she's unavailable today because she's spending the rest of the day with her mom at the emergency room; Carol fell in the tub and may have broken her shoulder. She promises she'll be here bright and early tomorrow.

My last night at Rocky's house is another lonely one. Rocky is again staying late at the studio. Rico is due back from his road trip later tonight or tomorrow and, if I don't see him before I leave, I'll call and tell him that Rocky knows he's told me about him. I can only hope he'll understand.

I make myself a sandwich and watch the news as I continue packing.

All the stories involve murders, alleged rapes, kidnappings and corruption. Congress is investigating the deaths of the nine hundred twelve men, women, children and infants in Jamestown who died by poison. Yesterday, the California Congressman and four others who were investigating the cult led by Jim Jones were found shot to death.

The only international news is coverage of the political situation in Iran, snippets of film footage of a country in turmoil. I think of Jamsheed. Things look dismal for the shah. Members of his government have resigned. The nightly curfew has been restored throughout the capital city of Tehran. I hope Jamsheed's parents have already fled the country and are safe in California.

I, too, am fleeing and will relocate. Like them, I'm escaping a potentially violent situation and about to start an unknown future. I watch the melee captured on film, distracted by the emotional riot in my own life.

Removing my clothes from the closet, I take in Rocky's scent. I can't wait until all this is out of my sight.

I look around me as I pack. Everything I loved, everything that brought me pleasure, now makes me sad. And the person who brought me more happiness than anyone is now causing immeasurable pain.

<hr>

I finish packing and hope to bury myself in sleep. I affirm that tomorrow I'm leaving this house because I'm a survivor, yet part of me wonders if my future will be worth surviving past my time with Rocky.

I hear Rico coming in through the front door and I'm glad he's home, relieved to know that in my absence, Rocky's brother will be here for him.

Soon, I'm asleep.

I have a nightmare.

I hear a thumping. I adjust myself, refusing to wake up to the noise. But it doesn't stop. In fact, it gets louder. Rocky isn't in bed. I get out of bed to see what it is. Someone's knocking at the front door. Maybe he's lost his key.

I make my way into the living room.

In the dark hallway, I sense rather than see Rico trailing me; he's heard the noise too. I turn on a lamp in the living room. I guess that it's probably somewhere between 2 o'clock and 5 o'clock in the morning.

I open the door. It's dark outside. The cold stillness of very early morning is in the air.

Two men, strangers, stand before the open door. One wears a dark uniform and in the dim porch light I see a badge shine in the reflected light. My first thought is that they've come to arrest Rico for the weed. Then I think, it could be coke; it's Rocky they're looking for.

As I start up the ladder of fear, I connect it to the fact that Rocky isn't home.

Rico is at the door now with me and he's answering the men's questions. Rico is unafraid; he knows the language of search warrants. The man asks Rico his relationship to Rocky. When he politely asks my relationship to Rocky, Rico answers for me. I register his calmness. I am unable to speak. He asks if anyone else is in, if Rocky's parents are there. Rico shakes his head. Now he, too, smells fear.

The man speaking has a space between his two front teeth and a scar running down his cheek. As we hold our eyes on him, I feel the strangest sensation, as though I'm about to burst open.

I watch the words form in the man's mouth as his lips move, forming words I don't want to hear. My heart has stopped beating. I want to close the door on these men, but we two stand transfixed, a captive audience, praying the talking man will stop making words before he says something horrible that he can't retract. But he's mouthing more words, one after the other, words I have dreaded for these past weeks. He finishes with a weak apology.

I can't find my breath. He's done this before at other houses and he will do it again. But for Rico and me, it's over.

The unthinkable has happened.

At Rico's request, I stay at the house with him until he finds a new place to go.

Nights, I find myself listening for Rocky's van to pull up in the driveway and when I awaken, I expect to see him already up, showered and dressing for the studio.

When Rico decides to room in with two of his band members in Manhattan Beach, I must face the reality of my own unknown future.

I must be strong if I'm to go on.

2 6

GONE

*R*ocky is gone.

Just like that. Like a candle snuffed out, a song cut off.

Rocky Calvo Borinquen, February 21, 1954 – December 23, 1978.
Named after another Rocky who didn't know his own limits. *He was a little hard to handle. Couldn't stop himself.*

Seeing him buried was hard. I stood there with Nora and Jonah and Paul, Rico and his band as well as the members of NightFlight and various other musician friends of the brothers and the studio musicians who were working with him on the album. Even the producer shows up.

I will never again visit his gravesite.

Rocky's death was unnecessary and unfair.

With him gone, the world has lost some of its meaning.

True, I had planned to leave him. But I had hoped he would save himself, possibly *because* I left him. His death has plummeted me into the depths of the very pain I'd hoped to avoid by leaving him.

These first tears I shed are tears of shock, loss and grief. They're angry tears, too. Rocky was so incredibly stubborn. He didn't even try to help himself and in the end, he let us both down.

There are tears shed in remorse, as well. I feel I failed him. There must have been something more I could have done to convince him he needed help.

Maybe he didn't love me enough to try. Maybe I wasn't worth it. So, my mourning combines grief and a feeling of loss with painful disappointment, agonizing frustration, and more doubts about myself. I, too, let us both down.

Though Rocky died the night those two men came to our door, I'd lost him weeks before to his addictions and his denials. What happiness he brought into my life was impermanent and now he's gone.

I worry about Rico. Now that The Rock Man is gone, he's alone in this world. I phone him and leave a message to assure myself that he's doing okay but he doesn't return my call. He probably has no place in his life for me now that Rocky's gone. I pray he'll be okay. I pray he'll forgive me one day for breaching his confidence. Neither of us saw Rocky alive again after the morning I confronted him with what I knew.

The only person I can share my sadness with is Nora. Thankfully, Carol welcomes me into her home – again! – even making sure I eat, despite an almost non-existent appetite and the pain of her damaged shoulder. She wears neither a cast nor sling.

Nora's concern for me is apparent. She's here for me as always and comforts me.

She was there, watching my relationship with Rocky disintegrate. She watched as I struggled with his downward spiral, his surrender to addiction, his denial and finally, his ultimate and senseless death.

And though she's always believed Rocky wasn't good enough for me, she's never once mentioned it. She's been a remarkable friend and I wonder when *she* will abandon me.

We're having coffee at her breakfast table. I'm picking at a piece of apple pie that Nora has put in front of me.

"Jolie, I know you're really strong, but you've been through so much, I'm worried about you. Are you really okay?"

I shrug. "The truth? I don't know. I just want to space out. Right now, all I want to do is bury my head somewhere and forget all this."

For the umpteenth time I try to make sense of it all. "He was so *perfect*. Everything he said and did was like no one else. He made me feel like we had a chance together. It's just so hard to believe he's *dead!* He's gone forever, just like that. It's just too crazy to believe."

"What can I do?" Nora asks.

I look up at her. "You? Nora, you're great. You're the best friend I could ever have. There's nothing you can do. I just have to go through this. Maybe I just need time."

Nora nods. "Do Phil and Stella know?"

The idea that I would tell them is ludicrous. "I haven't talked to them and I'm not going to."

"Are you going to move back home?"

"I'm never going back to their house. There's no way I can live with them. They think I was wrong to be with Rocky. I can't tell them how he died. And I can't go back to the way things were."

She squirms in her chair. "But maybe now that he's gone ... " She trails off.

"Even without Rocky in my life I'm not the daughter they want me to be. I never was and I never will be. It'll just be the next thing that makes me want to leave."

I try to still the anger that rises up as I think about Phil and Stella. I'll just have to get used to being on my own, forever.

"You can't imagine what it was like to live with them, to have parents like them.

"Stella tried to wrap me up in plastic like she wraps up her dishes, her furniture and everything else. She nagged me about what I should wear, how I should brush my hair, what to say on the phone, how to smile, what kind of bra to wear ... I can't live suffocated like that!

"And Phil's all about being Jewish! 'Date only Jewish boys or I'll kick you out!'

"What difference does that make to me? It makes a difference to him, not me. Maybe my real parents were Christian or Buddhist or some other religion. I have no idea *who I am*."

I chuckle. "You know, he's actually convinced that the U.S. is full of anti-Semitism. He thinks the government is out to kill Jews! Can you believe that? And I'm tired of being hit by him or being afraid that I'm *going* to be hit by him."

"Jolie! Your dad hit you more than that one time? You never told me that! I thought that time with Rocky was the only time!"

"Well, I'm telling you now. He'd beat me. And Stella would just watch him."

I know all this is so different from Nora's home life, I wouldn't blame her if she didn't believe me. "We just didn't connect at all. They barely connect to each other! They want me to be like they want me to be, and that's not going to happen."

As I speak to Nora about them, their very recollection upsets me. "Nora, you know me. I'm always going to have to do things my own way. That's how I am. It's not a good thing because I have only myself to blame for my fuckups and my heartaches. But, hey, if I ever do anything right – and there may be a slim chance of that happening – that will be my doing, too.

If I can't live my own life, what's the point? Besides, it's not like they're my real parents."

Nora's quiet for a moment. "So, what will you do?"

I look at her blankly. "I haven't a clue. I have to do something."

"Where will you live?"

I shrug and swallow the last morsel of pie. "Someplace really, really cheap."

"You know, I've been thinking about moving out," Nora says. "I mean, it's about time. I'm a big girl now." I nod absently. But when she looks slyly at me and follows with, "I'd want a roommate," I smile and get up to hug her, holding on to her tightly as if holding onto of a life raft.

"Oh, my god, that would be so great!" I say. My enthusiasm quickly dies. "What am I thinking? I can't share an apartment with you. I can't afford what you can. I can't afford anything nice."

"My parents can."

"For you. But they're not going to pay for me. I have to pay my own way and you won't want to live in what I can afford."

"I'm not moving without you, Jolie. Anything's fine with me, as long as it has two bedrooms."

We spend the rest of January hunting for an apartment, and the whole time I wonder if a two-bedroom apartment exists in the city that I can afford, and that Nora could possibly be okay living in.

With more free time on her hands, Nora spends more time shopping for apartments. I search when I can. Weekends, we hunt together.

The second weekend in February, we come face to face with a miracle. We both fall in love with a two-bedroom apartment in West Hollywood that's in a two-story building north of Sunset Boulevard on Larrabee Street, just a short climb from the world-famous Sunset Strip, that portion of Sunset Boulevard that has made the boulevard world famous as the magnet that draws the young and the hip. Larabee is a steep street that dead ends a block above the apartment building, which has four apartments. The one that's available has a huge brick patio that wraps around it with a totally amazing view of the city.

Nora insists that since the larger of the two bedrooms will be hers, it justifies her decision to pay sixty percent of the rent, so, it's affordable. I can't believe that such a great apartment, just a stone's throw away from the Strip, with Gazzari's, Whisky a Go-Go, the Rainbow Room and so much more.

As we drive by the Rainbow Room, I share the trivial fact with Nora that in 1953, Marilyn Monroe met Joe DiMaggio, that famous baseball player who was to be her second husband, on a blind date at the Rainbow Room. Thank you for that, Stella.

We're as excited as two kids walking into Disneyland as we sign the lease. The landlady, a tall, big-boned redhead wearing a tight purple dress and very high heels scrutinizes us.

"I won't stand for illicit practices going on in my apartments. Two good-looking girls like you. Don't think I was born yesterday." She gestures up and down the street as she says this, as if to imply that Larrabee is rife with call girls. "No funny stuff going on here. I won't allow that in my building." She waves a finger at us, as she collects the first month's rent and security deposit.

Back at Nora's house, I thank Carol for letting me stay at her home for so long. And then, for a change, I help Nora pack and on March first, we move in.

Thankful that I have possession of the pink slip to my Benz, I sell it and buy a much less valuable used green Spider Fiat convertible and learn to drive stick shift.

While Nora lives the carefree life of a UCLA student, completely supported by her parents, I take a full-time job as a hostess at The Pelican, a restaurant on Sunset Boulevard and register for evening classes at Santa Monica City College.

I don't particularly want to be around people and keep pretty much to myself for the first months, making a continuous unbroken circle from Larrabee to Santa Monica College to The Pelican and back to Larrabee. As a result of our different lifestyles and schedules, I don't see all that much of Nora either.

It's Saturday, the ninth of May, Nora's nineteenth birthday.

She and Jonah are celebrating with a party at the apartment tonight. It will be my first social affair since Rocky's death and I have mixed feelings about it, which is not a surprise as these days I have mixed feelings about everything.

Anyway, I need to be alone for a while and gather my thoughts. I decide to take an early morning walk.

Outside, the morning breeze greets me as I walk down the hill to Sunset and head east. Last night's rain, a rare occurrence in the city, has left the morning streets dark in their wetness. The air feels crisp and clean.

I arrive at Whisky a Go-go. I linger alongside the front door of the club and turn to look up at the yellow and black striped awning. I'd been inside once with Rocky, afterwards, the one time I saw him drink wine. It seems so long ago! The waiter had refused to serve me, so Rocky ordered a glass of red wine and we shared it.

So much has happened since then! I wasn't even living with him then. A tremendous wave of grief overtakes me, and I begin to cry uncontrollably as rainwater that has collected on the awning above falls on my face and runs down my cheeks. I can't stop crying.

People passing by don't seem to notice me.

With my eyes dripping tears, I look up at the signs in the front window advertising the current show at the Whisky. I expect to see my reflection in the glass but it's Rocky's image I see there, and he is looking at me. I turn around but there's no one behind me.

I turn back to the glass. He's still there, his hands in the pockets of his pea coat. He looks like he did those nights near the end, when he came home stoned and drunk, sickly pale, with dark circles under his eyes. But this image is even paler, the ghostly color of death. I shudder. I feel goose bumps. The hairs on my neck rise. Then suddenly, he's gone.

Why was he there? Was he reprimanding me? Could I have done more to prevent his death? Does he intend to haunt me? I rack my brains even now to find something more I could have done and come up with … nothing.

I want to go home. I'm emotionally drained. Turning back towards Larabee, I suddenly have so little energy that walking is an effort. I'm trudging, dragging one foot and then the other. Then, with every few steps, words, and then phrases – lines – flow into my consciousness:

The ground I walk on shakes beneath my feet. Step.

As I walk on Rocky's hills, Step. Slower step.

I wonder why I haven't died.

These are definitely not lyrics, yet I want to stop and write them down in the pad Rocky gave me. I still carry it in my handbag. It would be pointless; I can't share them with him. I'm tired and I'm melancholy and I wonder if this is what it feels like to be old.

My childhood years all drifted by. Dragging.

Life was sweet and simple then.

Now alone, and without love, Dragging step, dragging step,

I wonder why I haven't died.

I rest against a storefront and record the words in my book after all, as I know Rocky would want. I focus on the strangers moving past me, going their various ways.

Look at me. I'm old with wisdom in my eyes.

Yet still I do not understand.
I wonder why I haven't died.

I wonder how many of the people driving by have lost their loved ones to a death so untimely. Funny, you can't tell by looking at someone. They all keep moving.

I drop the pad back into my handbag and think about that. I'm one of them. I, too, will keep moving.

A ray of sunshine, the shooting beam of bright light that comes only after a rain, has found me. I lift my eyes to the sun, then continue on and come to a shop window displaying brightly colored blouses. I stop to look.

I glimpse myself in the window and I'm acutely aware of how young I look. I gaze at myself. Suddenly, Rocky is back, this time at my side, and this Rocky is the Rocky I first met. He's smiling and looking at me with so much love. He throws something up into the air like he used to throw his keys – but whatever it was, it doesn't come back down. He salutes me then turns away, and I know he's leaving me forever.

I feel so much lighter. A veil of understanding and acceptance has fallen over me. I can't measure my love for Rocky by his inability to deal with his illness or by his lack of courage to combat his addiction. I loved him. I was leaving him because I didn't want my life to slip away.

He's gone forever. But I'm still here. I can't – I won't – let my life slip away. Forever grateful, I'm ready to leave him to rest in peace and resume life amongst the living. I will make something of my life.

I make my way back to our apartment to help Nora and Jonah prepare for her party. I hike my purse strap higher up on my shoulder and stand taller. I feel the breeze shuffle my hair. At the corner, I pause to wait until the traffic light turns green, then cross to the other side. I'm glad Nora is celebrating her birthday.

We both deserve a good time.

27

PARTY TIME

*O*ur apartment is crammed with people.

Nora has instructed Jonah to invite as many of his friends as possible, hoping one of them will spark some interest in me. So far, nothing.

Thanks to Jonah, our DJ for the evening, the music of Queen fills the apartment and spills out onto the patio. *"We will, we will rock you."*

I venture outside squeezing my way between guests to enjoy the night air. The clouds that were apparent earlier in the day have given way to a view so clear that the city's lights glisten like thousands of tiny white and yellow diamonds laid out on a dark velvet tray.

"Hey." A tall guy has maneuvered his way through the crowd to join me at the black railing. "Here you are. Great party."

It's the guy with the dog who lives in the building up the street, one of thousands of good-looking actors-in-waiting that freckle Los Angeles. I greet him. "Hi, Holden. It is Holden, right?"

As always, he's wearing a tight Tee shirt. This one is red with an imprint of an open-mouthed shark and the word "Jaws" written above it, all in white. Like the other Tees I've seen him wear, it shows off his muscles.

"Right. Great party. Nora invited me yesterday when I was walking Bazoo."

Nora and I often have abbreviated conversations with him on the way to and from our cars as he's walking Bazoo. He looks back into the living room and again says, "It's really a great party."

"Yeah," I look around at the crowded patio. "Nora and Jonah know lots of people. Looks like they're all having a good time." I return to lean forward on the rail.

"And you? Are you having a good time?" I nod. "You sure? All good?"

The question makes me smile. "All? That's a big question."

"Yeah, I guess it is." Then he turns to face me, leaning his side against the rail. "You know, I've always thought of you as a beautiful sad girl. I know why you're beautiful. You've got long legs, you're slim and shapely, great features, wild coloring …"

"Well, thank you."

"No, really, your coloring is fabulous! I've never seen anyone with coloring like yours." He reaches toward my hair. "You've got this long, rich brown hair happening with those hazel eyes … and that unusual skin color. I'm not sure how to describe it."

And then he tries to do exactly that. "What would my agent call it? Tawny? Dusky? Swarthy? Olive?" He actually swoons then, circling his torso dramatically. "And then, to top it off, you underplay it all. See what I mean? It's a killer. So, the *beautiful* part is easy to figure out. But I can't figure about the *sad* part. I mean, why a girl that looks like you could be sad. Then again, I may be wrong; but I don't think so. It may be just a hunch – or maybe I'm psychic. I've seen so many psychics, I wouldn't be surprised if it's rubbed off on me." He laughs.

"That's quite a mouthful," I say.

"Okay, guess I'm wrong." He turns his attention to the view of the city's lights. "Pretty night out. A view like this … it looks like a diamond-studded black blanket."

"Wow! So, you're a poet too," I say.

He rolls his eyes. "Thanks! You know, going back to your great looks. For the longest time, I've wondered if you're Italian." When I don't respond, he asks, "Are you?"

196

"No, I'm not," I say. I'm surprised he would think I'm Italian. People usually guess I'm French, probably because of my name. "Why did you think I'm Italian?"

"You have this sort of exotic, super sexy thing about you."

I smile at the thought that Italian is 'exotic' to him.

To my surprise, I resolve right there and then that that I will not hesitate to say I was adopted. I answer him bluntly. I "Well, actually, I don't really know," I say. "Maybe I am Italian." Holden squints in confusion. "I'm adopted."

I'd always felt those two words stigmatized me. But, after all, it's not as though I've committed a crime. Besides, I've concluded that my own feelings about having been adopted dwarfs what others might think about it; their feelings just are not that important to me anymore.

"I don't know where my real parents are from or even who they were." Though the words fall easily out of my mouth, they still bore into the familiar hole in my soul.

"Hey," Holden says, standing taller. "You were adopted. Cool."

"Cool?" I chuckle at his unexpected reaction. "Where are you from, Holden? What kind of a name is that?"

He shrugs. "I have no idea. Maybe British? It's not my real name."

"Don't tell me you were adopted, too!"

He laughs easily. "No, I changed my name. My real name – are you ready? is Sol Horowitz." He laughs as if Sol Horowitz is a funny name. "I changed it to Holden Mannix about six months ago."

"Why?"

"A psychic told me that the vibrations of the name Sol Horowitz worked against fame." He smiles. "First, I changed it to Kamil LaRue. That was a real hit with the ladies, but – well, after two years, I still didn't see a glimmer of hope for any success or fame. "So, I changed it again. This time, I ran it by a numerologist as well as a psychic and we came up with Holden Mannix."

I'm intrigued. "And? Any luck?"

"Well, I've had a few callbacks. And ... " a sly look, eyebrows raised, "I'm hopeful."

"Great. Anything big?"

"As a matter of fact, yeah ... well, maybe." Holden's wrings his

hands. The gesture reminds me of something Phil would do, anticipating his first bite of a juicy steak.

"A movie?"

"No, television … a pilot."

"You fly?"

Holden laughs. "No, a pilot is like a test show. They shoot an
episode, maybe a few, and if the big guys like it, they air it. If viewers
like it, it becomes a weekly show."

"Oh, that sounds really exciting."

"We'll see. They've called me back twice and my agent is excited."

There's a shadow of a smile on his face as he turns shy. "But I'm
trying to stay cool, you know? These things are like that." The hands
are still moving, as if washing them with neither soap nor water.

"What's your role in the pilot? Or, I guess, what *would* be your
role?"

"My character's not a nice guy. He lives with this girl and makes it
with all her friends behind her back. It's a nighttime soap." I say nothing. This is not a storyline I have any interest in.

He leans back. "Did you watch 'Dallas' last night?" I shake my
head. "Too bad. Well, 'Dallas' is a five-part a mini-series. The first part
was just on last night. You should watch it if you can. It's about a
family that lives in Dallas and it's a soap opera. My agent says if 'Dallas' gets good ratings, it'll be a weekly series and if that happens, *this*
pilot will fly, too. So, I'm waiting."

I nod. "Well, I wish you luck."

"Like I said, you can't get too excited about callbacks and stuff like
that, or you'll be sorry. But between you and me?" He suddenly takes
me by my shoulders. "I'm shitting my pants."

I laugh. I find him somewhat endearing. "I'll keep my fingers
crossed double for you. That you get the part … and that no one finds
out you've dirtied your pants."

Holden laughs with me. His laugh sounds a bit like a machine gun.
If he ever becomes famous, that signature laugh will doubtless be
impersonated.

"Have you thought of getting an agent?" he asks. "Or, do you have an agent? You are one of the hottest women around. You know, movies, television?"

"No, that's not for me," I say.

"Modeling?" he asks.

I shake my head with feeling. "Uh uh."

"Okay. But you really are hot. I mean, I see all these movie types, models and actresses and whatever. But you – you always look great. Even now, in a simple miniskirt and top you look better than most girls do after lots of girl-fussing."

I thank him. We continue talking. Sol-Kamil-Holden tells me that he'd been meaning to stop by our apartment under some pretext and ask for my phone number and my astrological sign.

"After Nora saw me walking Bazoo this morning and invited me to her party I went home and gave Bazoo an extra treat."

He asks my astrological sign. I don't tell him that I don't believe in astrology. "Guess," I say.

"You're a Virgo; definitely Virgo." He points to himself. "I'm May fifth, a definite Taurus. You could be a Taurus too, cause you're so earthy." He looks at me, his hand at his chin, as if he's deciding whether he likes the couch he's just moved, in the new corner or the old. "But, no, you're a Virgo! You're shy, really organized and practical. Right? And you're ruled by Mercury, so you're intellectual and analytical. You're a perfectionist. Right? Am I right?"

I don't relate to any of those traits. "Yup! You got me! Exactly!"

I'm enjoying myself. Holden is amusing, almost childlike and his talk is light, about astrological signs and TV pilots — my God! he's actually changed his name *twice* in his search for a fame vibe.

Encouraged, he continues. "And, let's see … you're future-oriented. You know what you want to do with your life."

That's definitely pushing it. This time, I respond honestly. "Maybe soon," I say. "Right now, I have no idea what I want to do. I know it's not modeling, movies, or TV. Other than that, I only know I want to find my real parents, and that's about it."

"Well, then," he says, "I'm sure you will. Are you working on it, making any headway?"

"No." I'm suddenly serious. I will squeeze the facts out of Phil and Stella very soon. Meanwhile, I need to change the subject.

"Tell me about you, Taurus Holden," I say.

"Ahh, Taurus … ruled by Venus. I'm super sensual, highly sexual and I love comfort." He gloats. "What else do you want to know?"

"What about fame and fortune?"

"Al Pacino is a Taurus."

"Well, say no more!"

"Yeah."

This brainless, entertaining banter is just what I need. Holden's easy to keep happy. And when he makes a casual move to take my hand for a few seconds, his masculine warmth reverberates through my body. I'm reminded of how long it's been since I have been touched by a man.

So, when Sol-Kamil-Holden asks for my telephone number, I gladly gave it to him, and when he asks me to dinner the following night, I accept.

28

MISS JOLIE

J've passed Dan Tana's many times while driving on Santa Monica Boulevard, but I've never been inside.

Walking in with Holden, I immediately like the atmosphere of the place, and I'm apparently not the only one. Every table is taken, and the bar is crammed. I spot a famous aging male singer at the bar with a very busty blonde about my age.

The waiters wear tuxedos. The food they serve is yummy Italian. I start with a Caesar salad doused with garlic, then follow with a scrumptious shrimp scampi along with intermittent tastes of Holden's yum veal scaloppini marsala.

Our conversation over dinner is, of course, light and easy. Once again, I'm again enjoying myself in Holden's company. He tells me he's missing an episode of "Dallas" to be with me.

"You know, this place is a hole for movie actors," he says.

"It doesn't look like a hole to me."

"Well, they recently turned away Richard Burton."

"Really! Well, then I guess we should feel pretty good."

"Angie Dickenson eats here. So does Jack Nicholson and Johnny Carson – not that Carson is a movie star, but still … "

"I'm impressed," I say. "And I like the food."

"There's the story about Drew Barrymore. Her parents supposedly brought her here when she was a baby and changed her diaper on the bar."

I chuckle at the thought that something like that has become a legend. "I think of all the places I'd probably had my diaper changed, and no one cared." I say.

It's Holden's turn to chuckle. "Yeah. Me too."

I decline Holden's offer to go next door to the Troubadour after dinner to hear a band I've never heard of. Musicians mean Rocky and it's too soon to expose myself to that. Meanwhile, craving physical contact, I want to feel more of Holden's body heat.

"Let's go home," I say.

We drive back to Larrabee and Holden stops in front of my apartment building. When I ask why he's parked so far from his building, he says he's taking me home. I move to get out of his car.

"Okay, I guess you're calling it a night 'cause you're tired."

He hurries to correct me. "No, I'm not tired at all. I thought you said you wanted to go home."

"I meant to your house. But-"

Before I finish the sentence, we're parked in Holden's garage.

"This is great," he says. "Really great! I thought I was going to take you home and thank you for a great time then come home, go to bed and fantasize that you'd come home with me."

As we exit the elevator, I hear Bazoo barking, and I wonder if he's been barking since Holden left him, or if he's barking because he knows Holden is back. I'm immediately thankful that none of my neighbors have barking dogs. A miniature Sheltie is there to greet us with barks, whelps and a wagging tail when Holden opens the door. Unfortunately for Bazoo, Holden leads him into the kitchen and closes the door.

Then he returns to me. Wordlessly, he takes my face between his hands and brings his lips down to mine. My sexuality, igored for eons, comes alive.

Rocky wasn't motivated to reform even when the drugs and alcohol made it impossible for him to perform. Now, in Holden's muscular arms, feeling his strong body and the warmth of him, his desire for me is palpable. Repressed sexual feelings rush at me, flooding me, and I'm drowning in my own need.

I feel Holden's welcomed erection and I unbuckle his belt. I'd rip his pants off, but he stops me. He removes my top. Slowly. Deliberately. Left in my bra, he runs his hand up my arm to my throat, then down to my cleavage. I hear his shallow breathing and feel his hot breath on my face.

"Your skin is so soft, so smooth," he says.

I want to get on with it. "Take your clothes off," I order as I reach to undo my bra. By the time it drops, Holden has taken his shirt off. His hands are on my breasts, and I respond to the warm heat of desire exploding in his hands. His mouth is about to follow but I push him away. "Take your pants off," I say.

With his pants down and hanging between his legs and his beautiful erection pointing our way, he takes my hand and leads me through his living room and into his bedroom. As I fall on the bed, I'm fleetingly aware that a digital clock somewhere reads 11:10 in green. I sink into physical bliss.

I sigh in pleasure as Holden licks, kisses and gently sucks my breasts, then leaves them to kiss my mouth. He glides my pants off followed by my panties. I hear him catch his breath. He's suddenly motionless. I raise my head and look down at him, wondering what he's doing. He's staring at my body. Looking up to see my expression, he whispers, "You're beautiful!"

I expect him to kiss me down there so I'm surprised when he lays against me, holding me fast, anxious to enter me. I surprise him by pushing him away and sliding down his body to rest my head on his loins. I hold his hot maleness in a tight grip. I put my lips to him, encasing his swollen hardness in the wetness of my mouth. I need to obliterate the memory of the last time I did this, that bafflement, that helpless feeling of failure. Holden's gasps reassure me.

He soon reaches for me, pulling me up, easily bringing me to him. With my head hovering above his, he brushes the hair off my face and kisses me, and, as our tongues explore one each other's mouths, he sort of rotates us around, so I'm on my back. With our lips still joined, he finds his way into my most private part. We both let out a cry of pleasure.

The sum of emotions I've repressed for so long are given free rein. Rage, loneliness, hurt, and simple, pure need find their way to the surface. My nails dig into his back. I'm possessed. This is a new Jolie.

I've never experienced sex like this.

Rocky made love to me like he did everything: gently, slowly and luxuriously. But Holden is a cross between an animal and a gymnast. And it becomes obvious that he's also a performer. I only know I need a good fuck tonight, and Holden is the man to give it to me. He's a healthy young male, and I'm about to find out that he is both able and willing to present me with multiple erections.

I enjoy multiple orgasms.

He lays beside me and asks what's got to be the most ludicrous, unnecessary question I've ever heard — like he wants to confirm that he's cinched the part. "Did you like that?" he says.

"Very much," I coo.

"Good. Next time, I'll be able to hold back longer. But first, I'm going to get us a cold drink."

He jumps out of bed, giving me the chance to fully assess his naked body. He looks like a beautiful statue of a young man that's come to life. I admire his body, muscular, smooth, almost hairless, and nearly perfect. The guy is undoubtedly a looker. Those deep-set green eyes and strong jaw probably look really good on film. I smile at the thought that Holden, obviously so highly sexual, is now in my life and lives just steps away.

Then, just before he leaves the bedroom, he stands in front of the full-length mirror set within his closet door and I peer at him as he goes through a series of Mr. World poses, flexing his biceps, then his pectorals and other nameless muscles. What's strange is that he doesn't know I'm watching him, so he's not doing this for my benefit; I think he gets off on himself.

He tears himself away from the mirror and leaves for the kitchen, whistling. While I wait for him, some part of me is trying to make sense of the fact that I've abandoned myself so completely to Holden. How am I able to physically enjoy another man so much after Rocky?

He's back, holding a tall, iced drink, and I'll be damned if he doesn't put the drink down on the dresser to pose in front of the mirror again! He sucks in his already perfect abs before returning to me on the bed. I don't like all this mirror stuff.

"Wow! Seeing you laying naked there like that ... your body's glistening from our sex ..." He nods. "You're gorgeous!"

He stands above me, takes out a piece of ice and runs it slowly around my breasts, in circles, teasing my hardened nipples.

"You realize you're my girl now, don't you?" he says.

I instinctively move away. The ice cube moves with me, dripping down my breasts towards my navel. I like feeling. And I like letting Holden pleasure me.

I'm certainly not about to be his "girl" – or anyone else's girl for that matter. But he has another lovely erection; this is definitely *not* the time to argue the point. He turns me around and takes me from behind and my juices are everywhere.

Amazingly, the more he fucks me, the more I want and, true to his word, this time he fucks me longer. I come again. He finally falls on the bed and reaches over to his nightstand drawer to get a pack of cigarettes. He lights one and offers it to me. I refuse it, glad it's not weed.

He exhales. "Ms. Jolie, you are one horny girl."

I turn on my side to face him and shrug. "What can I do?" I say playfully.

"You can definitely get me going. Damn, Jolie! You are a gorgeous sexy tigress."

"And you, Mr. Holden are a horny guy."

"But I don't scratch," he says, turning to show me the red lines I've made on his back, reaching down almost to his waist. I've never scratched before.

"I know," I say. "I saw that when you got up. I'm sorry!"

"We may have to cut your nails, Ms. Jolie." *He's got to be kidding!* He finishes his cigarette and he's at me again moving between my legs, fondling me there and I love it. "You have a lovely pussy, Ms. Jolie."

"Mm. And you have a lovely dick, Mr. Holden."

Incredibly, Holden's lovely dick is again almost fully erect! He almost tosses the cigarette into the ashtray on the nightstand and we have sex again. Then he peaks and collapses alongside me, breathing deeply.

"Holden, you are an animal!"

"And you're the answer to any man's dream," he says. "No matter what I do to you, you come."

He picks up his cigarette from the ashtray, takes a quick hit and puts it out. He gets up to go to the bathroom. *Oh my god!* He's doing it again! He's standing in front of the mirror flexing his muscles! And ditto when he comes back from the bathroom! That Mr. World thing! *Damn!* It's so ridiculous that I want to laugh out loud and tell him he's a joke! The guy can't pass a friggin' mirror without posing and admiring himself! There is zero chance that I would ever take him more seriously than an occasional fuck.

When he returns, he takes the last sip of melted ice left in the glass, then stretches out beside me with one hand behind his head. "You know, you remind me of my very first girlfriend," he says.

I rest my head on his arm. "Was she still walking when you left her?"

Holden laughs. "Her? What about me? I was seventeen. She was Swedish. Her name was Inga. She used to say, '*I vont you,*' like Greta Garbo. '*I vont you, now!'* I swear, I think that's actually all she ever said. I was constantly fucking her! She wouldn't leave me alone. She had a way of getting me hard again and again – even when I thought I was dead, just by saying that. '*I vont you, now!'* It was like a Pavlovian reflex."

I would have thought they were perfect for one another. "Why did you break up?"

"Are you kidding? I had to. I couldn't take it anymore. My life had stopped. No friends, no homework. My grades dropped. Man! I was always exhausted. You know I'm sexy. I mean, I like sex a lot, but shit, Inga – Inga was truly *insatiable.*"

"She sounds like quite a woman."

Holden grunted. "Yeah, quite a woman. She was sixteen."

Now that I'm sexually spent, I'm tired and ready to go to sleep. I swing out of bed.

"Bathroom?" Holden asks lazily.

"Home."

He sits up. "You're spending the night."

"No."

"It's okay, really. I want you to."

"Impossible."

I'm looking around the room for my clothes. Remembering the sequence of events, I grab my pants and head for the living room.

"Why impossible?" Holden asks.

"Out of the question," I say, shaking my head.

In the living room, I grope the wall for a light switch but can't find one. Behind me, Holden turns the lights on. I march across the room, picking my clothes up off the floor as I go.

"What's the sudden rush?" Holden asks.

"No rush, " I say, "it's just time to go home."

"You can't go!" Bazoo whines and scratch at the kitchen door. I but Holden doesn't seem to care about his dog just then. "I want to spend the night with you," he says.

As he's becoming more insistent, I'm becoming increasingly anxious to get away from him. "Sorry."

Bazoo's incessant scratching bothers me, so I open the kitchen door and the dog runs out into the living room, wagging his tail and jumping on me. Holden doesn't try to stop him, and I struggle to dress. At last, my shoes are on and I head for the door.

"Well, at least let me walk you home," he says.

"It's no problem. Really. I practically live next door. I'll just roll down the hill."

"Hey, come on. There's no way I'm letting you walk home alone."

Though I don't wait for him, he's there alongside me anyway, a pair of pants thrown on and Bazoo on a leash. Along the way, he continually tries to persuade me to change my mind and return to his apartment. "I promise you'll be comfortable," he says. "I'll hold you all night. We're a couple now. That's where you belong."

Oh my God, get me out of here! I repeat that it's impossible.

I'm in a hurry to get home. The short distance to my apartment takes forever. Holden has a tighter hold on my hand than he has on

Bazoo's leash, and the dog stops to sniff and do his thing at every single tree, every single bush and every fucking blade of grass.

Finally, we're at my door. I find my key and insert it into the lock then turn to Holden. "I really had a great time. Thank you." I let him kiss me, enjoying the knowledge that this is last of him.

With his arms at my waist, he smiles. "You know, I can stay here with you, if you want," he says. "I'll take Bazoo home and be back in a second. That way, tomorrow morning we can continue where we left off."

As great as my sexual appetite was earlier, I'm now equally put off by the idea of waking up next to Holden. I'm super impatient to get inside. I want him to *go!* "Thanks, but I have to get up real early tomorrow. I have a lot to do."

He hugs me. "I'll miss you," he says. Then he kisses me again, this time more passionately.

I break away from him. "I need to pee," I say.

"Okay, Ms. Jolie," he says, grudgingly, "Well, I guess this is goodnight."

"Goodnight, Holden."

"I'll call you tomorrow," he says. "We'll do something."

"I'm busy tomorrow."

"Okay, that's right. Well, I'll call anyway just to hear your voice. And there's always tomorrow night."

My hand is on the doorknob. Before I can turn it, Holden has his hand back on mine, stopping me. "Jolie," he says, "I'm really glad about tonight. Are you?"

He sounds so earnest, I can't say no. "Sure."

He relaxes. His hand comes away. "Good," he says, looking into my eyes. "I know it's the beginning of something really special for us, for the two of us. I'm sure of it." He's caressing my shoulder.

The doorknob turns and I step into my apartment, ready to close the door on him. "Goodnight, Holden."

I shut the door and lock it, then lean against it and sigh in relief. Thank God that's over!

As I start for my bedroom, I realize I'm starving. After that sexual workout, I crave food. I devour two pieces of soft white bread smothered with peanut butter and honey and down a glass of chocolate milk.

I know I'll sleep well tonight. My body is more relaxed than it's been in a long time and pleasantly exhausted, even too tired to take a shower. I crawl into my bed, looking forward to a delicious hot shower in the morning after a great night's sleep.

I close my eyes, drifting off when my phone rings. I answer automatically, wondering would call at such a late hour and why. "I'm in bed. I smell you on the sheets. I really wish you were here with me, Miss Jolie."

I'm enjoying a morning cup of coffee with Nora and Jonah.

"I can't wait to hear about last night," Nora says. It's a question.

"We know you got home pretty late," Jonah adds. "We heard you coming in. So, you had some fun?" He's as hopeful as Nora. They're actually cute and have about as much subtlety as a pair of hovering parents.

"It was okay."

Nora is passing a meaningful look to Jonah. "Okay as in, you'll see him again?" She asks.

"I don't think so," I say.

Nora looks disappointed. "Why not, Jo?"

Jonah answers for me. "Nora, the president is probably okay, too," he says. "Our Jolie just wasn't blown away by the guy."

Nora's smirking. "Yeah? Well, I'll bet the guy was blown away by our girl."

And blown away I suppose he was, for minute later, the phone rings.

"I just woke up. I miss you already," Holden says.

"I was just on my way out the door."

"Were you lonely last night? Did you sleep well, all alone? Or were you as lonely as I was?"

"I'm sorry, Holden, but I really have to go."

"When will you be home?"

209

"I don't know."

"Well, I'll be thinking of you until I see you later. I'll call you. We'll get together," he says.

I make the 'crazy' sign to Nora and Jonah. "I'm sorry. I'm busy tonight, Holden. Why don't I call you?"

In fact, I actually do go out to do some errands. When I get home there are three more messages from Holden and two hang-ups on my answering machine. I leave for the Pelican without answering his calls. I know I'll be talking to him sooner or later; probably sooner; it can't be helped.

I have to make Holden go away. It's a shame I can't use his services again. He wants too much from me – way, way too much.

The thing is, I know he won't go away without an explanation. I'll have to tell him something that will push him away. And that won't be fun. I won't say I just ended a relationship. That's none of his business. I'll say I just don't want one. I won't say he's way too sticky and maybe a little nuts. His girl? And what's with all the phone calls?

I'll tell him that I wish him all the luck in the world in his career. I hope his psychics and numerologists will pull through for him. I really do. If his acting is as formidable as his fucking, he won't need much luck. But I'm done with him. He has to stop calling me.

My face-to-face explanation comes within 24 hours. He's at our door, unannounced. He's come to see why I haven't returned his calls. He's worried, concerned that something may have happened to me, and anyway, he was walking Bazoo. So, here he is.

"I don't think we should see each other again," I say.

He looks amazed, flabbergasted. "Hey, that's crazy!" I shrug. "Jolie, I'm in love with you."

I scoff. "In love with me?" I say. "Holden, you don't even know me."

"I've been in love with you since the first time I saw you," he says. "Maybe I didn't know you then, but I do now."

"I doubt it's love."

"It is! Jolie, I love you! And I know we're supposed to be together. We're meant for one another." He two hands are in his hair, pulling, and I get that he's frustrated.

"Okay," he says, "I know I'm not everything you want right now, but one day, I will be. This is my time! The planets are lined up. I feel really good about the pilot. Things are happening for me. Trust me, the negative vibes around me are fading away. They're almost all gone." He takes hold of my arm and shakes it. "It's happening for me, Jolie! I know it! I feel it! I know you feel it too! That's why you're not making any sense! You're talking crazy."

I smile, shaking my head. "I don't think so."

"Oh, wow!" He throws his arms up and spins around. "Tell me you didn't enjoy the other night."

"I did," I say.

"I know you did! And I know you really like me, maybe even love me, too. You're just in denial. Virgos do that. Don't do that."

I've been standing with my arms crossed, trying to be patient as he's gone through his tirade, trying hard to persuade me to change my mind and "be his girl."

"You're afraid I'm a player?" he says, "I swear I'm not. I'm an actor, yes, but I'm a one-woman-man. Honest!"

Though I have no desire to hurt him, I need to inject a note of reality into this melodrama. "Look, Holden. I don't love you. I was horny and there you were." His face falls and I feel really, really bad. He looks so hurt! But he's forcing me to do this. "And you were great. Really."

His hands reach for his head, as if he's poised to do sit-ups. "You're kidding me. You're talking like a guy. Like I was just a fuck." I just shrug. His arms fall to his side, waving me off as they do. "Well, the hell with you, Jolie. I'm not going to beg."

He storms to the door, pauses a beat then turns. "I'm giving you one last chance to get together with me. I'm the best thing going. After last night, you know that. This is a once-in-a lifetime chance. So, what's it going to be?"

"Find someone who appreciates you, Holden."

"Fuck that. You know what your problem is, girl? You don't know what you've got here," he says pointing to himself. "Look at me," he says. "Girls go ape shit over me. And I'm going to be a star! A fucking star! And soon! You get that? I'm going to be everywhere you look, TV, those fucking billboards on the Strip … and I'll be in movies one day. And I'm asking you to be my supporting star, My Girl!" I'm silent. "You think I'm going to beg you? Look, I'm asking you one last time. You want me?"

"You'll be a great star one day. I wish you all the luck in your career, Holden. And I know you'll make some girl really happy."

"Fuck this," he says.

He walks out leaving my front door wide open. On the patio, he turns to me a last time. "If you ever get horny and want another good fuck, call me. I'll see if I can fit you in."

Through the last week, I've answered the phone to silence two or three times a day, and I've had umpteen hang-ups on my answering machine.

I'm washing dishes when I get a delivery of two-dozen long-stemmed red roses set in a vase. I read the attached card before ripping it up. *"Tonight is our one-week anniversary. I miss you and I forgive you. Call me. Love, Holden."*

I put the flowers on the table and try to forget about them, but I can't.

Finally, I throw them in the trash.

29

INVISIBLE

*H*e plays with the wire, moving it this way and that in the keyhole.

The door opens with a click, the only sound in the still afternoon. He steps inside and quickly closes it behind him, then simply stands, surveying the room. He's in no hurry. He knows she is at work, and he saw her girlfriend drive away with her big boyfriend.

He's been here twice before. The first time it was crowded with people. The second time there was only the two of them. The room is smaller than he'd realized, the furniture more modest, standard inexpensive rental.

He scans the room. He doesn't see the flowers. The vase on the counter is empty. He walks through the living room and stands in the tiny vestibule facing a bathroom. There's are doors on either side. He opens one. The fragrance signals this is her room. He enters. The bed – her bed – has a simple headboard and two pillows encased in white and a fluffy pink bedspread covering it. He walks over and gazes down at the empty bed and his fingers glide over the pillow where her head has recently lain.

He notices the very small, framed photograph on her bedside table. It's a photo of her, locked in the arms of a swarthy, dark-haired guy wearing glasses and an earring. They're both smiling. He picks it up. *Who the hell is he?*

He picks up the scarf laying alongside the photo. It's mustard colored and incredibly soft. He puts it to his nose. Her fragrance rushes to meets him. He inhales deeply. He puts the scarf down and approaches the dresser. He opens the top drawer; it's filled with stacks of colored tops. He closes it and opens the second drawer. When he sees the mix of silk, lace and cotton lingerie in various colors, he realizes this is what he was looking for. He spots the panties he thinks she'd worn that night and brings it to his nose hoping her scent is there, but there's only the faint smell of soap. He puts the panties in his pocket and closes the drawer. He catches his reflection in the mirror above the dresser and his gaze locks onto eyes that stare back at him reproachfully. He opens the drawer, replaces the panties then shuts it.

As he moves to her closet, he notes that the answering machine by her bed shows five messages received. His hand moves to the machine, but he quickly withdraws it and slides the closet door open. His heart swoons. He yearns to see her in every skirt, every pair of pants, every dress and blouse that hangs there. He recognizes some. He wants to see her model every pair of shoes set on the closet floor. He sighs as he slides the door closed.

There's a small maple desk set against a wall. It's as tacky as the rest of the furniture in the apartment. A blue book lays on it, *The History of Philosophy*, and alongside that is a brochure that reads, *Santa Monica City College Catalog of Spring Classes*.

The lined loose -leaf paper that she's written on captures his attention. Her penmanship is elegant, the letters long, well-proportioned and lean – like her.

One sheet has something that looks like a poem written on it. He moves, positioning himself to read it without having to touch it. He reads.

Invisible.
I am invisible.
I wander through life unseen,
Untouched,

Uncared for,
Uncaring.

You see me.
You touch me.
You cover me with kisses,
Fill my hollowness with giving.
Your touch brings me to life;
Your love brings me to love.

And then you're gone,
Invisible.
Where is love?

Well, I'll be Goddamned! What do you know? She writes poetry!

He looks back at the photo of her, smiling in the arms of the unknown man he despises and anger bubbles inside him. *Why can't she see that her love is standing right here, damn it!* He slams his fist against the wall. *Damn you! This is fucked up!*

He must quell his anger.

He stomps back to the living room and paces there until he's calmer. He sees several more books on the coffee table, all text books. He sees a sweatshirt hanging on a chair, and he can see the Rams logo on the front. It belongs to her roommate's big boyfriend; he's seen him wearing it.

The sight propels him to scope the living room again then return to her bedroom, his eyes moving rapidly but carefully now, anxious to see if he'd missed any signs of another male in the apartment. He finds none.

He opens her closet again, this time sliding open the other door. Everything there is hers. He takes a final look around the room she was so anxious to return to, the bed she chose over his, committing every-thing he sees to his memory, making an imprint in his mind of the face of the man he loathes captured in the photo. *Could it be her brother?*

Retracing his steps, he steps into the small kitchen, opens the refrig-erator and peeks in. It's moderately well-stocked. He slaps his forehead. *What the fuck am I doing?* He swings the door shut and stands before the empty sink, looking down into it. *Jesus Christ, she's made me nuts!*

He heads for the front door. The ebbing afternoon, taking daylight with it, makes the apartment look a bit more forlorn to him now than when he entered. He's almost at the door when he stops. He wants something of hers, something to remember her by. He deserves that much.

He moves back toward her bedroom, his mind on her lingerie but when he returns to her dresser, he stops and stands there, conflicted. *Fuck her! I want her so much! I won't stoop to that! But she's mine! No, I can't! Oh, God, she's driven me crazy!*

He is confused. He's suddenly afraid. He doesn't fear being caught; he fears the pull that's brought him to this. He must leave this place immediately.

He fumbles as he tries to open the door and almost pulls the door-knob off as it opens. He's outside then, not a moment too soon, and shuts the door behind him.

His hands go to his temples, pushing, squeezing, trying to squeeze thoughts of her out of his mind. He breathes deeply and walks across the brick patio. He remembers the night they were together at that railing, the night sky clear and filled with stars and below them, the lights of the city, dazzling. The view is clouded now. There will be no stars out tonight. He descends to the pavement.

He's going home to feed his dog and his dreams.

30
MOTHER'S DAY

1979

*S*ince I saw Holden's signature on that card with the roses, I've been thinking about the influence of a name and wondering how my name might be influencing me and my life.

Holden changed his name to heighten his chances of success. Is there anything to that?

What was my mother's name? My father's? Had they given me a name at birth different than Jolie? Has my name affected my life?

I'm more determined than ever to demand answers to these and other questions about my adoption from Phil and Stella. I just need to figure out how I can get them to sit down with me and answer my questions when I haven't even seen them or spoken to them for so many months. I'm nervous about contacting them after so much has happened. I know I can't approach Phil. I should start with Stella. She'll be easier to talk to, more receptive and open to reconnect with me. She'll calm Phil down. Then I'll grill them.

I work the brunch shift today at the restaurant. I'll go to the house after work and make peace with Stella. I'll take her flowers. After all, it's Mother's Day. It would be great to find out who my real mother is on Mother's Day.

Before leaving for The Pelican, I call their house. There's no answer. I don't leave a message. I'll call again during my break.

The restaurant is unusually busy this Sunday, with a storm of reservations made for brunch. I'm standing at the podium, reviewing the list of reservations, crossing out the "no shows" – those parties that are more than a half hour late – and putting a check by the names of those who did show up and are waiting for a table, adding the number of people in their party.

Though my head is down, I can see a man standing in front of the podium, wearing the same blue shirt tucked into the same brown trousers, with the same belt that Phil wears. I look up to see Phil. Before my surprise wanes, I notice he's unshaven. His eyes are red and swollen and I see tears on his cheeks.

"Your mother's dying," he says. "She wants to see you." He's wiping tears away with his hand.

My body tenses. I'm scared. If Phil has found me, it must be something serious."Why?"

"She's got cancer." I stare at him. The breath goes out of me and I instinctively hold on to the podium. My tears are automatic. "She doesn't have much time," he says. He looks away. His voice is raspy. "Her lungs."

"Where is she?" I ask.

"Cedars." It's whispered.

Tears immediately fill my eyes. I reach for two napkins from the nearest table and hand Phil one. "Can I see her?"

He nods. "She wants to see you."

Cedars-Sinai Hospital is less than a mile's drive from the restaurant.

218

On the way, Phil brings me up to date.

"She complained her back hurt. Every day. Aspirin didn't help. You know your mother; she don't take aspirin for nothing. But she hurt so much. Eventually, she tried all of them. Nothing worked. She had *a lot* of pain."

He looks at me and finds my eyes. "She's been really sad since you left. You were her life. You go off and …" he turns back to the road, sighs and wipes his eyes.

"Anyway, I was gonna take her to France. Cheer her up." He looks at the dashboard and chuckles softly. Something like a smile appears on his face, as though he's seeing something smile-worthy there. "That Stella!" he says. "She's talked about going to France since I can remember. She's always wanted to go there." He's somber again. "She was so unhappy after you left. She missed you like you can't believe. So, I thought," he slams his hand down on the steering wheel, "Okay, France will cheer her up."

He repositions himself and fixes a stare somewhere in front of him. "She – we – kept hoping you'd come to your senses, come home." He looks at me. "You still with … him?"

"No," I say.

"Good," he says. He turns his eyes back to the road. "Tell her. It'll make her happy."

"When did you find out about the cancer?" My heart is thumping and I know I haven't yet heard the worst of it.

He turns to me, his head hung down. "I says to her, 'Go see the doctor, Stella. Go before the trip. You want to see some *fakokta* French doctor that don't even speak English?'" His eyes have widened and now they shift hurriedly from side to side. "She was too busy buying *schmutzahs* for the trip – like she's going to a fashion show, for Chrissakes! Skirts, pants, blouses, shoes – what do I know?

He glances at me. "She says it's nothing, probably the diet pills she's been on." I know she's been on those pills forever. He continues. "So, she stopped taking them, but still hurts. Her head hurt, her chest hurt, her back hurt … " He's gripping the steering wheel tightly with both hands. "God! She was coughing like there's no tomorrow. Finally, *I* made the appointment." He's looking out his window.

I look out my window. The world around me looks unchanged; but my world is out of synch.

"Doctor says she's gotta take tests," he continues. "So I take her here and there for tests, so many goddamned tests. Meanwhile, she's in so much goddamned pain – poor kid! – I cancel the trip." He rests his wrist on the top of the steering wheel and shakes his head. "Boy, how she got mad at me then! She wanted to go so bad she could have killed me!"

Stopped at a red light, he takes his hands off the wheel and wipes tears away with his shirt sleeve as new ones rush to take their place. I offer him a tissue from the box of Kleenex in the car. He doesn't take one, doesn't even look at it. I take out two.

He continues. "The doctor calls. Says he wants to see her. Right away. Says to bring me." He sighs. "Your mother tries to hide she's scared. But she keeps asking me, 'Why does he want *you* to come?' I says, 'For Pete's sake, Stella, how should I know?' I'm supposed to be a mind reader?" The question hangs.

Then he's quiet until we stop at the next red light. He shakes his head slowly and looks out his window. When he speaks again, he's nodding strenuously. "Well, we found out. Yeah, we sure did." He slaps the steering wheel again and makes a noise like a monster's chuckle, then goes quiet.

"Go on, Dad."

His body writhes, as if it's painful to force the words out, words he doesn't want to say, words that rekindle memories he doesn't want to relive. "Stella keeps asking me what the doctor wants to tell her. When we get to his office, a woman takes us into the doctor's fancy-shmancy office, smiling all the way, like it's just any other happy meeting we're having, and we sit down. He's sitting behind his fancy-shmancy desk." I'm held in suspense as Phil pauses and looks around. He sighs. "And he says … he … says, 'Well, Mrs. Gold, I've reviewed all your tests. I'm sorry.' – No, no, he's, '*deeply* sorry' — 'I'm *deeply* sorry to tell you this,'" he says." Phil swallows hard. "'but the tests show you have lung cancer.'"

Phil slams his hand on the steering wheel, yet again, as though he's smacking the doctor, and wipes his eyes with his shirt sleeve. "And then he says," Phil's voice is a mix of misery and parody as he tries to sound as schooled as the doctor. "'And, as your doctor, it is my unfortunate task to inform you that there's not much we can do.'" He pauses for a moment and sobs.

I put my arm on his and squeeze. "I'm here now," I say. "I'll be with you … and Mom."

He goes on with his story, and I'm not sure he's heard me. "'It's progressed quite a bit and … and it's … '" He breaks down again, sobbing. "'… it's too advanced.'"

His shoulders are spasming. I move my hand up to his shoulder in an attempt to comfort him; there's just so much I can do, sitting alongside him in the car.

Meanwhile, neither of us notice that the light has turned green, and we're startled by the cacophony of horns behind us.

"Fuck you, schmuck!" Phil screams, into his rear-view mirror. He flicks off the guy behind us. "You're in a rush? What are *you* in a rush for?" He sits back in his seat and starts driving again, wiping away his most recent tears. "It's *my* wife that's dying! And he's in a rush!"

I hold the ball of wet tissues in my hand and take out three more. "What else did the doctor say?" I ask. I need to know. "What about therapy? Surgery? Radiation? Chemo?"

Phil shakes his head. He's so sad, much sadder than the night he learned that his father had died. "The big doctor!" he says. Then he repeats my question. "What else did he say?" Phil scoffs. "Nothing. The big doctor sat there with his hands folded on his big desk, a big somebody. I says to him, 'What do you mean 'too late?' You're a doctor, ain't you? She's sick; fix her,' I says. 'Money's no object. Just tell us what to do, where to go.'"

"And?" I wait.

Phil's eyes travel from one end of his front window to the other end. "That miserable son of a bitch! He sits in his fancy office with all his goodies — he's got a fish tank in the wall, for Pete's sake! The big doctor!" He looks down again and this time, I follow his eyes and see wet stains on his pants. When he continues, he makes the doctor sound sissy stupid now, sing-songy, like a school child in the playground. 'I'm afraid it's too late to do anything. I told you, it's quite advanced.'

221

Slumped over and weeping, Phil's anger flares again. "Fuck you and your high-and-mighty speech, doctor," he says. Then his voice chokes and I see his chest rise and fall. "He says, 'I'm afraid there's not much we can do.'"

He turns to me. "The bastards only fix you when there's nothing wrong with you!"

My heart breaks."Poor Mom."

He sniffles and shakes his head. "Stella's sitting there like she's already dead. Doesn't say a word, just stares at the doctor. I says to the guy, 'Come on, there must be something we can do here. Anything.' But the bastard just sits there, using big fancy words. Says his doctor pals – his *colleagues*, yeah, that was the word he used – they *confirmed* everything; her file, her tests, and there ain't nothing they can do."

We're at a stop sign at the entry to the hospital's parking lot. Phil brakes. His hands drop to his sides. He's looking straight ahead at nothing, as pale and as miserable as a man who's just received a death sentence and, in fact, he has.

He grips the steering wheel again. "The big *makher* looks straight at your mother, says, 'My advice, Mrs. Gold, is to put your affairs in order and spend the time you have, enjoying each other.' I went to pieces. I wanted to kill the son-of-bitch bastard. I wanted to go over there and wring his goddamned doctor neck.

Phil is muttering to himself as though he's forgotten I'm in the car with him and hasn't heard my soft weeping. We've been blocking the entryway to the parking lot. Sitting here, the two of us crying, it hasn't occurred to to us to continue past the stop sign.

"Your poor mother could hardly speak," Phil says. "'You mean I'm going to die?' Stella says. The bastard just looks down at his folded hands with the manicured nails on his big important desk and says nothing. Doesn't answer her! I wanted to get out of there before I threw up, fainted or had a heart attack.

"Then the son-of-a-bitch nods. He *nods!*" He looks at me as though he needs to know that I see how horrible the doctor was, as though I agree that it was his fault Stella is going to die."'I'm afraid so!,' he says." Red as blood, Phil looks at me and repeats, *I'm afraid so!*" He sobs. He sighs.

He goes on. "Your mother's still staring at him, just sitting there staring at the lousy S.O.B! I try to hold her hand, but she pulls away and says, 'When?'"

I turn away from Phil and cover my eyes unable to imagine what what must have been like for my mother. I can't imagine her having the courage to ask that question; I can't even bear to hear the answer.

Phil raps his forehead with closed fists as he continues, his voice faltering. "Again, he doesn't answer her. He doesn't even look up at her." He wipes away tears with his palms. "So, she asks him *again*."

I can't bear to hear this. I don't know how much more I can take. I want to open my car door and run. But I need to hear this and I need to support Phil.

"He can't look her in the eye. Instead of answering," he says, "he starts to play with his pen – his goddamned pen! 'No one can predict that, Mrs. Gold,' he finally says, without even looking at her. The big doctor squirms a little in his seat and then he says, 'you should begin straightening out your affairs without delay.' He sounds like he's recorded that, like he plays it all the time." He's shaking his head again, slowly, as if in disbelief. "I'll never forget the way he said those words. *'begin straightening out your affairs without delay.'*"

I clutch my cheeks, my stomach, hurling. I can't seem to catch my breath. The several cars now lined up behind us, waiting to enter the lot after us, blast their horns. The attendant is approaching. Phil jerks the car forward up to the gate. He has to open his door to reach the ticket that spits out. Entering the lot, he turns down the first aisle of parking spaces so erratically that his tires screech. I brace myself, taking hold of the dashboard with one hand, my door handle with the other.

"Straighten out affairs!" He sounds as angry as he's ever been. Angrier. He hooks the car into a parking space without slowing down. "We're supposed to sit and listen to this *goniff*? Stella's supposed to sit there and hear she's dying?" He grabs hold of the steering wheel with his two hands. his eyes opened wide and talks to the car's roof through mournful sobs. "Why couldn't he tell just *me*? Why did they have to tell *her* she's dying? She didn't have to know!"

My heart is breaking for both my parents. I reach over again to take hold of his arm. "Maybe another doctor somewhere can do something," I say. I want to sound soothing, but I don't; I sound scared.

"I told him. I says we'll find a better doctor, a real doctor. He had an answer for that too. You know what the fancy doctor with the big fancy desk says?"

"What?" I ask.

"The bastard says. 'You can go to doctor after doctor, but I assure you they'll say the same thing.' He *"assures"* us!" Phil wipes his wet cheeks with his shirt sleeve again. "Listen to this. You know what the genius says? He says, whenever he tells someone they're dying, they don't want to believe it. No kidding! That's something, huh? He had some big fancy word they taught him in medical school for that, too. They taught him what to say when they made him a doctor. I'm telling you, the guy's a goddamned genius!

"Who the hell wants to believe they're dying?" He looks at me then. "Do you?" he asks. I don't answer. "I want to be there when the S.O.B. finds out *he's* dying of cancer and see if *he* believes it!"

"Dad, why can't they do anything?"

The breath goes out of Phil. He turns the engine off. He sounds exhausted. Depleted. Hopeless. "The cancer's gone too far. It's spread from the lungs to the rest of her body. He had a word for that, too, '*mast*- something.' That's why her back and the rest of her hurt so much."

We sit there, gazing vacantly, Phil's keys on his lap. Now I know everything – or enough.

My body is limp. "Poor Mom." It's an effort for me to speak. "What did she do when he told her?"

Phil shrugs, his gaze down, speaking as if in a trance. "She just sat there, like a ghost."

"I can't believe they don't even *try* to do something," I say. Ridiculously, I think my brilliant idea can remedy this horrible situation. "Why can't they at least *try* radiation or surgery or something? Anything!"

Phil's expression is blank, his eyes, dull. "Nothing to do. He gave us something for her pain and sent us home." He sighs. "She took it, and then took more and more. The pain got so bad, I didn't know what to do." He's remembering again. "I couldn't stand seeing her like that." He looks down at the keys on his lap then outside his window. "Here they give her all the morphine she needs."

And then I dare ask the question I couldn't believe Stella had the courage to ask. "How much longer?"

Phil suddenly, abruptly opens his door and gets out of the car. I hurry to get out as well, not wanting to miss the answer, in case he gives one. We meet and together, we make our way down the lot to the front door. I'm almost a half-head taller than him; either he's shrunk or I've gotten taller. "Days ... hours ... minutes." He stops in his tracks and looks up. "God forgive me! I should have done something."

I've never felt as close to this grieving man as I do right now. He's questioning himself and I know exactly what he's feeling; I've felt it, too. "Dad, what could you have done?"

He doesn't answer right away. One hand is at his forehead, stretching toward the middle of his hairless head, the other is clutching the car keys so tightly in his fist that his knuckles are white. "Taken her to the doctor sooner ... Pushed her harder. Instead, I let her go out and buy all that *khazari* clothing until it was too late. If only I'd known!"

"You can't blame yourself, Dad. You couldn't have known. How could you have known?" I take his arm in mine and hug it tightly. Please, don't blame yourself."

He reaches for my hand, grasping it as we enter the hospital. Realizing that all this time Phil has been alone in his grief, I feel a rush of compassion and I'm grateful that I'm here with him now to share this sadness with him.

We're the only two people waiting for the elevators. When he turns his gaze up, I assume he wants to see what floor the elevator is on, but then he says, "What will I do without her?" and I realize he's addressing the heavens. My heart goes out to him. "Your mother's a good woman," he says. "She doesn't deserve this."

The elevator arrives and we step inside. Before he pushes the button that will take us to Stella's floor, he takes my arm and looks me in the eyes. "She loves you. You have no idea how you changed her life. Tell her you love her."

As we walk down the hospital corridor, I try to look straight ahead, not wanting to peek inside any of the open rooms we pass, bodies lying helpless, ill or broken, possibly dying. A posted sign tells me we're in the cancer ward, and I wonder if this is the wing reserved for the terminally ill.

As afraid as I am of what I might see in the rooms we pass, I'm terrified of what I'll see in Room 887. But when I enter Stella's room, I'm surprised. Stella doesn't look all that different from the last time I saw her, about nine months ago. Her face is thinner, and she looks tired. But her hair is styled and lacquered as always, and in lieu of a hospital gown, she's wearing the purple duster I recognize.

Phil enters a step ahead of me. Then Stella sees me and her eyes light up. I waste no time moving to the left side of her bed to kiss her cheek. "Hi, Mom." I try not to look at the row of bedside monitors set up on the other side of her bed that beep with green lines and tiny red flashing lights.

"He brought you."

Two thin plastic tubes are lost inside Stella's nostrils and a bag of clear liquid that hangs from a tall metal pole runs through a tube into her left forearm. Her right arm reaches out for me. There's a small white device laying on top of the sheet.

"How are you?" she says.

"I'm okay. How are you? Are you in pain?" I'm hardly breathing, but I'm smiling. I'm determined not to cry.

"No, honey. They have me on morphine." She holds up the small device. It's connected to the tube running down from the IV bag. "See this? When I need more morphine, I press this button. See?" She's pressing down on the button. Then she says, "Sweetheart, push that lever so I can sit up a little." When I elevate her, I see the lines that pain has etched onto her face. Her breathing is shallow. She looks me up and down.

"How are you, my pretty Jolie? You've been gone so long. Didn't you miss me? You never even called home." At that moment, I so deeply regret not having kept in touch. I don't tell her that I'd called home soon after leaving and that Phil hung up on me before I could speak to her; it's likely that Phil never told her about that call.

"I called your apartment a few times," she says, "when I found out about this," she explains. Phil's head springs up in surprise. I'm surprised too. "You think I wouldn't want you here?" She goes on. "I got your number from Carol. But you never answered and ... well, I didn't want to leave a message. Never mind. You're here now, thank heavens."

Oh my God! I had assumed that all the hang ups and the lingering wordless messages I'd gotten on the answering machine were all from Holden! I so grateful to Carol for giving her my number. "I would have come sooner if I'd known," I say. "I was going to visit you today anyway, to wish you a Happy Mother's Day." I swallow my motive in planning the visit. "Happy Mother's Day, Mom." I bite my tongue hard to keep from shedding tears. "Sorry I didn't get a chance to buy you flowers."

"Thank you, honey. They wouldn't allow flowers in the room anyway." I finally scan the room; there are no flowers in sight.

"You look so pretty," she says with a smile. "I like that sweater."

"I know. I like it too. You bought it for me."

"You look real nice," Stella says.

"I have to dress for my job." I sit gingerly on the bed. "Is it okay to sit here?"

She nods. "Job?"

Phil answers her from his seat across the room. "She's a hostess at some restaurant."

"No school?" Stella asks.

"It's Sunday, Mom. I have school. I'm taking night classes."

"Night classes? Why night classes?" Before I can answer, Stella asks another question. "And that boy ... "

"I'm not seeing him anymore."

She grimaces and her shallow breath slows. She pushes the button she's holding. "That's good."

She stretches her hand down the bed sheet to find mine. "You're a smart girl, Jolie. I told your father you wouldn't stay with him." She stops talking to push the button on the device and takes several breaths. I watch her relax a little as the morphine flows through her. I see the easing of pain reflected on her face. I've never seen anyone in this state.

"Jolie," she asks, "why night class? We have money, sweetheart. Your father has money. You don't need to work. Why didn't you just ask your father for money?"

I shrug. The answer seems obvious. I didn't ask because he'd made it clear that as long as I chose to live elsewhere and date Rocky, he'd give me nothing. His money, like his house and their love, had always come with strings attached. Now Stella is implying that I'm wrong; that there would have been no strings. Yet, coincidentally, I've just told her I'm no longer with Rocky. More accurately, he's no longer with anyone.

My mother's giving me a pitiful look. She tightens her hold on my hand. Then she actually says it! "We love you so much, honey. I've always told you that. We couldn't love you more if you'd been our own child." I try not to show that my insides are cringing. I maintain a poker face out of respect to this dying woman.

She turns to Phil. "You give her as much money as she wants. You hear me, Phil?" The sternness in her voice causes her to stop, breathe, and push the button for more morphine before going on. "I don't want my daughter working! I want her to have enough money to go to school. I want her to –" she pauses again, takes a breath and continues in a softer voice. "– to have a college education without ever worrying about money. You give her as much as she needs – and more. You hear me? Promise me, Phil. You hear me?"

"Yes. Yes, okay!"

She looks back at me and speaks in that weakened voice. "Are you really okay?" she asks. I nod. "Good." The smile she tries to show me is barely there. She pats my hand and strokes my arm. "You're a special girl, Jolie. You're pretty. And you're smart, too. You can do things I never could. My beautiful little girl!" She barely manages to get that out before her hand withdraws to press down for more morphine.

"Maybe you should rest now, Mom."

Stella shakes her head and takes a tighter hold of my hand. "No, I want to talk to you, Jolie." There's a pause while the morphine begins to do its thing then she goes on. "You can be somebody." The fervor in Stella's weakened voice surprises me. She's never talked to me like this. "When I was your age, women married. If they worked, they were secretaries or salesgirls. In today's world women do everything." She gestures to the hallway visible through the open door. "I see women doctors all day. They're so sure of themselves. You could be a doctor."

I can't be around sick or dying people. I hate hospitals. I can barely tolerate seeing Stella with tubes in her nose and something in her arm. "I don't think so."

"Okay, so you won't be a doctor. But you do something worthwhile. You hear me? Whatever you want. You make something of yourself."

"I'll try." I say. She pats my hand.

"Have you eaten, Stella?" Phil asks.

"They brought me something, but I'm not very hungry. What I want is a cigarette."

"Now don't start that again," Phil says.

Stella's body starts to move under the sheet. She pulls out her nose tubes and lets go of the morphine control and takes hold of the mattress. The combination of moving even slightly while speaking is obviously exhausting, and she pauses after every few words to breath. "I've been smoking for forty-five years. Now, all of a sudden I'm supposed to stop?" She looks at me. "I'm dying of cancer. What difference does a cigarette make? Can you tell me that?" Managing to swing her legs onto the floor, she freezes in pain.

"Mom! Push the button." I don't see the device. "Where's the button?" It's lost in the bed sheets. Frantic, I jump up and start shaking the sheet. Phil is looking for it, too. I find it and put it in Stella's hand. She pushes the button down twice. Soon, her face relaxes some.

"Where do you think you're going?" Phil asks her.

"Where do you think? There's a sale at Saks?" I notice that she can't keep her head up.

"Very funny," Phil says. "You need the toilet?" His voice rises and his arms go out at his sides like wings. "For Pete's sake, where's the goddamned nurse?"

"They have other patients, Phil," Stella says. As Phil heads for the door, she tries to turn her body to see him but can't manage it. "Aw, leave them alone, Phil!"

He hesitates and then returns to her. She's sitting on the side of the bed, trying to get up. "I'll help you," he says.

She gasps. I can't stand the sight of this new Stella. I keep my finger down on the "Nurse Call" button. My mother is on her feet, precariously hanging onto her husband, and now I see how much weight she's lost. I'm shocked. Her purple duster hangs on her emaciated body. Her exposed arms are just bones.

As Phil and I start to help Stella to the bathroom, a nurse enters the room. "Let me help her with that," she says, hurrying up to us.

I watch as the two women go into the bathroom with Stella's IV trailing. When they emerge, the nurse helps Stella back into bed, and she immediately reaches for the morphine button. The nurse reinserts the nose tubes then checks her watch. "You should rest now, Mrs. Gold." She picks up the sheet of paper on the tray by Stella's bed then speaks to Phil. "She didn't eat her lunch today. She's weaker for that. She needs to rest."

"I should leave," I say. "Rest, Mom. I'll be back later."

Phil speaks to the nurse. "She ought'a eat something."

"Ah, what's the point?" Stella says to no one in particular. She's still holding onto the morphine control with two hands.

I kiss her forehead. "I love you, Mom. I'll be back soon."

I wait in the hallway for Phil to say his goodbyes to her and lean against the wall, overwhelmed.

⁓

Phil has to be at work every day and often nights, when the theaters are busiest, as well, so, though he visits Mom daily, I spend more time at the hospital with her than he does.

I want to be with her as much as possible these last days. Maybe I'm compensating for feelings of guilt. I want this time with her to be our best. I want her to know I care.

I've already brought a hair blower, a teasing comb, hairspray and some makeup to her room. Her helplessness is overwhelming. She sleeps a lot, but I stay in her room while she's asleep, thinking. It hasn't escaped me that her last days have come so soon after Rocky's passing. Rocky, unable to stop his murderous ritual of drugs and alcohol, Stella, unable to stop her lethal smoking habit.

Strangely, surprisingly, in her final days, my gratitude to this dying woman, the only mother I have ever known, grows daily.

Phil tells me his cousin Maury will be coming to visit Stella today and I resolve to make it obvious that she is loved very much. She must look cared for.

I haven't yet had to use the hair styling tools – Mom's lacquered French roll still looks perfect – but I apply lots of blush and a slight touch of soft green shadow above her lid. I don't have any red lipstick in the shade she wears, so I go downstairs to the shop on the hospital's mezzanine floor and buy a bright red Revlon lipstick. She smiles when she sees it and wants to look at herself in the mirror once it's on, but I don't have a hand mirror; it's just as well. I'm not anxious for Stella to see how much she's changed. I assure her she looks good.

Minutes after I'm done, Maury and Marie walk into the room with their stupid daughter Marissa. The day she called me a monster and I learned what it meant to be adopted was the last time I played with her and haven't spoken to her much either. Older than me, Marissa is now in her early twenties, and I still can't bear to look at her. She doesn't speak a word the whole time she's in the room other than that half-assed "hello" to the woman lying on her deathbed. It's way obvious that she's here only because her parents insisted she come. She has no love for my mother. I'm sure the same is true for Maury and Marie.

The tension in the room between Phil and Maury is palpable. When Phil opened his own theaters, Maury turned cold toward him. He's accused Phil of having suffered "a shameful moral lapse" for "catering to the maladjusted homosexual community," but Phil attributes his chill to jealousy. Stella agrees with Phil, and so do I. Today, I'm ready to defend Phil if needed. I feel I owe him and Stella that much. Their visit lasts about fifteen awkward minutes and they're gone.

I stay with Stella as long as I can. Her strength has diminished quite a bit in these last few days. I sense her death might come anytime now. I'm not familiar with the way death comes, and I'm scared. Before every leave-taking, I make sure to tell her how grateful I am for all she's done for me and to let her know I love her.

Her eyes have sunken in their sockets even further today. They're smaller than ever under drooping lids, and they look dreamy and glazed over.

"Mom, I owe you so much! You've been a wonderful mother. I had a great childhood and so many advantages because of you and Dad. I know you love me and cared about me, even though I haven't been the easiest daughter to raise. I've said and done things that hurt you. I'm so, so sorry. I never meant to hurt you."

I wonder if she fully understands my words, but then she says,"I know, Honey. I love you so much. I always have. From the minute I saw you in that crib."

I yearn to ask, *What crib? Where?* But I'll wait and ask Phil after ... later. I've been in this room with Stella for hours at a time but haven't asked her a single question about my past. I'm afraid that the subject will upset her. The thought that I may not see her alive again propels me to leave her with a smile on her face.

"Mom, I love you very much. I'm adopted, but I couldn't have loved you more if you were my real mother."

3 1

BURYING GOLD

*S*tella makes it through one more day before taking a turn for
the worse.

She develops a high fever and breathing becomes difficult. She's
put in an oxygen tent. The doctor tells Phil that her end is imminent.

Phil relays the news by phone to family members in New York.
Within twelve hours, Stella's younger sister Sophie and her husband
Bernie are at Cedars along with Phil's brothers, Mort and Sol.

She falls into a coma and dies at 3 a.m. Friday morning, May 20
and, though it's the middle of the night, Phil is at her side when she
passes. He spends many hours Friday in the room with his wife's lifeless body.

I have no desire to see Stella dead.

~~~~~~~

Jewish burials are not permitted on Saturday, the Shabbas, so Stella's
funeral is today, Sunday.

Family and friends have congregated in a chapel on the grounds of
Mount Sinai Cemetery in Burbank for the service. Phil and I, along
with the rest of the family, are seated closest to the casket that's

covered with white flowers and flanked with large wreaths and bouquets in softest yellow, pink and white.

The rabbi's introductory words, meant to comfort, urge us to view Stella's death as part of God's greater picture. Then Stella's younger sister, Sophie, goes to the microphone. Aunt Sophie will be the sole speaker other than the rabbi.

I can't speak. My emotions are too high, and my thoughts about Mom are too jumbled. The past is too close to the present, and I can't trust that my words will come out as I'd like, so I will say nothing. Phil is utterly incapable of speaking.

Aunt Stella first speaks of their shared childhood, then continues:

"I loved my sister. Stella was a kind woman. She was gentle and loving. She was always a wonderful sister, a good daughter, a good wife and a very caring mother. She overcame her share of challenges. My sister lived through every mother's worst nightmare, the loss of a child, yet she went on …."

What? I spring up. *What did Sophie just say? The loss of a child?*

There is a movement throughout the room, the give-away that others assembled here have, like me, just heard this for the first time. My mind has disintegrated. *The loss of a child?* Part of me wants to demand an explanation from Phil right here and now, but I refrain. I will have to wait.

Holding a white handkerchief at his round face, Phil has broken into a new round of wailing. His bald head only partially covered by the black yarmulke, bobs up and down. I can't confront him now.

As I sit quietly, questions stick out in my mind like thorns on a cactus.

A child! Stella had given birth to a baby then watched it die! How old was the baby? Was it a girl or a boy? How did it die? There's so much I don't know. I am suddenly aware of how little I've ever really known about this woman, about this couple that raised me. I lived with them as their child, yes. But what do I know about them? About their past? How they met? What their dreams were? About their child…

With questions rushing at me and clouded in confusion, I don't hear much of anything else Sofie says until she's almost done:

"... and in the end, it was only cancer, insidious cancer, that she could not conquer." She leaves the dais.

The rabbi leads the room in a short prayer, then announces the names of the male pallbearers who will carry Stella's coffin from the chapel to the hearse and then to her gravesite. He ends with the announcement that Phil and I welcome the mourners to our home following the gravesite services.

I can't be of out here too soon. I need fresh air and answers.

The pall bearers assemble alongside the casket. We start to file out of the chapel, Phil and I following behind that dark, mahogany box carrying the the woman I called "mother" to her final resting place. I whisper to Phil. *"What child?"* He doesn't respond. He doesn't react at all, and I don't know if he hasn't heard me or if he's ignoring me.

He begins to wail anew and I move to comfort him, but Aunt Sophie gently nudges my arm. "You go on. I'll stay with him." I want to ask her about the child. Instead, I leave them and walk ahead.

Outside, I'm hit by the bright sunshine on this brisk day. Mourners approach me with words of sympathy, their eyes conveying compassion. They mill about, mingling with friends and chatting, while we wait for the coffin to be loaded into the hearse.

Nora, Jonah and Paul, my Triumvirate find me. "What did she mean about the child?" gushes Nora.

"I have no idea!" I say. "I've never heard anything about a child!"

Sophie approaches and I introduce my friends to her. "How are you holding up?" she asks me. I shrug and nod.

"Your father's driving to the site with Bernie, Mort and Sol . Why don't you drive up with me and Maury?"

I really don't want to be ride up with Maury, but I want to stay close to Sophie, so I agree.

We're behind the car that carries Phil, which is immediately behind the hearse in the cavalcade of cars making our way up the gently sloping road. Sophie sits in front with Maury and I'm in the back with Marissa. Maury's wife, Marie, hasn't attended today, resting after having had a hysterectomy yesterday.

I'm so frustrated. Sophie is sitting not three feet away. I'm staring at her back, but there's no way in hell I'm asking her about the child with

Marissa here. I don't want the bitch to know I was surprised to hear about it. And it rankles the hell out of me no end that Marissa isn't asking about the child 'cause it almost certainly means that she knows all about it. If she didn't, she wouldn't be sitting here, cool as a cucumber. *She'd* be asking Sophie – or me – all about it this minute. Stella probably told her mom and her mom probably told her idiot daughter. It occurs to me that Marissa might even have known about the child as far back as when she called me a freak on my fifth birthday.

We make our way to the top of the gently sloping road, passing people assembled at other burial plots and gravestones as they try to relate to a dead person, meditate at a grave marker or kneel to lay flowers on the grass as I'd done at Rocky's grave. Now, I will bury Stella.

I soon realize that Jewish burials are filled with rituals. The family gathers around the rabbi. He pins black mourning ribbons on each of us, then immediately rips it.

"This ribbon is a throwback from generations ago," he says. "When a loved one passed, mourners would rip their clothes to show their grief. Today, we wear this black ribbon and rip it to symbolize that grief."

The rabbi pins the black ribbon onto the collar of my sole black dress, rips it, then pins one to Phil's black suit and rips that one. I notice his suit is new and looks expensive. It fits him well.

The rabbi recites more Hebrew prayers. Then Stella's casket begins to be lowered into the earth. It's so surreal! Tears quietly fill my eyes. I hear Phil's sobs. Sophie has put her arm around him. The rabbi continues to recite prayers throughout the casket's descent.

The mourners begin the ritual of covering the casket with dirt. Two shovels stand ready in the black hills on either end of the grave. Phil is first. I take my place behind him. A loose line forms behind us. Another, forms on the other side of the grave by the second shovel.

There are beads of perspiration on Phil's forehead. He wipes his face with his handkerchief, smearing his sweat and tears, then replaces it in his pocket and slowly, reluctantly, fills the shovel with dirt. He stands at the edge of the hole and looks down at the box Stella lays in. He barely moves his arm. He simply stands there, his head in his other hand, trembling, crying helplessly, and I am as helpless as he is, with no idea what I can do to comfort him. The rabbi takes the shovel from his hand, sticks it back into the mound of dirt, puts his arm around Phil's shoulders, and walks him away.

It's my turn to pour dirt down onto the wooden box. The closest thing I've had to a mother is about to be buried, gone forever.

Why does everyone leave me?

3 2
TEA WITH SOPHIE

*W*e arrive back home after the funeral.

Yesterday, Sophie had covered all the mirrors in the house with sheets. "The mourning period is a time for meditation. We're supposed to be thinking about the meaning of life and death. We'll be thinking about Stella now and forgetting about ourselves and our own vanity."

The mourners find their way to our home. According to tradition, neighbors, friends and acquaintances who were not at Stella's funeral can also join to pay their respects to us.

Today is the first of seven days of "*sitting shiva*," the Jewish tradition meant to comfort a bereaving family at what is thought to be the hardest time of their loss, the beginning, the first seven days. Whether that's true or not, only time will tell.

Our visitors sit and talk with us. They tell us how lovely the funeral was, how well the rabbi spoke, and how nice Sophie's eulogy was. No one mentions a child.

They've brought food with them in hopes the bereaving family will be able to mourn their loss without the distraction of preparing meals. Emma, Stella's housekeeper, will stay here serving with her daughter and her niece until nine o'clock. Throughout the afternoon and into the

239

evening, people laugh, they cry, they share stories about Stella. No one mentions the death of a child.

At sunset, the rabbi leads a *minon*, a group of ten men which includes Phil, through designated prayers followed by the Kaddish prayer, the traditional prayer for the dead. The rabbi will be here to repeat this for the next six evenings while the flame on the white memorial candle will burn continuously in memory of Stella's departed soul.

All this religious protocol, these prayers – it's all totally new to me. Hearing the words, *"Magnified and sanctified be God's great name throughout the world which God created and governs by divine will,"* my ears burn.

Do I believe these words? I'm not at all sure that I believe in God. I fell that something greater than me has been making my life difficult. Is it God?

If there's a God that is governing the world by divine will then that God directed my parents to abandon me. And directed that Phil and Stella adopt me. It would mean God said, "Hmm, I think Jolie will meet and fall in love with Rocky and I'll give Rocky this condition and he'll hurt someone very badly and then kill himself." What God would do that? And would he be *magnificent* and *all-loving*?

Wearing torn black ribbons, taking turns throwing dirt on the grave, *sitting shiva*, covering mirrors, and having *minions* are one thing, but if being Jewish means that I believe God decides everything that happens to us, I guess I'm not Jewish.

I make my own choices and those choices affect my life.

I wish I knew if my true parents were Jewish. Maybe they belonged to Jim Jones' church and poisoned themselves... or maybe they have no religion at all.

The evening prayers end. The rabbi leaves and the remaining guests depart.

This first evening of *sitting shiva* is over. The New York guests are all staying at the house. Sophie and Bernie are in the guest room and Mort and Sol, in my room. I'm glad Phil won't be alone.

My heart goes out to Phil. I never realized how much love he had for Stella. He has lived in deep sorrow, lost in a sea of sadness since his wife's diagnosis and drowning in it since her death.

What would it have been like for me if I'd buried Rocky after having loved and lived with him for as many years? He needs to be brave, to accept that he can go on without her.

Maybe sharing Stella's loss will bring the two of us closer.

It's been a long and difficult day.

The men are all about to retire for the night. I hug Phil.

Sophie tells Bernie she will clean up a bit before joining him and I realize here, at last, is my chance to question my aunt in private. I, too, stay and clean up.

We're carrying the first of the remaining dirty dishes into the kitchen. After depositing them on the kitchen counter by the dishwasher, Sophie says, "I cannot believe how well organized my sister was."

She opens the cupboard above her head exposing dishes cover in plastic and shakes her head as if in wonder. "Look!"

Does she think I haven't looked?

I lean against the counter. "Aunt Sophie, tell me about the child that died."

Sophie closes the cupboard door. "What do you want to know that you don't already know?"

"I don't know anything. They've never said a word to me about having a child."

Sophie's eyes register her surprise. She quickly looks away and starts back to the dining room. "Oh, I didn't know that."

I follow. "I don't know why they've kept it from me."

Sophie busies herself collecting more plates. "Well, I know they had their reasons. I see I've made a mistake and I'm very sorry. I shouldn't have mentioned it."

"But you did, and now I want to know."

She nods. "Well, honey, you should ask your father about that."

I trail her back into the kitchen, the few plates shaking in her hands. She deposits the dishes next to the others on the counter.

"Aunt Sophie, Dad's so sad he can't talk to anyone about anything right now. You can see that. Please, tell me."

Sophie turns to head back out of the kitchen. "If Stella didn't tell you, I don't think she'd want me to," she says.

She bears the signs of a long, hard day. Again, I notice the spot on the bodice of her black dress where some lasagna has fallen. On the black fabric, the spot is the darkest purple. Strands of her brown hair come undone from the pins of her low bun.

I take a gentle hold of her hand. "Stella's gone and I need to know. Please, tell me. I have a right to know. Did I have a sister? Or a brother?"

She sighs seeing my confusion and sighs. "They had a son. He died before they adopted you," she says matter-of-factly. She purses her lips. "He wasn't really your brother because, if he'd lived, they'd never have adopted you." She delivers this life-changing news and walks out of the kitchen.

I am transfixed; stunned. "Their son died, so they adopted me?"

"That's right." Sophie looks at me. Then she looks at the dirty dishes and sighs, probably deciding they'll stay there overnight. She wipes her hands on a dishtowel and turns to me. "That's right," she repeats. "They had a son named Jeffery and he died. That's why Phil wanted another boy."

I'm mortified. "He didn't want me?"

My mind tries to take in what she's said. My parents didn't want me and neither did Phil. He wanted a boy.

Is that why he was the way he was with me? Did he hate me? Resent me? Did he think of his dead son every time he laid eyes on me? Did he think of the boy they could have adopted in Jeffrey's place instead of me? *Oh, my god!*

Sophie smiles, quick to try to reassure me. "Oh, it wasn't you he didn't want, honey. He was upset and just wanted another son, that's all." That's definitely not comforting.

I am so hurt. I turn belligerent. I want to force her to tell me how and why I ended up here. "So why did they adopt me?"

Sophie looks away and grunts. "It's a long story."

"Please, Aunt Sophie! Please, tell me!"

My aunt seems to be turning it over in her mind. Her eyes travel as eyes do as when contemplating what to do. Finally, she clasps her hands and surrenders. "Well, honey, if I'm going to tell me whole the story, I'm going to need a cup of tea."

The kettle is still hot.

Aunt Sophie makes herself a cup of tea and sits at the kitchen table. I sit across from her, bracing myself to hear that Phil hadn't wanted me; I wonder if Stella did.

This is what I've waited my whole life to hear. I'm about to learn the answers to all my questions.

Sophie takes a sip of her tea and sets her cup down. "What do you want to know?" she asks.

"Everything!" I say.

Though I'm anxious as hell to learn the names of my biological parents, I forego asking about them. She's begun to tell me about my adoption and I want to know that whole story first.

I take a breath and try to at least start off relaxed. "How old was Jeffrey when he died?"

"Thirteen. He'd just had his bar mitzvah."

"Was he sick?"

"No. He wasn't sick, he died out on the water. On the lake."

"What lake? Where?"

"In Florida. In a boat."

"Florida? I thought Phil and Stella had lived in New York, then moved to California and adopted me here."

She's shaking her had. "No, no. They lived there. They'd just moved down there from New York. Phil had built Stella a very beautiful house there. It was the last thing he ever built."

"Phil built a house?" I ask incredulously.

"Your father was a very successful contractor."

I gasp. "Why did he stop building?"

She shrugs and takes a sip of tea. "I don't know.

She puts her cup down. "No, that's not true. Of course, I know. He retired. He'd made enough money not to have to work. Then, when Jeffrey died and they moved here, they left most of what they had behind, and he had to work again, almost start over. So, he started working with Maury."

A bell rings in my head as I remember the successful renovations Phil had made in the theaters. So, Phil had become successful twice.

"Tell me more about their son. About Jeffrey."

"What do you want to know?"

"What happened to him?"

"I told you. He died out on the boat."

"He drowned?"

"Honey, no one really ever found out. He was on their boat and well, he just disappeared."

"They never found him?"

"They found him," Sophie says softly. Then repeats herself. "They found him."

"Did the boat sink? Was he alone or with my parents?" I ask.

Sophie shakes her head and looks away. "He was alone. Phil never forgave himself for that. The two of them had gone out on the lake and then he went inside and let Jeffrey stay on the boat. It was the first and last time he ever did that."

"Oh! Poor Dad!"

"Poor Stella! My sister was crazy with grief. Well, they both were. Oh, honey, you've never seen people like that. Phil blamed himself – and she blamed him, too. I thought they'd never make it through. Just goes to show, you never really know people."

She shakes her head and sighs. "Stella blamed herself, too. She told me afterward that she'd been stupid for letting Phil act so foolhardy with her son. I told her she couldn't have prevented it, but … anyway, that's the story."

"Poor Mom! It must have been awful!"

Sophie's takes another sip of her tea then looks up, inspecting the ceiling.

"*Ay!* It was," she says. "She was misery personified. Phil, too." She shakes her head. "And now he's lost Stella." Then, as she lifts her cup again, she mutters, "Let's hope he doesn't try killing himself again."

I can't believe my ears. "What? What did you just say?"

"Nothing, child."

"You just said you hope he doesn't try to kill himself *again*. Dad tried to kill himself? You mean when Jeffrey died?"

"Forget it, honey."

"Aunt Sophie, you're kidding me, right? You tell me my dad tried to commit suicide and then you say, 'forget it'?"

"What difference does any of that make to you? It's history. Stella did the right thing not to tell you. You're young. You have your life ahead of you. What happened back then means nothing to you."

"I don't understand how you can say that. Don't you see? You're talking about the closest thing I have to family. Do you know what it's not to have known any of this?"

Sophie sets her cup down. She shifts in her chair. "I'm definitely talking too much."

"No, Aunt Sophie, you're not! Tell me what you were talking about with the suicide thing."

Sophie plays with the rim of her saucer. The house is silent and dark except for the light coming here in the kitchen. Then she sits primly, her mouth set, her hands resting on the tabletop and breathes deeply.

"Well, Phil and Stella flew back to New York with Jeffrey's casket. They never returned to Florida.

"Oh, what a terrible time! My poor sister! She was hysterical. After we buried him, we found a small apartment for the two of them. It was nothing, just small and dismal, nowhere as grand as what they'd been used to. But it was close to us – to Bernie and me and our parents, Stella's and mine; Phil's family, too."

"And?"

"We wanted them near us so we could take care of them, make sure they ate, take them food and – well, you know – keep an eye on them."

As she goes on with the story, her eyes travel around the wall in front of her as though she's watching her memories unfold like a movie projected there.

She looks back at me. "Well, it was just so terrible! *Nothing* could shake them from their depression. They wouldn't be comforted by any*thing* or any*one*, and certainly not by each other."

She pauses, shakes her head, and then goes on. "They were *ab-so-lute-ly* desolate." She shakes her head. "I tell you, child, they were a total mess! They didn't go out, they didn't bathe – they never got out of their pajamas!" She waves her arm, as if trying to wave away a memory that too clear.

"And Phil – he was half dead. He'd just lay on the couch in that living room day and night. Stayed away from everyone and never spoke a word. They both blamed him for the boy's death and neither of them were about to forgive him."

My aunt is lost in her memories.

Mesmerized, I wait for her to continue. "Stella lay in her bed clutching a photo of Jeffrey, crying and calling his name, as if he'd hear her and come back.

"Day became night... night became day... days became weeks, but nothing changed. The tears and the blame and the misery went on and on."

Sophie sighs again and frowns. "We'd *force* them to eat." Her eyes find me. They look sad.

She sighs deeply. "Then one night, I suppose Phil thought he'd found a solution to their misery. While Stella lay in bed – he never left the couch, you see ..." she stops and puts a fist goes over her mouth.

"Go on. What did he do?"

"God forgive him. It was a small one-bedroom apartment, so depressing. We should never have let them stay there. We should have found them someplace nicer or kept them with us."

"Aunt Sophie, what did Dad do?"

She bites her lower lip then pours it all out at once, as though if she were to stop for even a second, she would stop forever. "He shut all the windows in the apartment, put a towel under the front door and then – God forgive him! – he turned the gas on and went back to his couch to wait."

I crunch my face and shut my eyes. "Oh! How horrible!"

"Yes, it was." Her fingers return to the saucer's rim. She sips her tea. "I suppose he thought it was the best thing for him and for Stella."

"Thank God they didn't die! Stella didn't know?"

Sophie looks at me slyly. "Child, I've always wondered about that. She said she didn't. But I wonder if she would have done anything about it if she had known."

"What happened? I mean –"

Stella nods. "A neighbor was in the hallway at the elevator and smelled gas. She rang their doorbell and knocked and when no one answered, thank God, she called the police. They were rushed to the hospital. And then the hospital called me."

"How could I not know this? It's a terrible story! Thank God for that neighbor!"

After a moment of silence, I ask, "Aunt Sophie, why didn't my mom leave Phil after that?" Sophie looks at me like I'm crazy. "I'm not saying she should have," I hurry to add, "but you said she blamed him for killing their son, then he tried to kill them both. You said you were surprised they stayed together. Why did they?"

Sophie lifts her eyes to me. "Stella leave Phil? Impossible! My sister would never do that. It wasn't like today's world where women are independent. Back then you lived your whole life with the man you married, for good or for bad, better or worse."

I digest these words and recoil at the idea that anyone would stay with a person they abhorred, simply because they'd married them.

She continues. "And she'd just lost her son. What would she do without Phil? She didn't have a college education. She'd never worked a day in her life. She wasn't young. I don't mean to be nasty; I loved my sister. She was a good, good person. But it would have been stupid to leave Phil." She adjusts herself in her chair. "Stella wasn't stupid!"

I recall Stella's words to me in the hospital as she lay on her deathbed, how she had urged me to get an education and make something of my life. She had wanted me to understand how important it is not to be so dependent on a man that I couldn't leave him and take care of myself. Now I see where Stella was coming from.

"Okay, so what happened then? Why did they want to adopt me?"

Sophie looks at me with sad eyes. "Sweetheart, I wish it had been their idea, but they were both just so horribly depressed." She sighs heavily. "They weren't thinking at all." She's downed the last of her tea and now she's toying with the empty teacup, looking inside it.

"So? What happened?"

"While the two of them were in the hospital, we all got together. The two families – ours and Phil's. We had a sort of emergency meeting. We agreed it would be best for them to leave New York. There were far too many memories for them there. After all, Jeffrey was born in New York and grew up in New York. Everyone they knew there had known Jeffrey. We all loved him and missed him too – he was a dear, sweet boy – but we were all constant reminders of him. And our being there for them hadn't helped. So, we thought maybe they'd do better without any of us around, just the two of them. Things certainly couldn't get any worse than they were. You have to understand, honey, we were desperate. They had just tried to kill themselves – or Phil had tried to kill them.

"We thought, that perhaps, if they were forced to live by themselves, without us to lean on, they'd come to see that they needed one another. Maybe someday they'd even come to care for one another again. We hoped that alone, in a new setting, a fresh start, their shared loss and grief would bring them together. There was nothing else we could think to do."

There's a missing piece. "Aunt Stella, why didn't they tell me about Jeffrey? Why did they keep him a secret from me?" When she doesn't answer, I say, "Don't you think they should have told me?"

She seems to be weighing something in her mind. Then she bites her lower lip and looks down at her lap as she speaks. "We made both of them take a vow, sweetheart. A vow on Jeffrey's soul in front of the Torah – may he rest in peace all these years – that they would not mention his name again once they left New York."

She look up at me. "That's why they never told you about him, child." Then she shakes her head in dismay. "I guess I thought they couldn't keep that vow. Shame, shame, shame on me!"

I'm stunned. "And did the family decide they should adopt a child?"

"Well, actually?" She has her finger in the cup handle, moving it around on the saucer. "That was my idea."

I'm shocked all over again. "Your idea?"

"Uh huh," Sophie allows herself a cagey smile. "And apparently a brilliant one."

"Why?"

She shifts again, then says, "It was for Stella. I know my sister. She was a terrific mother. There was nothing she wouldn't do for Jeffrey. She lived her life for him. For Phil, too, in many ways, but not after Jeffrey died. She didn't want anything to do with him after that. So, she hadn't only lost her son, her whole life had lost meaning. She had no one to live for. Stella needed to feel needed."

Aunt Sophie leans towards me and her face takes on its youngest aspect, her eyes bright. "Jolie, when we were growing up, Stella was always mothering me. When we got older and I started dating, she'd make sure I was okay, you know?

"When I got serious with Bernie, she begged me to be careful not to get pregnant. She said it might push Bernie away; Mother never talked to me like that."

"You loved her," I say.

She nods. She sighs. "Ahh, memories!" She sighs yet again. "Old age has so many of them!

"When I married Bernie, Stella and Phil hadn't yet met. Our parents took Bernie and me aside and begged us … *begged* us … to just prolong our engagement and not marry until Stella married. She was older than me and they didn't want her hurt. You see, she hadn't yet had a boyfriend.

"You know what that sister of mine did? She saw how happy I'd been when I told her Bernie had proposed and that we were getting married. She kept asking us what date we'd set for the wedding and we couldn't give her one. I think, knowing our parents, she guessed what they'd made us promise. Maybe not.

"Anyway, finally, one Friday night when we were all assembled for Shabbas dinner, she quietly took Bernie into another room and grilled him. Yes, she did! She asked him what he intended to do for money, how he planned to support me, asked if he drank, had a gambling problem that we didn't know of, then threatened to rip him apart if he was ever unfaithful to me or ever hurt me. After that, she asked him what the hell he was waiting for.

"She made him promise that we'd set a wedding date right then and there that night. Sure enough, as soon as dinner was finished, Bernie had me sit down with a calendar. He said we had to decide on a wedding date then and there or it was off so, we decided on a date.

"Do you believe that? I'll never forget the look on our parents' faces when we told them. Stella was so happy! She was the first to hug and congratulate us. I think she was as happy as I was."

It wasn't easy for me to imagine the Stella I knew to be that compassionate to the young lovers. "That was really cool," I say.

"Now I didn't know about that talk she'd had with Bernie. She never, ever told me, even after the wedding. It was Bernie who told me, and only some time after we were married. And mind you, he made me promise not to tell Stella that he'd told me, and in all these years, I never did. Now, I wish I had.

"I wish I had thanked her for being such a wonderful sister and had told her how much I loved her and how much I appreciated all the things she did for me."

I'm trying to reconcile what I've just heard about my adopted mother with the woman who I know stood motionless while Phil hit me and watched silently while he called Rocky despicable names and threw him out of the house. I'm flabbergasted.

I shake myself and push forward, bringing myself back to my aunt. "So, you adopted me for her?"

Now it's Sophie's turn to be surprised. She moves to the edge of her seat and takes my hand, looks into my eyes. "No, honey. Don't you know how you were adopted?"

Sophie's question and her compassionate expression break through layers of pain, baring my loneliness and feelings of abandonment. I shake my head and I'm suddenly in tears.

My aunt stretches to take a napkin off the table and hands it to me. She pats me gently on my back while I wipe my tears away. "There, there," she says.

I regain my composure. "Aunt Sophie, I have no idea where I came from. I've always hoped that one day Phil and Stella would tell me. Stella's gone! I was going to beg them to tell me just before I found out about the cancer. Now she's gone! So here I am, clueless. I have no idea who my parents are — or were." My chuckle sounds ghoulish through my sorrow.

I appeal to her. "I have two mothers, I have no mother. Please, help me?"

Sophie gets up and comes to me. She sits on the chair closest tome me and hugs me close. "Hush now, honey. Don't cry, Jolie. You've gone through a lot today. I'll tell you everything I know, and I hope it'll help you." She closes her eyes and swallows. I think she's remembering — or, deciding where to begin and how to tell me.

"When I came up with the idea that Stella and Phil should adopt a child," she says, "I needed to be sure that they adopted a child with a good background, one that had come from a good home. She moves her head this way and that. "Lots of children are born to parents that are addicts, or insane, or abandoned by sick or homeless parents. I needed to be positive that they wouldn't adopt any of those." She leans into me and holds my hand. I know she's trying to be as gentle as possible with me while trying to make me understand.

"Do you see what I mean?" I nod. "All those things increase the risk that the baby will have problems in the future." I nod again.

I've just learned more about my adoption than in all the years I've searched for information about them, and more information about Phil and Stella than in all my years of living with them.

She bends he elbows and her hands extend out as she gestures ignorance. "Well, where do you find a child to adopt that comes from a good background? I mean, the *right* child."

"I don't know," I say. "Where?"

"Well, I did some research." Her fingers tap my hand then she eyes me as if she's about to share an important secret. 'I knew there were homes for pregnant girls and that some were for girls who were from rich, well-to-do families – their daughters got pregnant, too!

"I mean, back then, we didn't have birth control pills and God knows what else! If a girl found herself pregnant, she couldn't have an abortion. Did you know that Jolie?"

I'm almost too nervous to think. I just want her to get on with it. "I guess," I say.

"Abortions were one hundred percent illegal. Lives were ruined from pregnancies out of wedlock and many girls died from illegal abortions.

"Anyway, what I did was, I called all these homes for pregnant girls, all around the U.S. and I asked about their services and how much they charged. I told them I was calling for my daughter. A lot of them cost a pretty penny, but a few were outrageously expensive." Sophie gloats. "Those were the ones that interested me. I wanted the one that catered to girls from the wealthiest families in the country, and I found it: the most expensive home for unwed mothers in America."

"That's where I was born?" Sophie nods. "My mother's family was that wealthy? Who was she? Where was I born, Aunt Sophie? Tell me where! New York?"

"It was in Dallas. Dallas, Texas. I remember the name even now, because it sounded so pure and sweet: The Abigail House, Abigail's Home for Unwed Mothers.

"That woman, Abigail, took good care of those young, spoiled, rich girls from all over and made sure their babies were taken care of, too.

"She must have had a good heart – and I'm sure she got paid a pretty penny."

I sit there, staring at my aunt. On the same day we've buried Stella, I'm finding out so much about her, about me, and about my birth mother!

I brace myself for the big one. "What's my real mother's name, Aunt Stella? Who was she?"

"Well, sweetheart, Stella was your real mother. She mothered you like no one else could have. But, are you asking who gave birth to you?"

"Yes," I say. "You must remember that."

"I never knew her name, child. I have no idea who she was."

My disappointment is extreme and obvious.

My aunt reaches across the table and takes my hand. "Honey, they don't tell you that. I'm sorry. I'm sure that Stella didn't know either. Neither does Phil. She told me that the name of the birth mother, like the name of the adopted mother, was never disclosed; one never knew who the other was."

I simply refuse to let it end there. "Do you know anything about her? You must know something." Sophie shrugs and shakes her head. "Was she American?" I say. "How old was she? Why did she give me up?" Sophie is still shaking her head.

Damn! I've hit the same goddamn wall again! Despite all the information that Stella has given me, I still don't have the single piece of information that's most important to me.

"I want so much to know who she was," I say between clenched teeth, "I can't stand it!"

Still holding my hand, Sophie looks at me affectionately. "I'm sorry if you're disappointed, Jolie. But I have told you everything I know to tell."

All I can do is continue to try my hardest to get more information from her. "So, you're the reason they adopted me."

"Well, yes and no. I sent them to Abigail's but when they got there, they chose you from amongst all the other babies there. Imagine that, Sweetheart! Stella saw you and couldn't resist you."

"But Phil wanted a boy," I say. That seems to explain so much.

"Yes. But Stella wanted you, and only you, from the moment she saw you."

A sad little smile forms on my face. Stella really *had* loved me in her own way.

"Aunt Stella, do you remember *when* I was adopted?"

"Let's see. That would have been sometime in the summer. So, I think it was around September of 1961.

"You were a beautiful baby, Jolie. Stella sent me a photo of you almost immediately." She laughs. "She was always sending pictures of you. You were a beautiful little girl and now you're a beautiful young woman. She was always so proud of you."

"She was a wonderful mother to me. But I really want to find my birth mother ... " I think to add, "now that Stella is gone."

"I wish I could tell you more. I've told you all I know," she repeats.

"And I really appreciate it," I say. "You've told me so much, Aunt Sophie. I never knew any of that."

"Well, I hope I've done the right thing to tell you. I know that what I've told you is terribly important to you, and I do want to help you."

She scrutinizes my face. "Are you all right, child?" I nod. "You must be emotionally exhausted. What do you say we both go to bed? You've had gone through more than enough for one day. After all you've been through these last weeks with your mother sick and dying and then today, and now, finding out about Jeffery and your adoption - it's an awful lot for one day!

"I'm tired, too. I know Bernie is sound asleep. He'll be up early tomorrow and expect me to be up with him."

We both push our chairs back and get up. I give her a big warm hug. It's not her fault she doesn't know the name I so badly want to know. "Goodnight. Thank you so much for everything. It means so much to me to finally know everything you've told me."

"I hope I've evened up the score a little with my sister for her talk with Bernie. He's been a wonderful husband."

We smile at one another, then she adds, "Jolie, maybe we shouldn't mention our little talk to Phil."

"Okay."

I watch Stella's younger sister, so different from her, walk away. Then I set about cleaning up in the kitchen a little bit more.

I won't be able to sleep anyway with so much to think about.

33

MANIFESTING REALITY

$\mathcal{F}$or the remainder of the time *sitting shiva*, Phil is inconsolable.

"What will I do without her?" "I should have taken better care of her." "I'll never forgive myself." "Oh, my poor Stella!"

I listen but say nothing. I watch as everyone else tries to comfort him, to talk him out of his desperate sadness and cease his sobs. Nothing stops his tears. I sit by him and hold him, sometimes putting an arm around his back, sometimes rubbing his neck, but I say nothing. We will have time to talk later when we're alone and these first tears subside.

I decline his invitation to resume living at the house on North Beverly Drive. As soon as *shiva* is over, he presents me with five thousand dollars cash for no reason at all, and, true to the promise made to his dying wife, he insists on paying for fall classes.

"Come to me if you need more," he says, handing me the cash. "Remember what your mother told you. Finish college."

I quit my job at The Pelican and immediately race to Century City to buy a dress I know Nora will love, wrap it special and present it to my roommate with a card that reads, "To the Best Friend Ever. I love you, Jolie."

When I tell Nora about the money that Phil has given me and his promise to give me more, the first thing she says is, "Does this mean you can afford to pay for an apartment by yourself now?"

"I guess. Why?"

"Jonah's wants me to move in with him."

"And you never told me? You actually stayed here just to help pay for the rent?"

"I wouldn't dream of leaving you in the lurch. And it's not like I didn't love living with my best friend. But it's okay to go now, right?"

I am moved to tears. I plant a kiss on my soon-to-be ex-roommate's cheek. "You really are the bestest friend in the whole wide world!"

Norah moves in with Jonah and I move into a one-bedroom apartment in our building that miraculously becomes available. For first time in my life, I'm living alone.

I continue mulling over what Aunt Sophie has told me. It dawns on me that I might have enough information to find my mother.

This is what I know: First, I was born at Abigail's Home for Unwed Mothers in Dallas, Texas; second, I was adopted around September of 1961; third, Phil and Stella Gold adopted me.

With that information, I should be able to find the records.

My heart is pounding.

I'm sitting in the middle seat, seventh row on the right side of a Delta airplane.

I'm biting my lip and clenching the armrests as the plane starts down the runway. I hear the engines' roar and my heart speeds up.

The girl who's sitting to my left in the window seat, is about my age. She's wearing baggie jeans, a sweatshirt and flip-flops, and she's reading Judith Krantz's best-seller, Scruples.

The woman on my right, sitting in the aisle seat, is probably in her early forties, wearing a three-piece, turquoise suit and is already busily writing in a spiral notebook.

When I feel the airplane's leave the ground and hear the wheels retract, I squeeze my eyes shut. My stomach turns.

The turquoise woman says, "Nervous?"

I'm not sure who she's speaking to. I open my eyes. She's stopped writing, and she's looking at me, smiling. Her face is angular and striking. Her skin is chocolate-colored, and it looks like the only make-up she's wearing is red lipstick and a black liner that highlights her huge, dark brown eyes. Her black hair is pulled tightly back, and the large gold hoop earrings sway as she moves her head.

I'm surprised that though she was so busy writing, she can know that I'm nervous. "A little," I admit.

"First time flying?"

"No. I'm always nervous. At least this flight's not too long." I hear my own breathing, deep and heavy.

"It may help to distract yourself. Did you bring along a book?"

"No." I see the woman smirk as if my failure to bring a book on board shows a lack of intelligence. I immediately resent her.

The fact is that I didn't think to bring a book with me because I plan to use my time in the air to pull my thoughts together. I'm not at all sure why she thinks it's her business if I did or didn't bring a book with me, or that I'm nervous. I'm glad when I see her resume writing.

I tried to contact The Abigail Home in Dallas by phone and was told that there was no such listing in the Dallas directory. When I questioned Sophie about the exact address, I wasn't surprised to hear she didn't know it. She was only certain of the name, Abigail's Home for Unwed Mothers, and its location in Dallas.

I gave up on long-distance research and decided to fly to Dallas.

As soon as we land, I'm going to go straight to the Dallas Hall of Records to get the address. Then I'll see the place where I was born, and hopefully speak to Abigail and convince her to show me my records. With the information I have, she should be able to find the names of my biological parents in my file, or at least, my mother's name. Even if the Home is no longer in business, she must have the files someplace.

The plane angles. We must be turning. I peek out the window. All I see below us is the Pacific Ocean. I see the golden-white cover created on the ocean by the reflection of the morning sun. The thought that I'm sitting in a piece of metal, carrying a hell of a lot of weight fly over that ocean, scares the living bejesus out of me.

I wish I hadn't just looked out the window. I start to feel nauseas. I'll feel better when we are flying over land. Then, I wonder if I would have a better chance of surviving a crash over water or over land and, within seconds, despite the refrigerated air inside the cabin, my palms are clammy. I run them across the skirt of my new three-piece suit.

My stomach is churning. I look around me, but I can't see much of the other passengers from my vantage point. I glance at the girl to my left reading by the window, distractedly wondering if she is headed to Dallas or Fort Worth, headed for a vacation, or returning home. She glances at me and I quickly look past her to the view out the window. The plane's wing is still tipped. We're still over the ocean.

Shouldn't we have circled by now? I close my eyes and pray.

"How are you doing?" Turquoise asks.

I turn my head to look at her. "Maybe I should have brought a book with me."

She puts her pen down. "Are you going home for the summer?"

"No. I live in L.A."

"Oh," she says, "is this your first trip to The Big D?"

"Yes. Do you live there?"

"No," she says. "I live in Pennsylvania."

"Is this your first time there, too?" I ask.

"Heavens, no! I've been there several times. My work takes me all over."

"What do you do?"

"I'm a therapist."

"A traveling therapist?"

She nods. I'm mildly curious.

"Okay, cool. So, is there anything special about what you do? I mean that you travel?"

Her smile broadens and her eyebrows go up, making her eyes look even bigger; she's pretty. "Well, there are others that do the same type of therapy, but they don't most won't travel to their clients like I do."

"What kind of clients do you go to that need you to travel to them?"

"Well, CEOs, business people, actors, sports competitors, the elderly, cancer patients …"

I'm no longer clutching the arm rests.

"That seems like a lot of people. What kind of therapy you do?"

"Well … let me ask you this: Have you had any therapy yourself?.""

I think of Gloria at the Maple Center who told me I should be wondering why I was in a relationship with an addict. "No. But I'd probably like to. I think it would help."

The woman closes her notebook and drops it into the large attaché under her seat, replaces her tray into the upright position, settles back into her seat, and entwines her long fingers. I notice the diamond ring on the middle finger of her left hand. It is not a small stone.

My breathing has relaxed.

"Well, let's see if I can explain this in a few minutes."

"The basic premise is that everything is energy. That gives you untold power to change your situation because you're only dealing with energy and you're the creator — or the director if you will — of what you want or need."

I am completely mystified. "Huh?"

She puts her elbow on the arm of her seat and tries to get comfortable. "Can I ask your name?"

"Sure. I'm Jolie Gold."

"Pretty name. Okay, Jolie. Imagine that every feeling, emotion, idea, belief and memory, and every part of what you call yourself is a part. Just a part. Of course, you can see then, that you have lots of parts because you have lots of emotions — you have a part that's joyful, a part that's depressed, you may have a part that manages your time for you — lots and lots of parts - every thought as well as every single emotion and memory."

I nod.

"Aside from all these parts, you have a Self. That's that part of you that some call, the Soul. It remains untouched, regardless of which of your parts is being 'triggered' at the moment or, to but it another way, what part you're 'blending with' — whether you're blending with the part that's feeling loss, creativity, happiness, anger, or whatever other part it may be.

"The Self is non-judgmental, calm, curious, compassionate, and does not blend with any part, but rather connects to that part through a sort of focussed meditation that calls up that part. Then Self acknowledges that part without too much blending, so it's a lot like Self is watching a movie. You make the movie.

"Self connects with that whatever part you want to work on, perhaps a part that's been triggered and uncomfortable — say, like bitterness. Self acknowledges that part and offers compassion, curiosity about what's burdening it, listens as the part tells Self what it needs to unburden, and Self unburdens it. The part has all the answers you need."

I'm listening with some understanding, but my understanding is intuitive. "It sounds interesting." She nods. "Can I ask your name?"

Her smile is glowing. "Yes, of course. I'm Erivista Light. Glad to meet you, Jolie."

"Hi, Erivista. Cool name."

"Thanks. I like it. Turns out that when you unburden a part, you can generally choose to unburden it in fire, water, air or light. So, I connect to my last name."

"The whole thing sounds interesting. I've never heard of anything like it. And you're a psychologist?"

I notice that my stomach feels better, and my arms are no longer clutching the arm rests. My breathing is normal.

"I'm a licensed psychotherapist." I'm impressed. "I find so many of us need someone to talk to, someone to have a dialog with and someone to guide them to feel more at peace." She nods. "In the end, it all comes down to the same thing."

I wait for her to continue, but she doesn't. "What's that?"

"We each have a tremendous amount of control over our lives and our bodies. We can decide what we experience as our reality."

"That's it?"

She nods. "In a nutshell. Unfortunately, most of us don't use the power we have to live as we want. We fall into the role of victim. We think we can never amount to anything because of how we were brought up, or because of what we have or don't have, what someone did or didn't do to us. There are as many so-called reasons to be in a victim role as we can creatively conjure up and all of them are there to protect you from feelings that are worse than feeling victimized."

I think about *my* life. I've believed I'm a victim of the my mother who abandoned me, and of Phil's beatings as well as Rocky's senseless death. I also think of Phil and Stella and I realize that they considered themselves to be victims of Jeffrey's death, of anti-Semitism, maybe even of one another, and God knows what else.

"What's worse than feeling you're a victim?" I say.

"Oh, maybe feelings of self blame, depression, remorse, guilt, shame, fear, self worthlessness, envy, jealousy, self-hatred, … to name a few. All depends on the person and their parts, maybe all of those, and more." She pauses, then goes on.

"What I'm saying, Jolie, is that if you think and act as like you're the victim of someone or something else – something outside of yourself, you're giving away your power. But, if you believe that you're responsible for what happens to you, regardless of your individual history or your environment, you can start the process of change." You can start to unburden the parts of you that we generally try to hide and run away from despite the fact that our Souls can take care and unburden anything through compassion, caring, curiosity, clarity and love.

That part I intuitively understand.

"People who are diagnosed with a disease or who have suffered a loss often think they have to stop living life. We all have our own worst scenario that can make us as much a victim as the abused child."

"So, is there any hope for me?" I say, trying to sound light.

"Well, since this is a short flight, I'd say the least you can do is meditate and do a lot of visualization to manifest what you want."

"Visualizations?"

She nods. "Simply visualize what you want or need and believe it will manifest. You'll eventually realize it's all just energy that you direct.

The stewardess comes by with a snack and requests for drinks. My neighbor accepts a bag of peanuts and coffee. I want only water. I'm anxious for Erivista to continue and she does.

"Are you aware of the studies done that show the power of positive visualization on disease? Your thoughts that are instructed by your affirmations and your visualizations move energy. What better proof do we need of the mind's power to form our reality?

"When we realize that we have a huge influence over our bodies and our lives, we'll begin to *direct* that power to bring us happiness and peace of mind."

Her bag of peanuts falls by my foot. I bend to retrieve it and notice she's got great legs and wearing expensive designer shoes.

The flight attendant comes by to collect trash. I look out the window and immediately avert my eyes. The plane is passing through clouds in the blue sky. I want to hear more. I turn back to her.

"Well, I'm going to think about what you said."

She chuckles. "You're already living what I've said." I'm sure my surprise is written on my face. Erivista says, "That's right, Jolie. You're already using your mind to create your reality. Right now, at this moment. We all are. The trick is to use it far more than we're doing at present and to use it in a way that benefits us. That's how dreams manifest into reality."

"Wait. I'm using it now?"

Erivista nods. "Absolutely, Jolie. It's what's called "synthesizing intent into reality." It's a fancy phrase for a simple concept. You create your reality in your mind. Your mind has so much power.

I'll give you another example: you wanted to go to Dallas. Well, you're going! Everything lined up to allow you to go today. It's really so simple. You create your reality in your mind. That's what vision boards are all about.

"Here's another example of how the mind works. A while ago, you looked out your window and you got nervous."

"Yeah."

"But then we began talking and your nervousness subsided. Am I right?"

"Uh huh.

"Why? Nothing's changed. I hate to remind you, Jolie, but we're still thousands of feet in the air." My heart flutters.

Erivista reaches for my hand. "But you weren't nervous anymore. Why? Because you focused on my words rather than on your fear. That, too is a lesson. We choose our perception and in doing so, choose our life. It's remarkable, really. You have unlimited power, endless ability to exert control over your life. Recall it's all energy.?

Oh, my god! She's right! I haven't been afraid since I focused on her. I've just been concentrating on what she said. *Wow!* "That's so far out! You're right. What's that called again?"

She smiles. "Synthesizing intent into reality. Or just manifesting reality. Science is discovering just how remarkable our mind really is. The power of positive thinking, positive visualization – and, unfortunately, negative visualization – are all very strong and shape our reality. In essence, visualizing something can make it happen."

If what she's saying is true, the success of my trip to Dallas can be assured right here in the air! I phrase my question carefully. "What if what you want depends on other people?"

She has a smooth laugh. "Most of what happens to us depends, to some extent, on other people, no? But your positive thoughts and your visualizations will set things off that will allow others to cooperate and do what's needed to make what you want come to be."

I think of my conversations with Aunt Sophie. I wanted this and it helped make it happen. If she hadn't mentioned a son, I wouldn't be here. I wiggle in my seat.

"Okay, Erivista. Here's one for you. I want to find my parents. You're saying I should visualize them. But how can I visualize someone if I don't know what they look like?"

She draws back a bit, momentarily surprised. "You've never seen your parents?"

"No, I was adopted. So, I have no idea what my real parents look like. But I want to find them."

"I see. Well, Jolie, let's see. You can do a few things. Rather than picturing a particular person's face, picture yourself feeling like you've accomplished what you set out to do. Try to really feel the satisfaction, feel the glow of love and the glow of belonging to your birth parents. Reuniting with them.

"Make a list of the things you want to do with them, places you'll go with them and the things you'll talk about with them. Be specific. Visualizing yourself with a man and woman who love you. Their features may not be distinct. Maybe they're a large label across them that reads, 'My parents' or 'Jolie's mother' and 'Jolie's father.'

"And remember to affirm your beliefs. That's by using affirmations."

She counts off on two fingers. "Turn desire to reality by visualizations and repeating positive affirmations. Words have tremendous power. Repeat and visualize often that you *will* find them. Say your affirmations out loud so you hear the words. Repeat it silently, too, so that the idea is planted firmly into your deepest subconscious. And do lots of visualizations.; they're super powerful because you're already there in the visualization, so it can happen. You can manifest being there."

I feel my heart start to pump in excitement. Erivista continues, "You can be so very positive you'll meet your parents that you will be guided to that meeting."

"*Guided?* How?"

"Both consciously and unconsciously. Your actions (the visualizations and affirmations) and the forces at play in this universe about which we know so little, will guide you to them. Some call it 'divine intervention,' some call it 'higher self' or 'psychic self.' Whatever it is, just keep in mind that it may not happen overnight; you're not roasting a turkey. But you can be sure it *will* happen."

"That's incredible! Everything you're saying is totally incredible!"

A voice comes over the loudspeaker. "Ladies and Gentlemen, this is your Captain speaking. We're heading toward the Dallas-Fort Worth area. We will be preparing to land in approximately 10 minutes. Those of you on the right side of the cabin may be able to see a small body of water. That's Mountain Creek Lake. We'll be passing over the Cockrell Hill area in just one or two minutes.

"The weather in Dallas is 87 degrees and sunny and visibility is clear. For those of you who would like to set your watches, the time in

Texas 10:20 a.m. Please note that at this point your seat belts must be securely fastened. Our stewardesses will be passing by to make sure that your seats are in the upright position, tray tables up, all items stowed under your seat or overhead and all aisles and overhead compartments cleared for landing. You'll be hearing more from us when we're on the ground. I'd like to wish you a pleasant time in the Dallas-Fort Worth area, and we thank you for flying with us today."

"We're there already?" I ask, daring a peek out the window.

Erivista moves to readjust her attaché under her seat, and I realize she hasn't written since our conversation began.

"I'm sorry if I kept you from working," I say.

"No problem at all. It must have been important for you to hear what I had to say. It wouldn't surprise me at all if your thought patterns directed our seats to be adjacent today. I think you've been looking for answers for a long time, Jolie."

"I have been looking for years. That's why I'm going to Dallas."

"You're looking for your parents?"

"Yes."

"Well then, I have every reason to believe you will find them. Hopefully, you believe that too. If you do, and you focus your mind, if you ask it to work in a way to bring you what you want, I'm certain you will. But remember, patience is the key. Patience and some work. It may not be immediate – like I said, you're not cooking a turkey – but it will happen."

The plane begins its descent into Texas. My mind is filled with all I've just heard. I can perform magic! I'll easily find my mother and father. I just have to visualize them and *believe*.

I'm so engrossed in these thoughts that I'm surprised when I hear the wheels touch down and brakes pulling back. As we disembark, I thank Erivista effusively for our talk.

Her last words to me are, "Good luck, Jolie, and don't forget to be patient."

And then we separate.

34

A HARD LANDING

*S*itting in the back seat of the cab on my way to the Dallas Hall of Records, I review my conversation with Erivista.

Oh, shit! I cannot believe I didn't even think of asking for her business card! The woman gets paid to speak the way she spoke to me, and I didn't think to ask for her contact information! I'll have to be a lot smarter than that while I'm here in Dallas.

I close my eyes. As per Erivista's instructions, I imagine myself with my parents. I visualize a picture of myself with two figures, a man and a woman. 'Jolie's Father' is written across one, 'Jolie's Mother' across the other. My heart fills with a warm happiness and I grin. *I will find my mother. I will find my father. I will find my parents.* I repeat the affirmation softly and continually until the cabbie stops curbside at my destination.

———

I walk into the Hall of Records and approach the clerk's window feeling confident.

A petite woman out of Stella's era approaches wearing a tight black skirt with a flowered blouse, ruffled around the collar, down the front, and at the sleeves. The top of her wide black belt is lost under her midriff bulge. Her strawberry-blonde hair is in an up-do, similar to Stella's French twist but lacks the lacquer to hold it in place. Her black-framed eyeglasses slant up at the ends and connect to a gold-colored link chain. I hear her chewing gum snap. She comes to the window and asks how she can be of help.

I tell her I need the address for Abigail's Home for Unwed Mothers. She directs me to take a seat in one of the chairs along the wall while she searches the records on. I wait. My elation crescendos, realizing I'm a step away from Abigail. By the end of the day, she'll have located my file and passed me the name of the young unwed girl who gave birth to me.

I know it's possible that a file that old is in storage; Phil said that one of Stella's doctors had her file in storage after only seven years, and it took a day to retrieve it. If that turns out to be the case, I'll spend the night here in Dallas.

I close my eyes and resume my visualizations until the clerk's voice calls out to me. I spring off my chair and hustle to her window.

"Miss, this here name ya'll gave me? This Abigail's Home for Unwed Mothers? It no longer exists."

I smile. She must be mistaken. "That can't be."

The clerk perches herself on a high stool and faces me across the window counter, snapping her gum. Her glasses are dangling from the chain, resting against her chest. "Honey, I just looked it up?" As she pushes a sheet of paper through the window, I connect her accent to Mrs. Rutherford, and I know she has nothing good to tell me.

"Isn't that what it says here?" she says. "Abigail's Home for Unwed Mothers? On Gibble Road? The owner? This Jane Albright? It says she sold the land in 1968? to Pauly Development? Only single-family houses out there now? And the place you asked for? Must have been razed, torn down?"

I want to reach through the bars of the window and shake her. "But this is wrong! There's no Jane-whatever. The owner is Abigail some-thing-or-other. I'm sure of it!"

The clerk looks exasperated. She stops chewing her gum. She replaces her glasses onto her nose and eyes me. I'm sucking in my lips;

I'm confused. Abruptly, she gets off her stool, and returns to the files and the woman at the back of the room with the sheet of paper in her hand.

I close my eyes and try to clear my mind to calm my anxiety. *It was Abigail, not Jane! Sophie was so sure!*

The clerk returns, once again her glasses dangling. She's shaking her head. My heart drops. The sound of her snapping gum, the way her jaws move under loose skin when she chews, irritates me. She takes her place on the high stool again and addresses me. And the accent bothers the hell out of me.

"I'm sorry, Miss? But ya'll have some misinformation? There's no record at all of ownership by anyone named Abigail? The name of the place was "Abigail's?" But the records? They show the property was deeded to Jane Albright in 1956? 'as a single woman?' Then – as I've already told ya'll – she sold the property in 1968?"

Damn! Damn! "Can the records be wrong?" I ask.

The clerk looks up at me over her glasses and chews her gum a minute before answering. "Well, it's rare? Sometimes we'll see multiple records of sale for the same property? And you know someone's going to get sued? But that's not the case here? I checked on the recordation? Everything looks neat as a pin?"

She must be wrong! Why would the record show a 'Jane' as the owner of Abigail's? Jane must have been Abigail's partner. I'll go to the property on Gibble and find out what's happening.

"How far away is Gibble Road?" I say.

"About an hour? It's off Apache Highway? West of here?" I make no move to leave. "Well, if I can't help ya'll with anything else … ?" The woman begins to move off her stool.

"No, please, wait!" I'm pleading.

The slow, unhurried way she looks up at me, without moving back onto her stool, tells me she doesn't want to hear that.

"What else do ya'll need?"

"I'm looking for my birth certificate," I say.

"Your name? Identification?" I bring out my California driver's license and show it to the clerk. She puts her glasses on and looks at it. "Is this your father's surname?"

"I'm adopted. Gold is the name of the people who adopted me. I'm trying to find my real name. It would be on my birth certificate."

The woman eyes me. Your mother's name?"

"I don't know. That's what I'm trying to find out."

She takes her glasses off and smiles. "Then how can I help you?"

"What do you mean?" I say.

With her hands at her hips, she peers at me. "Miss, if ya'll don't know the name as it appears on the birth certificate? It's impossible to find it?"

"Don't you keep records of adoptions? Adopted babies?"

"No. Not here?"

"Well, where would are they?"

The clerk shrugs. "Can't say as I know? Somewhere else? Another department?"

"Doesn't someone else here know?"

"I'm sorry? I don't think so? Now, is that all, Miss?"

How dare she be so unhelpful! She can't just dismiss me like this. "What do you mean you don't think so? If you people don't know, who knows?"

The clerk's eyes become hard. She stops chewing. "I said, I don't know? And I will not take rudeness? I've answered your questions? And now, Miss, if there's nothing else I can do for ya'll? I've got work to do?" She gets off her stool and walks to the back of the room leaving me stranded at the window

I exit the Hall of Records and descend the steps to the street with weakened knees. I feel like I'm falling into a hole.

Outside, though the sun flaunts its heat in eighty-seven degree weather, and despite my three-piece suit, I'm chilled. I loiter, not sure what to do next. I want to bury myself somewhere and cry. Everything in my life ends up so fucked up. I always start out hopefully and I'm always let down.

Maybe I won't even bother going to Gibble Road. With my luck, nothing good will come from it. But how can I *not* go? I'm here, in Dallas for the day, I have the address and it is only minutes before noon. That means it's almost two o'clock L.A. time. I realize all I've had today was a quick cup of coffee at the airport and the water I drank on the plane. I need to eat and replenish my strength. Then I'll go to Gibble Road.

I enter the first coffee shop I pass, take a corner seat at a Formica-topped table and order a turkey sandwich along with a 7-Up with extra ice.

Waiting, I look at the people in the coffee shop. There's a man at the counter wearing a 10-gallon hat. Though his back is to me, I can see he's got on jeans and a short-sleeved shirt with tan-colored boots. He's the first Texan I've seen that looks the way I'd pictured a Texan to look.

My sandwich arrives. I take a hungry bite, welcoming the soft white bread that fills my mouth, the taste of mayonnaise and the moist turkey. This is good. They've used real turkey, not processed.

Turkey ... someone was just talking about turkey ... *cooking a turkey* ... Erivista! She said finding my parents takes patience.

"It isn't like cooking a turkey." Erivista! The woman gave me false hopes about stupid visualizations ... If I just *want* to find my natural mother badly enough, some unknown magical force will lead me to her!

What bullshit! And the woman gets paid for that? I put down my glass of soda angry at my gullibility. Patience! *Right!*

A woman is sitting at a table at the other end of the small coffee shop gazing at me, the sort of absent-minded stare that makes it obvious she's daydreaming and not really seeing me. She's an attractive brunette who looks like she's in her late thirties, maybe early forties. She makes a nice appearance. Her menu is closed and set on the edge of the table. She's alone, but there's a second menu on the table and two glasses of water.

As I eat my turkey sandwich, I'm comforted by her eyes on me and I move into my own daydream, one I've experienced before, when drawn to other strange women. Any minute now she'll come up to me.

"May I sit down?" she'll say.

I'll nod, enjoying her fragrant scent. She'll sit, take a few seconds to get comfortable then smile, reach across the Formica table and take my hand.

"I've been watching you," she'll say. "You don't know me but we're

271

not strangers." Her smile will change from warm and friendly to intimate and reassuring.

"I don't mean to shock you, but, well … the truth is … " She'll throw her head back and her thick hair will settle on her shoulders. "I'm your mother."

We'll stand and embrace, overwhelmed with happiness. The tears on our cheeks will mingle.

I watch a man walk up to the brunette's table. He bends down and plants a kiss on her cheek, ending our separate reveries. Her face breaks into a lovely smile as he sits down opposite her.

My sandwich is finished. I slink myself out from behind the table feeling stronger now that there's food in me. I go to the cashier, a tall, scrawny boy, who's ogling me. I pay my bill and ask if he would call for a cab.

As I leave the coffee shop, I smile at the woman who could have been my mother.

I've been in the taxi for almost thirty minutes.

The driver stops on a street lined with carbon copy stucco houses, all small and square. He peers at me in the rearview mirror. "201 Gibble Road?"

"Yes."

He nods. "Well, this is it."

My heart sinks. This is new construction. "Where? Which one?"

"Right there, Miss, the one with the bike in front. 201 Gibble Road."

"Can you wait here for me for a few minutes?"

He shrugs. "You're paying for my time."

There's no name on the wooden mailbox. At the front door, I cross my fingers, take a deep breath and ring the bell. No one answers. I ring again. The door opens. Though it's a weekday afternoon, a boy of about ten, wearing blue and white striped pajamas holds onto the doorknob.

"Hi, do you live here?" *Stupid question!* The boy nods. His eyes are swollen, his nose is a raw red.

"Is your mom or your dad home?" He shakes his head. "You're here alone?" He nods, bringing the Kleenex he holds to his face. "Will they be home soon?"

"Mom went to get medicine." Could he be Abigail's family?

I bend over, so I'm his height. "I need to ask you a question." He nods cautiously. "What's your mom's name?"

"Trudy." His voice is hoarse, as if it hurts him to talk.

"Do you know anyone by the name of Abigail?" The boy squints and pokes his head out me like a little turtle. "Abigail," I repeat. The boy smiles as though I'm teasing him and shakes his head shyly. "Are you sure?" He smiles wider. "Maybe that's your grandmother's name?"

He chuckles. "She's Marian."

"How about the other one?"

"She lives in Germany."

"Your aunt?" He coughs and shakes his head. Just then a sneeze catches him, a monstrous sneeze that releases a river of water from his red nose. He tries using the Kleenex in his hand, but it has fallen apart, so he puts his nose to his pajama sleeve.

I am desperate. I want to ask his teacher's name, his next-door neighbor's name and ask if he has second cousins. "You don't know anyone at all named Abigail?"

The boy shakes his head. When he separates from his sleeve, his face is a mess but he's still smiling. "That's a funny name, Abigail."

"Do you know anyone named Jane?"

My heart leaps when he nods. Then he says, "She's in my class." I slump. There is nothing left to ask here.

"Hasn't your mom taught you not to tell strangers that you're home alone?" The boy nods.

I bid him adieu and return to the waiting cab.

"Where to?" the driver asks.

"The airport." I still have time before I'm scheduled to leave. If I can't get on an earlier flight that the flight I'm scheduled for, I'll wait at the airport.

Is this really the end of my trip to Dallas? The clerk at the Hall of Records had said the property was sold to Pauley something. The names *Abigail* and *Jane Albright* are racing one another, swimming laps back and forth in my head and I don't know where to get the information I need.

Checking my watch, I say, "I've changed my mind. Instead of the airport, please take me to the city library."

⤬

I approach the long brown counter the librarian sits behind and wait for her to acknowledge me.

I guess her to be somewhere between fifty and sixty years old. She's overweight, and her thin, dirty blonde hair is held back at her temples by two clips, one in the shape of a red heart and the other, a rainbow. She looks up. Her mango lipstick is applied over chapped lips.

"Hi. I wonder if you could help me?"

"Certainly?" Another one that talks in questions. "What can I do for ya'll, Miss?"

"I'm looking for information about a place called Abigail's Home for Unwed Mothers. It was here in Dallas and sold to a company called Pauley something." I repeat, "I need information about it."

"Well, now, if that don't sound familiar?"

"Pauley?"

"No, that Home place."

My heart leaps. "You know Abigail's Home for Unwed Mothers?"

"Why, honey, everyone who lived in Dallas then knew that Home? That place helped put us on the map? Not exactly in a good way? It was a legend in this city? But it fell out of use in the late '60s?"

"Did you know the owner? Abigail?"

"Why, heavens, no? I had no use for a place like that? We were church goin' people? God-fearin' people? And I was a good girl? But honey? Like everyone else, I heard about Abigail"

So! Her name *was* Abigail!

The librarian leans in, inches closer to me. "When she sold that house and all that land to those developers? Everyone was mighty upset? Yessiree? I mean, we didn't like what was goin' on there? But the place was pretty as a picture? All open and green everywhere?

"She sold her ranch too? A huge ranch with acres of land? With all kinds of trees and creeks running through it? Once she sold it, the trees were gone?" She slaps her sides. She's making slashing motions through the air. "Chopped down? Every one of them?"

"And then almost overnight, up came all these look-alike homes and tall buildings? Concrete roads and White Castle? Carnation restaurants? Howard Johnson motels? I'll bet she made a pretty penny off *that* sale? Yessiree."

Thank you, God! "What was Abigail's last name?"

"Hmm." She closes her mouth tight and pushes her lips up towards her nose. No, don't recall as I ever heard it?"

"Do you know where she is now? Where I can find her?"

"Nope. Haven't heard hide nor hair about her since then?"

As I'm wondering what to do next, the librarian speaks again. "So ya'll are trying to find her?"

I nod. "It's really important."

"Well, honey, you can try searching the microfiche for an article about the sale? Maybe there's a mention of where she went? I'd think her last name would be there? Let's see ... it was 1968? the same year my daughter got married? Don't know that ya'll will find what you're looking for? But we won't know 'til we try?"

"Right. According to the Hall of Records, she sold the property in September of 1968."

She moves to stand up. "I'd start with the Dallas Morning News? Let me get the microfiche?"

She finds the spool of microfiche and gives it to me, leads me into a small room and shows me how to load the film onto the machine. Projected in black and white is every single page of the Dallas Morning News from 1968.

I fast forward to September. I study every page and every article carefully. A headline from September 16 catches my eye: "Development Company Set to Revamp City."

A spokesman for Pauly Development, the largest developer of urban buildings in Texas, confirms the company has purchased 250 acres of land, the largest single sale in Dallas in over 20 years. The company plans to develop single-

family housing projects, as well as commercial retail sites and office buildings.

Anticipating strong public opposition to the loss of open spaces, the company is presenting a detailed plan for modernizing Dallas, claiming the project will enhance residents' lives, add to city tax revenues and heighten the city's attractiveness to tourists and industry.

Construction plans and permits are already underway.

The purchase includes the former site of a ranch that housed unwed mothers-to-be as well as the sprawling Albright Ranch. The owner of the land, Jane Albright, was said to be pleased with the sale.

That's all it said: *"The owner of the land, Jane Albright, was said to be pleased with the sale."*

Okay, so now I now know that Abigail's was on land owned by Jane Albright. I need to know her relationship to Abigail. Was the land Jane's and the Home Abigail's? Did Jane run the Home? Or did Abigail? Maybe Abigail managed it and Jane, as the owner of the land, was her partner. Which of them can tell me what I need to know?

I scan through the rest of the month's paper half-heartedly, hoping to spot a follow-up story on Abigail or Jane Albright, owner of the land. I find nothing.

Despondent, I return the microfiche to the librarian, as she's finishing up with another visitor. "Anything there?" she asks. Before I can answer, she reads my dismal look. "No?" I shake my head.

"Well, let's see honey?... have ya'll tried the phone book?"

"What would I look for? Abigail Home no longer exists, and I don't know Abigail's last name. All I have is the name of the previous owner of the land."

"Well, we've got these here telephone books going back 20 years? Maybe ya'll should try looking up the number of some of the names you got there?"

"Okay, I will. Thank you for trying to help me."

She shrugs. "Honey, that's what they pay me for? Wait here?"

She disappears around a corner and comes back carrying a Yellow Pages, far thinner than those we have in Los Angeles.

"Here's the 1968 Dallas phone book? It's got businesses and residences?" she passes it over the counter.

I take a piece of paper from the counter and sit at a nearby table, find a pen in my handbag and open the book to businesses that start with 'A.' *Damn!* Abigail's Home for Unwed Mothers is not listed. It had already closed by 1968.

I turn to private listings and find my way to 'AL,' only a page away in this thin book. I glide my finger down the column, quickly finding 'Albright, Jane.' *It's there!*

I jot down the number and check it three times. I'm about to close the book when I think to look under 'P' for Pauley Development. Oddly, it's not included. I return the telephone book to the librarian.

"Any luck?"

"I found a listing for Jane Albright. Is there a telephone nearby?"

She directs me to a phone booth alongside the restrooms and wishes me luck. I insert a dime and dial the number. It rings. I wait.

A woman's voice: "Hello?"

I try to keep my voice loud enough to be heard over the phone and free from quivering. "Hello. I'm looking for Jane Albright."

"Well, you have the wrong number." I read her the number on the paper. It matches. "That's the number, but there's no one here by that name." We hang up and I stand there, deflated yet again.

The librarian has stepped out of the ladies' room and stops when she sees me. "No luck, honey?" I shake my head, my eyes glued to the floor. "Well, let's go see what else we've got."

I'm tired and distraught. I wait for her to lead the way and I trudge along beside her.

"Okay now, let's see? She sold the land in 1968? Hmm ... Let's see." Her hand goes to her cheek, her pudgy index finger falling on soft pink flesh.

"Have ya'll been to the Tax Assessor's office?"

"The Tax Assessor? Why would I go there?"

"Well, honey? They keep a record of all property sales? And they have information about both the buyers and the sellers? Maybe this Jane Albright was married or had children? Or maybe she had the property in the name of a trust? Those rich people do fancy things with their money? There should be an address and phone number? Maybe even a name of someone who would know how to find her?"

Hope, just too stubborn to die, swells again. "And where is the Tax Assessor's office?"

"Downtown? next to the Hall of Records?"

"Thank you so much. What's your name?"

"Celia?"

"Thank you so much, Celia."

"Good luck, honey," Celia calls to my back.

At the Tax Assessor's Office, I'm met at the window by a no-nonsense bureaucrat with shirt sleeves rolled up.

I hand him the notes I've scrawled, *Abigail's Home for Unwed Mothers* and *Jane Albright Ranch sold to Pauley Development in September of 1968.* He takes the note and gets right to work as though he's been waiting impatiently for me to get there, leaving me at the window then hurriedly returning with a file in hand as though he's being clocked.

When he speaks, I'm initially thrown for a second; his sentences end with periods.

"It's all right here, Miss. All the parcels were simultaneously conveyed to Pauley by the owner, the name you have on your notes. Jane Albright's name appears as the sole owner of all the land, except for one two acre parcel that was subdivided in 1964 and put into the name of a Dean Stanton. There was an improvement on that land, probably a residence." He held up several papers. "You can get a copy of all this for a five-dollar fee if you'd like."

"Yes, please. Does it have an address or phone number for Jane Albright or for Dean Stanton?"

"This top sheet shows a phone number."

"Yes, I want that too."

I hand him five dollars, he in turn hands me my copies and I run out into the hall and enter the nearest phone booth. I am so nervous that, as I try to bring money out of my change purse, I can't get a hold of a coin and finally empty out the change purse on the small corner bench inside the booth. The coins go rolling everywhere. I leave them where they fall and pick up only the coin I need, drop it into the slot and dial Jane Albright's number.

Wait! No! This is the same number I called at the library! Damn!

I hang up and scan the paperwork, looking for the sheet with Dean Stanton's number. Finding it, I say a prayer and let coin drop into the slot. I dial the number and hold my breath as the phone rings once … twice … and then someone picks up.

"Hawwo?" It's a little girl.

In the background I hear, "Tiff, who is it, sweetheart? Give Daddy the phone." The tone is loving. *Is it Dean Stanton?*

For a moment there's silence except for the sound of my heart beating loudly. I hold my breath, and with closed eyes, I say a quick silent prayer. Then I hear a mellow voice on the other end of the line. "Hi. Can I help you?"

"Hi. I'm looking for Dean Stanton."

"Well, you found him." I can hear the smile in his voice. It's as if I'm an invited call he's been expecting. I find myself smiling as well.

I sink onto the floor of the small booth, pushing more coins onto the floor on my way down and let my breath out in an inaudible, "Wow." He will have the answer.

"So, what can I do for you?" he asks.

"Well, I'm actually looking for Jane Albright."

There is a sudden heavy silence. I think we've been disconnected, but then I hear the little girl in the background, and I wonder at his reaction. Did I enter a forbidden zone? And if so, *why?*

I go on, "Do you happen to know how I can reach her?"

A second's pause. "Can I ask why you want to find her?" His voice is far cooler now, curious and cautious.

"It's kind of personal." I pause then, but he offers nothing, so I add, "but if it will help me get to her …" I start. "I was adopted from Abigail's Home for Unwed Mothers and I'm trying to locate my birth mother. I can't find Abigail because I don't know her last name and that's why I need to talk to Miss Albright."

Laughter erupts on the other end of the line as if he's just heard a great joke. Eventually, the laughter dies down. "I'm sorry, so sorry. I didn't mean to laugh. Really. It's just that it's still hard for me to believe Jane fooled so many people, so well, for so long. I thought I was the only one. I guess I never truly stopped to think about all the girls and families she tricked."

"What do you mean? I just want to talk to Abigail."

"There-is-no-Abigail." He makes a separate sentence out of each word.

My smile fades along with my hopes. "No Abigail? My Aunt Sophie said she spoke to Abigail."

"There was never an Abigail, only Jane. Jane *was* Abigail. Your aunt wasn't the only one who spoke to Abigail. *Everyone* did. They all thought they were speaking to a sweet, big-hearted woman who cared about girls in trouble and about what happened to their motherless babies when they were really talking to a heartless bitch! Jane only cared about money."

"Jane was Abigail?"

"I was the biggest fool of all. Strung me along for years, telling me how she wanted a baby and a family. Turns out, she couldn't *stand* babies. She hated every one of those babies. She sold those beds to the highest bidder then sold their babies to the highest bidder."

I shut my eyes and shake my head. I can't believe what I'm hearing. I put the phone to my other ear. "You were married to her?"

"For almost six years," he says, drawing it out. "It took me that long to figure out her game." He snorts. "That's how dumb I am." Then he chuckles. "But I'm okay now, married to a peach with two great kids. You heard Tiff, my niece on the phone. She's here visiting, playing with my kids. They're all great. Life is good."

"Do you know how I can reach your ex-wife?"

"Last I heard, she was somewhere in Europe. Hooked up with a count or something, French, I think, probably living in his castle."

Tears sting my eyes. This is the end of the line for me. My heart is skipping all over as I try one last shot with Dean Stanton on the phone. My heart's pounding so fast, it's an effort to push the words out.

"Do you happen to know what she did with the records? I mean from the Home. All the papers about the adoptions. It's so important to me. I'd do anything to find my papers, Mr. Stanton. *Anything!*"

His voice is soft and gentle, trying to soothe me over the wire. "Look … what's your name?"

"Jolie. Jolie Gold."

"Look, Jolie. Kids are everything to me. Family is all-important. It's all I ever wanted, so I can only imagine how you must feel about your situation and how badly you want to find your mom and dad.

"If there was anything at all I could do to help you, I would. But there *are* no records, Jolie. I don't think there ever were. Jane didn't give a shit about any of that. Jane only cared about the ledgers and as soon as the land was sold, she tossed all the ledgers out. I'm sorry, Jolie, but there's nothing I can do to help you."

I don't have it in me to get up and hang the phone up. When the line goes dead, I just let the receiver go; it dangles, swinging. I just sit.

I've reached the end of my search and discovered that there's nothing to find. My heart feels heavy. I take several deep breaths, but it doesn't help. A knock on the glass door startles me, upsetting me further as it brings me back to awareness of time and place. Someone's waiting to use the phone booth. I pull myself up off the floor and replace the receiver. With my hands shaking, I take my purse and exit.

"Miss, are these your coins?"

I don't look back. There is nothing left for me to do but to head back to the airport and home.

On the flight back to L.A. as I take my seat and fasten my seat belt, I am filled with anger, resentment, and incredible frustration.

I'm helpless. All my hopes have been crushed. An elderly man sitting in the window seat holds a copy of the Wall Street Journal. He looks at me and smiles as I take my assigned seat next to him. I will not be available for conversation nor will I look out the window.

I fasten my seat belt. Dean Stanton's words haven't stopped circling round in my mind. *She sold babies to the highest bidder … There was no Abigail! She only cared about ledgers … She tossed everything … She sold babies to the highest bidder.*

I sigh and sigh again, as my body still fights to calm down. Then as the engine roars and the plane alights, my fear of flying kicks in and compounds my misery. I just want to give up.

I need to occupy myself, distract myself from the failure of the day. The stout man sitting across the aisle passes me a big smile. I pretend not to see him. I plug in the earphones provided and close my eyes.

Turning the dial, I hear music, but I'm not in the mood music. Then a deep voice captures my attention. I lean back and listen to the taped commentary.

"As the first half of 1979 nears its end, we approach the end of this decade. With that in mind, let's travel back through the events of the last six months, to review the major news stories in the United States and around the world, take a second look where we've been and perhaps get some idea of where we're all headed in the months and years to come. This is good. I may be able to concentrate on it and distract myself from myself for a while.

"The year began with the establishment of full diplomatic ties between the US and Red China. We witnessed an oil spill polluting the waters of the Atlantic Ocean and the Gulf of Mexico. Biologists and oceanographers are concerned about the impact spills such as this will have on marine life.

"February 1st saw Patty Hearst of the respected Hearst family, earlier convicted of bank robbery, released from prison.

"Moving forward, for our next story of the year, we go backward in time to review events. Fourteen years ago, students on the Kent State campus protested President Nixon's decision to bomb Cambodia. In response, the governor of Ohio called in the National Guard to quell the demonstrations. Almost immediately upon the Guards' arrival on campus, two men were bayoneted by members of the National Guard and when the facts came to light, it was discovered that one of the two dead men had been a disabled veteran who had provoked the Guardsmen merely by yelling at them. On the second day following the arrival of the Guard, 13 unarmed students were injured by a barrage of bullets fired directly into the crowd by the Guard. Four of those students died. Although experts agreed that the evidence pointed to the conclusion that the shooting Guardsmen had aimed for specific individuals, none of the Guardsmen were punished either civilly or criminally. In fact, there was absolutely no immediate threat to the Guardsmen. Of the students who were shot, the closest was as far as 60 feet away; the furthest was 700 feet

away. All the students were unarmed. However, as all the Guardsmen were wearing gas masks at the time, their identification in photos was rendered impossible. This January, 14 years later, justice, slow to appear, showed its face when the state of Ohio agreed to pay six hundred seventy-five thousand dollars to the families of those who died or were injured in the Kent State University shootings.

"Moving on, in Cambodia, Pol Pot who has earned his place in history among the most brutal of leaders, alongside Hitler and Stalin, ended his regime with the fall of Phnom Penh, that country's capital city.

"On January 16th of this year, the shah of Iran, Mohammed Reza Pahlavi his wife, Empress Farah Diba and their four children, left his throne and his country behind forever. His abdication was the result of widespread rioting and anti-government demonstrations in Iran. The deposed Shah's request to enter the United States was rejected and the former monarch and his family traveled to Egypt. Within weeks of his departure, the revolutionary forces in his country took control under the leadership of the Muslim cleric, the Ayatollah Ruhollah Khomeini and the country officially renamed the Islamic Republic of Iran. It is feared that members of religious minorities, those with political differences, those with ties to the West and to Israel as well as friends of the former regime are all in danger of imprisonment and death under the rule of the fundamentalist leadership."

My thoughts jump to Jamsheed and his family as it does whenever I hear news of Iran. I pray they are all safe. Hundreds of families have probably fled the country and thousands more still hoping to escape.

"In March, radiation was released in Pennsylvania when an accident occurred at a nuclear power plant at Three Mile Island on the heels of the newly-released hit movie, "The China Syndrome," premised on a cover-up of dangerous faults existing at a U.S. power plant. Also in March, the U.S. space probe, Voyager, revealed photos of Jupiter's rings.

Internationally, Israel and Egypt signed a historic peace treaty.

"Britain has a new Prime Minister. A woman, Margaret Thatcher, became the new British Prime Minister when the Conservative Party won elections on May 3rd.

"On June 18 of this year, as a result of President Carter's meeting with

Leonid Brezhnev in Vienna for SALT talks, the United States and the Union of Soviet Social Republics agreed to limit the manufacture of nuclear arms."

The plane hits turbulence and bounces. I clench my eyes and grip the armrests of my seat. I switch channels. I have heard enough about the world and now I want music. I'm listening to the Bee Gees sing "Staying Alive" and my thoughts go to Nora, Jonah and Paul. Then the sound goes dead. In its place comes the captain's voice, announcing our imminent landing at LAX.

I take a deep breath and let it out slowly.

I continue to focus solely on nothing but my inhale and exhale until I feel the plane's wheels hit the ground. I did it. I flew all the way home without giving in to my fear of flying. On my return from Dallas, fresh with disappointment, I call Sophie. She shares my surprise and consoles me.

But she has nothing else for me.

35

BEDLAM

*B*ack in L.A.
 Depressed.

Hit a wall. *The* wall.

No where to turn.

Discarded by a mother who was young, unmarried and pregnant.

Who was she? Why didn't she keep me? Did she want to? Where was she born? Who was my father? Were my parents in love? What is the heritage I've lost?

The feeling of elation I had while listening to Erivista Light, thousands of feet in the air, has long since vanished, replaced with feelings of isolation and desolation far greater than that which I had before my trip to Dallas.

First, I had the hope that I would find out answers from Stella and Phil. Then I got answers from Sophie, and my hope grew exponentially; I had someplace to start from, a place to go to find answers. Erivista fed me more hope, picturing people wearing banners and thinking about how I'll feel and what I'll do when I find my parents. And then that day in Dallas running from one place to another until finally – *finally!* – locating Dean Stanton and finding out all my hopes ended in a pile of ashes.

I will never know who my real parents are. And so, I will never know who I am.

Sophie consoles me and, of course, Nora is sympathetic. But I continue to sulk.

I'm glad that Nora is living with Jonah. Much as I love her, I need my privacy. I want to sulk in private. I'm depressed. I decide I no longer give a good goddamn! It's bullshit. Everything is bullshit. So, I will do whatever the hell I feel like doing. I will go crazy.

Thanks to Stella, Phil is giving me more that what I need in the way of cash. I start classes at UCLA in September. Some of my classes are so large, they're taught in small amphitheaters. I'm doing well in all of them. Now I realize the importance of money and I definitely want a job that will pay a lot. Like Stella said, I want enough to be financially independent.

My life is about school and dating. That's all. I'm dating a lot. Men have become my drug of choice, distracting me from the pain of my depression. There are a ton of guys at UCLA – and everywhere else.

I think about Holden. I haven't heard from him. Maybe he's struck it big and moved away. That night I spent with him has changed me. I'm what you might call 'promiscuous' now, sleeping with lots of guys. I'm a regular *femme fatal* leaving a path of broken hearts behind me.

It's no problem hooking up with a guy. While most girls – including Nora – emulate The All-American Super Model, Cheryl Tiegs, or are still into the "Annie Hall" thing, wearing ties and borrowed suit separates, my look is super feminine.

My darker coloring and soft, feminine choices in clothing makes me stand out; guys love it. I can afford nice clothing now and I pretty much buy whatever I like. I dress in the softest silks, cashmeres, and suedes. My signature gardenia perfume leaves a sweet scent wherever I go.

I get off on the different ways guys try to get my attention. I find it amusing.

They send me flowers, buy me gifts, and take me on short weekend trips to places like Costa del Mar, Las Vegas, Santa Barbara and La Jolla. They show up at my door with candles and dinner from some of the finest LA restaurants. Some write me poetry. I love the attention. I know they do it to sleep with me. Guess what? I want to sleep with them just as much.

I play with them, sleep with them if I want to, and leave them when I tire of them. No emotional attachment for me. Nothing heavy, nothing serious. Not interested, thank you in exposing myself to the possibility of pain, heartache, or disappointment. Like the song says, "I'm through with love." I'm no longer vulnerable. I'm strictly in it for my own agenda.

My motto? "Keep it light."

"So, I was at Le Dome with Damon-"

Nora interrupts me. "Who's Damon?"

"It doesn't matter," I say. "Anyway, we sit down and order drinks when he sees two of his friends walk in with dates. He'd mentioned one of them to me before and wants to invite the four of them over to join us. I say okay, so we're moved to a larger table. The six of us are at a round table. We have drinks, all kinds of cocktails, appetizers, salads, then dinner – you know, the works. I had a great veal Oscar. A few have wine with dinner, whatever. Later, we all have coffee and dessert and some of us have after dinner drinks-"

"Did you have their banana tart? Yum! It's the best!"

"Yes, listen! So, the waiter comes over to our table – actually, he comes to me. He's holding a small round tray with a bottle of champagne on ice, and he leans over and says to me, "This is for mademoiselle.""

He hands me a small piece of paper that's folded in half. I ask him who the champagne is from. He's still bending over me and whispers, "It's compliments of the man across the way." I follow his gaze. There's a man at a table, not far from ours.

"Who was it?" Nora says.

I say, "There's this man sitting alone at a table facing me. Damon's busy talking to his buddies, and the two girls are trying not to look like they're craning their necks to hear what the waiter was saying to me."

"Did you know the guy?" Nora asks.

"Never saw him before in my life."

"Wow! Okay, go on."

"I smile at him and read the note I'm holding. Are you listening?"

"Yeah," Nora says. "Go on! What did the note say?"

"It said, *I've enjoyed my dinner far more while enjoying your exquisite beauty. If I may have your number, I would very much like to call you.*"

"Oh, wow! A real weirdo!" she says.

"I don't think so," I say. "He's just European. He was even wearing a beret.

"So, listen! Here comes the best part! The waiter leaves, and then he comes back with our bill. I take the bill and and ask the waiter for a pen. I turned it over – it was a huge bill for everything we ate and drank, the drinks, appetizers, dinner, desserts … Everything for all six of us!" I'm laughing as I remember the scene.

"Go on," she says.

"I wrote my name and phone number on the back of the bill and gave it to the waiter and told him to give it to the guy."

"Oh, my God! *No*, Jo!" Nora screams into the phone.

"Oh, it was fantastic! Listen!

I watch him as he goes up to the guy. He bends over and says something and hands him the bill. The guy picks up our bill, sees my name and number on it and gives me a big smile along with a little nod. I smile back, and I gesture for him to turn the paper around. He does and realizes it's our bill."

"Jo! What did he do?"

"It was fucking great!" He was so totally cool! He didn't even really look at it, I mean, he didn't look at the total and react or anything. He just put it down on the table and nodded to me, still smiling and nodded at the waiter to leave it there!"

Nora gasps. "Are you telling me a stranger paid the bill for the six of you?"

"Yes! Nora, it was like something from an old movie.""

"I don't believe it. And I don't believe you did that!"

"Believe it."

"What did Damon do?"

"What could he do? He was talking with his buddies when the

champagne came. He asked our waiter for the bill, not realizing he'd had already brought it. The waiter told him it had been taken care of. He couldn't figure it. None of the guys were really paying attention.

"I just told him it was taken care of. He looked at me in total amazement. He thought I'd paid. And the girls – well, they didn't know what to say, so they said nothing – they must have known I didn't pay. None of them had read note the guy had written or seen what I'd written on the bill when I gave it back to the waiter.

"All night, Damon kept saying he couldn't believe I paid for. I just shrugged and said, "Why not?"

Nora and I are both laughing.

"That's amazing!" Nora says. Then, "Jo, you didn't give him your real number, did you?"

"Of course, I did," I say.

"Oh, shit! He'll call you!" she says.

"He already did," I say. "I'm meeting him at his hotel today."

"You're meeting him?" She can't believe it.

"Yeah. At the Beverly Wilshire," I say.

"What are you meeting him for?"

"A cup of coffee," I say.

She repeats, "A cup of *coffee?*"

"I don't know. Maybe we'll go shopping," I say.

"Jolie, you are nuts!"

"Don't be silly, Nora!"

"I'm not silly,"Nora says. "You're out of your mind. You can't meet a total stranger at his hotel."

"I'll be fine," I reassure her. "It'll be fun; an adventure. But I gotta go. I'll talk to you later."

"Fun?" She says it like she's I've just told her I'm going to the front lines of war. "Be careful, Jo! Call me. I'll worry."

"Right. Check. And he will." I chuckle. "Get it? Write check? Anyway, I will. But he's expecting me. Give Jonah my love."

An hour and a half later, I'm inside the Pink Turtle at the Beverly Wilshire Hotel, the same Pink Turtle where I'd first met Rocky for coffee and apple pie.

My hair is down and I'm wearing a soft pink silk dress with heels. As I approach the entrance, I recall how I'd hidden myself before going in that day to meet Rocky.

I'm not the same girl I was then. I've grown up. There are no stars in my eyes. Determined to push the memory aside, I go in with a smile on my face and walk up to the table where Erick Bromm sits.

Erick already has a cup of tea in front of him. He's nice looking, definitely distinguished looking. He's got chestnut brown hair, brown eyes and an awkward nose, and he's impeccably groomed. He's the sort of man who has weekly manicures, regular appointments with his barber, custom-made clothing – the best of everything. He's wearing an elegant charcoal suit. I may be underdressed but, hey, he's a businessman and I'm a college girl.

"Forgive me for starting without you," he says as he rises to welcome me. His build is average. His English is perfect, with only an accent slight, enough to draw attention to his European roots. When he smiles, I note that his teeth are straight and almost white.

Since he's drinking tea, I order a cup of Earl Grey and decline his offer to order any food. As we drink our tea, Erick tells me he's here from Switzerland on business. He has a wife and daughter in Zurich. Tea and coffee finished, and those disclosures out of the way, I suggest we take a walk.

"It's such a lovely day," I say.

"Every day is like this in your city, no?" he says.

I nod, feeling a bit foolish. "Well, most. Would you like to take a walk?"

"Of course."

We walk out onto Wilshire and I lead us west toward the department stores.

Erick tells me he's in town to attend a series of business meetings with a group of men seeking venture capital to create a U.S. division of a multinational trading company. I'm not sure what 'venture capital' means, but I know they want money and they're hoping to get it from

Erick. At each intersection, he gently takes hold of my arm, guiding me across and soon we're standing in front of the window displaying men's wear at Saks Fifth Avenue.

"Do you mind if we go in?" I ask. I make certain that we enter through the men's department. As we pass the counters, Erick shows a passing interest in a light blue sweater and I insist on buying it for him. "Something to remember me by." He accepts on condition that I allow him to buy me something.

An hour and a half later, we leave the store with his sweater and my pair of butter-soft leather boots in a caramel color and a size 4 camel-hair coat to match. Though guys have bought me gifts, the extent of Erick's repeated generosity so soon after meeting is sign that records will be broken.

We return to the hotel and say goodbye as we wait for the valet to bring my car. I go back to my apartment, but only to drop off my bags, shower again and change clothes. Erick has invited me back for dinner. I wear my new boots with a short silk moss green dress and pin my hair up.

After a touch of makeup and a spin in a haze of my perfume, I drive back to the Beverly Wilshire.

3 6

THE MIDAS TOUCH

I enter the hotel, make my way to the elevator, and ride up to the hotel room of a married man who's more than twice my age; Erick is forty-three.

The thought excites me. I'm not the least concerned about what might happen. I'll simply take it as it comes and enjoy the moment.

The suite is elegantly furnished. The living room is barely lit, the curtains, drawn. There's a small table in the center of the room covered with white linen and set for dinner for two, with white roses in a vase between two tall candles waiting to be lit.

Erick leads me to a bar where champagne awaits, chilling in an ice bucket. I recognize the label. It's the same champagne he'd sent to my table at Le Dome.

"I apologize for the champagne," Erick says before expertly popping the cork. "It is not my preference, but I'm afraid, it is the best the hotel has to offer." I take the glass he holds out, the tiny white bubbles bursting amid the soft gold liquid.

"Let us drink to friendship," Erick says, raising his glass. Our glasses touch.

"To friendship," I repeat.

As I continue enjoying my champagne, Erick carries the ice bucket holding the champagne to the bedroom and sets it down alongside the large bed. And so, without a word, he has made his intentions known.

I don't wait for him to come back for me. I go to him.

There is only a dim light seeping from the living room into this room. I walk up to him, expecting him to take me into his arms and kiss me, but he does neither. He doesn't kiss me, hold me, caress my hair, or stroke my face. Rather, he stands in front of me and reaches behind me. He unzips my dress as expertly as he uncorked the bottle of champagne. Then he moves the straps off my shoulders, and they fall at my arms. His touch gives me goose bumps.

His silent, domineering manner makes my breath heavy and my heart pump faster. I feel warmth taking over my groin. My dress falls to the floor. My lace bra showcases the swell of my breasts. Erick sees this and his tongue slides out to wet his lips, but he doesn't touch me. His eyes flicker. His gaze is moving slowly down my body to my silk panties, looking at my every inch as if appraising a piece of art.

I sense his desire growing beneath his calm, steady gaze and I become hotter. Neither of us speaks. Erick unbuttons his shirt still gazing at my silk panties while I stand still as a statue feeling my private parts beginning to moisten.

Erick takes his shirt off. He unzips his pants, and they fall to the floor. He is not wearing underpants. He turns to pick up his pants and I see that he's completely erect. I hear myself swallow. He folds his pants and sets them on the wooden valet standing by the wall, then hangs his shirt alongside it. He lines his shoes up with his socks inside them. All this time, my eyes remain fixed on the size and swing of his perfect erection. He's through putting away his clothes.

He comes to me, his erection almost, but not quite, touching me. He's already made me feel that I'm there for him to have at his leisure and the effect on me is more erotic than any foreplay could be. I'm going out of my mind. I want him. Badly.

He cocks his chin ever so slightly toward my panties. Without a word, I slide them off. He sets me on the bed so that I am sitting on the edge with my feet on the floor. I start to lie back but he stops me. He keeps my heels on, then gently separates my knees. The feel of his touch on my skin feels good and I close my eyes in pleasure. I relax completely, anticipating more. He enters me with his fingers, and I gasp. Some part of me is embarrassed, knowing how wet and ready he finds me.

He lays me back on the bed and enters me. There is an immediate sensation of something close to an electric shock. I feel my sexual juices flooding. Then, as he continues moving ever so deliciously, he speaks, a whisper at my ear. "What are you doing tomorrow night?"

We make love, mostly silently, on and off throughout the night. I've never been with an older man before. Afterwards, I assume that his age is part of his sexual appeal. He's also the first lover I've had who's married – as far as I know – so maybe I'm also excited by the illicit nature of what we're doing.

All that aside, he's an insanely good lover and his apparent feeling of entitlement is incredibly erotic. At some point, I have a fleeting image of him as a spoiled and lustful ruler, and I am his favorite sexual toy, a sexual object capable of giving him great pleasure.

I groan in multiple climaxes. He tells me to stifle my groans and that only excites me more. Tonight, I learn that power is a tremendous aphrodisiac. I am no longer anything if not his.

Morning comes and I'm smiling. Though I've barely slept, I'm full of energy. Erick orders room service and I eat all my French toast, bacon, hashed potatoes and fruit salad. He laughs and says that with an appetite like mine, it's remarkable that I'm slim.

He has an early business meeting downstairs this morning, but he wants me to spend the rest of the day with him. I agree. I'll happily miss my classes.

While he's at his meeting, I go home to shower and change. I also check my mail and get the messages off my answering machine. There's a message from Nora. She's concerned because she hasn't heard from me since I first went to meet Erick. I call her back and leave a short message, simply to reassure her that I'm alive and well. "I'll tell you more later."

I change into a dark green suede skirt, the camel boots Erick bought me, with a simple beige camisole that has a green trim and a leather jacket that matches the boots.

When I get back to the hotel, Erick's is in the suite talking on the phone to Switzerland. He is wearing the light blue sweater I bought him.

"What would you be happy to do today?" he asks me when he hangs up.

"Whatever you like," I say.

"Do you enjoy museums?"

"I haven't been to a museum for ages," I say.

"Then we shall go."

I've never before appreciated art as much as I'm enjoying it with Erick. He seems to know something about every artist whose painting hangs at the Los Angeles County Museum of Art. He tells me about the artists' lives, how the eras they lived in affected their work and their unique painting techniques.

We leave the museum and lunch at a mediocre restaurant on Wilshire Boulevard. Erick suggests we return to Beverly Hills and window shop, which, I discover, means buying whatever is in a window that either of us likes.

After cruising Rodeo and Beverly Drive, we stop for a cappuccino at an outdoor café on Canon Drive, our last stop for the day.

Erick has his arm around me. Shopping bags of all sizes are strewn all around us, on the two empty chairs across from us, on the ground, as well as on the table. Erick is explaining what venture capital is. He investigates new businesses that need money and decides whether or not he'll invest in them, or perhaps, simply loan them money.

There's a screeching. Everyone in the café, including the two of us, looks up to see a silver Mercedes limo bolt down Brighton Way. It turns right on Canon Drive, brakes to a stop and swings into a parking space two cars north of us.

The driver, a young Asian man of slight build wearing a black suit, gets out of the car and hustles over to the curbside back door. Whoever is sitting in the back is not getting out. A large black hand appears, reaching out of the open window, long fingers laden with rings, and waves away the driver; he opens the front passenger door next.

A tall black man exits from the front passenger seat, wearing a black leather jacket and black leather pants. At least ten gold chains hang from his neck. A black fedora sits on his head. He's extremely thin with super long legs.

Erick and I watch as he goes to rear of the car. The driver lifts the trunk open. The tall black man brings out two shopping bags. The driver steps back up onto the sidewalk and stands alongside the car's rear door to wait.

Erick is fingering the necklace he's just bought me with one hand. His other hand is around my shoulders. The necklace is gold with alternating coral and lapis set in into a beautiful gold chain. He compliments me on how it looks on my neck.

"Thank you, so much. I just received this as a gift, just a few minutes ago from a dear friend. I'm glad you like it."

I glance up. The tall black man is J-walking, crossing Canon Drive, moving away from us, heading to a Cadillac parked on the other side of the street. He's carrying the two large shopping bags he took out of the trunk. Apparently, the limo stopped on Canon Drive to deliver these two bags to the driver of the Caddy across the street.

Funny, the Caddy looks exactly like Phil's. The driver of the Caddy exits the car and – *oh, my god!* It's Phil! I'm sure it's him! I don't believe it! I'm watching *Phil* get out of his car, reach into his sport coat, bring out a manila envelope and give it to this tall skinny guy.

In all these years, I've never run into Phil anywhere. I want to call out to him but – *oh, fuck!* I'm with Erick! I can't call attention to myself!

Oh, shit! Has he seen me?

I hurry to hide behind a large shopping bag I put in front of my face. While Erick enjoys his cappuccino, I peek out from behind the bag. Across the street, the black man has put his two bags down on the sidewalk and is opening the manila envelope Phil just gave him. He's fingering what's inside then closes it. He comes back across the street to the limo.

Thank God, Phil has his back to us! He's looking down into the two bags the black man left on the sidewalk. He picks them up and carries them to his trunk, puts them inside and slams it shut.

Back at the limo, the guy is handing the manila envelope to the large black hand with all the rings that's re-emerged out the window then sits back in the front seat. The black hand waves. The driver hustles around to the front of the limo, gets back into the driver's seat and takes off.

I sneak a look at Dad. He's wiping his forehead with the palm of his hand, a sign that he's nervous or worried. He's at his car door and opens it. He's getting inside. But just as he's about to sit down, with one leg inside the car, Phil turns his head and looks straight at me, so perfectly on target that we actually make eye contact!

Shit! It's as if he knew I was here all the time! Yet, though he's looking right at me, it's as if he doesn't recognize me. He probably thinks it can't be me sitting her with Erick and all these bags.

I wonder about what I just saw. The scene was so bizarre! Just the fact that Phil isn't at work at this time of day on a workday is weird. What was he doing in Beverly Hills? And what could my bigoted father possibly have to do with a black man?

I can't think about it right now. Erick is talking to me.

"Is anything the matter, Jolie?" he asks.

"Nothing. I'm just tired. It's been a busy day for me: the museum, all that shopping ..." I smile. "And I didn't get much sleep last night."

Erick suggests I go home and rest for an hour or two, shower, dress for dinner and return. He asks where I'd like to go for dinner. I suggest we stay at the hotel.

By the time I arrive home, I've put the strange run-in with Phil completely out of my mind. I'm thinking about the fact that Erick hasn't shown the slightest interest in where I live.

I turn my attention to dressing for the evening. I decide to wear the dress that Nora bought me for Christmas, the one I never the chance to wear for Rocky. The coral and lapis necklace Erick bought me today goes well with it. I recall trying the dress on in Rocky's bedroom the day of the Jonestown massacre, that last day I was there. The last day of Rocky's life. I was so certain Rocky would love it on me.

How strange life can be, that moment connecting to this one.

In the hotel's dining room, the maître's d' greets Erick. "Good evening, Mr. Bromm."

Our waiter knows him, too, and paws us with service.

Over dinner, I stay clear of his wife but ask Erick about his daughter, and I'm shocked when I learn that she's only a year older than me. She's currently in France, studying art and design.

I wonder what it would be like to have a father like Erick, not only wealthy but worldly too, so cultured, so sophisticated and so elegant … and so sexy.

For the millionth time, I wonder how my own biological father compares. Is he more like Erick or Phil?

"Are you sighing?" Erick asks.

"Your daughter's a lucky girl," I say.

He laughs. "I'm not sure she would agree." Then he takes a bite of his fish and says, "Did I tell you how lovely you look tonight?" I smile.

"I have something for you." He waves his empty fork. "You shall have it after dinner."

Erick has already bought so many things for me that I can't imagine what more he could give me. Up in his room, arranges me, still fully dressed, on the bed as though I am his to do with as he likes, and again, I am impacted by the sheer arrogance of the man, the attitude of a king that I find irresistible.

"See under the pillow," he says charmingly.

I lift the pillow to find a small blue Tiffany's box tied with the signature white ribbon. I open the box. There's a pair of diamond earrings inside, studs. Erick watches my eyes stretch open as I squeal in delighted surprise. I try to get up and hurry over to a mirror, to put the studs on and see what they look like on me, but Erick has other plans. He makes me lie still and he puts them through my ears and fastens them in the back. With my earrings on, he strips and enters me.

In the morning, when I go into the bathroom, the flash of the earrings catches my eye. I love them.

Erick invites me to join him in the shower. Under the falling water, I find a single white hair on Erick's chest, bend and kiss it. He gently lifts my head, pulls my hair away and grins at the sight of the sparkling earrings amid the drops of water on my face. We kiss then he arranges me against the shower wall with takes me with my back to him.

Erick has several meetings that day with attorneys. I leave him and meet Nora for lunch. Nora hears an account of my last two days, sees the diamond studs, and hears me rave about how much Erick knows about art.

She eyes me cautiously. "Since when have you been into married men?" I shrug. "You're falling for this guy, Jo. Are you in love with him?" I don't answer. "Oh, my god, Jo, you're falling in love with him!"

I'm irate. "No, I'm not. I'll never fall in love again. And certainly not with a man who's unfaithful to his wife!"

How could she think I'd be so stupid? I continue in a calmer tone. "I'm not in love, Nora. Part what I like about Erick is that he's married. There's no chance that this is anything but a fling. And he's so different from the guys I've known. He makes them seem like little boys."

"Jo! He's old enough to be their father. He could be your father! He's forty-seven!"

"He's forty-three."

"Whatever! I just hope you know what you're doing here, Jolie."

"I do."

At eight thirty, I drive to Chasen's on the corner of Beverly Boulevard and Doheny Drive to meet Erick for dinner.

Chasen's is one of the older restaurants in Los Angeles, where the who's who of the city meet to dine. I'd always thought the restaurant was a bit too dated and uptight when I went there with Phil and Stella, but tonight, with Erick, the restaurant has come to life. We sit side by side at a red leather booth across from the actor who plays James Bond and I stroke Erick's thigh as we enjoy our steaks.

"Tell me," Erick says, "I wonder Jolie, a girl like you, what will do you with your life?"

The fork I'd been directing into my mouth freezes. I put it down and think about an answer. I tell him the truth. "I don't really know."

Erick nods. "I think this is, perhaps, the ideal time to be a young woman in your country."

"Why do you say that?"

"The women of America are doing so much to advance themselves," he says. "They will be the prototype for the women everywhere. Because of them and their dedication, their demonstrations," he waves his arm in the air, "the things they do, women's liberation, now many things are possible for a woman like you. This is not the case in all countries."

"Well, I know I'll do something substantial," I say. "I just don't know what." It bothers the hell out of me that I can't come up with a better response. God, how I wish I had some direction!

"I am certain you will find the right thing."

After dinner, I'm back in Erick's hotel, back in his bed and back in his arms. Having sex with Erick makes me feel like a goddess and a whore. And now, knowing that his daughter and I are so close in age, I wonder if Erick fantasizes that he's having sex with her. Whatever the combination of our fantasies, it works for me.

I awaken smiling.

Erick isn't in bed. Guessing he's in the shower, I roll out of bed to join him; he's not in the bathroom. I look in the living room; no sign of him there, either. He must have gone to the lobby to get something or to one of his meetings.

I'm heading back to bed, deciding to wait for him there when the doorbell rings. Ah, he's back! Wearing only a smile, I open the door. The housekeeper has come to clean the suite. I quickly hide behind the door. "Please come back later," I say.

"I'm sorry to have bothered you, Miss. We were told the people in this room had checked out." The woman rolls her cleaning cart away from the door.

Checked out! I laugh to myself. I notice Erick's attaché isn't in its usual place on the dining room table which confirms he's at a meeting. On the way back to bed, I go to the bathroom to pee and notice that his toiletries and shaving bag are gone. I go back into the bedroom and fling the closet door open. Nothing there! I open the dresser drawers. Empty!

I flop onto on the bed, stunned. Erick is gone! He left! Just like that! Without telling me he was leaving, without even waking me to say goodbye! I'm sure he has no idea where I live and never even bothered to ask my last name. I doubt he's kept my phone number. The only time he called me was that first day.

I get up off the bed and shower. My clothes are neatly folded and sitting on a chair by the door to the bathroom. I dress, then go to the mirror along the low dresser and see the sparkle at my ears. I will always have these diamonds to remind me of him.

I sit back on the bed and wonder. Why would he leave like this? Does he do this sort of thing and leave like this wherever he travels? Did he think I'd cause a scene? I shrug and shake my head. I'm unable to come up with an answer.

I need the small hair brush I keep inside my purse. I go looking for my purse and find it sitting on a side table in the living room. There's a business card laying beside it. I pick it up, wondering if Erick has left me his card so I can contact him, but no, the name reads, "Solomon and Wise, Attorneys at Law." He left it behind because he no longer needed it. But he's so orderly, why didn't he throw it away? Why did he leave it by my purse? And why is this the *only* thing he's left behind? I drop the card into my purse. If I should ever try to contact him – though I can't imagine why I would – perhaps these attorneys will know how to reach him.

Searching inside my purse for my hairbrush, my hand hits something unfamiliar. I bring it out. it's a plain, white envelope, sealed and unmarked but for the hotel's insignia. I sit on the couch and open it.

There's cash inside! That's all, no note, no card, nothing else. I count out fifty crisp one hundred dollar bills. Five thousand dollars!

I smile, then chuckle, then let out a loud hearty laugh. I hold the bills over my head and throw them up into the air, letting them cascade down around me. I'm laughing so hard I need to sit down for a second before I collect the money and put it back inside my purse. I find my brush and brush my hair. I'm humming.

As I open the door and leave the room, I'm singing. It's the first time I'm singing since Rocky's death.

I know the words well.

I am gliding, yes I'm flying, soaring free and high above…

37
GOLD DUST

*A*fter those few days with Erick, I'm looking forward to catching up with my classes and relaxing at home.

I put the business card he left inside the Tiffany box and put the box and the envelope with the cash Erick gave me in the back of a dresser drawer. I haven't taken off the earrings.

I'm studying when the phone rings. I let the answering machine pick up and hear Phil's gruff voice.

"Why haven't you called? I left you a message *yesterday*. Call me!"

I call Phil. "Hi. Was that you I saw on Canon Drive?"

"Yeah, that was me."

Together, we ask, "Who was that man?"

"I'm coming over." I hang up.

I drive to the house on North Beverly Drive and ring the doorbell.

Phil answers the door, dressed for a typical Saturday around the house. But he's working his hands in his pockets and his face is flushed, the tipoff that something's wrong.

When I say hello, he turns his back to me and walks into the living room.

"Are you okay?" I ask.

"Who was that man?" he asks.

"What man?"

"Don't play dumb with me, Missy." *Missy!* He hasn't called me that since the day he kicked Rocky out of our house and I moved out. "Who was that man I saw you with?"

"A friend." I should have thought this out before I came.

Hands still in his pockets, Phil screws his head toward me and says with all the sarcasm he can muster, "A *friend?*"

"Yes. An international businessman. He was visiting from Europe. His name is Erick." Though I think I'm making things better by giving Phil these details about Erick, letting him see that I know him well and that he's a substantial person, every word makes Phil angrier and angrier until he is ready to burst. But by then, it's too late. He's grasped the picture all too well.

"And where did you meet this *international businessman from Europe?*" He has me there. I shrug. "And what do you and this *international businessman from Europe* talk about?"

"Things. Art. Women's rights."

Phil extricates his hands from his pockets and pushes my shoulders back. It's not forceful enough to knock me over, but I flinch. I wave his hands away. "Don't do that!"

"You're still a slut. A prostitute," he says.

"I'm not a prostitute!"

"I saw those shopping bags. For Chrissakes, you think I'm stupid? You think I was born yesterday? How old is this dick, your john?"

I don't answer. He comes at me again, but I hurry to put distance between us. "Stop! Don't you hurt me!"

He chases me and strikes a blow to my ear. The sting is so bad that I pull my hair away to put my palm to it and when I do, Phil grabs my ear.

"Well, would you look at that, Missy! These are real?" I don't answer.

"You're a filthy slut, a no-good hooker. You disgust me!

International businessman!" His eyes are big circles and he's that shade of purple.

He wipes his forehead. "It's a good thing your mother isn't here to see this. Don't I give you enough money? Do I ever say no? All you have to do is ask. I give you more than you need. You needed these?" He's talking about the diamond studs.

"I'm not a prostitute," I say.

"Ahh, you'd have broken your mother's heart." He softens when he says that and for a moment, I think he might cry. But then he booms. "You seem to do real good hooking! Business is good! Well, good for you, Missy! No more from me, not one red nickel, not a cent!" He is shaking his head grandly. "Not one lousy penny. I'm through giving you my hard-earned money. Let your johns support you."

"I'm telling you, no one supports me! Only you."

"Well, count me out," he says, "You've seen the last penny you'll ever see from me."

"But you promised Stella!"

"Listen to you, you ungrateful whore! Even now you can't call her your mother," he says. "After all she did for you. Get out of my house. Get out of my sight."

I'm in shock. I didn't expect anything like this to happen when I came here. "I'm sorry, Dad."

I am losing whatever father I have because of a simple coincidence in time and place. He's kicking me out. I'm leaving this house ... again.

"I'm going. But can you please tell me what *you* were doing there?" Phil is staring at the wall. He has his back to me and though he hears me, he doesn't respond; but his shoulders move.

"I didn't know you knew anyone with a Mercedes limo," I say. Silence. I can see his hands moving nervously in his pockets again.

I won't stop. "Who was the black guy with the rings and the skinny guy with the flashy pants? You paid him, didn't you? He gave you bags with stuff in them. What did you buy from him?"

Instead of an explanation, he responds with only a gruff, "Get out."

38

NORA'S VISIT

I've given up trying to find my parents.

I finished finals at UCLA and did well. I've taken all the general requirements and need to decide on a major. I have no idea what that should be.

I have this gnawing feeling that I'm supposed to *do* something, but I have no idea what; nothing I've learned is anything I'd want to pursue.

Strangely, though I never felt truly connected to either Stella or Phil, now that they're both out of my life again and Rocky is gone, I feel more isolated and alienated than ever.

Now that it's summer and classes are finished, I'm working full time, hostessing at a popular new café on Sunset that serves only organic food. I share in tips with the waitresses to augment my weekly salary.

For the first time, I'm fully supporting myself, so I'm looking for a better paying job. I'm not even able to make ends meet without using the little money I've saved from what Phil so generously gave me every few weeks, and I won't touch the money Erick gave me; I'm saving that for an unforeseen expense. I find a second job at the library on San Vicente Boulevard.

I speak with my aunt Sophie, pretty regularly. She knows Phil won't talk to me or even see me now, but I haven't told her why. She watches over him, calls him often, and tells me how he's doing. I relate to Aunt Sophie more than I ever did to Stella. She's easier to talk to.

〜

Sprawled on my couch with the television on, watching the news on Channel 7, I thumb through the catalogue of classes for the upcoming fall quarter.

Since the night I met Jamsheed, I've been following the news in Iran, and the lead story catches my attention. The Shah of Iran, Shah Reza Pahlavi has died!

After having been ousted from his throne and exiled from the country he ruled, he came to the U.S. for cancer treatment. The news anchorman recalls the Shah's history in exile and goes on:

"While in exile, the Shah entered the United States one last time to obtain medical care. In response, Iranians stormed the U.S. Embassy in Tehran, holding its employees hostage. President Carter's attempted rescue mission was aborted after several of the helicopters that were to participate crashed in a sandstorm."

After leaving the United States, the shah traveled to Egypt for asylum with his wife and their four children. He died of cancer there.

There are stories in the news that tell of Iranians, some likely in this crowd, who fled their homeland in fear of potential jail, torture, death, or simply discrimination and discontent, now that Iran is ruled by the Supreme Leader Ayatollah Khomeini and his band of mullahs who took power in the wake of the Revolution.

When I attended Beverly Hill High, there may have been one or two Iranian students. Six years later, the city, and likely Beverly High, is flooded with Iranians, most of whom seem to prefer to be called Persian rather than Iranian.

Their influx can't be ignored, particularly in Beverly Hills and Westwood. Because of my budding interest in Iran, I've kept abreast of the political instability there, and I'm fascinated by stories of Iranians who have left their homes and belongings behind, fleeing from the world created by religious leaders.

Iranian Generals and multi-millionaires now try to make a living owning sandwich shops or small markets and rug stores. Many who went to school here are now practicing dentists, doctors, accountants, and other professions,

Their wives — women who had servants and never opened a can in Iran are chopping vegetables, cooking meals and cleaning their homes.

I've heard that the new regime is anxious to oppress women. I hear bits and pieces of stories from Iranian girls who have found their way into the United States.

Males are forbidden to touch strange women in Khomeini's Iran. Mahnaz, a pretty, olive-skinned girl in my math class, told me that while she was still living in Tehran, she was deathly afraid to go out of the house because of the stories she'd heard from friends about the women's police who comb the streets looking for females, young and old, who show a trace of make-up or have hair showing out of their *chador*, that robe that covers them.

Mahnaz had stayed indoors for so long that one evening her mother forced her to go to a party at a friend's home. On her way, she wore the mandated *chador* in the street over her clothes, and, like the other girls, she took her *chador* off at the party. Once at their host's home, some of the girls applied make-up they planned to remove before leaving for home, and although listening to popular music is grounds for arrest, there was music at the party.

The police raided the home and arrested many of the kids, including Mahnaz. She was handcuffed and taken to prison, and there she was actually lashed for wearing make-up! Lashed for listening to music! Lashed for being in the company of boys who were not related to her without covering herself from head to toe with a *chador!* Lashed for dancing! Mahnaz was warned that the next time she broke these regulations, she would be dealt with far more harshly.

Imagine! For three days, her parents had no idea where she was. Soon after that, her family fled Iran. They entered the U.S. as refugees as I imagine Jamsheed's parents would do.

It's crazy nuts! Women in Iran can only ride in cabs driven by females, and there are even separate beaches for men and women! There's more, and it's all mind-numbing to me.

I passed by the Federal Building on Wilshire Boulevard yesterday on my way home from UCLA. There was a gathering of pro-shah Iranians, carrying signs, publicly mourning their shah's passing.

As I now watch the news clip highlighting the crowd, I try to imagine living in a country where listening to music is forbidden. I couldn't tolerate that. How can anyone?

And why are those who don't want to live by these rules stopped from leaving Iran? Why do they have to escape rather than simply buy a plane ticket and leave?

My thoughts are interrupted by the doorbell.

I turn off the television. It's Nora. "Hi, I'm on my way to Tower Records," she says. "Wanna come?"

"No," I say.

She comes in and notices the catalogue of classes laying on the coffee table. "You're making your schedule for next year?"

"No," I say.

There's a pause. Nora smooths her hair and looks around the apartment. "Listen," she says, "Jonah's coming home late tonight. Can you have dinner with me later?"

"No," I say.

Nora looks irritated. "Is something wrong?" she says.

"No," I say. "I might have a date."

Nora eyes me suspiciously. "With who?"

"Don't worry," I laugh. "It's not with Jonah."

"Another new guy?"

I nod. "Yeah."

She plops down on the couch. "Okay. Look, we need to have a serious talk, Jolie. This is not good."

If Nora's calling me *Jolie*, instead of *Jo*, it's serious. "What's up?" I say.

She shakes her head, then throws her arms up. She's frustrated. "You're going out way too much!" she says.

I sigh. I'm in the mood for this. "I've been home the last two nights," I say.

She slams her two fists down on either side of her. "I mean you're seeing way too many guys, Jo!"

I stand in front of the couch with folded arms. "Really!" I say. "When Rocky died, you pushed me to go out. You said it would be good for me and that it would cheer me up. Well, you were right! It cheers me up. So now you're telling me it's *not* good for me?"

"Come on, Jo, I never meant for you to go out with the whole world! And you're probably sleeping with all of them too." She waits a beat. When I don't correct her, she asks, "Aren't you?"

My grin widens. "Not *all*."

She looks at me like I'm an incorrigible child. "Okay then, most of them?" I smirk. "Jo, stop!"

"Why?"

Nora seems flustered. "For one thing, don't you get tired of it?"

"Why would I?" I say. "They're all different."

"But what's the point, Jo? You're nineteen. Don't you want someone to love you?"

"Trust me; they all love me."

"Jo, I'm serious. I mean *real* love. Don't you want someone to love? Forever?"

Her words hurt.

I need to get some water. "*Nothing* is forever, Nora. Not in my life, anyway. It's not a big deal." As I head for my kitchen, wanting to put distance between us and hopefully, change the subject, I ask, "You want something to drink?" Nora sighs and shakes her head. I'm surprised at how deep a hurt she's uncovered. I need a minute to myself.

I slam the refrigerator door shut, turn and confront my best — and possibly my only — friend. "Look, Nora, you've got your whole friggin' life together. It's perfect." I count on my fingers. "You've got great parents, you've got Jonah — you'll probably marry him and the two of you will live happily ever after — you're smart, you're gorgeous and you don't have a problem in the world. You never did." And then I add, "Geez! You even know what you'll do after college!"

Nora doesn't deny anything.

But she's hitting back. "You're right! You've had it much harder. I agree. My life's been great. I can't compare it to yours. So? You're going to hold it against me?"

She makes a haughty face. She gets sarcastic then. "Well, *excuse me* if you're a victim and I'm not!" she says. Then her tone changes, becomes — I guess you'd say, condescending."You're going to punish me, or whoever else, by sleeping with every guy that comes along?"

"No. But Nora, I have nothing else happening in my life. I have no idea where I'll be in three or four years, or even a year from now. I don't even know how I'll make the rent next month!

"I'm nineteen, and I have no idea what I want to do with my life. And anyway, if I did know, I wouldn't know how to go about it.

"My only family is Phil, and you know how he feels about me; he wants nothing to do with me. I've never made a difference to anyone or anything.

"And as far as being loved forever? You're kidding, right? I can't imagine what it is to be really loved for a day, let alone forever. I don't even know who I am or where I come from.

"Jesus, Nora! Just leave me alone! Let me be!"

"I love you, Jo. I've loved you for more than a day. You'll always have me. You know that. And I hope you know you could move in with me and Jonah tomorrow. We both love you. You matter a lot to me, and you've made a big difference in my life. You made a difference in your mom's life, too; she told you so, and your aunt told you so.

"And if I know you, you'll be fine. One day you'll be doing something great, something you love. You could write lyrics. You like that. And you know you're good at it."

As I look at Nora sitting there, waves of sadness wash over me. I shake my head. "I'll never write songs with anyone again. I'm angry. I'm working two jobs and spending all that money on my classes, books for school and gas to get to and from school. What a waste of money!"

I plop down on the nearest chair. "Oh, who gives a damn?"

Nora gets up and stands in front of me. "I just told you, I do! So does Jonah. So does my mom and so do your other friends. You care, too. You're not the kind of person who would be happy doing nothing," she says.

"Well, I'm probably going to end up doing exactly that." I say.

"It may look like that now, Jo. Remember, I thought I wanted to be a psychologist? And then a social worker, and then a *politician*?" I smile at the recollection of Nora, hell-bent on becoming a senator from California. "Who knows?" she says. "Maybe I'll change my mind again a million times before I graduate. And, by the way, who says I'll ever *hired* as a journalist?

"And Jonah! You think he was born knowing he wanted to be a sports broadcaster? And Paul wanted to be a musician before he decided to change to film. You just have to give yourself some time.

"Stop frowning! Don't be so glum. And don't forget, you're a year younger than all of us, and that counts for something, too." She bends over me, her two hands on the arms of my chair. "But please, Jo, meanwhile, please find one guy to stay with."

"Why, so he can die on me too?"

———

Nora finally left.

I'm curled up on the sofa again. I open the schedule of fall classes, but I'm too frustrated to go on. I throw the catalogue across the room.

How dare Nora judge me?

How can she think all I need is a boyfriend? Just because she's so fucking happy with Jonah ... Good for her! Jonah's a great guy and he'll make a great husband. I only hope she appreciates how incredibly fortunate she is.

But Nora's life isn't my life; it never has been. It's impossible for her to understand how I see things. Everything I've ever wanted has turned sour. The boy I loved died. When Stella died, I lost the only mother I've ever had. And if anyone might have had the clue, the missing link to discovering who I really am, it was her.

Oooh! I have so many good reasons to be angry.

Who the hell am I? Do I take after my mother or my father? Do I have their smile? Did either of them have a slight space between their two front teeth like do, or a crescent moon birthmark, like I have on my calf?

Were they stubborn? Did they have some illness that's genetic? Unlucky? I suppose my mom was. I mean, she got pregnant and had to get rid of her baby. Well, I know I take after her, that's for sure, cause I'm sure as hell unlucky too.

Sophie told me I was born at the most expensive home for unwed mothers in America. So, someone had a lot of money. Were they famous? Are they alive? *Who were they?*

God! I so want to know!

Stretched out on the couch, I close my eyes and try to empty my mind of thoughts that go keep going around in my brain like a carousel of worms.

Nora! How Jonah loves her!

I go down the list of the men in my life:

My real father? Never knew him. Was he in love with my mother? Were they together for just one night? Did he rape her? Did he even know she was pregnant?

Phil? A bigot who hit me and makes a living showing porn. He actually tried to kill himself and Stella! Was he really responsible for their son's death? Stella thought so and apparently, he did too.

Jay? My first real boyfriend. Asshole! He fucked some slut he'd just met. Had to do it with me there.

Rocky? My Rocky, the man I loved, the one I thought would save me. I wanted to be with him forever. He died on me. He didn't even try to save himself.

None of the other guys I dated before Jay and the string of guys I bedded after Rocky, starting with Holden? None of them worth a second thought, beyond passing sex or points on a scoreboard.

Oh, and Erick! The Married Man who travels the world and cheats on his wife. He deserted me like he was fleeing the scene of a crime, leaving diamonds and cash behind. How flamboyant! At least I still have the five thousand dollars he presented me with. And I still have the diamonds. I wonder if he leaves Tiffany earrings and cash for every

314

girl, like a signature goodbye. He probably gets a discount from Tiffany's for buying in volume.

My hands go to the diamond studs, overcome with a tremendous urge to take them off me this minute. It's as though he's branded me with them, left his mark on me like a serial offender would. I take off their backings as I make my way to the dresser and retrieve the blue Tiffany box from my drawer. I'm about to drop the earrings in the box, when I see the card there:

Solomon & Wise, Attorneys at Law

A Professional Corporation

317 North Grand Avenue, Tenth Floor

Los Angeles, California 90012

Bert Wise, Attorney at Law

(213) 555-5555

Senior Partner

I will call Mr. Bert Wise and get Erick Bromm's phone number and address from him. Then I'll call Mr. Bromm and tell him to go fuck himself and mail him back the earrings. He can give them to another girl. Or to his wife, or daughter.

I dial the number. A serious-sounding receptionist answers. "Good afternoon, Law Offices of Solomon and Wise. How may I help you?"

I don't know who to ask for. Should I ask for Bert Wise? I don't even know if they'll know who Erick is. This was a stupid idea. I'm just upset.

Meanwhile, the receptionist repeats herself.

"Yes," I say, hesitatingly. Could you tell me please, what kind of law office is this?"

"One moment please. Let me connect you with someone who can assist you."

I'm about to hang up when a new voice comes on the line. "Hello, thank you for holding. I'm Dan. May I answer a question for you?" Dan has a friendly voice; they're all so polite.

"Hi, I was just wondering what kind of law office this is."

"Sure. I can help you with that. We specialize in a variety of legal areas including mergers and acquisitions, various business matters, some tax and international trade." Well, that explains Bert Wise. "We also have attorneys with expertise in commercial litigation and experts in family law."

"Family law?" *Family law?*

"Yes," the friendly voice laughs. "I know it does seem odd. People are always surprised to hear that. The thing is, Mr. Solomon began his career in family law and, well, he's just never stopped practicing his first field of expertise. We have about eighty plus attorneys in the firm, but Mr. Solomon has always kept his interest in family law alive."

Bells ring in my head. "I see. Well, if an adopted child wants to locate their real parents, is that considered family law?"

"Absolutely."

The bells ringing in my head are deafening. "Can I make an appointment to see Mr. Solomon?" I remember to add, "Please."

"If you'll kindly wait one moment, I'll connect you to his scheduling secretary."

I make an appointment to see Irving Solomon Wednesday afternoon, September 5 at 3 o'clock.

39

SOLOMON'S COURT

I get to my appointment at Bert Solomon's office early.

As soon as I step off the elevator on the ninth floor, I'm in the reception area, a huge area, richly appointed with dark wood, rich red Persian rugs, healthy trees and impressive flower arrangements everywhere.

This is my first time ever in a law office and I'm a little intimidated. I approach a circular desk where two attractive receptionists sit taking calls, one white male and one black female. Both wear black. I wait. The male hangs up first and smiles at me. I give him my name, then take a seat by a large tree. There's a winding staircase in the waiting area opposite the elevator with a black iron railing going up, so I guess the office takes up two floors.

I see a variety of magazines set out on the tabletop in front of me, but I'm uninterested in them. I'm as nervous as I've ever been and full of anticipation. In minutes I'll be speaking with an attorney who specializes in finding lost parents. I'm bubbling over with equal parts of anxiety, excitement and hope.

I'm ushered into Bert Solomon's office. One look at the man and I like him. He's standing behind his desk, but he comes forward and extends his hand out to me. He's tall, older than Phil, has a slight paunch and hair almost all gray and scarce. He's wearing a light gray suit with a charcoal-colored vest that holds a watch chain. He looks like a good lawyer, whatever that means. Trustworthy.

I waste no time explaining why I'm there. Taking notes on his yellow legal pad, he asks me the details of my adoption. "I was born on August 27, 1961, in Dallas, Texas."

"How do you know that?"

"My aunt told me. She said I was adopted there."

He smiles. "How do you know you were born there?"

"What do you mean?"

"Well, Jolie – may I call you that?" I nod. "Oftentimes, children are born one place and taken to another place where they're adopted."

"I was born there. My aunt told me I was adopted from Abigail's Home for Unwed Mothers. My mother gave birth to me there."

"Okay then, that's a start. And do you know for a fact that you were born on that date?"

I nod. "That's my birthday."

"Of course, it is." He's smiling. I know he's trying to put me at ease. "It is possible however," he says, "that your adoptive parents set the date of your adoption or some other day of significance as your birthday? Adopting parents often do that. Have you seen your birth certificate?"

"No."

"Have you asked your parents for it?"

"When my adopted mother died in May, I went through all her papers with my aunt – her sister, Sophie – looking for it and anything else we could find about my adoption. We found nothing.

"I asked Phil – that's my adoptive father – if he had anything; he said he no. So no, I haven't seen it. But why would they change the date?"

"I won't speculate. Okay, we'll just have to see about that. But if we're not absolutely sure of the birth date, if we can't confirm it with a birth certificate, that makes it harder." He pushes back in his chair. His ballpoint pen is playing at his lips as he stares down at the legal pad in front of him with his notes on it.

"I know that Abigail's Home for Unwed Mothers was for rich,

unmarried girls who got pregnant." Attorney Solomon looks up at me. "I'm positive of that, Mr. Solomon, my Aunt Stella arranged the whole thing and she said she was sure of the name and the fact that the families were very rich."

"Well, then, we'll try to contact this Abigail's. See if it's still there, maybe it's changed to another business but perhaps it's a starting point to retrieving files."

"It's not."

"How do you know that?"

"I flew to Dallas. I tried to call, but I couldn't get the number from information, so I flew there and went to the Hall of Records. It's gone. The Home is completely gone. And it wasn't owned by anyone named Abigail either. According to the Hall of Records, it was owned by Jane Albright, and she sold it – or, well, the land it was on – to Pauley Development.

"I spoke with Jane Albright's ex-husband. His name is Dean Stanton. He doesn't know anything and says Jane Albright destroyed everything there was when she sold the property. I got these from the Dallas Tax Accessor's office." I hand him the copies of the documents they gave me.

The attorney puts his pen down and sighs. I don't like the sound of it. He rises. "Well, you're a resourceful young lady, Jolie. Okay, I have the information you've given me. Give me a few days, let me do some research and we can talk again."

I get up and take one of his business cards off his desk. He walks around and escorts me to his door. "By the way, Jolie," he smiles. "You're a student and unfortunately, our firm is not cheap. Do you mind if I ask you if you have funds?"

"Oh, yes, I have funds." He nods. "Goodbye Mr. Solomon, I'll wait to hear from you."

I don't wait long. Mr. Solomon's secretary called to arrange a second appointment for me at eleven o'clock this morning and I'm here, more nervous than I was on my first visit. My muscles are tight, and my neck is stiff.

I enter Mr. Solomon's office and he again rises to shake my hand. "Sit down, Ms. Gold." I sit in the seat I was in just two days ago wondering if there's any significance to the fact that he's not calling me by my first name today.

He sits behind his desk shuffling through some manila folders. "Here it is." He glances at me as he's opening the file he holds. "Ms. Gold, are you crying?"

I shake my head. "I'm sorry," I try to laugh as a tear rolls down my cheek. "I'm just feeling very emotional."

He tosses the file on the desk, pushes a button on his telephone and speaks. "Please bring in a box of tissues and a glass of water."

"I apologize, Mr. Solomon. I don't cry often. I'm just excited. I've waited a very long time for this." He sits back and frowns. "You did find my mother, didn't you?"

He shifts in his chair. "No, Ms. Gold." He picks up the file he'd been holding. "We've only done some research."

"Oh, well then, have you located Jane Albright?"

"No, I'm afraid you're way ahead of us."

Before I can ask why he's called me back without anything to report, there's a knock on the door and a woman walks in with a box of Kleenex and a glass of water, and puts both of them within my reach, on my side of the desk.

She looks at me with a tentative smile. "Is there anything else I can get for you? Would you like some tea or a cold soda perhaps?"

I shake my head and manage a smile in return. "Thank you, no."

"That will be all. Thanks, Nellie."

"What have you found?" I ask before Nellie can close the door.

"Well, Ms. Gold –"

"Jolie."

"Yes. Jolie. Well, Jolie," he says, opening my file. "We've researched the adoption laws of Texas. They have an interesting history."

He looks back and forth from me to the contents of the file and continues. "Early on, children born out of wedlock had the word 'Illegitimate' stamped in big letters across their birth certificates, which, I'm sure you can imagine, made life very difficult for them in those earlier days. So, there was a push to make adoption records confidential." I tense up at that last word.

"Those who pushed for confidentiality argued that it would save the illegitimate children much grief. From their perspective, if an adopted child was thought to be the *natural* child of the adoptive parents, illegitimacy could not be traced, hence the stigma would not attach.

"So, you see, the adoption laws of Texas in the early 1950s permitted the unmarried mother of an illegitimate child to prevent the adoption agency placing their child from ever disclosing the name of the natural parent – or parents – and also prevented disclosure of the adopting parents' identity to the natural parents."

I recall the day I packed my things and left home. "Stella – my adopted mother – always said she didn't know who my real mother was," I say. "But I didn't believe her. You said all of that was the early 50s. I was born in 1961."

"Well, now, mind you, none of those early laws impinged on the rights of the *child* to access that information."

I'm not surprised to hear this. I have every right in the world to access that information, even if my natural mother and my adoptive mother don't want to — or can't — know the identity of one another.

Mr. Solomon goes on. "In 1965, Texas further limited even the *adopted child's* access to their records, allowing that disclosure to the adopted child only where either the state agency or private adoption agency believed such information would be *"in the best interests of the child."*

I'm okay with that. It's undoubtedly in my best interest to find my natural parents.

He goes on. "In time, the distinction between the right of the *adopted child* to have access to that information and the right of the *public* to pry into the facts of the adoption was blurred."

I'm not sure I understand the effect of that last comment, but I don't like the way this is going. It's all about people not being able to find out what I want to know.

I'm increasingly uncomfortable. I'm squirming in my chair.

I'm on an emotional roller-coaster and I have no idea where I'll end up, but I'm beginning to sense that a heavy weight is about to fall on my head and crush my skull.

"Then in 1973, a law was passed that restricted *everyone's* access to records and after that, it made to difference whether or not you were a party to the proceeding."

He sees my puzzled look and explains, "A '*party*' means one of the four parents involved or the adopted child."

He sighs and goes on. "In short, at that point, *no one* could get any information without first securing an order from the district court."

I'm holding onto the edge of the desk. "Okay, do we need an order? Let's get an order."

He leans forward in his chair. "Well now, wait just a minute. Hold on. That 1973 law was *not* retroactive. That means it *did not* speak to adoptions prior to its enactment."

I think I'm confused and must look it because Attorney Solomon looks perplexed.

He shrugs and shakes his head. "They took away the power of the court to decide whether or not the records were in the best interests of the child until 1975, when the court was again given the power to decide whether or not to seal the files."

"What court? The Supreme Court?"

"No. I'm sorry. I should explain. The *court* is just another term for the judge. I'm talking about the judges in Texas. They no longer had the power to decide if the information was or wasn't in the child's best interest, but they could decide whether or not to *seal* the files in the first place."

I'm really confused now. I'm struggling to keep up with what Attorney Solomon is saying. I am trying to keep up. "Well, how do the judges decide what they'll do? If they'll seal the records?"

"That's what attorneys are for. Both sides try to make convincing arguments to persuade the judge. But that's all irrelevant. Because eventually, *all* adoption records in Texas were closed to *everyone*. They were *all* sealed. *All* agencies dealing with adoptions were *ordered* to keep all information strictly confidential – unless an order was obtained by a judge that allowed disclosure."

I feel like he just went in one big circle. "Okay, then we just need to get the order allowing the judge to disclose my birth parents' informa-tion." I don't like the look on his face. "I'm sorry, Mr. Solomon, but could you please tell me what all this means?"

"Well, that's the thing, Jolie. It's really not very clear."

He closes the file, gets up and circles to the front of his desk where he does something that's halfway between sitting and leaning on its edge. His arms are folded. "It might be said that adoptions that occurred *before* 1973 – like yours – would be subject to the laws that existed at the time of the adoption because, as I said, the *new* law was not retroactive.

"But the law in effect in 1961 did not allow for a hearing, so I'm afraid the courts could argue that you have no right to bring a proceeding requesting that your adoption records be opened."

The weight I'd been expecting has fallen. Anger drives me to my feet. I start pacing. "That's bullshit! I'm sorry, but that's bullshit! There is no way that they can hide those records from me. They're mine!"

Attorney Solomon's head hangs down. "I'm afraid that's exactly the situation here."

"But they're *my* parents! It's my right to know who they are!"

"I agree."

"How can you say you agree," I say, "when you've just told me I don't have the right to find out who they are?"

"Unfortunately, Jolie, too often there's a difference between a legal right and a moral right. They're not always the same thing. The law is sometimes arbitrary."

I'm on my feet. "*Arbitrary?* It's absolutely horrible! It's ridiculous! How can they do that? It's totally unfair! Why didn't someone stop them?"

"I'm sorry, Jolie."

"No! Don't be sorry! I don't want you to be sorry. I want you to do something about it. Fix the stupid law, change it if you have to. Make it fair! I'll pay."

I am so beyond angry; I may have a total break down.

"I have a right to know who my parents are and it's not their goddamned business." I'm circling around myself, ready to pull my hair out. I want to throw something.

"It's not just me, Mr. Solomon. There must be lots of other kids just like me, kids who don't know who their own parents are and want to find out. We all should be able to if we want to." I'm pacing, both hands locked in fists at my sides.

Mr. Solomon returns to his chair. I hurry back to stand in front of his desk and grab onto the edge. I lean into him. "Please! *Please,* help me!"

"Jolie, I'd really like to do that." He runs his hand through his thinning hair. "Maybe if I were several decades younger, I'd try."

"But it's so wrong! Don't you see that?"

"Yes, I do," he says. "I see it clearly. In my view, the law should allow someone like you to locate their parents. In fact I think courts should *help* them do so. This isn't the 1950s or the 60s, and I wouldn't be surprised to find out that lots of natural parents are trying to find their children as well."

For a second, I realize it's entirely possible that my birth parents have been. looking for me.

"Maybe," I say, "But the parents are the ones that put the child up for adoption in the first place! It wasn't the child. It wasn't *my* choice to be separated from my parents. So, I have a greater right to the information than they do."

Attorney Solomon's phone rings but I continue ranting, trying to communicate clearly. This could be the most important conversation of my life.

"Mr. Solomon, please understand. I don't want to move in with them! I don't want *anything* from them. I just want to know who they *are.*"

The phone is on the third ring when he picks it up, but only to order his secretary to take a message. I fall back into my chair. I cannot tolerate this goddamned feeling of defeat.

Goddamn it all! What am I supposed to do now?

Attorney Solomon is talking to me. I tune back in to hear him say, "… someone change the law."

"Who?" I ask. "No one gives a damn. No one understands. You have to be in my skin to know what it feels like."

"Then it'll have to wait until someone in your position *cares* enough to change it," he says.

"I care tons. But I can't change it."

He looks at me. "Why not?"

I push my head forward to look him in the eyes. "Mr. Solomon, I'm a nineteen-year-old college girl!"

Mr. Solomon taps his desk with both hands. "That, young lady, is exactly who it's going to take."

"I'm sorry but I don't see how you can you tease me about this."

He leans back in his chair, legs apart, arms open wide. "I'm not kidding," he says. "Change the law."

"That's really not funny," I say.

His answer is immediate. "I'm very serious," he says.

Is he serious? "Just how am I supposed to do that?"

"Go to law school. Become a lawyer. Petition the courts. Change the law. And I'll tell you, Jolie, it's not only Texas that perpetrates this sort of unfairness. I've come up against this sort of nonsense with the laws of other states, too."

My mouth is hanging open. I sit back down in my chair. "Are you seriously suggesting *I* can do it?"

He closes the file. So this is it. Even Attorney Solomon can't find my parents.

"I'm absolutely serious!" he says. "Who better than you? You're young, you're bright, you're resourceful … you said it yourself: only someone in your shoes can imagine how grievous a wrong it is to deny a child in your position access to that information."

He's serious! "You really think I can do it?"

"Yes," Attorney Solomon says. "Absolutely! And I'll help you."

A thick silence has fallen over the office. I'm digest all he's said. I have to think this through.

If that's what it takes to find my parents … why not? I have no pressing plans, there's nothing else I'm planning to do, nothing else I'd *rather* do. This would be a chance to do something good for myself and help other kids in my situation.

When I again speak, I've made up my mind. A new Jolie has been conceived.

I'm on my feet again, speaking with new resolve. "Okay, Mr. Solomon. Maybe you're kidding, pulling my leg, or maybe you're daring me. But if you really think I can do it, I'll try. I'm going to do it.

If I have to go to law school and become a lawyer to change those stupid laws, then okay, that's what I'll do!"

Mr. Solomon stands. "That's exactly what you'll have to do." When I reach for his extended hand, he sandwiches mine between his two. "Jolie, I have a feeling this is the inception of a wonderful legal career. Now, I can't guarantee that you'll ever find your parents. The laws already on the books may make it impossible for you. But, if it means anything to you, you'll be making it possible others to find theirs in the future."

I set my lips and nod. I say, "We'll see. Maybe at first, I'll only get to help others. That's okay; they have as much of a right to know who their parents are as I do. But I won't stop until I change whatever law I need to so I can know who *my* parents are."

Mr. Solomon reaches out and pats my shoulder. "Good. I have no doubt you'll be successful. Determination and anger combined with intelligence and resourcefulness is an excellent mix."

He looks at me, really looks at me with squinted eyes. "You know, Jolie, the firm could use a young person with your spunk around here. Not many of our attorneys have joined the firm in hopes of doing family law. Most are involved in business concerns. You might just be an excellent addition to our firm if you proceed with family law. It's always been an interesting area.

"I'm getting older. It's not easy for me to work as hard as I did when I was younger."

Now I glimpse the weariness of the man who's been a lawyer for the decades it's taken to establish this large firm.

He hands me a file. "Here, take this. It's your file. You can go over the information my clerks put together for me, read over what I've been talking to you about."

"Thanks."

"It's been a pleasure to meet you, Jolie. I'm sorry we weren't able to have more success in your matter. But I hope you'll remember the commitment you made here today.

"I promise you this: it won't always be easy. Law school is challenging, and the practice of law is more challenging. Meanwhile, stay in touch. Please call me any time, and definitely call if you need my help.

I'd very much like to stay abreast of your progress, so let's stay in touch."

"Thanks. Thanks a lot, Attorney Solomon." *I actually smile!* I finally know what I'm doing."

It's true. He didn't find my parents, but he's given me a future.

He smiles. "And don't forget you have a job here."

We say goodbye and I pass through the reception area and approach the elevator.

As I push the "down" button, a young man in a pin-striped suit catches up with me. "Ms. Gold, Mr. Solomon asked that I give this to you. He wanted you to have it." He hands me a single sheet of paper.

The elevator has arrived. I thank him, enter the elevator and read:

Concerning all acts of initiative, there is one elementary truth, the ignorance of which kills countless ideas and splendid plans: the moment one definitely commits oneself, then Providence moves too.

All sorts of things occur to help one that would never otherwise have occurred. A whole stream of events issues from the decision, raising in one's favor all manner of unforeseen incidents and meetings and material assistance which no man could have dreamed would come his way.

Whatever you can do or dream you can do, begin it. Boldness has genius, power and magic in it. Begin it now.

Johann Wolfgang von Goethe

40

BEHIND ME

I leave Attorney Solomon's office and drive back to Sunset Boulevard to start my shift at the restaurant.

Beside me, on the seat of my car, is the sheet of paper Attorney Solomon gave me with the quote from Goethe. I am aware that it echoes Erivista Light's message, emphasizing the power that comes with a firm commitment.

I'm feeling a quiet new excitement. My life has direction and meaning at last. I will become an attorney and fight for the rights of adopted children.

After work, Nora comes over and we share a late dinner, full of news about Jonah. He'll be interning with a well-known sportscaster starting in the Fall. I listen while preparing a large salad.

Though I'm dying to tell her my news, I wait until she's finished gushing hers. Only then do I recount the entire scene in Attorney Solomon's office, including – as best as I can – the convoluted laws of adoption in Texas. Hearing them, she hugs me sympathetically. She's on the verge of tears.

But then she hears of my plans to become an attorney and she goes wild, jumping up and down and throwing her arms around me, hugging me tightly, jumping again and hugging me again, squeezing me with love.

"Oh, Jo! You'll going to law school! Oh, I'm so happy! That's fantastic! I'm so happy for you, Jo! Oh, wait till Jonah finds out! Oh, Jo, that's so cool!"

Eventually, the jumping stops and the hugging is not quite as tight. "You'll make a great lawyer! I told you you'd figure out what you want to do." Then she grabs my arm. "Lucky me! My best friend will be an attorney! I'll be your first client."

I chuckle. "You'd probably be my only client, but I doubt you'll ever need me. I'm going into family law, remember?"

"Well, even if I don't need you, I'll find you business. Trust me: you'll be successful. And you'll change those terrible laws, that's for sure!"

"As Stella used to say, *From your mouth to God's ear*."

"Jo, it's really so wonderful! You'll be helping so many people!"

"It's so strange, it just *feels* right, Nora. I just wish I could do it all right now. But I have to get through law school first."

"Have you told Phil yet? Oh, I can't wait to hear his reaction!"

We talk about my future as we eat our dinner. I tell her all about Attorney Solomon's offer to help me and his offer of a job. I show her the quote from Johann Wolfgang von Goethe.

Dinner done, I'm getting coffee when Nora calls out. "Wow! Come look at this, Jo." She's focused on the TV that was on but muted, turning the volume up.

The screen shows a young woman about our age. The caption at the bottom reads, "Iran Today." Neither of us can take our eyes off the screen, mesmerized by the woman whose entire body and every strand of hair is covered by what looks like a black sheet. She's holding it closed tightly with one hand at her chin. All that shows is the woman's incredibly face, beautiful, glowing, radiant, and, obviously, without a trace of makeup.

Nora has turned up the volume. It turns out this girl is a student at the University of Tehran, and she's being interviewed by an American reporter.

Her English is lilting and perfect.

Reporter: "How do feel about the new laws mandating that Iranian women wear the chador?"

Beautiful Girl, smiling ethereally: "As a devout Muslim who has studied the Koran, I know that the word of Allah, our God, as written in the Holy Book is this: Whether a woman chooses to wear the *chador* or not is a question of her personal choice, a reflection of what is in her heart."

Reporter: "Do you wear the *chador* by choice then?"

Beautiful Girl: "Yes. My heart tells me to wear the *chador*."

Reporter: "So do you believe that a woman whose heart tells her not to wear the *chador* has the right not to do so?"

Beautiful Girl: "I believe such a woman must reach deeper into her heart and listen closer to what her heart is telling her."

"Wow, isn't she gorgeous?" Nora asks.

I agree that she is breathtaking and also extremely diplomatic. I'm actually more impressed by the way the woman seemed to dodge that last question than by her astounding beauty.

"Her answer sounds like double talk to me," I say. "I think she's afraid to say what she wants to. How can she be willing to be a second-class citizen in her own country overnight simply because she's a woman? How can she live like that, Nora? Could you?"

Nora shakes her head. Lost in the beauty and intelligence of the girl on television, our attention is jarred by the ringing of my telephone.

It's Aunt Sophie. "Honey, I'm worried about your father. He sounds terrible."

I motion to Nora to mute the TV. "Why? What happened?"

"I think you should go see him right away."

"He won't talk to me, Aunt Sophie."

There's a slight pause, then Aunt Sophie says, "Please. I'm worried, Jolie. Go over there and check in on him, make sure he's okay."

"Okay."

"Call me."

I grab my keys. Nora turns the TV off and we're out the door. I'm hurrying to my car as Nora calls out "Let me know what's going on."

Phil's Cadillac is parked in his driveway.

I don't ring the doorbell. Instead, I use my key to enter. Inside, the house has emptied the last light of day, replacing it with shades of nighttime.

"Dad?"

I know he's home but there's no answer, and that scares me. I move fast, heading first for the kitchen, sniffing for gas on my way. Thankfully, I don't smell any.

I see Phil sitting at the head of the dining room table. He's in the shadows, his head in his hands. I switch the light on and the crystal chandelier above us bursts into an explosion of light that reflects off the well-polished table and the plastic that – Stella would be happy to know – still covers all the dining room chairs.

"Phil?" He doesn't look up. "What's wrong?"

He passes his palms slowly across his forehead and glances up for just a second and I can see that his face is pale and there are dark circles under his eyes. He says nothing and I can't imagine what could have happened that would be this bad. Maybe he's just been told he's dying.

"Dad? What's wrong?" No answer. "Dad! What happened? What is it?"

He responds in a weak voice that's filled with dejection. "I didn't know. I swear. I didn't."

"You didn't know what?"

He slides an elbow off a pile of papers on the table. I walk around the table and reach for the top sheet.

United States Court
The People
v
Phillip Gold
Case Number 014598

Across from that, on the right side of the sheet near the top is a numbered list of 22 things, that I assume are alleged violations of law; I don't bother to scan them. Whatever they are, this is bad.

"What is this?" When Phil doesn't answer, I point to the long list of violations. "What are these? What does all this mean?"

"I'm ruined."

"Why?" Phil remains silent, looking down at the table, his head still in his hands. Then they move up to thread the sparse amount of hair above his ears and he shakes his head. "Dad, you have to tell me what's going on!"

He looks up. He looks absolutely terrible. "They've been out to get me for a long time. They got me."

I put a hand on his shoulder. "Who? Dad, who's been out to get you?"

"Sit down," he says. I pull a chair close to him and sit. I see he's aged in the months since Stella's death, even aged since I last saw him.

His voice is muffled and raspy. "A few weeks ago, three guys come in. They don't look queer; they're dressed normal – like me." His eyes settle on me, move to the wall behind me, traverse it, and return to me. I nod, encouraging him to continue. "They come in together, but they don't sit together." He pauses. "They were cops – undercover." He props his elbows on the table and returns his head down and between his hands but this time, he's shielding his eyes, hiding his face.

I didn't know what to say. "Did you know they were cops?"

Phil shrugs and looks at me. "How could I know? I figure maybe they belong to some kind of club for queers that don't want it known."

"So?"

Phil turns his head away and his shoulders jerk up. "So, nothing. They left. Next thing I know, they're back a couple nights later. These same three guys. I see them coming in. Then I see they're taking turns going to the john, coming and going the whole time. One goes, comes back, then the other one goes, then the next one goes. They just keep taking turns coming and going. No one can piss like that."

"Why were they doing that?"

Phil shrugs. "I figure they're looking for a poke in the john."

I'm totally grossed out. "Okay, go on."

"Then there's more of them coming in. Every night they're coming in like flies to shit. I tell Charlie, and he says the same thing is happening at the other theaters, men who don't look queer are going in and the same thing's going on there. Men coming in, going to the head and buying videos."

I recall that at some point Phil added videos to the items available for sale at his theaters' concession stands. I nod to let him know I'm with him.

But instead of resuming his sad tale, he sighs deeply and then he's quiet. I'm beginning to get the picture. Undercover cops have been spending a lot of time at his theaters. Whatever this is, it's a lot of bad.

I wait for him to go on but still offering nothing more, he closes his eyes. When he opens them, he sighs again and looks up at the chandelier.

"They got me, Stella," he says. "Yeah, they got me good." He looks at me and a light finally comes into his eyes. "You still think they like us Jews?" I try not to show how startled I am by the question; I won't agitate him any further. "You think they'd do this to me if I wasn't a Jew?"

"Tell me what they're doing."

More silence. Then the plastic squeaks as he moves off his chair. He stands and picks up the pile of papers but drops them back down. "Ahh, what's the difference?" he says, wiping his forehead with his hand. "They got me. I'm finished. It's all here. They got warrants for the theaters and the house – they got everything. The lawyer says it's all legal."

"They searched the house?" No answer. "What do they want to do to you?"

"They're closing down my theaters. They're taking me to trial. They want to put me behind bars, put me in the poorhouse and let me rot."

Alarms sound in my head. "Jail? For what, Dad?"

Phil's hand is again at his head, pushing his forehead up. He looks straight into my eyes. "They say the queers are dealing drugs and poking each other in the johns –" his voice starts to fade – "and jacking off in the seats." Then his eyes get big and round. He looks at me.

"What the hell am I supposed to do if a couple of queers want to jack off while they're sitting there watching a movie?"

"You need a lawyer, Dad." My mind immediately goes to the only lawyer I know.

I continue, bringing him up to date, hoping that I can give him some news to feel good about. "I haven't had a chance to tell you," I say. "I'm going to go to law school." I pause. There's no reaction.

"I know a really good law firm. I don't think they handle criminal cases, but I'm sure the attorney I know there can help you find the right one."

He looks at me in total disbelief. Apparently, he did hear what I said and the news does momentarily take precedence over his legal troubles. "Law school? What for?" he says.

"I'm going to be a lawyer." I say, edging a smile.

Phil's looking at me like I said I'd just had dinner with Stella before coming over. "You tell me jokes at a time like this?"

"It's true. I wanted to tell you. I'm going to practice law."

He slides his hands into his pants pockets. "We both know you can't go to law school. You're too busy playing hanky-panky with the boys. You'll never make it. They'll kick you out."

"Dad, I'm doing this."

"If you're dumb enough to try it, how will you pay, Missy? Weren't you listening when I told you? I'm not giving you a cent!" Then his face falls as he adds, "Anyway, there's no money. I couldn't pay for it now if I wanted to. I'm broke."

"I don't want your money. Just let me get you a lawyer."

"I have a lawyer."

"Well, what does he or she say?"

"What's the matter with you? I told you, he says all this crap is legal."

"Does that mean you're going to jail?"

Phil collapses back into his chair. "You're gonna go to law school?" His eyes are bulging out and his pale face is turning that shade of purple.

"I'm sorry, I don't understand. If you have a lawyer, why are you so sure that you're going to jail?" I repeat, "I'm sorry, I don't understand. Could you please tell me? Please?"

"Oh, Jesus!" Phil mutters, not trying to hide the fact that his patience is wearing thin. He starts to pace around the dining room, his fingers working in his pockets. "They want two trials." He gestures to the stack of sheets and holds up two fingers. This here is just one bunch: the feds. The lawyer says another bunch is coming from the state. They both want me."

I swallow and try to sound calm. "For what?"

Phil stops walking. He shakes his head and waves his hand in dismissal as if the charges are petty and so am I. "I told you! Listen! The feds say the queers are poking each other in the Tom Boy theater and selling drugs in both of them. And they say I broke some law about putting minors in porn films and crossing state lines."

I'm aghast. "You show kiddie porn?"

"No, *I don't show kiddie porn*," Phil says, mocking me. "I'm a Jew. Jews don't do that."

"But it's okay for a Jew to show minors in sex films." I can't help myself.

"Don't you start with me, Missy. I'm no pervert." He puts his hands back into his pockets, working them, and walks around the table. "I don't like no porno," he says. "Queers sicken me – paying money to see men poking men …. " He turns back to me.

"But business is business, and nothing pays like sex. Nothing! What I do and don't do's got nothing to do with anything. It's just business." There's a sudden glint of light in his eyes.

He slams his hand onto the table, and I'm startled. "Missy, *you've* been living off money from sex – queer sex! I could 'a made a fortune just selling videos of freaks that pee on women and stuff like that. Trust me, it would make your head spin. But I didn't do that. All I did was sell some movies to a bunch of queers that pay good money to see them."

I shake my head. His logic is beyond me. "Don't you shake your head at me!"

"So that's what you were doing on Canon Drive when I saw you that day?" He turns away in silent admission. "You were buying porn videos from that guy in the Mercedes." Phil still doesn't answer. "You bought kiddie porn?"

Phil screams, "I told you, it ain't kiddie porn. They ain't kids!"

His stubby hands fly out of his pocket and go up toward the chandelier then back down to palm his bald head. "One lousy kid! That's all! One lousy kid in one lousy movie. One goddamned kid in 'Behind Me' is under eighteen."

"Behind Me?" If the situation weren't so friggin' serious, I'd laugh. Phil gives me a warning look that's lethal. My expression remains serious.

"How the hell am I supposed to know he's a kid?" he says. Hands are back in his pockets and he's pacing again. "For Chrissakes, I'm not his mother! I didn't make the movie. I never even seen it. I never seen any of them. I told you, they all make me sick. I just buy them and play them for the queers that pay me to see them. And they buy them."

"Who's your lawyer?"

"Christopher Sanders."

"How did you find him?"

"I asked around. He's the only one that ain't a Jew. I figure since they're out to get a Jew, I got a better shot with a goy."

"Dad? You really think this is all about being Jewish?"

"You tell me, Miss College Student Going to Law School. They're going after us, owners of these theaters, closing us down," he points his chin to the stack of papers, "putting us on trial...," he shakes his head, "...ruin us all, put us all in jail. And who the hell are we? We're Jewish, every one of us! They're arresting Jews with these fancy search warrants and papers. Why don't they arrest the goddamn perverts, the queers? How many Jews are queer, for Pete's sake?"

I'm speechless. Phil is gazing out the dining room window. "Maybe I'll just sell the goddamned house and go to Mexico."

I'm amazed. "And be a fugitive? Come on, Dad! If this lawyer knows what he's doing, he should be able to prove you didn't know the guy was underage. And what about the drugs? You didn't know about them either, did you?"

Phil doesn't answer me. I assume it's because he knew about the drugs. Instead, he scratches his head and says, "I don't know what the hell to do. I mortgaged the house to remodel the theaters. I gotta sell it." He sits back in his chair, a defeated man. "The lawyer wants $50,000 for starters." I whistle. "He'll want more."

"That's okay. You have it."

Phil buries his head in his hands. When his hands come away, I see he's crying. "I've lost it all. Everything. Every penny."

I kneel at his side, my head at his chest and hold him as he cries.

4 1

TARNISHED GOLD

I don't care about the house.

I don't care about the money either; even if he had it, he's said he wouldn't give me a penny. I'm only concerned about Phil. I'm concerned about his state of mind. This is a man who once tried to kill himself. And now his Stella is gone.

The house I grew up in goes on the market and sells almost immediately. Phil moves into a studio apartment south of Pico Boulevard, where rents are cheap. His doctor puts him on an anti-depressant, and I wait for it to kick in and start its magic.

I wish he would let me put him in touch with Bert Solomon, but he's dead set against any help from me and refuses to even think of hiring a Jewish lawyer. All I can do is be there for him to talk to.

I guess he thinks I don't have the staying power to make it through law school. He doesn't know why I want it. He doesn't realize how badly I want it. I want it badly enough to sacrifice whatever I have to sacrifice and do whatever I need to do to make it through.

I've decided. First, I'll go through paralegal school so I can work as a paralegal while I go to law school at night. That way I'll work in Bert Solomon's law office and get practical experience while I'm in law school. My college average is above a 3.8 and I know I can ace the Law

School Aptitude Test if I study for it. I'll go to a law school that'll accept me without four years of college on the basis of super high test scores and my high grades in the classes I've taken.

My only problem is money and that's major.

I need money for paralegal school and the job I have now at the restaurant and the library won't come close to paying enough for my expenses plus paralegal school.

I think about my options.

Phil made a lot of money selling sex. According to him, it's supported us for years. Well, I'm pretty. Guys seem to like me. Maybe I can somehow cash in on the money-maker like Phil has.

Of course, I wouldn't do anything illegal. And I don't have it in me to do anything touch-feely. Maybe something that's just looky-looky? Do I have the guts?

Rocky got me over my stage fright. I wonder....

The phone rings. It's Phil. "I got the other bunch of papers."

"I'll be right there."

This time, I ring the doorbell and Phil answers. He shows me his back and we go into the dining room.

"Maury's a prick," he says.

"What did he do now?"

"I asked him for a loan; not a lot, $60,000. A *loan*! You know what the son of a bitch said?"

The apartment looks dismal. "What did he say?" My eyes scan the room. It's it looks like nothing has ever been put away. The convertible bed is open, the single sheet and blanket askew, clothing strewn about, dirty dishes in the kitchen, and now I notice the smell of rotting food.

Phil's arms fly up at his sides. "He says, No! He called me a smut peddler! Says I shamed the family."

The room is stuffy. I look at the windows. They're closed and the curtains are drawn. He flops onto the single chair that looks potentially comfortable.

"Says he wants nothing to do with me. Pansy! He talks like I'm Sturman, for Chrissakes!"

"Who's Sturman?"

He looks at me. "You never heard of The Jewish King of Porn? He sold comics in Cleveland. Then he figgers the money is in sex magazines. So he sells them instead. Now he's everywhere. He's got stores, magazines, the whole *megillah*."

"I've never heard of him." I go pull the drapes open then shake the window behind them open.

"Ahh, what difference does it make?"

He walks over to the fridge in the tiny kitchen, opens it and brings out a can of beer, pops it open and takes a long drink. I've never seen him drink beer before. Never.

Then he moves to the wooden table on the other side of the small room were the latest communication from the government sits. I join him and pick up a stack of papers as thick as the those that made up the Federal charges. This one looks equally serious with another long list of purported violations of law.

"Have you read this?" I ask.

Phil's eyes widen and his lips quiver. He waves at the papers. "You nuts? They make it so's only a lawyer can understand what they're saying." His hand glide over the pile. "The lawyer read it," he says. He puts his hands in his pockets and turns away. I say nothing. "They got me on chicken shit charges." I remain silent. His hands are working inside his pockets. He wipes his forehead. "They says I showed movies with minors. Sold videos with minors. Drugs in the theatre. Drugs sold there. Prostitutes and *solicitation* going on.

"Dad, why won't you let me talk to Bert Solomon? Maybe he can help. Those lawyers are really good. Maybe he has a friend who does this type of criminal cases. He may even know a really good one that's not Jewish."

Phil's anger rises and he booms, "No! Now you stop. Just stop. I told you, I want you saying nothing about this to him. Don't you start that again. Have you told him about me?"

"No."

"I don't want you saying one word to him. You hear me? Not a word. I have a lawyer."

"Yes, I heard you. But you're wrong."

I go to the sink. The smell is horrid. *Doesn't Phil smell this?*

I find some soap and a sponge and start washing the dishes that fill up the sink and sit on the counters. Phil doesn't stop me.

We're both quiet until all the dishes are washed. As I'm drying my hands, he says, "I'll do fine without this Bert guy. You hear?"

"Yes, Dad." He's walking away and I take the opportunity to open the window in the kitchen. The apartment needs fresh air badly.

"Dad, remember what Mom used to say? *Nothing's eaten as hot as it's cooked.* Things will work out."

Leaving his apartment, I try to believe that. I take the new batch of legal papers with me to copy and return as I did with the Federal papers. I also take two bags brimming with garbage to dispose of.

I've barely driven a block away from Phil's apartment when the clouds that have been gathering all day begin to emit drops.

I feel insulated inside my small car from the rain around me and from the sad mess I've just left behind. The gentle sound of the steady rain falling on my car's soft canvas top is comforting. I feel secure.

My thoughts seem to move with the rhythm of my windshield wipers as they move steadily back and forth, pushing away drops of rain that linger, join other drops, then cascading down my windshield. I realize I love the rain.

I approach the Sunset Strip where sidewalks have turned brown and glisten under the streetlights. Traffic is congested, cars bumper-to-bumper, as people make their way home at the end of the work week, hoping to pass a weekend that will justify the last five days they spent at work.

Partygoers are out, moving hurriedly on the Strip, trying to keep dry as they come and go to restaurants or find their way to the clubs and bars, enjoying the endless entertainment available to them.

The exuberant sound of people talking and laughing on the boulevard mixes with car horns and blaring music as proof that these people are resolved not to let something as mundane as some rain stop them from their merry-making.

I arrive home, tired and again, worried for Phil. He's having a hard time, and I know a harder time awaits him, alone in a depressing apartment. I'm afraid he will again try to end it all.

I'm relieved to see no messages await me on my answering machine. I'm too emotionally drained to speak more of Phil's troubles tonight. I'll call Aunt Sophie and Nora to update them tomorrow.

I take a hot shower and get into bed with a magazine. Thumbing sleepily through the pages of Vogue, an advertisement catches my eye, a photo of a woman holding a young girl in her arms, a toddler, smiling down at her. They're outfitted in clothes by the same designer. They both look almost ridiculously happy.

I fall asleep and dream of a beautiful woman. Her skin is dusky like mine, and she's wearing a low-cut white dress. There's a chain around her neck that holds two interlaced hearts.

She sits on a peach-colored couch brushing the long hair of a young me into a ponytail while singing a hauntingly sweet song to me, and when she's done, she ties a pink ribbon around the rubber band, then lifts me onto her lap and hugs me to her chest, stroking me lovingly. She's singing the whole time.

Then the song ends, and she puts me down. She gets up and moves gracefully to the window to her right. It's open. I'm too short to see over the sill. She smiles at me, then leans back – all the way back — and simply disappears.

I scream "Mommy!" and awaken in a cold sweat.

4 2

THE GOLDEN RULES

*T*he following morning, I take my coffee to the couch and leaf through the State and Federal papers.

I'm able to make enough sense of some of it to understand Phil's problems.

Apparently, the Commerce Clause in the U.S. Constitution gives the government the power to tell Phil what films he can and can't sell and he's being charged with selling videos and showing movies that are illegal; they show minors having sex. That's in addition to charged with harboring prostitution and allowing the sale of drugs in his bathrooms.

Sexual exploitation of children. Solicitation. Illegal Possession and Sales of Drugs

Defendant has given obscenity and child pornography, prostitution and distributors of illegal drugs safe refuge on his premises. He has opened a safe haven for pedophiles looking for illicit material, films with unlawful content, unlawful sexual solicitation as well as for distributors of illegal drugs.

Defendant cannot argue he was blind to either the illegal nature of the film shown in his theater nor to he illegal nature of the continuing activities on his premises.

345

The Court knows that past judicial decisions must be as relevant the outcome of a case as is legislation enacted by Congress.

A landowner may not use property for illegal activities. Further, landowners may not allow tenants to use property illegally. Defendant landowner may not use the premises for illegal activity such as the distribution of illegal videos and the publication of child pornography, prostitution and drug sales.

I guess they're saying that Phil, the owner of the building and the theater, allowed illegal activity on his premises. They have him as both the land owner and the owner of the theater.

In Grosfield v. United States, (1928), the landowner's tenant was illegally manufacturing alcohol on the premises. The Court denied the property owner the use of his property, despite the landlord's argument that he bore no responsibility for the illegal use of the property by his tenant.

The Court held that the landowner cannot prevail in his argument that he did not participate in the criminal act of the tenant. The tenant could have been ousted and the illegal use of the premises ended.

Thus, the owner bears the paramount responsibility to end the illegal use of his property.

So, they're saying that Phil *allowed* the illegal activity to go on because he could have closed his theater. Or policed it better.

Secondary liability extends to persons that condone illegal activity on their property as well as those landowners who, through their own inaction, encourage illegal activity. It is Defendant's "ability to supervise" which enmeshes him in liability.

Yeah. They're saying he condoned all the stuff, simply because he owned the place and didn't stop the sale of drugs and other illegal things going on. I picture Phil standing watch in the men's room to interrupt any solicitation or drug activity going on there, and I chuckle.

The film in which minors participated, whether volitionally or without their volition, was criminally produced for the purpose of being viewed for money.

Defendant's actions encouraged the continuing production of such illegal, obscene material. Defendant aided and abetted the illegal film production by providing a means to complete the unlawful activity by charging theatergoers and possible pedophiles a fee to view the illegal material in his theater, a safe sanctuary...

Defendant has allowed pedophiles and others to sexually exploit and abuse children and has aided and abetted in the distribution of illegal products in violation of federal laws...

So, he's also responsible for the fact that films with underaged kids performing sexual acts were shown. *Filmed?* Even if he didn't know they were underaged?

If theater owners refuse to show such illicit products, child exploiters would cease making them, for there would be no market and child predators may think twice before producing child porn. Kalm v. Harper Bros., 222 U.S. 55 (1911)

There it is. That's their case against him. It concludes:

It is one of the basic principles of tort law: The landowner is responsible to supervise his property to prevent illegal acts by any persons.

The landlord is in a position to prevent reasonably foreseen repetition of the illegal use of the property.

Here, Defendant was in the best position to refrain from displaying the illegal films, selling illegal videos and also to prevent the solicitation of sex in restrooms and the sale and use of illegal drugs on his premises and he must be punished to the full extent of the law.

That's why Phil says they'll take his theaters away. Would they actually send him to jail, too?

43

SWAN SONG

West Hollywood, 1980

The top of my green Fiat Spider is down.

Stepping over the closed door of the little sports car, I slide easily into the driver's seat, insert the key, throw the stick into first gear, and take off down the hill. In seconds, I'm leaving the Sunset Strip, heading west to the 405. I'm anxious to get where I'm going, so I'm glad to see traffic is moving easily on the boulevard.

I'm sure Tony is nervous because I'm running late. I don't care. I'm euphoric. Tonight is my swan song, my last night and the end to these last 10 months. After tonight, I can put it all in my past. It has served its purpose.

Chasing the late afternoon sun, I notice a Corniche traveling alongside me in the lane to my right.

It's a convertible, white, with a white interior. The top is down. The driver is a deeply tanned, movie star type. I set my sunglasses up onto my hair. Catching his eye, I smile shyly at the driver, and he smiles back, showing teeth that are whiter than the upholstery he's sitting on.

I slow down and he slows down to keep pace with me. I see silver creeping up his sideburns. I slow down even more; he follows suit. I speed up playfully, and he does too, enjoying the game.

We're approaching the intersection of Sunset and Beverly Drive, where there are tall palm trees and ample foliage. We're across from the driveway entrance to the famous flamingo pink Beverly Hills Hotel and not far from the house I lived in with Phil and Stella. I wonder what Stella would say if she knew her home had been sold to pay for Phil's legal bills.

Just as our two cars arrive at the intersection, the traffic light in front of us turns red. I stop, but my new road friend is busy enjoying the pretty girl in the sports car driving alongside him and isn't paying attention to the traffic light. He rear-ends the long, sleek, shiny black Mercedes-Benz sedan that's stopped in front of him. The driver of the Benz exits his car and storms toward the Corniche. He's waving a pad and pen in the air.

As the light turns green, I accelerate past the intersection and the two cars, throw my head back in laughter and give the Corniche a last glance in my rear-view mirror. I drop my sunglasses back into place, protecting my eyes from the glare of the descending sun as I continue on to the San Diego Freeway.

Once on the 405 heading south, I snap a cassette tape into the player, turn up the volume and start to sing along with the Doobie Brothers. *"Take this message to my brother... You will find him everywhere... Takin' it to the Streets."* I love the Doobies and I'm enjoying myself immensely. This is the last time I'm making this drive.

I had purposely chosen to work in a place that's in Gardena, a place where the chances are slim to none that anyone I know would ever see me there. People who live and work on the Westside in Los Angeles don't go to Gardena, nor do prosperous attorneys – although, I suppose, they could meet their client anywhere. But the odds are against it.

And, of course, I used a phony name – Sally Tract – as well as a phony address, and a phony social security number on my application. I don't expect they'll be sending me any mail. I make sure I get paid in cash.

Twenty minutes later, I exit the freeway and find my way to the parking lot of the Hole-In-One, a small building, the color of descending twilight. I park alongside the building, lock my purse in the trunk and hurry through the once bright red back door, carrying only my keys and a duffle bag.

As soon as I'm in the building, I begin to undo my top. By the time I reach the changing room at the end of the hall and the closet where I keep the box that holds my stage outfits, I already have my skirt zipper down, my halter-top off. My skirt falls, and I kneel down to put my duffle bag and keys on the closet floor, under the box for safekeeping. I hastily put on a pink G-string and the pink pants with the snap-down sides.

I hear the trademark knock on the door: one-two-three, hard and quick. The door opens, The stench of cigarettes enters the room. It's Tony.

"Late again, Pink. You're on in three minutes." He leans into the doorway, his hand on the doorknob.

"I'll be there."

"What do you want tonight?" he asks, eyeing me.

"Respect; Signed, Sealed, Delivered; and Last Dance."

I know Tony wants to linger, but there's no time. He has to leave to order up the songs I want played. He gives me one last look then turns away. The door slams shut.

I've managed to get the top half of my costume on. I unzip and kick my boots off to step into the pink, strappy stiletto heels. I hurriedly apply the fuchsia-colored lipstick I keep on the dresser and put on the large pink earrings there. I'm in full costume and ready to start the show.

As I quickly make my way down the hall to the stage, I pass Ruby. Ruby's a good woman who lives for her son Tyrone; he's all she talks about. She's in the flowered polyester robe she wears when she comes off stage. Her artificial lashes, theatrically long and full, frame her dark eyes, now wide with glee. She waves her zippered pouch at me. It's overstuffed.

"Weeyoo! It's payday, girlie! There's money out there tonight!"

I remember that first night I watched Ruby from side stage ten months and a lot of dances ago. She'd taken me under her wing and had shown me some cool moves.

"How's our little man?" I ask her.

"That boy's my angel," she says for the thousandth time as she nods her head. "Yeah, that's what he is. My angel."

"I'm sure," I say. I pat her on her arm and continue on.

I climb the few stairs to the stage, set the my robe and the plastic bag to put the cash in out of view, and take my position behind the curtain.

Thanks to the yellow lights set above them, these curtains look like rich red fabric. But those of us who work here know they're old, worn and dirty.

I take a deep breath. This is my last night on stage, and I will give it everything I've got. The men will love me all the more.

Damn! They'll miss me!

I hear a microphone announce "Here she is, The Hole-in-One's very own…Pink!"

The first bars of Aretha Franklin's "Respect" take up the room as the curtain rises and I begin to dance. The room fills with hoots, whistles and shouts.

"We love you, Pink!"

"Where you been keeping yourself, girl?"

"Pinkie, I love you!"

"I dreamed of you again, Pink!"

This first dance is my meditation. I close my eyes and let my body and soul become one with the music. Soon I'm no longer aware of anyone or anything other than the music. I don't see the men; I hardly hear their comments. When I'm ready, when I've transcended the tackiness – the worn out old wooden floor, the cheap curtains, the stench of beer and the boozed-up men – I open my eyes.

I strut from one side of the stage to the other and then down the short runway while I slowly untie my blouse, looking for the men waving bills. I go to those men and squat, letting them bathe in the excitement of inserting money inside the waistband of my tight flamingo pink pants.

When they successfully lure me to them with their folded bills, young and old, and whatever their color, they howl with excitement. They know they are the lucky ones – they get as close to me as any man in the room will. Their hands get to linger on me for a few savored seconds, grazing my tummy, my hips or the small of my back as they insert their cash. Some kiss the hand that's grazed my skin then groan and reach into their pockets to fish out more money.

Toward the back of the room, a man is looking at me through binoculars. I smile; this is *not* a large room.

I cup my breasts, encased in the hot pink demi-bra, and stroke the satin, enjoying the feeling of the soft fabric against my nipples, and the men's groans.

After circling the room, I return to center stage and slowly undo the pink rhinestone snaps of my pants down one side and then down the other, still dancing, kicking high. The bright pants fall to the stage floor along with cash. Then I strut around in my pink bra and thong and cup my breasts once more.

At the end of this first number, when the curtains fall, I quickly gather the cash strewn on the stage and stuff it into the plastic bag. I position myself for the start of the next dance. I've chosen a long song for this dance because this is when I seriously work the room in preparation for my third and final number.

The second dance starts. The men recognize my signature song and go totally nuts. Every time they hear the words, "*Signed, sealed, delivered / I'm yours,*" it's as if each man there imagines I'm signed, sealed and delivered to him. *Crazy!*

I shed my bra as tantalizingly as I know how. I know the tease is more titillating, far sexier than any display of flesh. So, I tease the pants off the men, doing and undoing the single large hook with my back to them. They've seen this before. They've seen other strippers do it and they've seen me do it many times before. They know I won't take it off quite yet. I play with them, tease them, mock them. I can feel them getting hotter, their blood rushing to their dicks as they go berserk with desire, hoping this time … no, this time … I'll let the damn thing drop. But I don't. Not until I'm good and ready. Not until they beg. By the time it comes off they'd elect me President of the United States if I were running.

I move to the pole. I have no idea why men like to see girls pole dance, but they do and in this dance I do a lot of that. Now I'm completely engrossed in my performance, loving the excitement I'm causing.

I leave the p0le and shimmy up to one man who shouts, "Two fins, Pink," thankful that I'm not a man and will never be as foolish as these men. After making his third deposit of the evening into the side of my already full G-string, the man falls to his knees and gently takes hold of one of my calves. I reach down and put a finger to his lips.

The excitement in the room grows. I move my finger up his face to his hair line. He dares to extend an arm in the direction of my breast. I take hold of his hair and pull. It's over in an instant. The guy goes from moans of ecstasy to a short cry of surprise and shoots to his feet. As the audience cheers, the man reaches for his wallet. *Nuts, no?*

Back on center stage, I lie down with my back on the floor and lift my legs, opening and closing them, flashing the bit of pink satin at my crotch. Oh, how they love this.

I just might miss this job after tonight. I stand, thrust my pelvis out and gyrate in hip-led circles on way, then the other. I break from the dance into a strut. I'm riding high on the power I have to make these men grovel and howl with every move I make, the power that comes from being a young, desired woman. I can't imagine who wouldn't love this. It's electrifying.

The second dance ends, I gather the cash and I'm ready for my final dance. This is the last dance I'll do in this place.

As much as the men loved the second dance, they love the third dance more. Tonight I've chosen – most appropriately – Donna Summer's "Last Dance," for my third and final number.

During the slow introduction, I shed my thong —slowly — one side down, the the other side down as the first side goes back up. It's like what I did with the bra — teasing mercilessly.

"Let me help you with that, Pink," says a jock standing along the runway, waving a 20-dollar bill.

When I turn, showing them my back, they know it's coming off. They're out of control. I finally turn back around to face them, covering my privates with my hands, smiling shyly, turning away from the audience. Then I throw my hands up and kick into high gear, moving in time to the upbeat disco rhythm.

I'm out to make the men to remember my last dance.

A surge of energy hits me and I repress the urge to twirl like a little girl. Instead, I turn my back to the men and wiggle my ass. The men start pounding on the tables. I parade down the runway and across the stage in only my high strappy stilettos, my body glistening, nipples erect. I walk with a bounce, letting my young full breasts shudder and my tight round buttocks alternate positions like a seesaw with every step. While holding my nipples between my fingers, I gaze out at the men with the same smile I'd flashed the Corniche driver. The men are all out of their minds.

About half the men have left their tables, no longer waiting for me to go to them in my vulnerable state; they've come as close to me as they can get. They're crammed at the foot of the stage and runway, and so close, that I just reach over and take the money they're holding out for me, one after the other.

A black man, about my age is standing at the other end of the runway. "Pink, Baby, forget these old farts. Come to me, Baby, I'm your Sugar Daddy. I gots two twenties for you, Baby." He's drunk, swaying on his feet. I make my way to him. His eyes are yellow. I turn around and, with my back to him, I squat down and take the two crisp bills from his hand through open knees, spread apart. He clutches his heart. "I've just died and gone to heaven," he says, "and I'm not fixin' to come back. Um hmm!"

"Forty bucks here for you, Pink." I go over to the two college-types in USC caps, likely, business majors who've pooled their resources.

The money is flying tonight, like Ruby said, and it's mostly fives, lots of tens and enough twenties. I take their money gladly. I deserve it.

I wonder at how foolishly they spend their money. I assume that most of these men are lying bastards, undependable to their core.

I wouldn't be surprised if there's a woman somewhere, waiting for every one of these men and for the cash they're giving me. She'll probably believe his lies: that he spent his money and the night out bowling with buddies, or stayed late at the office, or whatever.

I feel very little compassion for these women. They're suckers, and not very smart if they believe these jerks, if they depend on them. I have no more respect for them than I do for their pathetic men, lined up in front of me, anxious to give a naked stranger their money.

I know better than to ever commit to a man like any of them.

I don't respect them. I don't respect Phil, Jay, Rocky, Holden, Erick … my own birth father … I don't respect any of them.

And if one day some man should dare tell me that he's lost respect for me because of what I'm been doing here, well … I'd tell him I'm proud of who I am and what I did. I did this for only one reason and that's strictly for the money. I'm proud that I was able to get all the money I need to take me where I'm going.

The music stops, the curtain falls. I'm done with the only set I'm doing tonight. I leave the stage for the last time. As I cover myself with the short black silk robe, I hear the table-thumping cries of the men demanding more. I'm used to it.

I'm aware of the smell of my own fragrance, a mix of my signature perfume and perspiration. I throw my hair back, and as the men call me back to the stage, I think, *Right! Hold your breaths… Hah!*

Their noise is interrupted by the announcement over the mike that it's time for the next act, a debut from a new girl named Kimmy.

The men quiet down and the waitresses flood the room, busy taking orders for more drinks. I want to pack up and leave, but my natural curiosity holds me back just long enough to catch a glimpse of the new talent. I look on from stage side, recalling how I stood watching Ruby on my first night here, amazed at what she did, sure I never could. I stood frozen on stage. Ruby had constantly encouraged me.

The music starts and an Asian girl appears on stage, wearing a red strapless top and white short shorts. She's lovely, petite with long straight dark hair and small breasts characteristic of many Asian women.

As she begins her first dance, a man screams out, "It's a boy!" and I watch as laughter and hoots stop the new girl short. She stands onstage transfixed, a child who's forgotten her lines in the school play and wants to run to her mother. I'm afraid she's going to start crying.

I'm angered and disgusted by these men. Kimmy needs reassurance. I catch her eye and send her a big smile along with the "thumbs up" sign, but it doesn't help; she's badly shaken. In seconds I'm back onstage, still wearing my robe.

Donna Summers is singing, "Hot Stuff." I dance my way toward Kimmy. She gives me a tiny, tentative smile, more polite than welcoming, and very unsure.

I continue dancing, smiling at her and the men, predictably, whistle and call out my name. They're thrilled to see me back.

I face Kimmy as I dance, mutely inviting her to join me. She begins to dance. She nods, whether to signal her understanding or her appreciation, I can't say.

As the two of us dance, I sense a new undercurrent in the room, a new excitement. The men are ready for a novel act. I intuitively move closer to Kimmy and initiate a hip-bumping movement and Kimmy, aware that my presence has brought about this turnaround, happily gives me the reins, relaxing, ready to follow me wherever I, her savior, may lead her.

I continue smiling, knowing that I need to keep Kimmy feeling comfortable and safe. I gently reach for the back of her red halter-top and untie, then re-tie it. I move the zipper on the girl's shorts and toy with it, then eventually undo it, going low to coax them down and off, all while moving in rhythm with the music.

Tony, has hurried to side stage – he's either heard the men's negative reaction to Kimmy or their screams at seeing both of us on stage – and he's watching us.

The men are effusive.

"Yeah, Baby, work it."

"Yeah, Pink, show her how it's done."

"Ooh-wee! I need another drink!"

Eventually, I strip Kimmy of everything. It's against the club's policy to go topless before the second number but it was my decision. Let Tony fire me! *Hah!*

Meanwhile, the men – not expecting to see this amount of nudity in the first dance – show their appreciation, and money flies onto the stage as they whistle and slam down on their tables.

I shed my robe. We're both naked now as we dance, our bodies touching, our stomachs and breasts freely brushing against one another, and, at times, our lips only inches apart.

The men were wiggling in their seats, but now they're crowding the stage again, eyes glued on us. They want a closer look. We're being showered with bills.

When the music stops, I quickly take my robe and leave, leaving the money there for Kimmy.

I can hear the men whistling their approval of Kimmy and I'm glad I helped the new girl. It's a fitting way to take my leave.

44

EXIT

I sigh as I make my way back to the dressing room.

My time at the Hole-in-One is over, and I can't wait to get out of the place. Dancing here has sometimes felt humiliating, and sometimes, exhilarating, but it did the job: it paid my way through paralegal school. I'm a licensed paralegal.

Pink dies tonight.

I enter the small dressing room and close the door behind me, making sure it's locked. Tony doesn't know I'm leaving, and I definitely don't him barging in. I don't want a scene. I'll just leave quietly, then call and tell him I quit.

I toss the bag carrying my night's loot in the chair by the door then sprint to the closet to bring out my duffle bag. I'm dressing and packing at the same time. I take off the Chinese robe, moving fast. I want to get out of here before….

~~~

Shit!

One, two, three. The rapid knock then Tony's voice. "Pink? Open the door."

I throw the silk robe back on. "Who is it?"

"Who do you think? A Jehovah's Witness. Open the door, Pink."

I curse my luck on my way to the door. I unlock it and walk away. Let Tony open it for himself!

The stench of cigarettes enters the room. Tony drops a bouquet of flowers onto the side table by the door, pink carnations, wrapped in cellophane. He flicks his cigarette ashes into the cheap Hawaiian ashtray there.

"Pink, we need to talk. You were late again."

I'm moving. "Yeah, sorry, traffic."

He takes a drag off his cigarette and exhales in my direction, one hand in his jacket pocket. He's rocking forward and back again as he speaks. "I've told you before, you've got to be on time, Pink. This is a business. We've got a schedule. You can't be coming in late. The other girls don't like it. The customers don't either."

Since I'm leaving, this conversation is moot; but Tony doesn't know.

I'm moving things out of my drawer and closet, putting them into my bag. My silky robe loosens. Tony's eyes pick at my body like sharks' teeth, making me uncomfortable; I'm always uncomfortable when I'm alone with Tony. I want to get my clothes on. I find my bra. "The customers didn't sound unhappy to me," I say airily. "They sounded just fine."

"They were just glad to see you. But I can't reschedule the girls around *you*, Pink. That's no way to run a business."

He walks up behind me and I realize that the long mirror alongside the dresser has made turning my back to him pointless. "Here, let me help you with that." I suppress a shudder as he takes a hold of my bra.

I don't like Tony touching me. I put my arms through the bra straps, feeling as vulnerable as a dog accepting its collar. Tony's eyes wander over the reflection of my body in the mirror as he gathers my long hair easily with one hand and guides it off my back, his hand moving far too slowly. Then he fastens my bra. I almost trip over myself as I quickly move to pick up my panties.

"No wonder they go crazy for you," he mutters. He idly picks up one of the two books lying on the dresser. "I'm Okay, You're Okay. You're reading this?"

I don't answer. In my haste to cover my nakedness, I'm all thumbs and cannot, for the life of me, put my panties on. I finally give up trying and hurriedly put on my skirt without them.

"Anyway, that's bullshit," he says. "Most people are not okay. That's the whole trouble with relationships. People are all fucked up."

When I silently pick up the two books and put them inside my duffle bag, Tony notices. "What are you doing?" he says.

"Packing."

"Why?"

"I'm leaving," I say.

"You're quitting?" I don't answer him. "You're kidding, right?"

I take my pink chandelier earrings off and drop them into the bag. "Tonight was my swan song, Tony."

Tony grasps my arm. "The hell it was."

"Let go of me!" I pull away. He immediately lets go.

I back away from him and continue packing, throwing everything I see into the bag. In goes the stage outfit I'll never wear again.

"I'm sorry if I hurt you, Pink. You know I'd never do that." He sounds contrite. "It's just that this it's so sudden." He watches, fingering back his oily hair as I drop my robe into the bag.

"Why, Pink? What's happened?" I shrug. He chuckles. "Hey, don't misunderstand … about being late. Hell, it happens. There's no way I'd really let go of you. You're the most popular girl I've got." I'm silent. "I was just talking. You know-"

I check the dresser drawers. "I know."

"So, why are you talking like this? You can't just walk out." He points to the duffle bag. "Put this stuff back. Let's talk." He takes my robe out of the bag.

I kick off my stage heels. "Tony, I'm leaving." I add them to the suitcase, take the robe out of Tony's hands and throw it back in.

Tony's fingers again comb through his hair. He looks genuinely confused. "Is it the money? That's it, isn't it! No problem. I'll pay you more. You're long overdue for a bonus, Pink, a nice fat one." He opens his wallet and starts counting out bills.

I put my hand up and shake my head. "Don't, Tony. This is not about money."

His eyes are two question marks. "But you've earned it, Pink. The crowd out there loves you."

"They love any girl who gets naked for them."

"No! You're different, Pink. That's the whole point! There's no one like you. Do you have any idea how many guys asked if you'd be on tonight when you were late? Can you even guess?"

"Don't care." I scan the room one last time.

I sit down on the chair and begin putting on a boot. Tony grabs the bouquet of flowers he'd thrown on the table and shoves it in my face. "One poor guy brought you roses, for Chrissakes!"

I push the flowers away. I switch legs, putting on the second boot. Tony's still holding the flowers outstretched, like a young boy presenting a fist full of daisies to his first love.

"Pink, you know how I feel about you. I can be a real sweet guy. Stay. I'll set you up. I'll make sure you'll be comfortable. Real comfortable."

"I'm sorry, Tony. I can't." I stand up, eyeing the flowers and add, "Carnations."

"What?"

"The flowers. They're carnations, not roses."

Tony slams the flowers down on the dresser. "I don't give a damn if they're goddamned golden lollipops!" He's obviously at a loss. He swoops up the bag of cash and hurls it into the bag. "Don't forget this."

He lights another cigarette, inhales, rolls back on his heels, and gestures to the door. "Okay, Pink. You want to leave? Leave! Be my guest. I'll find some other young chippie to replace you. But you'll be sorry. I want to see you find another job like this," he says.

He sits down on the chair I've just left and crosses his legs, inhales again, exhales, and waves his arm around the room. "Make money at some other place like you do here. Come in late, no one hassles you-" He stops and looks up at me. "Moving to another club?" I shake my head.

"Has some guy been hassling you? Is that it? Tell me who. Just point him out."

I just want to get out of here. "No one's hassling me."

"Then what the hell is it with you?"

"It's just time to go. That's all."

"Time?" Tony stretches the word out. He stands, stabs the cigarette out on the ashtray at his side. "Time to go? What fucking time is that? Tell me. Time to leave the job of a lifetime?

"You sleep all day, come in at six, seven, four nights a week, you dance, have some fun – and get paid like a fucking queen."

His shoulders curve in as he shrugs, then his arms fly up. "Time? Time for *what*? What Pink? Are you getting married? Some jerk get to you?" I don't react. "Nah, you're too smart for that."

He crouches by the duffle bag, takes the bigger of the two books I've packed out of the bag, and eyes it. "What's this...?" Book in hand, he walks over and puts it down on the dresser. "The Complete How-To Guide for Family Law Paralegals." He's read the title on the cover slowly, as if he had trouble with the words. He flips through the pages. He sees my notes written in the margins and the yellow and pink highlights I've made.

A tide of anger rises up in him. He picks up the book. "What the hell is this?" He gestures to the bag. "Is this what all this is about?"

"Calm down, Tony."

"I can't calm down until I know what's in your head! Pink." He runs his fingers through his hair yet again, then paces around the small dressing room.

"Look, Pink, I've been meaning to talk to you about something. I know this guy who's in the movie business. He's been in here a few times to see me and he's seen you, asked if you'd be interested in being in a movie. It's a good opportunity. The money's good." He isn't expecting my laughter. "What's so funny?"

"You're talking about porn?"

"Yeah, but nothing raunchy. Baby, you're a natural. I saw what you did up there tonight with that new girl. That was great!"

"No thanks."

"Don't get me wrong, you wouldn't have to lick pussy."

"Shut up, Tony."

He sits. He's suddenly cool. "Oh, now it's 'shut up, Tony.'" He flicks ashes on red carpet and smiles, as though he's enjoying himself.

"I see. Making changes, huh? You leave here and that's the end of it. The new Pink. Quit stripping, no porn talk … you're going to be a *good* girl now, is that it? *Huh?* Gonna be a girl scout? *Huh?*Gonna go to church now? *Huh?*Join the choir maybe?"

While Tony is speaking, I put the textbook back inside the duffle bag, zip the bag closed and pick it up. He gets up. "Bye, Tony. Take care of yourself."

He stands, blocking my way to the exit out the door. "I just don't get you Pink. You want to hurt me, hurt me. Go ahead. But don't be stupid!"

I sigh. I look at Tony. I never dreamed of opening up to him, but now, standing here, ready to leave this place forever and knowing that I'll never see him again, I'm tempted to see if I can make him understand.

I put the bag down by my feet, take a deep breath, look up at him and begin. "You have a mother, Tony?"

"Yeah, I got a mother. Duh. Everybody's got one."

"Does she love you?"

"Yeah, I suppose so. Yeah, she loves me. So?"

"I have a mother, too. Like you say, everybody does. But I don't know who mine is. I've lived my whole life with strangers who never let me forget I'm adopted. They weren't horrible people. They didn't tie me to a pole and beat me to death or starve me. But they made it plain that I was not theirs." I see the look of curiosity on Tony's face. "My mother abandoned me. I don't know who she is."

Tony's face has softened. He shrugs and shakes his head. "Tough break, Pink, not knowing your folks. But you're young. Take my advice. Don't go through life feeling sorry for yourself."

"I'm not feeling sorry for myself."

"Not knowing who your mother is – I guess that can fuck things up," he says. "But you're smart, Pink. Don't let that get in your way. I mean, what's important is that you know who you are."

I'm obviously not doing a good job explaining myself. It may be

JOLIE'S STORY: MOON CHILD

impossible, but, for whatever reason, I want to see if I can make Tony understand.

"I've tried to find my mother. I don't want anything from her, not even her love. I just need to know where I came from, who I came from, my ancestry, my heritage ... my genes. I've done everything I could do, but in the end, I couldn't find her. Not a trace. You know why?"

"No. Why?"

"Because, Tony. I'm not *allowed* to. I have no rights. Nothing. Zilch. Zero. Nada. Kids like me, put up for adoption, have no rights at all. We are not permitted to find out who our birth parents are. What was my mother's name? What's my real name? Did I have a name my parents gave me that was different than the one I have now? Why didn't they want me? Love me?

"I feel like I don't *belong* anywhere. It's like I was just dropped here from another planet. I have no roots, no history. You can't know what that feels like. I'm totally unconnected. It's like I'm swimming alone lost at sea."

Tony looks like he's really listening. But I want him to do more than that. I want him to feel the magnitude of my emptiness. He puts his hands in his pocket and looks down, takes a few steps away and circles back. I turn to the mirror. "Why do I look like this?"

Tony answers. "Okay, okay. I get it." He comes and stands behind me then speaks to my reflected image. "Stay. I'll help you find your mother *and* your father. I'll hire the best private investigators in the city."

I turn to face him, and my laugh sounds maniacal to me. "And what will they find? Where will they look that I haven't? There are *no records,* Tony! None were kept. The place I was adopted is gone, demolished. There are absolutely *no records anywhere* of my real parents and nothing about my adoption. I don't even have a birth certificate! And if there were records, the court would have sealed them so no one could see them."

"So, how is leaving here going to change that?"

I pick up my bag. "I'm going to law school. I'm going to become an attorney and work to change the laws, so they protect adopted kids.

365

We haven't done anything wrong. It's not right to steal our history, wipe out our past and deny us knowledge of our roots. We have the same right as other children to at least know who brought us into this world."

Tony has followed me and now he asks, softly, "Tell me, Pink, when did you decide all this?"

I look away. Though I wonder if I've managed to make him understand, the bottom line is that it doesn't matter. Either way, I don't feel any better; I'm still caught in the pain of my truth. "A while ago."

He nods. "And where exactly does stripping fit in?"

I look up to meet his eyes. "I needed this job to get money to become a paralegal. I've done that. And, I've taken the test I needed to get into law school. I did well, even better than I expected. I have a job waiting for me as a paralegal while I'm in law school. I'm starting night classes soon." I smile. "So, I have to go. See Tony?"

Tony stands there with his hands in his pockets. He rises on his toes and back down, then smirks in resignation. He turns and scans the room. He notices my G-string lying bunched up in a corner by the dresser. I had missed it. He picks it up and hands it to me. "You almost forgot this," he says. As I shove it into the barely opened zipper, he says, "Maybe you'll wear it the day you graduate from law school."

He opens the door and follows me out of the room. Several steps into the hallway, I turn back. I want to return to the dressing room and retrieve the bouquet of carnations left behind. I ask Tony to hold my duffle bag.

I take the bouquet and notice the small card attached with a string to one of the stems. It says, "Pink, you are pretty. Please call me and I will make it good. 839-5278. Love Cecil." I remove the card, rip it in half, and drop it on the chair. I return, holding the flowers, to take my bag back from Tony.

Together we continue down the hall until we're at the back door that leads to the parking lot. With the bag in one hand and the bouquet in the other, I wait for Tony to open the door, but he hesitates, shifting from one foot to another. "This place won't be the same without you, Pink." He sighs.

"Now, you do real well in law school," he says. "I expect you to bring the house down. Show them what you can do."

"Thanks." I stretch up and plant a light kiss on his cheek. "Take care of yourself, Tony."

He wraps his large arms around me. "They'll miss you, Pink. I'll miss you." He comes away and says, shyly, "Maybe we'll have dinner sometime; you can tell me how you're doing."

I have no intention of seeing him again. "Sure. Thanks. I'll see you around."

"You'd better, counselor, or I'll spill the beans about your past." He smiles. "Of course, I'd first have to find out your real name. I know it's not Sally Thomas."

I gesture in the direction of the dressing rooms. "You'd better go make sure the show's going well. You wouldn't want the girls to be running late." He nods and opens the door to the parking lot.

Just before I walk out, I hold the flowers out to him. "Tony, these are for you. Give them to your mother."

And I'm gone.

The End

Enjoy the story of Jolie's birth parents in **Persian Moon- Layla's Story,** *and continue the saga of mother and daughter in* **Moonlight***.*

. . .

DISCUSSION

Thank you for reading *Moon Child – Jolie's Story*, Book One of the Moon Trilogy. Here are some suggested topics for discussion:

1. Why do you think the author began the story with Jane Albright?
2. Does Jane Albright remind you of someone you've known?
3. Should Jane's husband (Dean) have realized his wife's manipulations sooner?
4. Can you justify the laws of Texas surrounding adoptions in the 1960s?
5. Are you or anyone you know and adopted child or adopting parent? What is that like?
6. Can you understand Jolie's feeling of feeling unanchored?
7. What are your thoughts about how Jeffrey died? Was it due to foul play? Do you blame Phil?
8. Can you understand Phil's attempt to commit suicide?
9. Do you think Stella knew Phil had turned the gas on? If not, how would she have reacted had she known his plan?
10. Can you justify Phil's behavior towards his adopted daughter?
11. Why do you think the author used the fact that Stella wrapped everything in plastic as symptomatic of a part of

her personality? What other habits characterize her personality and insecurities?

12. Do you think Phil's paranoia that Jewish theater owners were being victimized due to their religion was well founded?

13. Jolie represents the woman who follows the dictates of her heart and fights for her right to live as she chooses. She takes a proactive role in her life and holds only herself accountable for both her mistakes and achievements. Do you identify with her? How? How much of that mind-set do you believe is a condition of youth?

14. To what extent do you believe a woman is a victim of her country? religion? era? lineage?

15. Do you believe a woman is today able to follow the dictates of her heart and free will as Jolie did, or is that impossible? Explain.

16. Could Jolie have done anything more to help Rocky with his addictions? With his refusal to accept his medical issue? Elaborate.

17. Why or why not do should Jolie have begun therapy as suggested by Gloria at the Maple Center?

18. How would you judge Jolie's experience with Jay? Rocky? Erick? Do you see similarities between these three men?

19. Do you think the hope of becoming an attorney is a good reason to turn to stripping?

20. Do you believe that Jolie can be an effective attorney? Why? Why not?

21. What are your thoughts about the scene when Jolie gets back on stage with Kimmy?

22. Why did Jolie feel it was important to make Tony understand her reason for leaving the Hole-in-One.

23. Since the time Jolie became an attorney, the laws of Texas regarding adoption have changed. Do you know someone who has benefitted from these changed laws? An adopted child? Adopting parents?

24. What did you enjoy most about Moon Child?

25. Do you think it is important to have read Persian Moon-Layla's Story, Book One to appreciate Moon Child?

26. Are you planning to read another book in the Moon Trilogy?

27. How would you compare Layla Saleh's early life to that of Jolie?

28. How did the early lives of Jolie and Layla affect their later life?. affect the goals and dreams of they

29. Do you relate more to Layla's mindset or Jolie's mindset?